Every Closed Eye
Ain't 'Sleep

Every Closed Eye Ain't 'Sleep

MaRita Teague

URBAN
CHRISTIAN

Urban Books, LLC
97 N18th Street
Wyandanch, NY 11798

Every Closed Eye Ain't 'Sleep

ISBN 13: 978-1-62286-816-2
ISBN 10: 1-62286-816-1

First Trade Paperback Printing October 2015
Printed in the United States of America

10 9 8 7 6 5 4 3 2 1

*This is a work of fiction. Any references or similarities
to actual events, real people, living or dead, or to real
locales are intended to give the novel a sense of reality.
Any similarity in other names, characters, places, and
incidents is entirely coincidental.*

Distributed by Kensington Publishing Corp.
Submit Orders to:
Customer Service
400 Hahn Road
Westminster, MD 21157-4627
Phone: 1-800-733-3000
Fax: 1-800-659-2436

Every Closed Eye Ain't 'Sleep

MaRita Teague

To courageous breast cancer survivors everywhere
&
To those who bravely fought the good fight

In loving memory
of
Gaile Teresa Owens Thomas

ACKNOWLEDGMENTS

I thank and honor God for being my source. He's allowed me to press forward and has created rivers in the desert. I am forever grateful.

Zedric, you are the beat in my heart. I love you. My three sons, Zedric Noah, Joshua Antone, and Zachariah Justice, I thank you for bringing so much love, purpose, and joy into my life. Mom prays that you always find purpose and strength in Him and who He has created you to be. Soar and refuse to give up.

My parents, Kenneth and Rita Hinton, thank you for your unwavering belief in me. Your sacrifices are appreciated, and I love you. My in-laws, Leon Teague and Evelyn Penn, thank you for your prayers, love, and support. I love you both dearly.

Thank you to Nadeen Gayle, Regina Brooks, and Chelcee Johns, of Serendipity Literary Agency. Nadeen, I am deeply grateful for your insight, guidance, and representation.

Joylynn Ross, I'm honored and thankful to work with you and Urban Christian/Kensington Books. Thank you so much for everything.

A special thank goes to Rita Hinton, Adrian Davis, Gloria McLeod, Lisa Downing, and Yolonda Tonette Sanders for assisting me through the drafting process. I appreciate the sacrifice and investment of your time. I also want to thank: Aleta Hinton, MiKelle Hinton, Landrian Hinton, Kandace Davis, CoRita, Elicia Hinton, CoRita Cornish,

Belleza Hinton, Autumn Hill, Peggy Etheridge, Cynthia
Puryear, Gloria Cannon, Pam Atkinson, James Penn,
Charlotte Teague, Lorra Hill, April Hill, Laila Jamison,
Fannie Tillman, Kennedy Goolsby, Leslie J. Sherrod,
Mata Elliott, Angelique Gayle and Darian Taylor of The
Gayle Agency, Carla Orton, Jeff and Rachelle McLeod,
Barbara Shackleford, Willis and Denise Turner, Robert
and Audrey Richardson, Juanita Wood, Dr. David Neff,
Courtney McGinnis, Michelle Hicks, Michelle Blackwell,
Pastor Ozell and First Lady Carolyn Northern, Dillon
Tillman, Pastor Tony and First Lady Joyce Campbell, Dr.
Elton and Lady Edna Amos, LaReta Blackwell, Kimberlea
Tillman, Tanya McGinnis, Yvette McGinnis and Crystal
Jackson for their influence and/or input. To The Temple
of Healing Waters, Superintendent Chad Carlton, and
First Lady Darice Carlton, thank you for your prayers,
love, and support.

Finally, I want to thank readers for making the writing
journey worthwhile.

CHAPTER 1

DESIREE

*Keep thy heart with all diligence; for out
of it are the issues of life.*
—Proverbs 4:23

Backing out wasn't an option.

For the third straight year, I didn't say no to my secret crush, Lionel Banks, who naturally possessed a charisma rivaling President Obama's. With aspirations to run for mayor, Lionel, the coordinator of the festival, treated every woman like the only one on earth.

Crush or not, I planned to run in the opposite direction of Lionel's cool and easy swagger this year. That soothing baritone had done nothing to offset my third straight financial loss from participating as a vendor at the Harlem Renaissance Festival, even if the vendor fees assisted Huntsville's inner city cultural arts program.

Enough was enough, I decided while putting the finishing touches on my booth area. This would be the last year. People wanted to buy ribs, grilled corn, and bootleg DVDs and CDs, not the handmade upscale jewelry I sold.

After hanging the final set of earrings up, I was struck by the massive chocolate-covered body headed directly for my booth. I held my sigh on the inside, and asked, "May I help you with something?"

"I believe you can, sweet sister." He cocked his head to the side, scanning my curves.

I placed my hand on my hip. "What exactly do you need?"

His squinty eyes hid when he smiled, the twinkle of mischief narrowly escaped. In spite of his dirty sneakers, a definite turnoff, his amber-scented cologne wafted through the air just enough to send a quick tingle down my spine. The muscle man clouded my good sense, and overlooking his shoes became easier as I reflected on my lonely days and nights. In mere minutes, as I had done too many times before, I threw my graduate degree–toting, upper class–reared and etiquette-trained self out the window, relinquishing my power to the inviting smile.

The dark stranger pretended to admire my jewelry and casually picked up a pair of iridescent purple and gold chandelier earrings, my personal favorite.

"These some nice earrings. You make these, girl?" The jewels sparkled, gleaming in the blazing August sunlight. He dangled them and grinned, obviously feeling my gaze.

Nothing irritated me more than a brother who talked like a caveman. As a college English instructor at an HBCU, I loved when men used correct English; yet, I couldn't deny that the man's charisma held me in a trance. "'Girl?'" I asked, looking behind me as if the mysterious "girl" would appear. "I'm nobody's girl, but I did make them," I said with enough attitude to run any sane man off.

He turned away grinning, holding his hands up. "My bad, my bad. Missus?"

I ignored his question and in a much too high pitch remarked, "Those took me the longest to make. Good taste."

Muscle man scratched his gleaming bald head. "People do always tell me that I got good taste."

I winced. Subject verb agreement is always a plus in a man but again I reminded myself that education wasn't everything.

His grin widened as he rhythmically moved his head to the calypso jazz resounding through the park, flashing his too white teeth. I couldn't help noticing that his top teeth were shades whiter and perfectly straight. The bottom row, the color of dirty snow, peeped through every now and then when he spoke. Had he whitened the top and not the bottom?

He flipped the earrings over to check the price and then gripped his chest as if he were having a heart attack. "Whew! You proud of these, ain't you, girl?"

I looked away and folded my arms. "If you don't stop calling me girl, we're going to have a serious problem. My name is Desiree."

He stepped back to examine the sign on the front of the table skirt. "Yeah, okay, Desi's Designs, I get it," he sang, mimicking my business name to the rhythm of the music. "Desi, nice to meet 'cha. I'm Taye, and I guess I'm gonna risk starvin' next week 'cause I just have to buy these earrings. See, it's my li'l sis's birthday. She just loves this kinda stuff."

Maybe he wasn't so bad, I thought, trying to grasp at words that wouldn't come while slowly wrapping his earrings in tissue paper and a customized box. He couldn't be half bad if he'd buy his sister a relatively expensive gift. I reasoned that even with his raggedy tennis shoes and poor grammar, he did have good taste. The earrings were the best I had on display. "Forty-four dollars and ninety-five cents," I said, handing the box to him. I made a point to brush his hand as he took the box.

He pulled out his weathered wallet and gave me two twenties and a five. "Keep the change."

I eyed him and shook my head. "Oh, okay then. I guess I can do a little extra for that whole five cents."

Listening to the tingle inside, I whispered, "One minute." I reached my hand out for the box, which he relinquished with ease. I wrestled under my table to find the box that held an assortment of ribbon and bows until I found the perfect piece of satiny royal purple ribbon. After taking entirely too long to knot the perfect bow, I returned the box. "Thank you for your purchase."

His smile had me in an emotional headlock, and his refusal to walk away from the table made everything worse. I tried to cloak my nervousness in a nonchalant tone. "I can't help you with eating next week, but I'm about to take a break. How about a hot dog on me?"

His silly grin said it all, so I asked the vendor next to me to watch my table as we walked to the hotdog stand.

I wasn't a fan of canary yellow on men, especially dark-skinned men, but the bright shirt clinging to his body warmed me hotter than the sun. Although it did bug me that Taye had a habit of rubbing his two fingers down his imaginary mustache, he stared at me like I was the only woman on earth as we sat in the crowded food court area.

I groped for conversation, which fell flat in a sea of one-word answers.

"So, are you from Huntsville?" I asked.

"Nawww." Taye wiped his mouth, perfectly content not to give up any other information.

"Where are you from?" I asked.

"T-town," he said with his mouth full.

I frowned, clueless.

"Girl, you ain't heard nobody call Tuscaloosa T-town?"

He shook his head, but I was the one in disbelief. *The word "ain't" and a double negative?* I had to remind myself that not even one man had even said hello to me in months.

I did like that he made me feel comfortable and pretty though. After a chili cheese hot dog, and an enormous funnel cake smothered in strawberries, whipped cream, and powdered sugar, he said, "I been trying to think of who you remind me of, and I got it."

I wiped the powdery sugar from my face. "Who's that?"

"Let's see. Anybody ever tell you that you could pass for a lighter skin-ded Gabrielle Union?"

I nearly choked on my drink. I hated when my people added Ds to words; and I looked nothing like Gabrielle Union. The only thing we probably had in common was our height. At five feet ten inches, I often found myself taller than some men.

Otherwise, I had traces of my mama's Lena Horne–like beauty. My hair, very long but more coarse than hers, fell across my shoulders, but my almond eyes, strong nose, and chiseled cheekbones were inherited straight from my father.

"Lips and eyes like an angel, and a brick house, too."

"Brick house? You are too young to talk like that. You sound straight old school."

"So, you like old school, Ms. Desi?" He surveyed my body and licked his lips like I was a piece of fried chicken.

"Well, not all old school is bad now, is it?" Flirting back with a man like Taye could be dangerous, but, as usual, I knew that I had the upper hand. Still, I heard Mama's voice, telling me, *Don't write a check that you can't cash.*

Taye stole the remaining strawberry on my paper plate, and popped it in his mouth like we were a couple—and we were.

I had decided not to tell Mama about Taye, but changed my mind after the good time we had while taking her to run errands. Then, my plan to tell her fizzled when she caught me off guard.

"Honey, I know you're probably still upset about the breakup with Jace, but I knew when you bought him those shoes that thing wasn't gonna last."

"Jace who?" I asked her with attitude. After a few seconds of silence, we both fell into a boisterous laugh, something we shared in common. I suddenly didn't have the heart to tell Mama that not only had I long forgotten about my ex of several months ago, Jace, but I had also moved on to Taye.

"Desiree, you are something else, girl. You always have a man, but goodness, your choice in men is terrible."

My smile faded. I knew she would go on her usual rant about my string of unhappy relationships. I didn't want to hear it. How was I supposed to know that I was only one of Jace's many girlfriends?

"Mama, before you start in, you need to think about the fact that the problem is not me. Look at me. I'm professional and fine as—"

Mama interrupted, "Don't say that."

"'Wine' is not a dirty word, Mama. It's in the Bible. Anyway, I'm trying to explain to you that it's the men who are the problem, not me. I can't help it if these guys lie and cheat. Do you understand the situation out there? All the good men are married, gay, or unemployed. How does a good woman like me navigate through all the mess that is out there?"

"That's simple, Desiree. The Holy Ghost will let you know who the right one is."

I wanted to tell her that the Holy Ghost didn't keep her from marrying my stepfather, but Mama always saw all of my shortcomings and none of her own.

They thought I didn't know it. But you can't hide certain things from a child. Even as an eight-year-old I could read the forced smiles and frosty glares written across their faces. And by the time I was twelve, it wasn't surprising when the pep in Mama's step fizzled out like flat soda.

Strange thing was, raging arguments or raised voices never shook the walls of our home. Silence gripped the rooms with so much strength that at times I imagined that hundreds of the sparkling crystals suspended on the massive chandelier in the foyer would crash onto the floor or maybe even the too perfect wedding picture cradled in the glass frame perched on the fireplace mantle might shatter into pieces.

Nothing ever broke though. Except, that is, on the day I left for college. My stepfather, who I call Dad, opened the front door to take my bags out, and the wind blew, rocking the chandelier back and forth. One crystal tear fell, splitting into tiny pieces. A tense gaze locked Dad and Mama in place for a few frozen seconds. An ominous chill surfaced at the unusual occurrence. Somehow I knew that something had shifted and things would never be the same.

I had nearly finished packing for my freshman year in college. Mama had rushed in, clutching the frame to her chest, and then thrust it toward me as if it were a treasure. I hadn't reached for it. She ignored my lack of desire for the picture of the two of them and dove into my suitcase.

"You just take this," Mama said, rolling the picture in one of the many granny flannel nightgowns she'd forced me to pack.

While she fidgeted, nestling the picture between the fresh pack of pastel-colored underwear and her secret beauty weapon, a jar of Nivea cream, she fastened on a grin. A failure at the art of contrived smiles, I couldn't drum one up to return the favor, even for Mama.

"When you get to missing us real bad and you feel like you can't make it, remember that we're praying for you and we love you, you hear me now? You're gonna make it, Desiree." Her body betrayed her words. The wet circles under her arms and weak tremor in her hands gave her away. Now I knew that she was either afraid I couldn't make it without her, or afraid that she couldn't make it without me.

Mama gripped my arms, and I melted into her much too tight and unexpected embrace, soaking in the smell of her almond-scented lotion and freshly flat-ironed hair.

I hated how she said "we" all the time. Not only had she forced my stepfather on me too soon after Daddy's death, but she also had refused to see that the gulf separating my stepfather from me was wide and long. And just as my mother felt indebted to Dad for taking such good care of us, Dad has always been especially indebted to me for being the keeper of his dirty secrets.

While Mama tried to figure out where I got my sassiness from, I tried to figure out where her spark was. Why she didn't do something about Dad was beyond me. Her spirituality had made her weak, and I refused to be a victim.

From almost the very beginning of their marriage they only tolerated each other. I, the go-between, buffer, and good daughter to both, stayed in the crossfire of the silent but deadly war. The weight of balancing the two of them bore my insides into almost nothingness, a faint reflection of the dysfunction between the two of them.

Mama, forever concerned with the outward appearance of things, didn't know that the weight I carried registered much heavier than the extra pounds she was so concerned about me having. I felt at least two tons on the inside. Behind the perfect façade, our house had been a model case for dysfunction.

If I chose bad men, then as far as I was concerned, Mama's as much to blame as I was.

CHAPTER 2

ISABELLA

*By him therefore let us offer the sacrifices of praise
to God continually, that is, the fruit of our lips giving
thanks to his name.*

—Hebrews 13:15

Two smells I hated were ones that reeked of cheap
cologne and a lowdown cheater. My husband wouldn't
dare wear anything inexpensive, but the stench of other
women burned the insides of my nostrils. I couldn't prove
it and stopped trying years ago, but I knew. The only bit
of satisfaction I got was that he had no idea that I was on
to him.

Equipped with a passionless marriage, a career that
never started, and not one grandchild to push on a swing,
I did the only other thing I did that made my heart sing
besides going to church and spending time with my
daughter. With my garden tools in tow, I searched for the
perfect spot to plant violet morning glories.

The grass, though wet and crisp with dew, never
needed mowing. Langley did take care of some things,
and in this case it was a lucrative contract for Redman's
Lawn Care to visit us every other week during the spring
and summer. The robin's egg sky, speckled with a dark
cloud here and there from last night's storm, painted the
perfect canvas for gardening. Although it had begun to

clear, from experience I knew Alabama's humidity would soon smother the faint breeze, so I dug out the old straw hat passed down from what had to be generations of women in my family.

I waved to Pete, a ruddy, red-haired young man, who made a habit of waxing his Mercedes early every Sunday morning. His wife, Melanie, had complained to me, "Pete is a real piece of work. He wanted that car so badly, but the only thing he does with the doggone thing is wash, wax it, and pull it right back into the garage. Whoever heard of not driving a car, ever, Ms. Isabella? And why wash it on Sunday? I have to take the kids to church by myself."

Pete probably liked waxing that car to relieve stress. I understood that because that's how I felt about gardening, but I also knew Melanie's pain. Getting my own husband to church had nearly been impossible. Langley viewed church as a big waste of time, especially at my church. The last time he attended, he yawned in agitation. "Don't these people understand that there are other things people would like to do on their day off? My goodness, the announcements lasted for almost twenty minutes. Totally unnecessary."

As I dug into the damp red clay, it relaxed me. Humming to the tune, "He's the Lily of the Valley, the Bright and Morning Star," I poured water onto the exposed roots and jumped, spilling way too much in the hole at the sound of my husband's voice.

"Why would you plant those, Isabella? And if you just have to plant them, why there?"

I held my hand to my chest. "Langley, you just scared me to death."

Without an apology, he stood, towering over me, impatiently waiting for a response that he wouldn't get. I felt small, like a child with her hand caught in the cookie jar once again. Staring at his perfectly pleated trousers and expensive Italian shoes, I caressed the heart-shaped leaves of the flowers, determined not to let him ruin my peace.

"Okay?" He blew out in frustration and drew his arm up to check his Rolex. "I've got to go, it's getting late, but please don't make the fence look country. We have the homeowner's association to think of." He began to walk away, mumbling something about how silly it was for me to cover up the fence we had paid so much for.

"When will you be home? It *is* Sunday," I called after him, but not caring, only wanting him to acknowledge the error of his way.

Without turning toward me, he said, "You know I golf on Sundays at the country club. Late again. I'll be back in time for the dinner party, of course."

He didn't dislike everything country because he married me and rarely missed an opportunity to golf at the country club. My husband was my cross to bear, and I was sure if Langley knew anything about bearing crosses, I'd have been his.

I, determined to buy more flowers to make the vines grow more densely up the fence, hoped that they'd be different than me and grow up and over the fence, not trapped and dependent on a stiff old board.

Things began to change for me in my late forties. Langley gently nudged me out of the office administrator position at his office, explaining that he had gained a level of success and stature that surpassed having his wife work as a secretary. I tried to protest, but Langley won, as always. I ignored the perky, young brunette who bounced into a position I had held for almost twenty years.

Langley encouraged me to rest and to enjoy the rewards of his hard work and my many years of helping his practice to grow. I threw myself into Desiree's world, church activities, volunteering, and more than my fair share of shopping sprees.

I pushed the final roots gently into the soil and patted dirt around it. After pouring a little water, I prayed for sunshine and growth for the morning glories and me.

My phone alarm rang, signaling it was time to get ready for church service.

"Morning, Sister Morrison." Pastor Kingston waved as he slipped his key into the side door of the church.

"Good morning, Pastor." I held on to my hat, trying to speedily get to the door while he held it open. "Come on, Sister Julia, and Mother Butler. Let me get your bags," I said, taking their purses. The crumbling cement in the parking lot, in desperate need of paving, had become an obstacle course for me but nearly impossible for the elderly women.

When we got up to the door, Pastor Kingston sighed. "I'm so sorry about that parking lot. Thanks be unto God though, because the paving company is coming early this week. We're finally going to have a safer walk for everyone."

"God is good!" Mother Butler huffed. "He knows what you need when you need it! Oh, Mother Jenkins comin' in in a spell. She gonna need some help now."

"That's right, Mother. He is good," Pastor said, sounding more encouraging than the lines around his tired eyes revealed. "I'm going to send Deacon Whitlow out to help the other ladies in, no worries."

I was just one in a sea of women without husbands at church. Some were widowed. Some were single. Some were like me. I hated being in that number, and I did have it better than some. Langley did show up on Easter and Christmas. Like all the others, I sucked it up and came to church faithfully anyway.

Purpose and hope filled the pews, at least most of the time anyway. In the small, dingy white building, in desperate need of a makeover, I felt alive and useful. There was always something to do.

I loved the members with the ferocity of a mother bear, but detested the condition of the building, which had been deteriorating at an alarmingly steady pace. Our building fund drive had been going on for years, but we always ended up having to invest in some other maintenance problem. There weren't enough chicken dinners we could sell to get the place in good condition. Whether it was a leaky roof, toilets that overflowed, the peeling paint on the walls, or a broken hot water heater, the church needed major renovations. Still, Pastor Kingston kept a positive attitude, always making sure that the church remained warm in the winter, cool in the hot Alabama summers, and, most of all, safe for all the parishioners, which was no easy feat.

The neighborhood had changed so much over the years. What used to be a safe, clean, and peaceful environment had become crime infested, ripe with drug use and theft. Pastor Kingston made sure that the trustees put hefty money into beefing up the security system.

After teaching my young women's Sunday School class, I rushed upstairs to get up to the sanctuary in time for praise and worship. While holding on to the rickety banister of the dimly lit, narrow staircase, my heel sank into a small hole in the aged wooden floorboard. I tried to stop myself from falling backward but couldn't.

"Sister Morrison, you all right now, I got you." Sister Wanda, a lanky but strong young woman known for her raspy voice and four-inch heels, deflected my fall, gripping me under my arms. The pain that shocked me between my arm and breast took the wind from me. I got my bearings, and pushed her away, maybe a little too abruptly.

"Thank you kindly, Sister Wanda. Honey, you're a lifesaver."

She belted out a hoarse laugh. "The good Lord is the one that saved you, but"—she bent down and pulled my shoe out of the crevice—"He didn't save your Stuart Weitzmans."

I lingered a bit on the top step, holding my chest.

"Sister Morrison, are you okay? What's the matter?"

"I have this pain here," I said, pointing Sister Wanda to the area where the pain seemed to be radiating. "I'm sure it's nothing though."

"Oh, Lord knows I didn't mean to hurt you. I'm mighty sorry if I grabbed you too hard. People always talkin' 'bout how small I am, but you a little bitty thang yourself."

I drew in a quick breath. "Now, Sis, I don't know about all that, but I do know you don't have a thing to be sorry about; in fact, I'm thankful to you. I could've really hurt myself something awful. The Lord has a way of taking care of His own."

"Yes, indeed He does, Sister Morrison." Sister Wanda rushed to the nearest closet for a folding chair. "You sit down a spell, Sister Morrison." She rushed to the kitchen.

By then, the throbbing pain dulled a bit.

My best friend, Alice, came toward me with a glass of water. "Sister Wanda just told me you nearly broke your neck. You okay, sugar?"

"I should've known that girl was gonna get you. I'm fine, but look at this shoe." I dangled it, exposing the mangled heel.

Alice threw her hand up in the air. "Better the shoe than you. Besides, I told you about buyin' them fancy shoes. When you gonna have some sense and dress like me?" She pointed her finger down to her practical comfort shoes, and we both laughed. I swatted her off playfully. One of the reasons that Alice and I were such good friends was because we're both comfortable in our own skin.

The pain subsided and nothing helped it more than a good dose of praise and worship. Even though Missionary Blithe worked my nerves in every missions meeting, I had to give her credit. Nobody could lead praise and worship like that woman. She knew exactly how to get the congregation in the mood to praise. Why she couldn't stay in her lane was a pure mystery to me. God gives people gifts. Most of the time, it's as clear as day what He's given them to do, but they want to do something else. God gave her that voice to sing, and she just wasn't called to fuss at the homeless for taking one too many canned food items from the food pantry.

Missionary Blithe eased her way into the slower-paced songs, gliding us right along into worship, but I did have to close my eyes so I wouldn't think about all the things Alice and I talked about. Alice swore that Blithe thought she was Dottie Peoples because so many people told her that she sang just like her. I guessed she figured she'd steal Dottie's hairstyles since she about had her voice. Dressed in her rhinestone-embellished suits and clear-heeled pumps, Missionary Blithe had her hair perfectly sculpted and gelled. None of her sweating or jumping around moved the large weaved bun on top of her head. Me and Alice always joked, "Just like a tree planted by the waters, her hair shall not be moved."

Gossip wasn't my forte and I knew it wasn't godly, but when Alice and I started going good, we got carried away if we both weren't prayed up. I kept my eyes closed, determined to stay focused on the Lord and away from "Dottie."

Just as I lifted my hands in praise, I felt the familiar sting in my breast area I had felt on the stairs. I thought maybe Sister Wanda had caught hold of me a little too tight. Or maybe I'd pulled it in the garden. I didn't know, but I eased back down onto the pew.

"Hey, Mama," Desiree whispered as she slid beside me. "What's wrong? You okay?"

"I'm fine," I whispered, "but why are you always late?"

"Oh, Mama, relax. I'm here in time for the message. I just wished I could've missed these doggone announcements," Desiree whispered back.

Missionary Purdy read the church announcements, nearly rocking me to sleep. We had invested in getting a big screen for announcements, and they flashed while she read. I truly didn't see the point in the big screen if she was still going to read them anyway. The church administrator had tried to tell her that they wouldn't need her reading services anymore, but she cried like a bee had stung her. Pastor Kingston stepped in, and we all had to continue to see and hear the twenty-minute announcements every Sunday.

"You look nice, Desiree." I tried to set it up so that I could tell her that her cleavage was showing. She would take it the wrong way if I didn't let her know that I thought she looked nice first.

"Thank you? I know that it's coming, so what's wrong with me, Mama?"

"I didn't say nothing was wrong."

"You set me up for it though. Go ahead."

Desiree got on my nerves. I wouldn't tell her about her cleavage or anything else with that attitude.

Her long hair hung down in waves so long that she could almost sit on them. Many people told us our hair was just alike, but hers was prettier, making it the envy of women, black and white. I only wished she didn't have to act like it. Don't get me wrong. I was glad that she was confident, but she's overweight. She called herself a curvy girl, but she needed to accept that she's too big. It just wasn't healthy, and she certainly shouldn't have flaunted it the way she did.

With peppermint breath, she whispered, "Thanks, Mama. I got this jacket from that boutique we like on Bridge Street. It's so cute."

How Desiree went from teaching Sunday School, singing in the choir, heading up the Pastor's Aid committee, and the list went on, to a late bench warmer was something I couldn't understand. When I tried to address it with her she got an attitude, and she got it honest, because I got an attitude right back with her. I knew she needed the Lord, and not just for show.

Pastor Kingston stood at the podium, signaling for the musicians to quiet. "I have a question for the congregation today, one that I want you to ponder before you answer. Is there such a thing as too late?"

I nudged Desiree. She rolled her eyes.

Pastor Kingston continued, "Some people say that it's better to be late than never, but I'm here to remind you that, yes, there is such a thing as too late. Get your Bibles and turn to Matthew 25. We're going to read the Parable of the Ten Virgins. The title of today's message is entitled 'Too Late.'"

Pastor Kingston's anointing to preach God's Word allowed him to reach everybody. At the beginning of the message, I just knew that this one was for Desiree, but by the end of it, the Holy Spirit let me know that it was just as much for me as for her; so much so that it scared me.

CHAPTER 3

DESIREE

Know ye not that ye are the temple of God,
and that the Spirit of God dwelleth in you?
—I Corinthians 3:16

Some overweight women spend their time dieting, depressed, and disgusted, but not me. I was proud of my curves, even if Mama didn't see the value in them. Her petite politeness had gotten her very little in the relationship department. I was comfortable in my own skin, and if a man wanted to be with me, he had to love all of me as is.

As Mama and I ate lunch at the food court in the mall, I stopped chewing.

"What's wrong?" She leaned toward me.

"Did you see that man over there in the baseball cap, staring at me?"

"You always think some man is looking at you, Desiree."

"I can't help it if men find me attractive, Mama."

"You are attractive, Desiree, but that long slit in your skirt is what he's attracted to, not you!"

I looked down, and shook my head. "I suppose you'd like me to put on a potato sack?" I hated having this verbal sparring with Mama. She made me feel like I was a teenager. It didn't matter though. As much as Mama and I got on one another's nerves, we were connected at the hip.

"Nobody said nothing about wearing a potato sack, but if you would just tone down some, stop showing so much skin, you'd probably have a better chance at getting a husband. You keep attracting the wrong men for the wrong reasons."

"That's your assessment, Mama, and I happen to disagree with it. I'm a professional woman who chooses not to be covered from ear to ear, but that hardly makes me a stripper."

"That's ridiculous to say, Desiree. I wasn't saying that at all and you know it."

Once again, I knew that it just wasn't the right time to tell her about my new relationship. If Mama couldn't get past a little slit in my skirt, she surely couldn't accept that I was dating someone who she would say was beneath me.

No matter what I said to try to bolster Taye's image in the eyes of my friends, nobody liked him. Geneva, the loudest and most unapologetically honest, never minced words.

As I rattled on about how wonderful Taye was, Geneva straightened her wig. "I don't trust that man, Des. Why do you pay for everything and why does he allow it? That's just crazy, girl! He is the man!"

Geneva taught developmental English, and we shared an office in the old gym with two other instructors, Phyllis and Zapora, who couldn't stand either one of us for no apparent reason. During my first year teaching, before Geneva joined the faculty, I hated going to my office. It was bad enough that the building sat perched on the top of the hill and we froze in the winter and roasted in the summer. What made it worse was that Phyllis and Zapora either ignored me or talked to me like I was stupid. Like Frick and Frack, I rarely saw one without the other.

Separate, each was bearable, but together their powers activated, zapping all in their vicinity to shreds, until Geneva got hired, that is.

On Geneva's first day, she sauntered in, totes in tow, with the scent of incense trailing her. "How y'all doing?" Geneva asked the three of us.

I jumped up, delighted that she would share the office. Phyllis and Zapora, on the other hand, glared at her like she was an alien.

Geneva plopped her bags down. "What's wrong with y'all?"

Phyllis put her hand on her hip. "Why nothing is wrong with us, what's wrong with you?"

With a neck roll uncharacteristic of a professional woman, Geneva said, "What's wrong with me is that look like y'all been sucking on some lemons. I don't have time for this foolishness."

That said, she told them to clear the desk that was hers, and she made herself right at home while they sulked.

I supplied Geneva, the sister I never had, with a weekly stash of her addiction: sunflower seeds and pistachios; and she listened to my plight as a single professional black woman. She claimed that her life was boring, which was hard for me to believe with a husband and four kids.

When I casually told her that I was thinking of asking Taye to move in temporarily with me, she shook her head. With perfect precision, Geneva spat the shell of a sunflower seed into the small wastebasket under her desk and swiveled her chair over to me. "Desiree, you confuse me."

"How so?"

She looked around to be sure none of the other professors were around. "You are one of the best educators here in the department. Everyone loves you, especially the students. You're smart. You look and speak like you're secure and confident, but, honey, what's up with your choice in men?"

I tried not to act insulted. I didn't like her grouping all of my men into one category. "Taye's not like the other ones I've told you about. He's different."

"I don't know who you're kidding. He's just like the other ones. If you want my opinion, no, don't even think about him living with you."

"He's lost his job, and I do care about him."

Geneva didn't say anything.

I added, "I don't want him to be out on the street."

She pushed herself closer and whispered, "Okay, you want it raw, girlfriend? You're crazy, I mean downright out of your mind if you continue to allow that man into your pocket. Now, the brother is trying to move in with you? I may not go to church every Sunday like you, but seems like I'm making out better than you when it comes to using wisdom. It's just not right on any level."

I did my version of a stare down, penetrating Geneva's large nutmeg eyes and flawless ebony complexion. Even with her lips pursed tight in agitation, she had the face of black Barbie. I could see why she had a good husband and four kids.

Geneva's eyes locked on mine until I gave in.

"Taye and I love each other, Geneva." I paused dramatically for effect and continued, "I know that I have a lot to offer. I have my own career. I don't need a man to take care of me, like Mama. I want a companion, a friend and father to my future children. No, he's not perfect but nobody is. If I don't compromise on some things—"

Geneva cut in, "Mr. Right can come right on in and swoop you up. Just please excuse Mr. Right now."

I held my tongue but only because I respected her. With a doctorate, husband and kids, and at least ten years on me, I had to consider her opinion, not like it.

With an air of resignation, I tried to change the subject. "So, did you get your performance appraisal from Dean Whitlow?"

Geneva ignored my attempt. "Desiree, you are special and, you don't have to compromise anything! Set that bar to the moon, girl!"

"Honey, the bar *is* set." I nodded to get her off my back.

She unshelled another sunflower seed. "I know you're a grown woman and all, but does your mama know how serious you are about him?"

I rolled my eyes.

"Mmmmm, hmm. So she doesn't even know about him?"

"What does my mama have to do with anything?" As the words spilled from my lips, I knew Mama always had a lot to do with everything I did, even at the ripe age of thirty-three.

Geneva knew how close Mama and I were. Certain things, my mother just didn't need to know.

Still, that night, I tossed and turned, knowing that if I intended to even consider allowing Taye to move in, he had to meet Mama.

During the drive to Mama's, Taye whistled like he didn't have a care in the world. Sweat poured from my palms. My heart raced, so much so that I could hear it.

I prayed in silence. *God, please let Mama like him, just a little.*

"Turn here on Refreshing Waters Place," I directed. "There it is, Taye. The number is 14273."

My heart thumped louder in my ear as we pulled into Mama's circular driveway. Then I spotted her, seated on a mat next to the flowerbed in her garden attire planting.

I exhaled deeply. Mama's initial impression of Taye would either make or break him. Mama was just that type. She sized people up quickly, and in spite of her devout Christianity, she didn't often give out second chances. She had little tolerance for people who she classified as riffraff.

I eased toward my mother, hesitating more with each step as she eyed Taye with a stony glare. I had tried to convince Taye to wear something a little more appropriate instead of the hip hop shirt and baggy jeans, but he had told me with his hands flying up in the air, "Girl, I gotta be me. You can stress all out over your mom if you want to but, shoot, she puts her pants on one leg at a time, just like I do."

I didn't say it, but I wanted to tell him that Mama didn't wear pants.

Mama didn't even take her gardening gloves off to shake his hand when I introduced them. She did, however, manage to get up from the ground, but out of no respect for my new boyfriend. She tilted the brim of her hat up and squinted to get a better look at him.

It didn't matter that I had only told her good things about him. Mama's flared nostrils said it all.

Taye took a deep breath and gave Mama that same silly grin he had given me at the festival. "Hey there, Mrs. Morrison. Nice to meet ya." He looked around bobbing his head and said, "This here is a real swanky neighborhood. Yeah, man. I could definitely see me and Desiree living large like this one day. What'chu think, baby?" He chuckled, not one bit derailed by Mama's glassy stare.

I cringed. Mama fluttered her eyebrows and frowned, still speechless but saying everything.

Pretending to examine the rhododendrons, I struggled to divert her attention. "Well, the flowers look so beautiful, Mama." I could've kicked myself for what came out of my mouth next. "Mama, Taye loves gardening."

"Really," Mama said puckering her lips. The lemon drop, as I liked to secretly call her, soured.

"Yes, ma'am. I love working with the earth." Taye bent down and picked up one of the flowers still in the packaging. "Look at that gold, kissed by the sun. Black-eyed Susan plants are so perfect to plant in late summer."

"You a farmer or somethin'?" Mama held her hand out firmly to get the flowers back from Taye, whose smile quickly dissolved.

I stood erect as a soldier, knowing right then that there would be no sweetness for Taye, only sour.

Taye lifted his mirrored shades, exposing the small beads of perspiration that had collected under his eyes, and reclaimed his smile. "I'm no farmer, ma'am, but I think in a past life I may have been." He chuckled at himself, something he was fond of doing whenever he thought he was being clever.

"Well, Ty, what do you do in this life?"

I rolled my eyes. "Taye, Mama."

Without correcting herself, Mama raised her eyebrows, waiting for a response.

"Well, I take care of this beautiful daughter of yours." Taye slipped his arm around my waist. I tried to look comfortable.

"How so?" Mama demanded.

I interjected, seeing the surprised look on Taye's face. "He has been so fantastic helping me with my jewelry orders; and, Mama, Taye cooks very well and takes care of my car—"

Mama interrupted. Then, it was her turn to chuckle. "Let him answer, Desiree."

Taye's once relaxed countenance transformed into a posture of defense and annoyance. "I'm between jobs, but I've been a sanitation worker for years. I got laid off awhile back. This economy is bad. You know how it is."

"So, you normally work with trash? Of course, Desiree is not one to wallow in the likes of trash." I detected the shrill in Mama's voice and closed my eyes.

"Oh, Mama!" I frowned, convinced that this was the nightmare I didn't want to live out.

Taye bit his bottom lip, attempting to refrain from saying something he might regret.

Taye and Mama exchanged icy glares for a few seconds until he let a whispered profanity escape from his lips. With a sudden pop, Taye snapped his sunglasses in two and stomped to the car.

I stood in silence as Taye gunned the car impatiently, signaling for me to get in the car. Mama knelt back down and continued planting, now almost pounding the dirt around the flowers.

"Desiree," Mama said, scolding me.

"Mama," I returned in the same tone.

"Don't get sassy with me." Mama's eye bore into me.

I stood up, now fuming. "You could've at least given him a chance."

Mama stopped digging and looked up at me. "Why is that boy drivin' your car? He doesn't have a car of his own?"

"Why? Why can't you just be happy for me? Everything isn't always what it looks like."

Mama turned to look up at me, and the coldness in her voice sent a chill down my spine. "My daughter is not trash."

I wanted to respond, but didn't know what to say. Anything I could say would come out wrong, disrespectful, and only make things worse. Taye gunned the motor.

"Talk to you later, Mama," I said, though gritted teeth.

I could've sworn that I heard Mama mumbling as I walked to the car. I swung the passenger door open and screaming rap music nearly shattered my eardrums. I muffled the sound by covering my ears, and yelled, "Turn that down!"

When Taye didn't respond, I added, "Please, Taye!"

Oblivious to my demands, Taye refused to turn the music down. I watched his temple pound. I choked back tears. We rode home with no words between us, only the loud hip hop music I couldn't stand.

Taye whipped my car into the cramped garage, barely missing the wall. He yanked the keys out of the ignition and threw them onto my lap. In his fury, he slammed the door behind him with so much force that a faint breeze whipped across my face.

Intent on gathering my own hurt feelings and coddling Taye's bruised ego, I nearly crept into my own home. Bent over in the refrigerator, I could hear Taye talking to himself.

Silly clichés, ones that nobody really wanted to hear when they're upset, flooded my thoughts. I wondered if I should tell him something like, "This too shall pass. Keep your chin up. Get back in the saddle. Mama can't judge a book by its cover." I definitely couldn't say that one.

Instead, with all the softness I could muster up, I lightly grazed his arm. "Taye, baby, Mama means well. She's just set in her ways. She'll grow to love you just as much as I do."

Taye opened a beer retrieved from a hidden spot in the back of the refrigerator. He knew I didn't approve of alcohol of any kind in my home, so I instantly got an attitude.

"What are you doing with that in my house?" I questioned with my hands resting on my hips.

He gulped down the whole can and let out a crude belch. "Don't you start tripping, and don't start nothin' you ain't got a mind to finish."

"What? Have you lost your mind? I need to go ahead and take you home, Taye. You need to cool off."

"You heard me," he grunted.

I raised my voice. "Listen, don't you dare threaten me. What I got a mind to finish is this relationship!"

"Do what you gotta do, 'cause this is your house, right?" he said with sarcasm.

I tried to calm the situation down when I saw where the whole thing was headed. I exhaled. "I realize that my mother may have offended you, but it wasn't me. You're disrespecting me, and I'm not going to put up with that. And what's with hiding beer in my refrigerator? We've talked about the whole beer thing before. It's unacceptable."

Taye slammed the can on the counter. "Girl, I'm so sick of hearing about how this is your house and all. You think I got memory lapse or something? Ain't no reason to tell me that all the time. Matter of fact, you never have a reason to let that come out of your backward mouth again."

"Backward? Get your stuff and get out of here." I grabbed his jacket and tossed it toward him. He caught it and threw it back at me with so much force, I nearly fell. For the first time, I felt fear with Taye.

I tried to think about what Jesus would do, what Mama or my friends would do, but I couldn't think straight. The insults kept coming, one after another. He ranted but wouldn't leave.

My ulcer gnawed, and I raced to my bedroom, closing the door behind me.

After downing antacids, I balled up on the corner chaise, grabbing the bag of chips I had stashed beside it. I had planned to watch television and just cool down. I knew that he'd leave when he found out that I wasn't going to let him take me there.

Taye had other plans though. He stormed in and flicked the television off, challenging me to say something. I refused to take the bait.

"Don't you ignore me!" His face contorted in ways I hadn't seen before.

He grabbed my arm and chips flew across the room, spilling to the floor. I struggled to pull away, but his grip got tighter.

"Stop it, Taye! Calm down! Stop it!" I yelled.

His breathing, irregular and frantic, put me in a state of panic. It was surreal. I felt like I was watching it all happen. His massive hands dug into my arms. I pushed him away with all of my strength, and I ran, crushing chips as I fled to escape in the bathroom.

He pounded on the door. My hands trembled as I turned the lock and pushed against the door, praying he couldn't bust through it. I turned the water on in the shower, hoping to drown the obscenities and pounding. Maybe if he thought I was taking a shower he'd just go away.

It got quiet, so I relaxed a little. Maybe he'd given up. Although uneasy, I decided a hot shower might loosen the tight knot in my stomach and give him more time to leave or cool down. As the steam billowed out, filling the room and steaming up the mirror, I turned the water off, straining to hear if he was still there.

I didn't hear anything.

I wrapped the towel around myself and slowly peeped out. Suddenly, the door smashed me in the face, and I was knocked to the floor. Reeling from the fall, I tried to gather my senses as blood gushed from my nose. Before I attempted to get up from the floor, he stepped on my hand and grabbed me, shaking me with the force of a major earthquake. I screamed. I cried. I tried to get away, but his grip locked me.

"Taye! Stop it! Please!"

Still, he shook me, and yelled, "You ain't better than me! You hear me? You ain't!"

I stopped fighting to get away, and I hissed at him, "I don't have any clothes on."

He seemed to come back to his senses, and let go, with one final push knocking me to the floor. Grabbing a towel, I wrapped it back around me. The tremor in my hands almost wouldn't allow me to get tissue off the roll to wipe the blood from my nose. He came toward me.

I wailed, "Go, Taye! I'll call the police. Just go!"

Like a bad Lifetime movie, in a flash his whole demeanor softened. "I'm sorry." He stumbled on his words. "I didn't mean—"

I yelled, "Get out! Now!"

He slunk away, shaking his head back and forth.

My nose didn't appear to be broken, and the bleeding stopped. I checked all over my body to make sure that I was okay. I wanted to call Mama. I needed to call the police. Instead, I sobbed while I got dressed, trying to figure out what to do.

After putting the deadbolt on the door, I went to dial Mama's number and hung up. She was right about him.

Then, I thought about calling the police again, but I didn't need all of that drama and confusion when I was the one who'd decided to allow him into my life in spite of all the glaring red flags. My embarrassment wouldn't even allow me to tell my best friends, Shay and Geneva.

Nobody could know what had happened. Hot tears stung my face.

My secret desperation to be loved by a man made me wonder just how low I could go.

CHAPTER 4

ISABELLA

*Trust in the Lord with all thine heart, and lean
not unto thine own understanding.*

—Proverbs 3:5

I acted like I didn't see Margie, my best friend Alice's daughter, rushing toward me after church.

"Mother Morrison, wait one minute!" she called to me. Now I had to stop. Panting, Margie sighed. "Whew! You're a hard one to catch."

I would have to let Alice know that her daughter needed better support in the chest area, especially if she was gonna be running after folks in church.

"Mother Morrison, don't you look so cute with your stylish pin. Oh, my! Look at that shoe with a little rhinestone in it, how cute! Did Desiree make that?"

She spoke to me in a condescending tone, like I was a ninety-year-old woman, hard of hearing. I was no spring chicken, but I wasn't old either.

"Thank you," I said, patting the pin. "Desiree is mighty talented, huh?"

Alice, a total wreck since her daughter's divorce, begged Margie to move in with her, and now Alice was in a different kind of misery. Margie lived on Alice's phone, and when Margie was gone, Alice was stuck as a built-in babysitter for her unruly grandchildren, who Margie refused to whip.

Personally, I thought Margie had way too much free time and she needed to find a job. Maybe when she did, she could shake loose of her nickname, Scoop. Desiree said that she gossiped about everyone to deflect attention from her own drama.

Like a whirlwind, Scoop chatted incessantly about who knew what. I was just glad that Deacon Albright had Desiree hemmed up in a corner so I could catch up to her.

"Well, Margie, I'm gonna be goin' now."

She rested her hand lightly on my arm, and said in a syrupy-sweet voice, "Mother Morrison, I wanted to tell you that Mama told me how much you wanted Desiree to meet someone nice, and I was praying about it, you know?" Her eyes widened, nodding.

I didn't say anything, annoyed that my oldest and dearest friend would share any of our personal business with her daughter, who even Alice admitted had a big mouth.

When Margie couldn't get me to respond, she mistook the red light for green and continued, "Oh, Mother, I just feel like the Lord dropped someone in my spirit for Desi."

As much as this child talked, I doubted if she ever got quiet enough to allow the Lord to drop anything in her spirit; but then again, who was I to judge? Still, my curiosity was piqued, and I gave in. "Who's this?" I asked.

Margie's chalky brown skin brightened and her smile widened so that I thought her parched lips would crack. "He's very smart, and he's got a fantastic job. He's from a real good family. He—"

I interrupted, "Please, get to who it is, Margie." I wasn't in the mood for the fluff.

Margie's shoulders drooped and she took a deep breath. "Okay, it's my cousin, Robert. He's moving here from North Carolina in a few weeks. He's thirty-five and wants to get married and settle down with a nice Christian woman like Desiree."

I squinted, skeptical that out of all the single women in the church she was close to, she chose Desiree, who could hardly be considered a friend. "Why didn't you talk to Desiree about it yourself?" I questioned.

She took a step closer and whispered, "I never know how she going to react to things. You know what I'm saying, Mother. She can be so guarded with me."

"I wonder why," I said with sarcasm.

"Oh, I have no idea. I've never been anything but kind to her. We're both in the same boat. Being single isn't easy, and I hope that she'd do the same thing for me."

"Margie, well, of course she would."

"I do want her to meet him. I think they'd really hit it off. We could be related! You and Mama would love that!"

My patience was beginning to wear thin. "Okay, well, I'll try to remember to mention it to her. I've got to get on home, dear."

"But, Mother, I didn't tell you what he looks like."

Without realizing it, she already had told me that he wasn't attractive by not addressing that issue immediately. I glanced at my watch to let her know her time was about up.

"I think he's just perfect for Desiree. He's very intelligent. He's a big guy, but he's nice looking in my opinion. He likes women like Desiree."

I jerked my head back. "What is that supposed to mean?" This time, without waiting for an answer, I told her, "Thank you for thinking of Desiree, and I tell you what, I'll mention it to her."

I started to walk away, but Margie followed. "I hope Desiree will give Robert a chance before some of these other church women get to him. You know how that is."

I stopped and opened my arms to give her a light good-bye embrace and got a whiff of her singed Royal Crown pressed hair. After telling her I'd mention Robert to Desiree, I flagged Desiree down in the parking lot.

"I tried to wait for you, but you don't know how to leave church, Mama."

"You need to learn how to fellowship again, Desiree. You rush in and out of here so fast; how in the world can you draw strength from other saints like that?"

"Anyway, Mama, what the devil were you and Margie talking about?"

I explained what the Lord had supposedly dropped in Margie's spirit about Desiree and Robert.

"Oh, no, you don't, Mama! You promised me after that disaster with Clyde, you would not try to set me up with anybody else. Now I have to look at that sorry excuse for a man every Sunday." Desiree breathed heavily, now upset.

"Really, Mama, what's she doing trying to set me up with someone anyway? She needs to try to give those two kids of hers some attention. Last Sunday, I couldn't believe those boys had on shirts and ties with dirt under their fingernails, and you don't even want me to tell you how nasty their ears are!"

"Oh, Desiree, that's awful! She's been through a terrible divorce, so we just have to pray for her. Alice does the best she can to help her, but Lord knows, you can only help somebody who wants to be helped." I cleared my throat for effect.

"I hear you, Mama, loud and clear."

"Well, it's the truth. She's all up in everybody else's business, but she needs to tend to her own."

"The answer is no, Mama."

"I said just as much to her. I just thought I'd mention it."

I knew that I had to find a way to get Desiree to meet him. It couldn't hurt, considering what she'd been dating.

***

After Desiree and I had Sunday dinner together, I came home, watched television, and just relaxed. Like I always did, I made a plate for Langley and left it on the stove. I never thought I'd be married to a man who insisted on acting like a teenager. He rarely made it home for dinner, but I always made it available anyway.

When I grew tired of television, I went to bed around ten. The sound of the garage door opening woke me up. I looked at the clock. I rubbed my eyes, thinking that it must've been the wrong time. *2:30 a.m.* Even for my husband, this was late.

I turned on the nightstand lamp and sat up, waiting for his entrance. I tried to mask anger as I heard him turn the doorknob to our bedroom.

"What are you doing still up, Isabella?"

"That's the wrong question that needs to answered, isn't it, Langley?"

"Don't start with me." He tossed his keys and wallet on the dresser and began to undress.

"Just how much do you think I'm going to take of this?" I asked.

He frowned. "Take of what? I told you that I'd be late."

"Where have you been?" I asked quietly, knowing that I'd never get the truth.

"I met with some of the fellas from the golf club. We had drinks, and we watched the game. Just go to sleep and stop the drama. I'm tired."

"You fail every test to prove that you love me and care about me."

He pulled his shoes off, then turned to me. "Stop testing me. I'm married to you. I take care of you. I always come home to you."

Instead of yelling, arguing, or crying with Langley, I had always deliberately chosen my course of action. I pretended that I didn't know, didn't care. Lately though, his actions had been more reckless and brazen, a blatant disregard for me and my feelings.

For years, I put up with his disrespectful treatment because I needed to break the family curse of broken relationships. I wanted the devil to know that he didn't have authority over the destiny of my marriage and family. Sometimes I thought it was the devil himself that took my first husband, Desiree's father, Ray, from us; but other times, I knew that God had allowed Ray to leave because it was his time.

Any way it went though, God blessed me and Desiree with another chance at a different kind of hope and happiness with Langley. I had to prove to myself, the devil, and the world that I could make a marriage work. Langley provided my daughter with a dad who loved, took care of, and lived with her. With Langley's behavior and Desiree's choice in men, I wondered how successful I'd really been though.

My grandmother, Honey, took me and my sister Josephine to church every Sunday. She fasted, prayed, and taught us about Jesus; that is, when she wasn't doing her other favorite things: gossiping, cussing, and drinking with her golden girls on the front porch.

Every now and then, when we thought they were too drunk to care about us listening in, my sister and I would press our faces to the loose screen door until Honey yelled for us to go read some Bible verses. She never appeared to see us but always felt our presence. "Just remember, y'all do what I say and not what I do!" rolled off of her tongue on a daily basis right along with, "Children should be seen and not heard."

As for my own mother, she didn't have time for Jesus, Josephine, or me. And I only remembered her taking me to church one time, a day woven into the fabric of me.

Josephine had wanted to go, but Mama snapped, "Girl, your daddy ain't dead. You stay."

My mama, grim and stoic, sat with me at the back of the church for my father's funeral. She refused to let me walk past the open casket to pay my respects, denying me one good look at the man who rejected us both.

I stared at the grainy photocopied picture of my daddy, Timothy Wayne Curtwright, on the front of the program. I figured he must've had a pretty rough life if that was the best picture they'd found. Leaned against an old Ford, my dad, a self-professed pretty boy, as Honey told me, smiled like death could never catch up to someone like him. His fair skin and deep dimples mirrored my own. When Mama caught me grinning, she snatched the program, mumbling something about me acting ignorant just like him, and who in the world smiles at the doggone funeral of her daddy.

"Sit up, Isabella. People lookin' at us," Mama snapped.

I wanted to hit her for taking my program away. *Give me the program back! I want to see my daddy!* I wanted to tell her. Instead, I sat up straight and pulled my dress down to hide my ashy knees, which would be another reason for Mama to be mad at me.

After the service, Mama rushed me out, pretending that she didn't hear someone call after her. When we got in the car, she grabbed my shoulders roughly, her eyes wild and swollen.

"I took you there so you'd see him, but he wasn't no good, Bella. What kinda man goes and drinks himself to death like a plumb fool?" she cried.

Mama choked on her saliva, coughing, tears springing up like a fountain. I sobbed too, but I was sure we had different reasons for crying. I didn't want a dead plumb fool for a father because I thought surely I had some of that same plumb fool blood running through my veins.

When we pulled back up to the house, Mama straightened herself up and in an angry whisper, she demanded, "I don't wanna hear nothin' more 'bout him, you hear me now? I done this for you, and it's over. Don't you go sayin' nothin' to Honey either. You ain't to do nothin' with the Curtwrights, you hear me, girl?"

"Yes, ma'am." I nodded dutifully, but cringed inside watching her fold our funeral programs. I took a deep breath. "Mama, can I please keep my program? I won't show nobody, and—"

With clenched jaws, she spat out, "No!"

She crammed the programs in her purse. I slumped in the seat, swallowed up in it and her. But I kept my word. Even when a girl named Sandy Curtwright, also in the fourth grade with identical dimples, introduced herself to me at the neighborhood community center, I didn't tell Mama. I didn't even tell Josephine. I told Sandy not to call again, but it was only after she'd told me I had at least three other siblings around the city with different mamas. It was too much for me to take. Besides, Mama had warned me, so I let it go.

Mama worked hard and played harder, staying out 'til the wee hours of the morning. Honey became the mama my own wouldn't be for me and Josephine, sacrificing her golden years to raise me. I guess that's why her heart broke over me marrying Ray and not a college man.

To make matters worse, because Ray couldn't be drafted to go to Vietnam on account of his flat feet, Honey scoffed, "That boy can do everything else. If he can run the streets, he should be able to run in the army. Least he could do somethin' that might bring some honor and dignity to our family by fightin' for the country."

As much as I didn't like Honey's tirades about Ray, I understood them. She and my grandfather had married and he had left her when Mama and her brother were young. Honey was tired of working so hard without having a lick of money, respect, or status. According to Honey, it was a white man's world and the only way to succeed was to get an education or a career in the military. To Honey, Ray had nothing.

To me, he had everything. What I had with Ray only comes once in a lifetime. I knew that. When he passed, I fell back on what Honey had taught me, waiting for a man who could give me and Desiree stability and security.

After living off of Ray's insurance money and odd jobs for a few years, I started taking a few classes, here and there, when I could fit it in. But I knew that I needed to get married again, and before I was thirty; or my options would be slim. Things weren't like they are now, when marrying after thirty is more of the norm.

Just as I planned, I waited until I was a few days shy of thirty years old and accepted Dr. Langley Morrison's proposal. Langley had replaced Desiree's former pediatrician, who retired. He didn't hide his attraction for me at the first office visit. He tried to find things to say, stuttering and stammering about Desiree, a perfectly healthy child.

Langley's face was one that you see and yet don't notice. Not unattractive but no Ray either. His gangly body and long face read dull as the day is long, but his eyes were kind; that is, behind the thick glasses. His hair, undoubtedly his best feature, was then wavy and dark as midnight in the Alabama woods.

Langley's looks had improved with age, like many men's looks do. Contact lenses, a few lines and creases, and wavy hair speckled with gray gave him the extreme makeover he had always needed. Even the fuller face with a little extra weight around the middle had helped his looks. It's a shame that women have to work harder the older they get and most men just seem to ease right into middle age and their golden years, looking mature while we get to be just old.

Honey never got to see what I was sure that she would think was my good fortune in marrying Langley. She passed away right before I met him. And Mama, a grief-stricken alcoholic, passed away from a heart attack the next year. All of my life, death had hovered over me, reminding me that nobody and nothing's here to stay.

Honey would've thought Langley walked on water. Lord knows, Langley thought he did. Thing was, the water he's walking on was drowning me.

It wasn't always like that though. When Langley asked—no, begged—me to marry him, I ignored my lack of enthusiasm and graciously accepted. What woman in her right mind wouldn't want to be married to a doctor? I had a little girl to think about.

In the beginning, Langley's captivation with me was dizzying. I would get dressed and feel his eyes just burning into me with desire. Even while I cringed inside at these times, because I knew that my heart wasn't in the whole relationship with Langley, I knew that I was making a better life for Desiree, and it made it manageable. Like a broken record, I'd say to myself, *he's a doctor. A doctor is in love with you.*

As the years passed, just like Mama had predicted, Langley, a doctor but still a man, didn't smile when he looked at me anymore. He'd settle for quick, hurried glances and wasn't too keen on conversing.

It took me turning forty to realize that I had made a deal with the devil. I thought I was the only one settling to make a better for life for Desiree and me, but I accepted the fact that he had married me for my looks. He provided all the finer things in life for us, and I, in turn, took care of his needs, managed the house, and provided him with the arm piece he needed for his social gatherings. By fifty years old,

I wasn't much arm candy for him anymore. Now, his need for me was no more than that of comfortable housekeeper. Although Langley didn't seem to love much outside of work and golf, I did believe that he truly loved Desiree. I could be thankful for that.

After Langley showered, he got in bed. We lay in silence, so much so that I thought he was asleep.

"Isabella," he said softly.

I just knew that the apology I longed for was coming.

"Are you ready for the dinner party tomorrow evening?"

"Oh, you don't know how ready I am."

Thankful Desiree had agreed to help, I nearly forgot how angry I had been with Langley.

We prepared the formal dining room, and I felt a twinge of excitement as Desiree showed me the centerpiece she made. The silk ivory roses in the fancy gold vase gave the otherwise stiff and colorless room a welcoming feel.

"Desiree, honey, I may need to keep this on the table always. It looks absolutely beautiful. The Lord's really given you so many gifts. I don't know what you're better at, the jewelry making or the floral arrangements. I really believe you got that from your Honey. Lord knows, I don't have a lick of talent for things like that."

My daughter's gloomy face brightened. "Thanks, Mama, but you know how Dad is about too much color. He can be so drab. I can't believe that you all still don't have one wall painted anything but white in this enormous house. It's just a shame."

"Child, you know as well as I do that he says the house will sell better if we keep the walls white. That was, what? Ten years ago?"

"I'd have to challenge him on that. He'd just have to come home and find at least one room painted my favorite color."

"Girl, you done lost your natural mind for sure." I smiled at the thought though.

The doorbell rang, and I rushed to let the caterers in, making sure to inspect the dishes: crisp duck breast with pink peppercorn sauce, haricots verts and red peppers, lemon bulgur timbales with chives, and raspberry tart for dessert. Not too bad of a menu for a gal from the outskirts of Dothan, Alabama. Not too many years ago, I couldn't even tell you what that was. After years of learning the ropes of becoming a Huntsville socialite and too many failed attempts at gourmet cooking, I had finally resigned and done like most socialites and mastered the art of menu selection, leaving the cooking to the experts.

Langley demanded perfection, and, at my age, I had discovered some things were better when you paid to get them done. My pride wasn't hurt one bit, anymore. Did the food really taste any better when I'd slaved in the kitchen for at least a day or two before one of his infamous dinner parties? Besides, at least I had one thing to discuss with the other doctors' wives, even if it was something shallow like which caterers were the best in the city.

Newly married, I had taken a stab at hosting one of Langley's dinner parties. I made the mistake of cooking my famous fried chicken, candied yams, potato salad, fresh cooked greens, honey-glazed ham, and buttery peach cobbler. Everyone at the dinner sang my praises, but Langley blew up.

"Soul food, Isabella? Really? This is not a backyard cookout; this is a professional gathering. Did you see how Dr. Upshire turned his nose up when he saw the pinto beans? Oh, and Dr. Garrison kept asking, 'Now what is this?' If you were attempting to embarrass me, you did a fine job!"

I remembered crying myself to sleep, but it didn't do me any good. At the time, I didn't understand. Now, I knew better. He didn't embrace his whole culture, just certain parts. He'd support and attend the United Negro College Fund benefits, black fraternity meetings, and all sorts of other clubs and committees for African Americans, but just don't cook him soul food, at least not in public. Don't remind him of his blackness unless it is going to make him shine.

Being married to Langley led me to a series of revelations. One of the first came when I realized how proud he was for being so light that people had to guess whether he was white or black. Another came after we had been married a year. He sat me down and said like he was explaining a diagnosis or something. "Isabella, you're a beautiful woman."

I felt warm on the inside as he continued. "You have an innate class and poise that is truly rare." I couldn't recall anyone ever describing me with words like class or poise.

He continued, "Well, this is difficult for me to express to you. I don't want to make you feel badly, but your grammar could use a little work. I know that you never had the opportunity to get a degree, by the way, which I think is totally unnecessary for you to have, but I was thinking that perhaps an English or maybe a speech class might do well for you." He loosened his tie and cleared his throat.

"What?" Tears sprang up suddenly, and my cheeks warmed with embarrassment. "What's wrong with my grammar and speech?"

Langley shifted around in his chair, clearing his throat again. "You don't speak horribly, but the Black vernacular is not appropriate in the circles in which we socialize."

"The black what?" I said, not knowing what the devil he was talking about.

Langley's frustration equaled mine. He put his hands up. "Okay, okay. Isabella, I just think that learning standardized English wouldn't be a bad idea. Maybe taking a grammar class could help?"

My back stiffened. "How do you think I got to be thirty-one years old without speaking standardized English?"

He jutted his chin. "You know what I mean, Isabella."

"I'm sorry, Langley, but I don't."

Langley stood up and dug his hands deep in his pockets, grasping for a way to bring his message down to my level. "The way you speak. . . . I just think you could sound a little more professional, a little less ethnic."

The fire inside of me extinguished the hurt. "Langley Morrison, if you don't like the way that I speak, you should've thought about that before you begged me to marry you."

That was the last time he ever spoke about me taking a class. Yet, that bothered me to my core. I spent years paying attention to the way he and other educated people spoke. I learned to leave certain words out of my vocabulary and include ones that I thought made me sound educated. Overall, I'd only noticed him wince every now and then when I apparently used a word in the wrong context. I guessed as far as my husband was concerned, I'd never quite measured up. To him, I was no more than an unopened glittery package with a big, pretty bow, but empty on the inside.

I knew that people tended to idealize loved ones when they're gone, but it had taken a lot of years for me to stop comparing Langley to Ray. Whenever Langley hurled one of his little nice-nasty insults my way, I couldn't help thinking about how Ray always seemed to be pleased as punch by my speech and just about everything else about me.

Ray's job was just that: his job. He was responsible and a hard worker, but family was the center of his world. Not

Langley. He did that job like it was gonna earn his way into heaven or something. He was really gone most of the time, but anytime I got lonely, I remembered the choice I made after Ray died. Langley took the struggle out of everyday, "trying to make it" living; but the thorn in my flesh got bigger by the day.

Only, the older I got and the more miserable Desiree seemed to be, the more I questioned that choice to marry Langley. My focus on breaking the family curse of poverty and broken marriages sure had helped to make me and my daughter two lonely people.

Thunder rumbled in the distance as I began to invite the dinner guests in. I smiled, welcoming them in to our shell of a home, but shuddered inside with a strange inkling that a storm was headed my way.

CHAPTER 5

DESIREE

Can two walk together unless they agree?
—Amos 3:3

The angry autumn rain pounded like a frantic drummer on my rooftop. I yawned and peeled back the sheer curtain, watching the neighbor's wet collie pick through the garbage strewn on the sidewalk by the ferocious wind whistling through the trees. They had forecasted rain, but Huntsville summer storms could instantly stir up a tornado.

I scanned the channels. No watches, no warnings. No easy way out of the date.

As if the gray day weren't enough to keep me stationary, *The Imitation of Life,* one of my favorites, would be coming on AMC. Another bad blind date was not my idea of fun; I'd have rather been alone.

Mama, however, refused to let Margie's request go. She had called three times.

"What do you have to lose, Desiree? Let's just forget about Margie. Besides, Alice says he's real nice. It's her nephew, for goodness' sakes. He's got to be worth something. Honey, he may just be the one."

I knew that my fate would be sealed with my mother for an eternity if I backed out. She'd never let me forget it, always dangling the carrot in front of a starving bunny, saying how I'd missed out on a potential Mr. Right.

The last time Mama called, she pulled the final trump card. "I know you are still upset about Ty, but you gotta let that go."

"For the hundredth time, Mama, his name is Taye. Anyway, I'm over him. I don't even think about him anymore."

I only partially lied to Mama, too. Taye did enough for me to be over him. His daily messages proved to be almost unbearable, but I didn't know it could get worse. The real trouble began when he stopped calling.

One night, I nearly drowned in a gallon of Blue Bell ice cream and a pecan pie. Another night, it was Thomas Pit's pulled pork sandwiches, smothered with sweet pickles and white sauce. After watching *Love Story* on a particularly difficult evening, I graded papers, popping Krispy Kreme donuts and Cheetos until I got sick. I knew that he was no good, but there were days when I missed him.

After one visit to a psychiatrist specializing in compulsive eating disorders, I never went back. Dr. Stein peered at me over her red bifocals. "Ms. Morrison, after reading through your paperwork and listening to your eating habits, I am going to diagnose you with emotional eating disorder, which quite simply means that you are eating for other reasons than hunger."

I wanted to tell her, "No kidding, Sherlock," but instead I nodded as if she were telling me something new. Dr. Stein rattled off her checklist, differentiating between emotional hunger versus physical hunger. "I need to make sure that when you find yourself eating to fill the void, in other words when you're not hungry, that you put a strategy in place to replace eating. For instance, when you want to eat, try taking a walk, calling a friend, or even replacing a healthy food for a comfort food."

Blah, blah, blah.

"Ms. Morrison, you aren't morbidly obese, but you are headed there if you don't get this under control. We will work on this together, and you just take this one day at a time."

She concluded her session by offering her positive, "textbook approach to end all sessions with" spiel. I let her finish, then asked, "Can you prescribe me some weight loss medication? Or, better yet, how about a recommendation for bariatric surgery or the lap band?"

She took her glasses off. "You're not big enough to have those procedures done. Besides, that wouldn't take care of the root of the problem."

I left, never to return.

The phone rang again. Mama always called again after we hung up. "Mama, please—"

When I heard the masculine chuckle on the other end, my cheeks warmed. "Oh, I'm sorry. I thought it was someone else."

"No problem."

"Robert?"

"Yes, Desiree, it's me. Remember, call me Bobby B. That's what my family and friends call me."

I cut to the chase. "How old are you?" I asked.

"Excuse me?"

"You must be younger than what I expected if you expect me to call you that with a straight face." I knew that he'd be offended, but I didn't care. Anybody bad and bold enough to walk around expecting people to call you something like that had to be ready for criticism.

Unfazed, he continued, "Hey, I'm just calling to let you know that I'm around the corner from your house."

I reapplied my copper coin-colored lipstick, the one I wore with everything, after bumping one last curl in my hair. Almost daily, I thanked God for giving me at least one physical trait of Mama's. My hair, freshly kissed with blond highlights from my favorite beautician, made people pay attention to me. There were the gentle pulls and flips from women, trying to not so inconspicuously detect if it was mine. And of course, men drooled over my hair, making me the envy of many women, even with my extra curves.

At Dad's request, Mama wore her long, straight black hair in a bun almost every day. When she unraveled it at night, Mama looked like a black, beautiful Rapunzel. I remembered asking her as a teenager why she always wore it up. She explained, "Desiree, sometimes you got to do what's necessary to make your man feel secure."

No enlightened woman in the twenty-first century would buy into Mama's philosophy about how to keep your husband happy and secure, especially since Dad didn't even seem happy.

The doorbell rang over and over again, like a kid playing with it. My stomach sank. He really was a kid. I inhaled, popped a Tums, and adjusted my plunging neckline. With my large bust, everything but a turtleneck posed problems. I practiced my smile and decided it was good enough to leave on when I opened the door, only to discover that the "Hello, Robert" that I wanted to come out wouldn't. Time stood still for a few seconds. Stunned by the innumerable freckles that covered his almost albino-like complexion, I stood speechless. Never had I ever seen any person, white or black, with so many freckles. Even his eyelids were covered with them.

He extended his ghostly chubby and freckled hand politely. "Nice to meet you, Desiree."

By Robert's smile, I sensed that he was pleased with my appearance. I, on the other hand, thought that he should be in *The Guinness Book of World Records* for the most freckled person. Still, I had been training like an athlete conditioning himself for a marathon not to quickly dismiss someone over superficial things like initial attraction. I'd try to have fun anyway.

My habit of imagining children with every guy I went out on a date with turned strange. We hadn't made it out of the door, and I'd already imagined consoling our future children from school bullies over their freckles.

"Please come in and have a seat," I finally managed to say. "Would you like something to drink?"

Robert was dressed appropriately in a golf shirt and khakis; that is, until he sat down, exposing his white athletic socks with black scuffed dress shoes. Without asking, he grabbed a few mints from the candy jar on the coffee table.

"No, thanks, but I hope you don't mind?" he asked as he held up his hand with the mints.

"Help yourself. I'm just going to grab my purse."

"Yeah, okay. How long have you lived here?" he called as I powdered my face, still trying to gather my wits from the freckles. I wanted to call Margie and tell her off.

I responded, "Oh, I guess it'll be four years in September."

"You like pink, huh?"

"Yes, how did you know that?" I smiled. My living room, decorated in muted tones of tan and chocolate brown, had just a hint of pink accents.

"Well, the throw pillows gave it away."

"Ahh," I said, "I forgot about those. Pink is my passion." I chuckled in my girly tone.

"That's a little weird but interesting."

"Weird? Really? A lot of women like pink."

"I used to be into color analysis. Hmmm. . . . Let me see. I think pink is the color that's supposed to neutralize disorder. I believe some prisons use it to diffuse aggressive behavior."

And he thinks I'm weird?

I walked back to the room, throwing my cape around my shoulders. "I see. You ready?" I asked.

"You really look nice, Desiree. I'm so relieved. I was afraid you might look, well, you know, not too good since it's a blind date and all."

"Thank you, Robert," I replied, wishing I could return the compliment.

He held his freckled, chubby index finger up in a scolding manner. "Uh, uh, uh. Remember, call me Bobby B."

"Sorry," I murmured, hardly sincere.

Lighter-skinned men had never been my cup of tea, but I was determined not to let the fact that he didn't look exactly how I pictured spoil my evening. His tightly coiled reddish hair and broad nose were the only things that gave away his ethnicity. I'd never seen someone so white.

Bobby B was indeed Bobby B and not Robert after all. When we got to his purple Geo Prism, a car I thought was extinct years ago, he didn't bother to open my car door. A pile of papers littered the passenger side seat, and I waited for him to clear it.

"Oh, just throw that stuff in the back seat," he offered, starting the car up before I had a chance to get in.

"If you want me to get in this car, you need to clear it off yourself," I said as kindly as I could.

He scooped up the pile and tossed it across the back seat.

When I got in, the smell of stale fast food and gas fumes hit me. He pushed a cassette tape in, and smiled at me, pointing to my seat belt. I buckled up, prayed that his car wouldn't break down, and prayed that nobody I knew would see me in his loud, outdated clunker.

"I didn't realize people still listened to cassette tapes."

"Yeah, I love my cassette tapes and VHS tapes. I'm old school, all the way, baby. It might be because my parents are older. They taught me to appreciate their way of doing things. My car is a little old, but it has a Toyota engine. I keep the oil changed, and I believe that this baby will run forever."

"Robert, I mean, Bobby, you're not that old school because you didn't think about opening my car door."

He turned the volume up, not bothering to address my comment. Instead of music coming through the car speakers, the roar of the ocean's crashing waves filled the silence. *He's trying to be funny,* I thought. I smiled and turned toward him, but he appeared to be in his own peaceful world. I'd always wondered what kind of people actually bought the nature soundtracks and now my questions were answered. I waited for him to turn it down or explain the significance, but instead, he remained silent. Why the guy wasn't the least bit interested in finding out about me or talking about anything was beyond me. Had Margie spilled every detail she thought she knew about my life?

"So, Bobby B, are you glad to be back in Huntsville?" I said, almost yelling over the ocean. He didn't respond so I spoke louder. "Bobby B!"

"Hey, yeah, what's up?" he asked as if I were disturbing him from deep thought as he reluctantly turned the ocean down.

"I was just asking whether you think you'll stay in Huntsville. I know you're from here, but most people from Huntsville can't wait to leave, at least for a little while."

"The Rocket City is A-okay with me." With that said, he turned the ocean sounds back up, and this time I figured I'd just let the waves roll.

Besides, when we stopped at a light, I caught a glimpse of his freckles again, and decided he looked downright creepy. From that point on, I decided to really avoid looking at him unless absolutely necessary. I wasn't in the mood to pry a conversation out of anybody, particularly somebody like him.

He pulled into the Olive Garden, and I tried not to be offended. He hadn't even asked me if I liked Italian. Although I did like Italian, Olive Garden ranked low on my list.

Bobby B got out of the car, and I groped for the correct lever to pull the door open until I realized that the handle didn't work. I had to knock on the window to get his attention.

I rolled down my window.

"Oh, I'm sorry about that. I need to get that handle fixed."

Fixed? This car needs to be put out of its misery. Without a hint of embarrassment, he opened the door and began racing ahead of me into the restaurant.

Bobby B's future in my world was on life support. He had swung his three strikes, and we hadn't even stepped foot inside the restaurant.

After we sat down, he folded his hands on the tabletop. "So, Desiree, how are things in your corner of the world?"

I resisted the urge to tell him we really were in two different planets. "Things are fine. What about you?"

A perky blonde whose ponytail swung long after she stood still came to take our order. "Hey, guys! My name is Meg, and I'll be your waitress tonight. Can I get you started on some drinks?"

"Can you bring out a large bowl of lemons with my water?" Then, he asked me, "Should I order you a bowl of lemons too? We can make some lemonade and save a few bucks on drinks."

Meg raised her eyebrows and then smiled just like they told her to do in training.

"I'll have ice water, please—no lemons."

Bobby stopped Meg before she turned to get the drinks. "Do I get that free salad and bread sticks with the spaghetti dinner?"

"Yep, you sure do, sure," the happy waitress chimed, rolling her eyes as soon she turned away from him.

I excused myself to the ladies' room but wanted to make a mad dash for the door. Usually, I drove my own car when I went out on a blind date, but since Bobby was Alice's nephew, I broke my rule and let him pick me up. Never again.

Over dinner, Bobby dulled me with his monotonous tone and incessant desire to inflate his already outrageous ego. And in spite of his Christian upbringing, Bobby didn't say grace before he dove at his plate with the vengeance of a quarterback ready to make a dash for the winning touchdown. He ignored my bowed head in prayer and inhaled his plate of spaghetti in minutes. My teeth inadvertently clenched at the sight of him snorting down his food, and the scary sound effects were enough for me to avoid eye contact from that point on.

After the earsplitting little squeals of Bobby's fork scraping across the plate to scoop the remnants of spaghetti into his mouth, he left a thin trace of sauce at the corner of his mouth and a few drops on his shirt to top it off. Only then did I really know how much I didn't like the guy because I had no intention of telling him. I reveled in knowing that he looked stupid, chatting incessantly about his achievements, and only hoped that I didn't look equally silly sitting here with him.

Since I had pretty much lost what little appetite I had, I asked the waitress to box the rest of my meal. Bobby took a swallow of his table-made lemonade. "I'm surprised that's all you're eating."

"Excuse me?" Although I had heard him perfectly, I didn't know exactly how to take that comment.

He chuckled a bit. "Well, you know what I mean, Desiree. You don't look like you miss a whole lot of meals. You're a healthy girl, and you didn't eat as much as I thought you would."

"Is that right? Well, maybe you should consider using one of those lemons on some of those freckles. Isn't that what they say?" I smiled.

Bobby B leaned back in his chair. "You have a pretty sharp tongue, don't you now?"

I said a quick prayer that the Lord would direct my tongue. The only problem was that when I opened my mouth, nothing came out. I took it as a sign, and instead opted for a look that spoke volumes. Mama had taught me the infinite possibilities of facial expressions conveying things words could never do.

A trace of pink flushed Bobby's speckled cheeks and he squirmed in his chair upon the realization that he had insulted me. In the awkward silence that ensued, the blond waitress tried to lay the bill discreetly beside Bobby.

He scanned the ticket and slapped the bill down on the table. "Whew!"

"What?" I asked, no longer attempting to hide my frustration.

"They raised the prices."

In my desperation to get home, I searched my purse for my wallet and slid twenty dollars in his direction to cover my portion for the bill, tip and all.

He smiled like he had hit the jackpot. "That's what I'm talkin' about. A woman who knows how to kick in and pull her own weight. Get it?" He emphasized the word "weight" and seemed tickled by his play on words.

When I saw him pull his tip card from his wallet, I had seen enough. I didn't wait for him to get up from the table. I headed for the lobby, wondering how much of *The Imitation of Life* I had missed.

When we got in the car, Bobby offered to take me to get ice cream, but I yawned and politely told him I needed to get home to bed so I could make it to Sunday School. Guilt struck me like lightning when I realized how easily that lie slipped out. I hadn't been to Sunday School in months, but I figured I'd better press my way tomorrow. Maybe this date was productive if I'd get back to Sunday School.

After pulling into my driveway, Bobby started to turn the car off with intentions, I guessed, of walking me to the door. Before he could take the key out of the ignition, I insisted, "Please, I'm fine walking myself in. Thank you."

"No, the pleasure has been mine." I wondered why he tried to mask the disappointment on his face by offering me a weak smile and his extended hand for me to shake. I gave him a limp handshake and tried to open the door, forgetting that I was trapped.

He chuckled. "You're trapped."

I didn't crack a smile. "Let me out, please."

When he opened my door, I bolted for my front door. *No second dates for Bobby B, the freckled wonder.*

CHAPTER 6

ISABELLA

A man who has friends must show himself friendly, but there is a friend that sticketh closer than a brother.
—Proverbs 18:24

Most of the time I wasn't even the slightest bit tempted to take even a sip of wine available at the numerous charity events Langley and I attended, but my mouth almost watered as the server offered up the grape juice–looking drinks on the silver platter. I couldn't believe how difficult it was to get an iced tea or a Coke. While Langley sauntered about the room doing his best to get everyone's attention, I knew he conveniently avoided conversing with me.

No matter how much I fussed at the beginning of our marriage about his lack of consideration and downright rudeness by leaving me alone at social events, he insisted I attend them with him. He also remained aloof and detached. Thank Jesus for the Holy Ghost, though, the only comfort I had.

The best thing about the night was the color. Women decorated the sparkling ballroom in their shades of coral and orange evening gowns, complementing the elegant apricot decorations. The charity ball, dedicated to raise awareness and money for multiple sclerosis, hardly made me think it was making anyone aware of anything but drinking and dancing. Seemed much more like a party to me, and I didn't consider the MS banner and small, untouched table of information in the entrance raised that much awareness, although I was sure it probably did contribute a pretty penny to help find a cure, which was most important.

It'd be at least an hour or two before Langley would be ready to leave, so I stepped out on the balcony for some fresh air. A million stars lit up the dark, clear night, and I couldn't help thinking about my first husband. On a night like this one, Ray and I would've sat on the front porch, hugged, or at least held hands, dreaming about our future. Life had so much more promise and peace when sharing it with a loving spouse.

Langley was too much of a realist to talk about dreams. To him, dreams were watered-down versions of goals. I still dreamt though, but mostly for Desiree to have a better life than me.

I removed the satin jacket to my simple but stylish St. John, ready to feel the air cool my arms. A loud cackle interrupted my quiet time, and I decided it was time to retreat inside. A white-haired, blue-eyed older woman dripping with diamonds clung tightly to her mate, a much younger man, reminiscent of James Bond. The woman pointed toward me. "Honey, can you get us some more to drink? White wine for me. What'll you have, Bruce?"

Bruce held his liquor much better than his counterpart because his smile faded quickly as recognized what she had said.

Bruce's face reddened. "Pauline, that's not one of the servers!" Pauline apparently found this hilarious and despite her old age, she giggled like a silly teenager.

"Oh, they are everywhere these days, aren't they?"

My eyes bore into Pauline. I considered giving her a piece of my mind but always held it together in a crunch. I represented Dr. Morrison and all other African Americans. Treating ignorance with ignorance only made things worse. With a deliberate about-face, I returned to the inside party but ready to leave.

To add insult to injury, I found Langley in the personal space of a tall, busty brunette. Now a woman can do many things in these kinds of situations and downright embarrass herself. Or she can take the high road, the one I chose. With a smile that overtook his usual grim countenance, I watched in horror as Langley flirted with the woman. I caught Dr. Summers, a colleague friend of Langley's, watching me with sympathy, and my face warmed.

I gathered myself together and raced out to call a cab.

During the ride home, I decided that was the last event Langley and I would attend together. I refused to let myself be served up on a silver platter for rejection, humiliation, and disrespect. I groped for a Word that would comfort me. The only scripture that came to mind was, "If the unbeliever departs, let him. God has called us to peace." Sure, the peace I wanted to give him was a piece of my mind, but what good is your religion if you don't exercise it in times of great duress? Pastor Kingston always said that. Besides, it's not like Langley's unfaithfulness was a newsflash. All the signs had been there. The new blow was how bold he'd gotten with it.

Who was I fooling though? Langley saw the faint dark circles under my eyes that even makeup didn't totally hide. He certainly noticed that my once long, dark hair grayed a little more with each passing month. I could hardly stand wearing the high heels he loved so much. The sag in my breasts, the small pouch in my stomach that no amount of exercise would erase, and the fine lines formed around my mouth in a smile clearly made me unattractive to my husband. I was sure. By the time I got home, my long list of imperfections and justifications for Langley's infidelity grew quite long.

After turning the alarm system off and starting up the spiral staircase, I reminded myself of the deal I had made. Langley wanted an arm piece. He needed a wife. What for? I didn't know. As for me, I wanted a better life for me and my daughter. Now that Desiree was doing well, I contemplated leaving. The Bible says you can do that when your spouse commits adultery, but as silly as it sounds, sometimes it seemed like more trouble than it was worth. I hadn't worked in years. What would I look like starting over at my age?

For the most part, Langley had kept up his part of the bargain. My friends, especially Alice, said they couldn't help but envy my life, and I could honestly say I wanted for nothing material. I got to play golf, a sport he schooled me in during the first couple years of our marriage, at the country club, go to the gym regularly, and get my hair done at least once a week. I went to the spa once every month or so, and I even gave in a few years ago to Langley's insistence on getting a housekeeper. If all I had to worry about was Langley's little flings, I shouldn't have been as miserable as I was. But I was.

Truth be told though, no matter how many Gucci and Chanel bags I owned, I could only carry one at a time. Shopping used to be my fix, but with age I'd lost my enthusiasm for it. The things that brought me joy now were the simple things. Going to lunch with Desiree, working in the church, planting in my garden, and slipping Alice a little extra money every now and then, that's what made me happy.

When I heard my cell phone ringing, I knew right away it was Langley. For a second, I considered ignoring the call.

"Isabella, where are you?"

"Do you really care?"

"Don't start," he answered, agitated.

"You're the one who's started something."

"I am not in the mood for this tonight, Isabella."

"What *are* you in the mood for?"

"Just tell me where you are."

"At home, Langley."

"How did you . . . Never mind. I'll be home in a few hours."

I started to protest, but changed my mind, resigned to my lot in life. The Lord would have to be the one to convict him of his ways, not me.

"Isabella, good Lord, did you hear me?"

"Why you insist on using the Lord's name in vain?"

"I don't have time for this. Good-bye, Isabella."

As I undressed and unpinned my hair, I thought about my youth. I would've responded differently to him some years back. I no longer had the energy or stamina for his crazy antics.

After a hot shower, I felt better and decided to check on Desiree even though it was late. When I picked up the phone, she was on the other end and the phone hadn't even rung.

"What a coincidence because I was calling you," Desiree said.

"And I was calling you! How was your date with Alice's nephew?"

"You don't even wanna know, Mama. All I have to say is please don't try to set me up like that ever again."

"What's wrong with him?"

"More like what's right about him."

"It was that bad? He's a professional and that's a step in the right direction. Just make sure that you, at least, gave him a chance."

"Mama, that's not the issue. He was that bad. You really confuse me. Do you want me to lower my standards like I supposedly did with Taye, or raise them? I'm confused."

"I don't mean lower them into the trash can. Set the bar high, but don't be unrealistic."

"Oh, okay, whatever that means. You raised me not to judge people, yet you do a lot of that when it comes to my choice in men."

Maybe she was right. "I'm not being judgmental because I want you to be equally yoked, daughter."

"Here we go." Desiree's voice trailed off.

"Here we go, nothing," I said, annoyed.

"Just see things the way they really are. Today is a new day. Men are different."

"Oh, I see, honey. Every closed eye ain't 'sleep. I know more than you think I know."

"Maybe what you know is still not enough."

I sensed that there was more behind her words. "What's that supposed to mean? If you want to tell me something, say it."

Desiree blew out a long breath. "I'm sorry, Mama. I just want you to understand that things aren't as simple as you seem to think they are. Times have changed."

"That's just it, Desiree. Our standards should be the same Christian standards you have been raised by all of your life."

"I appreciate the Christian values. Mama, you had me in church every Sunday, Bible Study every single week, and all of the extras in between. I know the Bible. I really do. I'm the last person you need to preach to. No disrespect, but how is all of that helping in your relationship with Dad?"

Shocked, I fell silent for a few seconds. Desiree and I didn't really discuss the state of my marriage much. I always made a point of not letting her know that things were as difficult as they were.

"Okay, if you must know, Desiree, the spirit of the Lord is the only reason why I could make it after your daddy passed, and He helped me to raise you by myself until I married your stepfather."

"Mama, I asked you a question. How has all that you know helped you? Dad won't even hardly ever step foot in the church."

"I am trying to help you from making some of the mistakes I've made. Can't you see that? God has helped me to see that it's not always about happy and lovey-dovey feelings. It's about faithfulness, commitment, and making the choice to love, in spite of whatever."

Desiree mumbled, "Faithfulness and commitment?"

I acted like I didn't hear her. I didn't want to delve into the place she was going, but my stomach dropped. She knew something.

"Anyway, Mama, I'm just saying that I'm tired of church, not God, just church. Over these past few years, I've noticed that so many in church are motivated by their personal agendas. It's almost worse than the secular world. People politicking over positions, power and prestige. People throwing off on other people every time they get a mic in their hand instead of just preaching and teaching the Word."

"Now, you can't say that about Pastor Kingston," I interrupted.

"Maybe not him, but most everyone else does it. It's a turnoff."

"I thought you were more spiritually mature than that, Desiree. You got to look past some things. Eat the meat and throw away the bones."

"Maybe I'm not even where I think I am. All I know is that I'm tired of church as usual. I want to feel like what I'm doing in church, what I know in the Word, is applicable to me in life."

I couldn't believe how she vented, but at least I knew how she felt. "Maybe you should talk to Pastor Kingston about how you're feeling. I'm sure that if you think I don't understand, he will."

She sighed. "I'm sorry. I'm not saying everything the way that I want to, but I do know that one of my frustrations is that we're supposed to be at church all of the time. Yet, the church is full of single women, not broke-down women, but attractive, saved, good women. You all have the women believing that Prince Charming is going to come charging through the door to marry them and it just isn't so. There are no available men at our church, oh, unless you want to talk about Deacon Bill, who hits on anybody in a skirt. And yes, there's Brother Alvin, nice looking and gay as the day is long. Besides, what good is all that churchin' if you do it like you do, and the path still leads to not being happy?"

"I've never said that I wasn't happy. I said that it's not always about being happy." I stammered. "I have peace and joy, understand that."

"Okay, Mama." Desiree sounded like she didn't believe me.

"Your point is well taken that people are human in church, that's why we need the Savior. I'd hardly say that the church is full of agenda-driven folks the way you say. The problem is that usually these people make a lot of fuss and the good folks just suffer long with them."

"Is that what it is?" Desiree said, not really asking.

"I can see where all of this could be a major problem if a person wasn't really grounded in the faith. A personal relationship with Jesus brings clarity to things that look a mess. You see people and things with new eyes. As far as the men in church, that's a problem. I don't know all the answers, but I know that if you'll just be faithful, God will give you the desires of your heart."

"Yes, Mama, I know that He will. So, where is Dad?"

I knew that she was changing the subject to end the discussion. "I left him at the ball. He had business to attend to."

She yawned. "Well, Mama, I need to let you go."

"Listen, you get some rest now, and we'll continue this conversation later."

My thoughts lingered on Desiree and then back on Ray. No way would I have had a conversation like this if Ray were alive. She wouldn't question how God operated in my life. She could see it in our love for each other and for her. We both showered Desiree with all the love we had to give. Seemed like we loved that girl so much from the day she was born, we barely had a bit left for each other by the time we put her to bed each night.

Ray used to go right for her as soon as he walked in the door from a long day at work. After lifting that heavy mail all day with his tired, aching feet, he'd drag himself in the door, find Desiree, and toss her in the air until she'd laugh so hard she'd cry. Before he knew it, he had regenerated some of the energy the post office had zapped from him.

I couldn't bear to tell him that I was a little jealous of him showing Desiree all that attention. Instead, I would tell him, "Ray, you ought not throw that girl up so high. You gonna shake her brain up somethin' awful."

He'd just laugh and wave me off. "What'chu talkin' about, woman? Now, Bella, this here ain't no ordinary gal. This is the prettiest and toughest gal in Alabama. She needs to be tossed around now while she's still little. Might as well get used to it. Lord knows, life will shake her up."

Being a widow at twenty-seven years old shook me up for sure and Desiree losing her father Ray was almost more than any of us could bear. Before Ray, life had already taught me to be a realist but a hopeful one. After

Ray's death I became a pragmatist, a word I learned from Langley, and I had lost my vision for myself. I clung to the small bits of hope, but only because of my faith in God and love for my daughter.

After Ray's death, in a flash, possibilities narrowed and closed like the iron curtain. In 1975, it was hard enough to be a black woman, but to be a single mother with no college education or money put me in a tough spot. I had been too entrenched with my family to even fully understand what all the fuss of the Women's Movement was all about. I was too busy fighting a bigger monster than being a woman. Racism made me feel like I was constantly walking a tightrope. Couldn't be too black or too white acting because you would easily attract the wrong kind of attention.

Honey had scolded me in no uncertain terms after Ray's death, "You go ahead and cry a spell, then wipe them tears and recognize you got a lot more than plenty folks do." She then whispered, "All you gotta do is look at Josephine. She got a much harder load to tow if you know what I mean. She'd be cute if the world didn't have you to compare her to."

Her false teeth slid out a bit and clicked. "You a pretty woman, Isabella, but pretty don't last forever. Look at me. I wasn't pretty as you, but I looked good enough. You need a man who got some money to take care of you and Desiree. You can grow to love a man if he got more than two dimes to rub together. You got a strike against you 'cause you got a chile, but you got Desiree the right way and, like I said, you look like somethin' special for now. Don't let that go to waste this time, girl. You got a chance to go ahead and make somethin' more of your life. Give that baby a chance to have what you didn't have. Give her a chance to go to college."

I had heard some form of this one way or another all throughout my life from my grandmama, and she'd liked to have had a cow when I married Ray. Against my dear grandmother's wishes, I chose love. Ray was love, as sappy as it sounds.

When we got married, Ray's parents were thrilled. During the ceremony, I was the happiest I'd ever been with the exception of the two times I'd messed up and looked at Honey. Her lips struggled to purse because her dentures didn't fit, and she sucked in constantly, mad as fire.

Honey had told me after first meeting Ray, "Lord have mercy on your sweet soul, you a silly girl, Isabella. I done taken care of you when my own daughter wouldn't and this is how you repay me. I got more than that boy, and I ain't got more than a hill of beans! He ain't got nothing, you hear me? Nothing."

Her head shook in an exaggerated motion. "Chile, you could have 'bout anybody you want with that face and good hair like that. God didn't give me no face like that, 'cause the good Lord knows I'da used it to help both of us." She sucked in her teeth one last time and plopped back in her rickety rocking chair on the sad, weathered porch.

Honey always got her way with me by making me feel guilty. It was always the same. I should've been more grateful that she sacrificed everything to raise me. I was what they call these days a people pleaser normally, but not this time. Ray made me feel too good to please Honey that time.

I remembered staring down the large hole on the porch like I always did as Honey spoke, but I didn't say one word. Back then, you didn't dare talk back or express your feelings like young folks do these days. Desiree didn't know how good she had it. Sure, it hurt that Honey couldn't stand my choice, but I also felt the woman in me rise to the occasion, determined to live the way I saw fit, poor or not.

Honey was wrong about Ray though. He made a better than decent living at the post office. We didn't have a house in the suburbs, but at least our house didn't have holes in the porch. After convincing her to come visit after we closed on the house, she sucked her teeth the whole time.

"Y'all ain't got no swimmin' pool?"

"Where's that electric dishwasher that everybody's talkin' about? What's the point of payin' all that money if you ain't gonna have one of them?"

"That yard is so small, you can't put no garden or tree. Just a shame."

On Honey's way out to the car, she almost hissed, "Y'all might get there if you take some classes at the college. Mabel's daughter got all the nice stuff. Lord, Bella, please don't go rush and have no babies. Go to school first."

As soon as she left, Ray threw the fruit bowl across the room and balled his fist. "That woman!"

I threw my arms around him, soothing his ego. "That's just how Honey is, baby. She doesn't mean any harm at all." And Honey didn't.

As much as Honey worked my nerves, I could never stay mad at her long. She was my mama since my own mama left Honey to raise me not too long after my daddy left. Apparently, when I was too young to remember, we all lived together. What I did remember was that Mama lived like someone had knocked the wind outta her sails. She loved my daddy, but he refused to marry her. According to Honey, Daddy was a stone that never stopped rolling.

Honey told me, "Good thing you don't 'member him, Bella. Some things is better left undone."

I didn't know what she meant then, but it made perfect sense to me now. My mind drifted back to Langley.

Some things really are better left undone and unsaid.

CHAPTER 7

DESIREE

Watch and pray, that ye enter not into temptation: the spirit indeed is willing, but the flesh is weak.
—Matthew 26:41

Shay was late for everything. I used to think it was because she wanted to make a grand entrance, but I'd come to the realization that a much larger and deeper-rooted issue was there. Our friendship had endured her eternal tardiness but at times only by a thread.

I knew once she sashayed through the restaurant doors, my aggravation would dissipate. Shay was just like that. People got entranced or entrapped, whichever you prefer, by her presence. Her face, a muddy brown skin tone plagued with scars from severe teenage acne, would be classified by most as average, but her sparkling eyes danced. Besides, what Shay lacked in the pretty department on the outside, she more than made up for on the inside.

Shay told me the story a million times. Her mother, confident, bold, and pretty on the inside, too, used to sing that Temptations song "Beauty Is Only Skin Deep" to Shay as a little girl.

I'm not quite sure that I would've come out emotionally intact with my mama singing this to me as a child, but it worked with Shay. In spite of her optimism, she, like me, told it like it was.

I had been waiting for her for twenty-seven minutes exactly, and the server kept coming to ask, "May I take your order now?" while glancing at her watch. As soon as I began to give my order, Shay breezed in at the other side of the booth, bringing with her the aroma of a lilies and lavender perfume. Without even opening the menu, Shay said to the waitress, "I'll get the pecan-crusted chicken salad and a glass of unsweetened tea, please."

"Yep," the clearly perturbed waitress answered, without bothering to scribble her order onto the pad.

Shay smiled, head cocked to the side. "Excuse me, miss, but your skin is just flawless. What do you do to keep your skin so clear?"

The testy waitress's demeanor softened, and she caressed her cheeks with both hands. "I guess it must be genetic because all I use is Ivory soap."

Shay's eyes twinkled and she batted her lashes. "I see."

"Well, I do drink lots of water," she offered.

Shay nodded, lightly tapping her hand on the table for emphasis. "It figures. Never used Ivory a day in my life, and I hate drinking water!"

The waitress smiled. "Just squeeze a little lemon in it. It helps the taste and adds antioxidants."

"I guess I'll have to try that if my skin can look as clear as yours. Change that iced tea to water with a splash of lemon," Shay complimented her.

I rolled my eyes.

As the waitress went to put in our orders, I shook my head. "You're a mess, girl."

"What? Her skin is perfect, almost as clear as yours, Des. Anyway, listen, Des, I am so sorry I'm late—"

"Talk to the hand." I took what I liked to call my "cleansing breath," and changed the subject. "So, what's been going on?"

"You see I got my hair cut?"

I frowned. "That's not cut; that's what you call a trim."

"It's cut in a totally new style." She tried to flip her stiff hair and said, "See all the layers?"

"What layers?"

"How can *everybody* else see the layers but you?" Shay asked, clearly annoyed.

"Maybe *everybody* wasn't honest with you." I pretended to look for something in my purse.

Technically speaking, you wouldn't call what Shay and I did arguing, but we teetered on the edge of an argument all of the time, and it was almost always about trivial things we barely remembered twenty minutes later.

She moped, biting her bottom lip.

I leaned forward. "Your hair is cute, Shay, layers or not."

"Thanks," she said, still a little smug.

Shay twirled a chunky red jasper necklace around her fingertips. When I ordered the red stones, I knew that I'd make something for Shay with them. Accented with the rustic metal circular centerpiece, I glued small chips of the red jasper and marcasite.

Shay had gone wild when she opened the box. "I don't care what that costs, Des. I gotta have it."

Of course, I never made a dime when it came to her. Her friendship and thanks always paid me plenty. Nobody got more excited about my jewelry than Shay. She had gotten me more orders than I'd been able to get for myself. Even though she wore the necklace with a green suede skirt and a burgundy turtleneck, breaking all kinds of fashion rules, she still wore it well.

After the waitress served our meals, I ate and Shay talked, ranting about her new dog, son, job, and other, less important topics.

"Des, since Reggie and I divorced, I've been going on this site called Christian Singles Get Together, otherwise known as CSGT. I've talked to some interesting men, and I thought it was a little weird at first, but guess what?"

I stopped chewing, eyebrows raised.

She didn't wait for me to respond. "I met this really nice guy, Paul. We've been dating for almost a month. So, last night we made it official. We're a couple!"

My mouth flew open. "Shay! A month? I've talked to you almost every single day, and you haven't mentioned Paul."

She waved me off. "I know. I didn't want to hear your mouth and your strong opinions. I knew that you'd turn your nose up at how we met. Now, I can take it, so whatever."

She had her nerve.

"A month? I thought we were friends." I couldn't believe her. "You got a little thirsty, didn't you?"

"See? You sound like one of your students. I'm hardly *thirsty*, Desiree. What I am is tired of waiting for a great guy to find me. It's been a blessing for me to take some authority over my choices."

"Quite frankly, Shay, I'm shocked that you would do that whole Internet dating thing. It's so, so beneath someone like you."

Shay held her hand over her heart. "Des, really? I'm not trying to make you feel bad, but let's talk about your success rate running into guys or even meeting them at church. I've raised the standard in my book. I've had the opportunity to find out a lot more about people on the site so that I don't have to waste my time with men who aren't about anything. Actually, what I'm doing is more efficient because I get to weed out the losers much more quickly."

I swallowed down a big gulp of water. "That is, as long as they're not lying to you."

Shay rolled her eyes. "You can be such a pessimist. We shop and pay bills online, and do countless things on the Internet. Why not date and use it for our advantage? It's not the taboo, scary thing that it was awhile back. Anyway, Paul is divine, and I wanted you to be the first to know that we are a couple. Don't hate."

"Girl, please. Nobody's hating on you. For real though, how do you know he's not married, gay, or crazy?"

She shook her head. "If you don't sound like your mama, I don't know who does. You take the same chance if you meet somebody at the grocery store, church, or anywhere else. Taye and Bobby B aren't exactly glowing examples of meeting good men. You can pick and choose what guy you date, and if you feel weird about someone, you just don't date him anymore. You cut out a whole lot of nonsense when you complete your profile. Like I said, everybody is doing it."

I couldn't stand how she said "everybody." Shay always liked to make me feel like I was totally clueless about things. At the same time, she did make a good point. Could dating a guy from the Internet really be as bad as Taye or Bobby B?

"I don't know, Shay. It sounds a little desperate to me, but I am happy if you're happy."

She picked at her food while she talked, which was probably why she was thin and I was not. Talking for her was the exercising that everyone else had to do. In lieu of eating, Shay ran her mouth.

"Well, I am happy, but you, my friend, need to get with the program, and stop waiting for good things to come to you. Honey, sometimes you gotta go after the good things. At least make yourself available so the good thing can find you."

I blew out a long, slow sigh. "Okay, Shay, so tell me about Paul."

"Paul's a private investigator. Isn't that cool? He lives in Decatur but works for the Huntsville City Police Department."

"Wow, I gotta admit, that is interesting."

"Des, you can do the same thing. If you want to meet someone local, you just make that preference when you set up your account. Girl, you need to get your life."

I chuckled as I dipped my last French fry in ketchup. My mouth still full, I said through my munching, "Now, you got a point there."

"That's all I'm saying. What in the world do you have to lose? Besides, you don't have to give anyone your real name or phone number unless you want to."

"So tell me more about this Paul character."

Shay grinned as she pushed her unfinished salad away and almost whispered, "Okay, he's thirty-nine, a little older than me, but so what, right?"

"So what, nothing, girl. That man is nine years older than you!"

"I'm mature. Anyway, he's very fair complexioned with dark features. He looks serious in a private investigator kinda way, and even has a thick mustache, but he's a lot of fun. Most importantly, he seems to be saved for real."

"Really? That's great. Okay, so, how many kids? And has he been married before?"

"I was getting to that. He's been divorced for almost five years, and has a twelve-year-old son who lives with him."

"If he's so saved, why'd he get a divorce?"

"What are you trying to say? I'm saved and divorced. You can be so dogmatic. People make mistakes, Desiree. And sometimes bad things just happen to good people. If you must know, his ex cheated on him. He works a lot."

I raised my eyebrows.

Shay drew her breath in, trying to be patient. "We're getting to know one another, and we've even had a little disagreement and straightened it out. It's like we were made to be together; at least, so far."

I loved Shay, but every now and then jealousy interfered with our closeness, sometimes with her but mostly with me. Paul did sound like a catch.

As I eyed the dessert menu, trying to resist the apple pie à la mode drizzled with hot caramel, I said, "All I know is that you better be careful. Those Internet predators can be sly and dangerous, Shay. A man can be anybody he wants to be on the computer."

Shay rolled her eyes. "We see each other all of the time! Just because you meet people on the computer doesn't mean they're psycho. Again, think about Taye, and he was pretty psycho in my book."

I was bothered by her bringing up Taye. I had eventually told her all about what happened with Taye. It stung for her to bring something so painful up like it was nothing.

"The thing about Taye was that I knew from the start that he was trouble. My loneliness took away some of my good sense," I admitted.

Shay conceded, "Well, I guess we can all make some crazy choices when we're needy."

"I didn't say I was needy. I said lonely."

"Tomato, tomahto."

"There's a big difference, Shay. I don't have any trouble meeting men. I have trouble finding the right one."

"Whatever, Des. I would love to argue with you further, but I have to pick up Stevie from school."

I decided against dessert, but only since Shay had to go. When I tried to reach for the bill, she grabbed it and tucked her credit card in the folder before I could object.

"You're such a sweetie sometimes. Thank you. I owe you one."

"No, you owe yourself." Shay whipped a pen out of her purse and signed the bill the waitress left, and on a napkin wrote: www.christiansinglesgettogether.com. Then she underlined it. "Try it!"

I only took the napkin because Shay had already paid the bill. Besides, I might want to look at the site, but inside I remained resolved. I'd never join a dating site.

CHAPTER 8

ISABELLA

*Thou therefore endure hardness, as a
good soldier of Jesus Christ.*
—2 Timothy 2:3

I missed my sister every day. Technically, she was my aunt, but with only ten years between us, we grew up at Honey's as sisters. Some days I missed her presence worse than others, and during the holidays it was definitely worse. Josephine loved Christmas. She'd come every year to help me decorate, and I'd do the same for her.

Jo had that special quality, the one that changes the atmosphere of anywhere she touched. Langley also had this power, only he often used it for evil. Josephine, bless her heart, used hers mostly for good. Just like the confrontation between a superhero and an evil villain, Langley and Josephine battled it out whenever they met. Somehow though, it never caused conflict with me and Jo, but it always caused a heap of trouble for Langley and me.

He would tell me, "You change around your sister, and I don't care for that one bit at all."

He was right. I did change around my sister. I changed into myself. I took the mask off, refusing to participate in Langley's shenanigans. Never one to argue much with Langley, I relished the times Jo would come and even the score between us, setting him more than straight.

Langley couldn't stand my sister and didn't try to hide it. He couldn't stand her honestly. It didn't help that Langley constantly helped her with finances, and Josephine didn't allow that to cloud her assessment of him.

"Is it necessary for your sister to be so very loud, Isabella?"

"Why must we be responsible for Josephine's inability to manage her finances?"

"It would be nice if *your* sister would respect our home and remove her shoes when she enters."

More than anything, Langley loathed Josephine's fearlessness of him, and I relished it. She would tell me, "The sun don't rise and set on him like you think it does, Bella."

Jo, never one to bite her tongue, didn't care who liked what she said. During one visit, Jo complained about her weight. Langley told her, "It's very simple, Josephine. If you exercise and cut calories, you will lose weight. We have to take the bull by the horns. We have to take hold of the opportunities that we have before us to make ourselves better."

Without missing a beat, Jo, hands on hips, with a bowlful of attitude, fumed, "Take the bull by horns? That's bull! But okay, Dr. Langley, you got yourself a point. In fact, I got a word of advice for you. Dr. Langley: why don't you trade in those Coke-bottle glasses for Lasik? That's one opportunity you need to grab a hold of."

I cut in, trying to avoid conflict, but Jo couldn't be stopped. That is, until lupus got a hold of her. Since Josephine's passing, Langley's behavior had gone from bad to worse. I had no more guns to draw. My defenses were zapped.

After stringing the last of the Christmas lights on the garage door, I opened the front door to hear Langley calling, "Isabella? Isabella?"

"Yes, what do you need, Langley?"

He came down the stairs with his unruly eyebrows frowned in a customary scowl I was all too familiar with. "What are you doing?" Without waiting for me to answer, he said, "It's much too early for Christmas lights. For Pete's sake, it's not even Thanksgiving yet." Without taking a breath, he asked, "Have you seen my black and gold cufflinks?"

"They're in the top small drawer of the armoire."

"How did they get there?" he asked, playing like he didn't know.

"I moved them because all of your other cufflinks were there."

Langley slid his hand over his mouth, stroking his mustache, something he did when he got angry. "Isabella, when I specifically put something somewhere, I expect you to respect my personal space. I mean, at least ask me if it's okay to move them."

I pulled my shoes off with an exaggerated slowness, praying that I could hold my tongue as I had trained myself to do so often with my husband.

"Isabella? Isabella! Did you hear me?"

"Yes, unfortunately, I did," I said avoiding eye contact.

"What's that supposed to mean?"

"That's supposed to mean that I'm just plain tired, Langley."

I walked toward the kitchen and heard him say, "Well, there we go. We actually have something in common for a change."

What did he have to be tired of? He did whatever he wanted to do, whenever he wanted to do it. But Langley had always been like that, charting his own course in life with no real thought of anyone but himself. He had never wanted his own biological children for that very reason. Desiree, well-behaved and obedient, offered him the satisfaction of saying that he had a daughter but without all the inconveniences.

I didn't know it when we married, but children were a hiccup to him, a detour, taking him away from his selfish ambitions. Sometimes I wondered if being a pediatrician had ruined his perception of children.

Determined not to let Langley ruin my holiday spirit, I decided to pull some of the decorations from the storage closet before Desiree arrived to help. On my tiptoes, I stretched and pulled the container toward me a little bit at a time. Once I had a good grip on it, I lifted and, without warning, a stabbing pain shot through the left side of my chest. The piercing pain took by breath away, causing me to send the large, heavy container plummeting to the floor.

Just as I clutched my breath, Desiree rushed in.

"Mama, are you okay?" she said, looking alarmed as she knelt down beside me.

"I don't know," I answered, wanting to reassure her. However, the pain had been so intense it took my breath away. Slowly, the stabbing pain dulled.

"You don't look good. Let me get you a glass of water."

I looked at her, still scared myself. "No, don't leave. Just stay here with me for a minute."

Desiree reached in her pocket for her cell phone. "I'm gonna call Dad. I just passed him on the way in."

I exhaled deeply, and grabbed her arm. "Don't call him. I'm fine. The pain is getting better."

"I still think I should call him."

"I'm tellin' you, I'm fine now. I guess I won't be trying to reach up for anything high and heavy like that again."

Desiree stood up with her hands on her hips. "Mama, why would you try to move this heavy thing? I told you I was coming over to help." She reached over to give me a hand.

"Thank you, baby. I've been having a little trouble lately, but that was the worst it's been."

"You think it's your heart?"

"I don't know but my heart doesn't hurt; feels more like my arm."

"Yeah, we're going to call Dr. Blevins's office right now. Where's your cell? Is he in your contacts?"

I nodded, pointing her to my cell.

Desiree left and returned with a glass of water and her cell phone to her ear. I sipped the water, silently fearful that the awful, familiar pain would come back. "They can see you tomorrow at three o'clock, Mama."

"It's gone now. Probably just a muscle spasm. Or maybe it's gas."

"You think everything is gas, Mama. I'm sure it's nothing, but let's be on the safe side."

Later that evening, I lit a few candles around the bathtub, something I did often when I wanted to relax. I lifted my shirt up over my head, but before I could get the shirt off, the plunging jab once again took my breath away. The stabbing pain bolted through my chest like fire. I dropped my arms down and grabbed my chest, this time scared enough to race for my phone. I dialed Langley's number as fast as I could. In my nervousness, I misdialed and had to try again. The phone rang and rang until his voicemail picked up. Without leaving a message, I began to cry softly and tried again. Something was wrong. Although the pain had already begun to subside, I dialed his number again. This time he picked up.

"Hello, Isabella."

Trying to catch my breath, I sniffed and tried to muffle my sobs. "Langley, something's wrong with me."

"What? What is it?" he said with more excitement than I'd heard in years.

"It's somethin' in my chest on the left side."

"Your chest? It could be your heart. I'll call 911," he said anxiously.

"No, it's starting to go away a little now. Earlier today after you left, I got the same real sharp pain. I don't know what's going on," I said, trying carefully not to breathe deeply as I sat down on the ledge of the bathtub.

"I'll be there in twenty minutes. Just hold on, Isabella."

"Where are you, Langley?" I asked.

"I'm not far. Just relax. I'll be there shortly."

"All right, thank you."

Even in my scared state, it didn't get by me one bit that he didn't answer the phone the first time I called and that he hadn't told me where he was.

I gave myself about ten minutes and decided I felt well enough to go ahead and take my bath. This time, I carefully finagled my shirt and bra off and examined where the pain had been. Everything looked relatively normal, but I held my hand over the top of my left breast where the pain had emanated from. I felt a dull ache and heat seemed to be coming from the spot, but I couldn't be sure.

It had to be a muscle I pulled or something, I decided, relieved that I remembered lifting some huge boxes of canned goods at the soup kitchen several days ago. I had carried them right on my chest, and I was confident I had pulled a muscle then.

After I finished undressing, I sank into the warm bubble bath, feeling better already. While I leaned my head onto the side of the tub, I closed my eyes until I heard a tap on the door that I knew was Langley. Before I could answer, he called my name, easing the door open with a genuine look of concern.

I sat up, startled that he would come in with me undressed and bathing.

He sat down on the ledge of the tub. "How are you?" he asked as he slipped off his cufflinks, rolling his shirt sleeves up.

"I feel fine now." I tried to hide my awkwardness while he felt my head, As he brushed my unruly hair back away from my face, it almost made me want him in a way I hadn't in a very long time.

"You really shouldn't have gotten into the bathtub by yourself, Isabella. Something could've happened."

"Well, I appreciate your concern, and I truly am sorry to bother you, but that pain was somethin' awful. It scared the daylights outta me for the second time today."

"You certainly need to get that checked out tomorrow. Well, I'm glad you're feeling better."

While I began to wash myself, he held his hand out for the bath sponge. "Let me help."

My stomach tightened, but I handed him my sponge. He began to wash my neck and bathe me with so much care I hadn't realized how much I'd missed this much attention.

"Where is the pain coming from again?" he asked.

I directed his hand near my breast, unable to ignore an unfamiliar spark ignite that I thought was long gone. He slowly held my hands in his, gently pulling me up out of the water. All of my usual feelings of self-consciousness about my aging body melted in his loving gaze. I'd even managed to block the image of him touching another woman like this.

Langley grabbed a towel from the linen closet and opened it up, holding it out for me to step into. Once he had me wrapped in the warmth of the towel, he held me and I relaxed in the shelter of his arms.

"I was so worried, Isabella," he said as he caressed my back.

"I'm glad you're home, Langley."

"You smell so good." He released the clip, and my hair, damp and heavy, fell down covering my shoulders. He nuzzled his face in my neck, stroking my hair.

I figured there wasn't much need for words. Maybe Langley did love me a little like a man was supposed to love a woman. I basked in the glory of the moment. Too many times I had taken the physical part of our relationship as a mere marital duty.

For once in a very long time, Langley wanted me. And, boy, did I need to be wanted.

CHAPTER 9

DESIREE

*And the Lord God said, It is not good that the man
should be alone; I will make a helpmeet for him.*
—Genesis 2:18

As a single woman, weekends could be the loneliest
times, especially ones without a date. On days like this,
I missed Aunt Josephine. When she came to visit or I
visited with her, I got to breathe. I picked up my favorite
picture of Aunt Jo and Mama, who, happy and light, had
her arms around Aunt Jo's waist. They both were laughing
so hard that they showed nearly all of their teeth. When
I asked Mama why they were laughing, she had told me
that Aunt Jo had just told her a dirty joke. I tried to hide
my shock. Mama didn't laugh too much and especially
not over anything dirty. But Aunt Jo had that effect on
her. She could say things to Mama that were off-limits to
the rest of world, especially when it came to Dad.

I wanted to bottle up the Mama who appeared when
we visited Aunt Josephine in Dothan, their hometown.
Just twenty miles west from the Georgia state line and
even closer to Florida, Dothan is one of the larger cities in
that part of Alabama. Mama and I visited at least several
times out of the year, but my favorite visits were in the
fall when we would attend the National Peanut Festival.
Mama always seemed to relax and let her guard down in

Dothan, so much so that I even asked her once why she loved going so much.

"Honey, you know that's my home, and my sister lives there."

She felt me waiting for more, so she added, "And because so many good folks come from Dothan. My hometown is straight from the Bible. I bet you didn't know that, did you?"

Mama tended to throw out little tidbits of information that you thought weren't really anything at all. But one day, my curiosity got the best of me and I did a little fact-checking, and discovered that Dothan is in the Bible, more specifically, in Genesis 37:17. It's not a lot, but Mama knew her Bible. I guessed it didn't matter if it's a different Dothan and it only reads, "let us go to Dothan."

Mama, Daddy, Aunt Jo, and just about everyone else I knew from Dothan really were good people. When I was much younger, I wanted to be good folk and come from Dothan too. I thought I even lied to some people in second grade, telling them I was from Dothan. As an adult, I understood that Dothan cradled Mama's innocence. Hope sprang up in her like daisies in the sunshine during our visits there. She and my biological daddy had lived and loved there until his job transferred them to Huntsville.

One time I had even overheard Aunt Josephine telling Mama, "Girl, I just knew you and Ray had no business going to Huntsville." (She didn't pronounce the I.) "That was too much stress on him. Bella, you always was tryin' to be somethin' you wasn't. Talkin' him into takin' that job was wrong. Trust me, he would've been alive if y'all had stayed."

A low groan escaped from Mama's lips, and I decided right then in my eight-year-old mind that just maybe Mama was the one responsible for my daddy's death.

Years passed before I realized that Mama wasn't responsible for my daddy's heart attack.

On the morning of my eleventh birthday, the man I knew as Langley stood hands folded behind his back, his face wearing a plastered, clinical smile. His voice, steady and authoritative, delivered the news much like a doctor would inform a patient that they had been diagnosed with an incurable disease.

"Desiree, first of all," he said, "let me say that I know things have been pretty challenging for you over the past few years. I know that the loss of your father has left an indelible mark on your life, and I could never attempt nor wish to impede upon your memories and wonderful relationship with him. However, we have to move on, and life will be so much easier for you now."

He sighed in frustration when he noticed the puzzled look on my face. He then looked to Mama for help. Mama squeezed me and began to rub her hands across my back. "Langley and I have been married for over a year now, and you're old enough to understand that it's just not proper for a young girl to call the man who is protecting, providing, and. . . . loving her by his first name."

Does she want me to call him Mr. Langley? Mr. Morrison?

"What do you think I should call him?" I stared up at her, hoping that she wouldn't say what I feared.

My stepfather began scratching his neck, shifting from one foot to the other uncomfortably. Mama let go of me, and said sternly, "We both feel it's time for you to call him Dad, dear. Your daddy will always be Daddy, but Langley, your stepfather, will be Dad."

My stomach balled into a tight fist. I bit my bottom lip until I tasted the salty blood pool in my mouth. They both waited for my response, but I didn't say a word.

Mama stood, clasping her hands together happily, seemingly ignorant of my hatred of the idea. I didn't want him to marry Mama in the first place. They didn't go together right. He was weird. Mama wasn't herself with him. I knew enough to know that she was settling. Besides, I didn't want anyone to marry Mama. She had forced me into a role that I didn't want, but even then, I knew fighting wasn't an option.

"Well?" Mama had asked, hopeful, grinning from ear to ear.

With both staring down at me with the full expectation of compliance, I murmured, "Okay," with as much enthusiasm as the slave Kunta did when his slave master made him say his name was Toby in *Roots*.

"Maybe we shouldn't press her on this, Isabella," Dad warned.

"Oh, don't be silly. If Desiree doesn't call you Dad now, she never will. I've read books about this, you know." Mama then said to me, "You know that you're Mama's angel?" I nodded in disgust. Mama had been so wrapped up in her new life that Mama's angel hadn't even wanted to tell her that she started her period. "Desiree, use the mouth the good Lord gave you, honey."

"Yes, ma'am."

She sat down on the couch and patted the seat for me to come sit by her. "Now, your daddy will always be your daddy. The thing is, he's gone on to be with the Lord." She sighed and her shoulders drooped. "He will always be Daddy, but Langley is Dad. You see, there's a difference."

"Yes, ma'am," I said, just wanting it to be over.

"We are going to start the legal adoption. There's really no reason for your name to be different from ours. Just start signing your name and introducing yourself as Desiree Morrison," Mama whispered, brushing back my hair. "This is wonderful for us, Desiree. God took the horrible situation we were in and turned it around for our good. Satan meant to sift us as wheat, but God had different plans." Her voice, suddenly less gentle, whispered, "You're a doctor's daughter now. Be thankful, Desiree. Be thankful."

"Yes, ma'am." I nodded like an obedient puppy, aching for my mother's approval. They both still looked a little stressed, so I fetched.

"May I please go see if Rolanda can come over. . . . *Dad?*" I asked.

Mama smiled again. Dad cocked his head to the side. "Isn't she a precocious child, Isabella?"

It's strange how things happen sometimes. Once I started calling him Dad, my fuzzy memories of my daddy sharpened. Dad's presence reminded me of all that my daddy was.

My daddy, Ray Lee Abney, lived a short but sweet life. He never raised his voice to me, but I'd heard a few heated arguments between Mama and him. Never nasty or physical, but there were at least a few times I pushed the pillow down on my head so tight in fear I thought I'd suffocate. They argued but always quickly patched things up.

Smelling of sweat, cigar, and Old Spice, he'd come home dressed in his blue postal uniform. His laugh, a muffled grunt reserved especially for me, Mama, and only his closest friends, could not be imitated. If I closed my eyes, I could still feel his ashy, rough hands patting, tickling, and even spanking me a time or two.

One memory of my daddy that was forever etched in my mind was when my uncle Fred, Daddy's brother-in-law, a man I hadn't seen since Daddy's funeral, drove his dusty old white pickup truck up from Tuscaloosa for a visit. Uncle Fred wore his large gap between his two front teeth with pride, and smiled wider than anyone I'd ever seen. He'd flip his baseball cap back and forth between the front and back as he talked. I remember asking, "Why do you turn that cap like that when you talk?"

Mama had tapped me. "That ain't nice, Desiree."

"Leave that gal alone now." Uncle Fred laughed. He took his hat off and planted the rather grimy-looking hat, tattered and sweat drenched, on my head. Fearful that I'd get tapped again, I resisted the urge to take it off but winced inside feeling the damp, dirty hat squishing my new pink satin ribbons. Uncle Fred chuckled when he realized he had won at making me mad. He chuckled and took it off. He scratched his head with the rim before putting it back on and said to me, "You ain't got no problem wearin' your ol' Uncle Fred's hat, do ya, gal?" His hearty laugh shook his whole chest.

"No, sir," I answered, trying to fluff life back into my ribbons.

His ebony skin glistened as he knelt down. "How'd you like to go for a ride in my pickup?"

I jumped up and down in excitement and ran to Daddy who stood close by. "Please, Daddy?"

Mama interjected, "You mean in the back of that pickup, Fred? Ain't no way she's doing that!"

My daddy kissed my mother on the cheek briskly. "Don't you worry yourself."

"She is not about to get in that truck with Fred, Ray!"

Daddy looked over toward me. "That's *my* girl, right there, *my* girl, Isabella Jean. Now, me and my brother are gonna take Desi out."

Before Daddy could scoot Mama out of the room, I heard her say, "You better be careful with my baby, Ray and Fred. I ain't playin' with y'all."

Uncle Fred, Daddy, and I headed out to the pickup truck and to my delight, Daddy lifted me up into the back of the pickup, then he climbed up to join me while

Uncle Fred got in the driver's seat. Daddy tucked me in the corner of the back of the pickup and sat down beside me, holding on tightly as Uncle Fred called out, "Hold on, y'all!"

Daddy and I laughed the whole ride as Uncle Fred hit every hill, pothole, and bump he could find. I was sure we couldn't have been going as fast as it seemed, but we bounced around in that pickup, having more fun than any amusement park I'd ever been to. I laughed until my stomach ached. When I saw the deep hill ahead of us, I crouched down while my father's big arms cradled me with strength and tenderness, a feeling I'd never felt from a man since. Before a steep downward thrust, he sheltered me tight, and I remembered being fearless, not one bit afraid of anything.

I couldn't remember having that feeling of being protected since Daddy, but I knew that I'd been on the hunt for it. I desperately wanted that feeling back. The closest way I'd get to it on this night would be the Word Network. Somehow, it always gave me comfort on sleepless nights, so I turned the channel to it. A young preacher joined by his wife at the podium implored the congregation, "*He* that findeth a wife findeth a good thing. Y'all hear that? *He* is the operative word." He stopped for a moment and stared up to the ceiling. "Amen, lights."

The congregation laughed and his wife, dressed impeccably in a green suit and matching earrings, lightly touched his arm, egging him on. "That's right, sweetheart." With their tag-team preaching style, his wife took over. "In other words, ladies, you let him find you. When you try to take the man's position and look for him, God's perfect plan is disturbed." That was so easy for women to say who were already married. I wasn't so convinced that that verse should be taken so literally. I mean, she wasn't being silent in the church, as another verse instructs.

I grabbed my sketchpad from my nightstand and did something I did often. I began to sketch a necklace that I thought might perfectly accentuate the first lady's green suit. Sometimes that happens. I see an outfit and I get inspired to create jewelry for it. I drew a large choker-like necklace and sketched a large oval that I imagined would be gold with a green jasmine stone. After I looked at the finished sketch, I decided that the preacher's wife could've taken her stylish suit to the next level with a necklace like this.

I tossed the pad away and still felt the loneliness, the void. I tried to go to sleep, but then kicked the covers back, realizing that I didn't want to sleep. I booted up my laptop to check my sites to see if I had any new orders. On eBay, I had an order for two brown zebra jasper hair combs and a leather turquoise belt, necklace, and earring set. On my Facebook page, I had no new orders but I did have an outstanding order placed for a rose quartz necklace and earring set to fill. It looked like my Saturday was going to busy.

Before logging off, an ad at the top of screen struck me. It read, Lonely? We've got the answer. My curiosity got the best of me so I clicked, only to realize it was an online dating site. I surfed a bit on the site and decided it was a sorry ploy to get money. Then, I remembered the site that Shay had written down for me on the napkin. I decided that it wouldn't hurt to look at the site she had been on to meet Paul. Nobody had to know. I found the napkin buried in the side pocket of my purse.

Once I typed in www.christiansinglesgettogether.com, the home page showed one Caucasian couple embracing, one African American couple staring into each other's eyes, and an Asian couple holding hands and smiling. The blinking icon at the bottom read, Enter for a change in your life. I clicked and actually looked over my shoulder to make sure no one was looking at me, even though it was silly; I knew was alone. After I clicked on Enter, the next screen read, Free 30-day trial offer. No obligation.

For a brief second, I thought about the scripture the pastor on television had read about the man being the one to find the wife, but I rationalized that I wasn't finding anyone. I was simply letting myself be seen by men who might not otherwise know I exist. How could a man find me if he didn't know I existed?

After filling out the general information, I had to choose a screen name. After hashing through a litany of screen names, I settled on Jewels4Him. Next, I went on to complete my personal profile:.

Hair Color: Brown
Eye Color: Brown
Height: 5' 6"
Ethnicity: African American

I paused when I read Body Type. My choices were: slender, athletic, average, few extra pounds, and big and beautiful. How in the world was I supposed to answer this? I'd always been aware that I was a bigger girl in the eyes of some, but being curvy in all the right places had plenty of perks. I didn't see myself as big. Big, compared to whom? I didn't like how the whole "Big and beautiful" description sounded, so I opted for "a few extra pounds," but who was I kidding? I had more than just a few extra pounds to work with. I hated how people always put others in annoying categories and boxes, but I had to check something, so a few extra pounds was what it was.

I went down the list, answering the host of questions, such as: What's your marital status? Do you smoke? How many children do you have? How would you describe your looks? It wasn't difficult to answer this one. I checked the Gorgeous box. After entering that I was an entrepreneur (I knew that I needed to be careful about announcing my teaching profession), I read, relationship expectations: serious relationship, casual relationship, e-mail pal. Initially, I checked serious relationship until I reconsidered and changed it to e-mail pal. How could I know if I wanted a serious relationship? I wanted to get married one day, but didn't want to attract desperate men or stalkers. Besides, what did men think of women who actually checked serious relationship? I didn't feel desperate, just lonely.

Next, I downloaded a picture of myself, the only one I had already scanned in my computer. I was sitting in the fellowship hall at church after Faith Lewis's wedding, and I looked fabulous in my silk teal matching blouse and long, floor-length skirt, accented by a teal glass beads and Egyptian coin necklace ensemble I created. My hair, newly relaxed, hung down long and straight past my breasts, framing my round face.

I thought I was finally free to search through some of the guys, but the next screen read, I am looking for . . . Then, I had to put in qualifications I was looking for in a man. I thought an age from thirty-four to forty-five would be reasonable. With marital status, I didn't care whether the man was never married, divorced, or widowed. As long as he wasn't married or separated, I figured it would be okay. *Ethnicity.* I hesitated. I preferred African American men, at least I thought. No white guy had ever even approached me. Not wanting to eliminate my chances of finding Mr. Right, I checked Any. I wanted him to be local, so I checked that box. As for height, I figured as long as he was taller than me, I wouldn't care if he was a nice guy. Last, I checked that he could be any build.

When I finished, I saw, Congratulations! You're now ready to search profiles. I clicked on View Profiles and scrolled through what seemed like endless pictures of men, mostly scary or unattractive looking. There was Iceberg, a light-skinned brother with a not-so-surprising doo rag on his head, and TrickD, who exposed his coarse chest hair, and I began to wonder if this was actually a Christian site. I mean, it just didn't look good for me. I scrolled through many average-looking men, but I did a double take at BBlessd until I clicked on his profile and noticed that he had cut women out of his pictures because I could actually see part of a female's arm or dress or something. Even though it was late, I was convinced that I needed Shay to share in my laughter so I picked up the phone.

"Hi, Desi!" she cheerfully greeted me.

"Hey, Shay. Sorry to call you so late. You busy?"

"Naw, just talking to Paul on the other line and sitting here giving myself a pedicure. It ain't pretty."

I chuckled. "Okay, so call me tomorrow."

"Hold on, girl. We were just getting off the phone anyway. He's gotta work in the morning."

When she clicked back over, I wasted no time telling her the news. "Guess what exciting thing I've been doing?"

"Let me guess: makin' some funky new jewelry or watchin' somethin' on TV. Oh, I know, what did Judge Mathis do now? I've never seen a sister so in love with a TV judge."

My voice sank. "Shay, you really know how to make me feel good. Believe it or not, that's not my only idea of excitement."

"What?" she sang into the line like I had sparked her interest.

"I signed up."

"Signed up for what? You already told me about the gym," she said.

"You know, for that site you told me about."

It got quiet and I couldn't hear the scratchy sound of the file against her nails. Shay's high-pitch gasp hurt my ear. "What? You did it? I never thought you'd do it in a million years! You're on your way now, baby."

"Girl, calm yourself. I haven't seen one man who looks even remotely interesting."

"Oh, calm down. You don't need ten, just one. You just got on."

"Seriously though, Shay, some of these dudes just look plain scary."

"Wait a minute, you're online now?" Shay asked.

"Yeah."

"Oh, give me a second and I'm gonna get on my laptop and look with you."

I heard Shay rustling to get her laptop booted up. "Girl, you gotta check this one guy out. His name is JamN4Jesus. He's must have about ten pictures of himself. In one, he's on the keyboard. He's on the saxophone in another one and playing the bass in another and—"

"All right already, I get the idea," Shay interrupted. "Okay, I'm all booted up and logged in the site."

I heard Shay typing away. When I heard her holler, I knew she had found him. "He just knows he's got it goin' on, doesn't he?"

Shay and I stayed on the phone for two hours, laughing and looking at profiles together. She had asked for my username and password, and being the novice I was at Internet dating, she logged in as me and sent at least four men what they called "flirts." Even though I had mentioned that I thought the men were attractive, I had no intention of making the first move to get to know any of them. Shay had other plans.

"I can't believe you sent them flirts, Shay! I shouldn't have given you my password. I'm so embarrassed. Don't do that mess, girl!"

"It's no big deal, Des. It's Internet dating etiquette."

"You know I've been raised the good old-fashioned way. A man should make the first move. He's the one who's supposed to pursue, and I don't even know how I feel about the whole thing of being on the Internet anyway. My mama would kill me. She really would."

Shay let out a tired sigh. "Well, your good old-fashioned way is gonna cause you to be single at forty. You act like you have to tell your mama everything. Don't tell her. She wouldn't understand anyway. You can still be saved and get in the way of a blessing." She paused for a second and continued, "Besides, Des, no offense or anything, but the men who have been chasing you lately are not what I'd call cream of the crop men."

"Thanks for the reminder." She did have a point though.

"I'm sorry. All I'm saying is that you need to take more control over your life instead of just running into men. Just give it a chance. You may get lucky like I have with Paul."

"Lucky? I'm not trying to get lucky; I'm trying to get blessed with the right person," I reminded her.

"For goodness' sakes, girl, that's what I meant. Paul is so wonderful. He's taken his profile down since we've started to become serious, but I'll e-mail you a picture of him. I can't wait for you to meet him. I stepped out on faith, and He did it."

Shay always tried to put a religious spin on things to get me to sign on, but she wasn't really that spiritual. However, I didn't want to limit my options, and I couldn't help thinking that I didn't want to put any limitations on God. Maybe I did need to put myself out there and try to have a little more control over my dating situation.

After winding down from our Internet profile searching, we got off the phone. It had been fun, but I began to question whether I should even have a picture on the site at all. A saved, professional, classy woman, like me, on a dating site? Was I compromising my standards, and more importantly, the Lord's standards for me? I just didn't know. Yet, the twinge of expectation settled me, and I knew that whatever was coming had to be better than my current state.

CHAPTER 10

ISABELLA

*Be careful for nothing; but in every thing by prayer
and supplication with thanksgiving let your requests
be made known unto God. And the peace of God, which
passeth all understanding, shall keep your hearts and
minds through Christ Jesus.*

—Philippians 4:6–7

Pain shot through my breast with an intensity that
almost took the wind outta me. Now I regretted that I
hadn't gone to the doctor several days ago when I'd had
the first episode. Not only was my armpit sore, but my
whole breast area hurt. I reached under my nightgown
and touched where the throbbing pain attacked. The
small area felt lumpy, hard, and hot.

Of course, a woman always thinks about cancer when
something isn't quite right, but I'd always been so good
about getting mammograms. In fact, I just had one a few
months ago. Plus, nobody I could think of in my family
had ever had it. It couldn't be cancer.

I sat up and squinted to focus on the digital clock. Four
o'clock in the morning. Something just wasn't right to
wake me up out of my sleep like this. I raced to the bathroom and examined the breast. When I unbuttoned my
gown, I gasped. The red, circular area had changed and
now looked a little like the skin of an orange. *What kind
of allergic reaction would only appear in this one area?*

I didn't go back to sleep, counting down the hours until my nine o'clock appointment with Dr. Blevins.

Just as I left the doctor's office, my cell phone vibrated.

"Hey, Mama. You feeling better?"

"Well, baby, I've never been so relieved in all my life. I was fretting over that rash on my breast for nothing. I'm just leavin' from Dr. Blevins's office. He examined it and said he believes it's a spider bite. Says there's not much you can do for it, but he gave me some kind of prescription for a cream. The only other thing he mentioned that it could be was something about 'calcifications in the breast tissue,' but according to him that's even less serious than a spider bite."

"I wish that you would've allowed me to go with you."

"Honey, now that I know it's nothing, I'm fine now. I'm glad you didn't come over a silly spider bite. No need for you to miss work over that."

"Call the exterminator, Mama. And, I know how you are, so just make sure you actually use the cream."

"You know how terrified I am of spiders? I already called. They'll be out tomorrow. As much as this thing is hurting me? Trust me, I'm going to use the cream until the tube is gone. Dr. Blevins said it must've been some kind of spider though."

Days passed, and with no signs of the cream working, I decided that although Dr. Blevins meant well, his seventy-plus years had maybe caused his skills in diagnosing to be a little rusty. I needed a second opinion, and my much younger OBGYN, Dr. Perkins, would surely get to the bottom of it.

To my surprise, Dr. Perkins had a cancellation and got me in the next day. They were efficient but lacking in the courtesy department. The receptionist couldn't be more than twenty. She didn't even look up when she gave me the old, "Sign in, and I'll need your insurance card and license." No greeting or anything, certainly cold and dry as they came. To make things worse, the waiting room experience felt like her: no frills, no small courtesies. No plants or pretty pictures to look at, and not even one *People* or *Ladies' Home Journal*.

The breast pain subsided a bit, but that always seemed to happen by the time I get to the doctor's office. Things seem so bad until you get to the office. I was inclined to cancel my appointment and leave, but my thoughts were interrupted by a soft-spoken nurse calling my name. I got up and followed the kind voice into the examining room. After taking my vitals, the nurse said, "Okay, hon, just take off your shirt and bra and slip the gown on. Dr. Perkins will be in shortly."

I took my shirt and bra off, struggling to figure out how to get into the paper gown. I didn't know if the opening was supposed to be in the front or the back. To kill time, I read magazines and every poster in the room:

Get Your Annual Pap Test.

Did you get your daughter the HPV vaccine?

Pregnancy and Parenting: What You Need to Know.

I shivered, wondering why they would tell you to undress and blast the air conditioning while making you wait so long. After nearly thirty minutes, with a light tap on the door, Dr. Perkins breezed in, extending her cold hand.

"Hello, Mrs. Morrison. Please forgive me for making you wait. Today has been such a busy day." The pale skin on her face looked so transparent that tiny veins peeked through in spots, but her smile was warm and professional. My attitude with the staff instantly evaporated because of her kindness.

She flipped through my charts. "Mrs. Morrison, what brings you in here today?"

I explained the pain, and she nodded, and put the chart down. While she washed her hands, she made small talk. "Now, I've known you for, what? Three years or so, Mrs. Morrison? I can't believe that I hadn't thought of asking before." She didn't wait for me to answer the first question. "I've just got to ask if you're any relation to Dr. Langley Morrison?"

"I'm afraid I'm guilty. He's my husband. How do you know him?"

"Small world. Why, I just heard him at a conference in Fort Lauderdale a few months ago. Very good information he gave about juvenile diabetes, and very good golf game, I hear." She smiled.

"Yes, that's what people say, but I'm not a huge golfer myself," I said.

"Okay, let's take a look." She examined it closely and her small talk ceased. While feeling under my arms and neck, she said, "Hmmmm. Your lymph nodes are swollen." She examined the breast area again, frowning.

"So, what do you think? My general physician said that it was a spider bite, but it seems to be getting worse. The cream he prescribed isn't doing a thing. It's quite painful and it itches, too."

"Mrs. Morrison, we're going to need to do a mammogram. It could be an infection, and I'll give you some antibiotics for that. I think that I'm going to also have you get an ultrasound. I'm going to schedule you for tomorrow if you can do that."

My stomach tightened. "So, it isn't a spider bite? It's an infection?"

She sat down on her stool. "It's just not consistent with an insect bite. I'm skeptical about an infection, but I just don't know for sure. I don't want to alarm you, but we need to rule some things out."

I tried not to sound nervous. "Some things like what, Dr. Perkins?"

She took a deep breath and shifted around on the stool. "I don't want to jump the gun, so don't get excited. We just need to be sure that there's not a malignancy."

"Oh, no worries about that, Doctor. You can see on my chart that I just had my mammogram a little while ago. Clean as a whistle."

"I did see that, Mrs. Morrison, but unfortunately, mammograms don't detect all types of breast cancer. Let's not rush to make any conclusions though. Like I said, it very well could be an infection, but I'm going to go ahead and have the receptionist schedule your tests for first thing in the morning."

She stood up after I reassured her that I could make it, and patted me on the back before leaving. When I checked out at the front desk, the once rude receptionist morphed into the sweetest thing I'd ever imagined, which frightened me almost as much as Dr. Perkins did.

When I got home, I started to call Langley, but I remembered that he would be in session for his conference. Besides, after our night of coming together, he had stiffened and changed right back to the same old man I'd grown to dislike and distrust. Clearly, since I'd interrupted his outside action, I was just convenient.

Not wanting to worry Desiree, Alice, or anyone else I loved and cared for, I prayed, long and hard. I thought of Hezekiah. So I reminded the Lord of how faithful I'd been. I told Him that if He didn't let this be cancer, I'd never give Him another complaint about Langley, Desiree, or church folks. I repented for gossiping and letting the sun go down on my anger, especially when it came to my husband. I knew that I hadn't done all the good that Hezekiah had done when he asked God to lengthen his days, but I had been faithful. After the prayer, I listened like Pastor Kingston had instructed us to do after prayer. Silence. As I got up from my knees though, a still, small voice, pressed me to prepare for what was coming.

"Isabella! Isabella, wake up!"

I rolled over slowly and irritably, smelling Langley's always much too loud cologne. "For Pete's sake, what is it?"

His face grimaced and I sat up. "How many times have I asked you to park all the way over to your half of the garage, Isabella? Is it too much to ask for you to stay within your line? If my Mercedes were to get dinged, it would be your fault, and I would be livid!"

"Welcome home, Langley. I thought you weren't coming home until tomorrow." I rubbed my eyes to focus.

"Did you hear what I just said?" he asked, ignoring my sarcasm. "And why are you asleep in the middle of the day?"

"You mean to tell me you woke me up about this nonsense? We have a four-car garage. Surely you have enough room."

He slipped his shoes off. "That's not the point. The point is that I've asked and now I'm telling you, do not go over the center line in the garage again."

I thought about arguing with him but remembered what I'd just prayed and decided to let him have this one. "I'm sorry, Langley. I'll try to be more careful." I didn't feel like arguing with him. I'd learned that it wasn't worth the trouble. As he undressed, he never mentioned the conference and he didn't ask about my breast pain. Instead, he rattled off a long laundry list of things for me to do.

"Don't you think you need to write this down or something? You've been mighty forgetful lately."

I sighed, shaking my head no.

He snapped his fingers and said, "I know, I'll message you the list to your phone. Oh, and do you mind preparing me a late breakfast?"

It didn't matter that his list had been the same for nearly thirty years. He insisted on torturing me with reminders, instructions, and lists. It was like the other night didn't even happen. He wasn't a husband, but a drill sergeant, teacher, and on good days, a coach or parent.

As soon as Langley rushed out, I made my way to church, hoping to at least catch the end of noonday prayer.

Once I made it to church, gently pushing through the double doors of the sanctuary, I met Pastor Kingston and a few prayer warriors on the altar. Muffled cries could be heard echoing throughout the sanctuary, and only when I got closer did I recognize that the cries and groans were coming from Mother Georgia.

"Oh, Lord, we thank you for helping us to be long-suffering with the members who won't take the time to come to prayer. Lord, bless those who are only interested in pleasing themselves and not you. Help us to be patient and tolerant of folks who don't know the way. Help us, Lord!"

One of the reasons I had slacked off from coming to prayer was exactly because of the few who prayed like Mother Georgia. I hated when people used prayer to vent their frustrations with others from the church and it disgusted me to think that folks would use prayer to lift themselves up and put others down. I didn't have time for this. As much as Desiree had worked my nerves about colorful opinions about church, she did have valid points, especially about situations like this.

I tried to keep my eyes closed, but I peeked to see if Pastor Kingston would allow this to go on. Georgia continued in almost a wail, "We cry out to you, Father God, and we ask for you to help us to intercede for those who don't want to pray. They doin' something of everything else, but prayer. Watchin' these reality TV shows, going to the clubs, drinking and partying like you ain't coming back. Give 'em a mind to pray like us. Give us strength for the journey to bring 'em in, Lord!"

Pastor Kingston tapped Mother Georgia, but she acted like she was caught up in the Spirit. "Hiya! Glory, Lord! Hey, hey, heyyyyy! Gloryyyy!"

When Mother Georgia sensed that the amens and hallelujahs had stopped, she simmered down, and Pastor Kingston ended the prayer. "We thank you, Lord, for your grace, mercy, and loving kindness toward us. We thank you for being an ever present help in the time of trouble. You are our peace, our way maker, and our everything. We can do nothing without you, Father. We thank you for this time of fellowship and communion with you. Jesus, we ask you to forgive us of our trespasses and lead us into your will and your way. You know the burdens we carry, and we cast our cares on you, God. Heal, deliver, and set us free. Amen."

Pastor Kingston caught me on the way out. "Why, Sister Morrison, how are you? Been quite some time since I've seen you at noonday prayer."

"Why yes, it has been, Pastor. I'm glad that I came today. Your prayer blessed me." There was no way I could tell him that I was tired of Mother Georgia's long and dreary prayers. He would surely think I was shallow as a pie pan. Truth was, though, that the woman either irritated us or put half of us to sleep. Everyone knew she was sending messages to the congregation and not praying to God.

"Well, praise be unto God. You're an anchor of this church, Sister Morrison, and your presence is needed." He rested his hand on my shoulder. A soothing chocolate man, slight in build, but big in character, the members loved Pastor Kingston, and he fondly always referred to his "sweet members."

"I'll be coming more often. I really will."

Pastor Kingston smiled, and his face, weathered and long, but kind, asked, "So, how's Brother Morrison doing? You both have been on my mind lately."

I felt a little uncomfortable and tried to avoid eye contact. "Langley stays busy, Pastor, but please continue to pray for both of us."

"Well, I won't keep you, Sis, but you call me if you need me." He hesitated, searching my face for something more and added, "I'll be praying for you . . . both."

I always got the feeling that Pastor Kingston knew more than he ever said in words. I thanked him, but walked out of the sanctuary with an uneasy feeling.

CHAPTER 11

DESIREE

Be strong and of a good courage, fear not, nor be afraid of them; for the Lord thy God, He it is that doth go with thee; He will not fail thee, nor forsake thee.
—Deuteronomy 2:6

Last week Mama told me about a girl who was getting into her car late at night when a maniac waited under her car, grabbed her by the ankles, and pushed her in the car, only to abduct, rape, and strangle her to death. I gasped in horror while Mama nodded her head and in her customary serene voice said, "Now, calm down, I didn't mean to scare you, but you just be careful and don't be going out late at night by yourself."

Mama has a knack for unloading on me, getting me worked up and then, on the turn of a dime, trying to calm me down.

Darkness, unsettling creaks, and whistles of the wind scared me. Instead of it getting better with time, I knew it was worse. I didn't want to be alone. But, I didn't want to settle either. I told myself sometimes that I had to settle like Mama did or be alone. Then, other times I told myself, *but if settling means that I could potentially have a man like my stepfather, I know that I can't. I won't.* Instead, since my late twenties to now, I was permanently coupled with Mama. She was my long-term relationship. When I ran into people without Mama, they asked questions like they would ask about a spouse.

"Where's your mama?"

"How's your mom?"

"What's your mama up to these days?"

They looked around and asked, "Is your mom here?" However, Mama's presence in my life didn't quell the nagging desire to fill the void that only a man could. I wanted to fuss about how my husband bought me a vacuum cleaner for our anniversary and tell my girlfriends how he didn't help change the baby's diapers. I wanted to be busy with finding new ideas for dinner menus, keeping up with the laundry and making sure that I kept myself desirable for my man. And yes, I even wanted to sit next to my man, my husband, at church when the Word was going forth. Normal or not, I dreamed about these types of things almost on a daily basis.

Instead though, Mama was him. We never spoke it aloud, but we both knew that I had to make up for what my stepfather wasn't to her. If I didn't listen to her, who would? Without me as a dinner and shopping partner, she wouldn't have one. Even with her closest friends, she was only totally herself, well, mostly herself, with me. It drove me crazy that while she steadily picked apart every man who got close to me, she refused to see her own marriage for what it was. Sometimes I didn't know if I wanted a husband more for me or to escape from Mama.

I flipped open my laptop to see if I had any e-mail or "flirts" from the dating site. I thought I was seeing things. Six flirts and two e-mails. Shay's dating system breathed a faint breath of life into my dating life, which had been nearly on life support.

Before I knew it, I'd spent the whole morning looking at the profiles of the men who had flirted, read the e-mails from the two who had sent them, and finally got the nerve to e-mail back the one man who looked relatively attractive. A police officer, Victor's skin looked like a peppermint patty: smooth, dark, and shiny. His nose, extra wide, fit his full face and lips. Although his double-breasted suit was dated, I couldn't help taking in his bulging muscles. I took a deep breath and typed.

> Hi! My name is Desiree. Thanks for responding to my profile. You wanted to know something about me, so here goes. Obviously, I'm a Christian since I'm on a Christian site, but otherwise, I'm a teacher and like reading, making jewelry, and listening to Gospel jazz. How long have you been on the site? What types of things do you enjoy doing in your spare time? Take care.

He responded instantly.

> Let's IM each other, okay?
> —Victor

I nearly squealed in delight and clicked on my instant messenger. I read:

> Desiree, nice to meet you as well. I've been on the site for a few months, and it's been pretty cool. About me . . . well, I work a lot so I don't get much of a chance to log on, but so far, it's been pretty good. On the weekends that I don't have my children, I like to play basketball or just chill out with my partners. I enjoy almost all sports, except for maybe golf, and believe it or not, I cook some mean lasagna.

Victor and I messaged back and forth until my fingers cramped. When I let him know I had to go, he asked for my number. I wondered for only about a half of a second if I should, but I gave it to him. When I checked the time, I realized that I'd spent hours on the site. Saturdays were generally my most productive day to make and fill jewelry orders and I had blown this one away.

After showering and getting dressed, I began the tedious job of cleaning up the mess I'd made in my studio. Crystals, gems, leather, and metal scraps were strewn across my jewelry bench, polishing station, and lapidary beading area. After tidying things up, I worked on an order from an elderly woman from the Miami Beach area. She wanted four jewelry sets that were no longer in stock, which meant I'd have to work nonstop for the rest of the day.

After about an hour of working, I sighed in frustration when the phone rang. I knew it had to be Mama; she was the only one who called during the day on Saturdays since everyone else knew I ran my jewelry business then. Startled at hearing a deep baritone voice on the other end, I nearly dropped the phone.

"Hello, may I speak to Desiree, please?"

"This is Desiree." I tossed the jewelry aside and walked out of my studio, pleasantly surprised.

"This is Victor. We met online a little bit ago."

"Oh, hi. How are you?" I asked, trying not to sound shocked. I thought maybe he was a little too thirsty calling so soon.

"I know I said I would call later, but your picture is so beautiful. The messages between us seemed to be flowing so I thought I'd call before someone else caught your interest." He chuckled.

Momentarily speechless, I laughed. "That's fine." I didn't quite know if it really was fine or not.

"Did I call you at a bad time?" he asked.

It had been so long since any man had rung my phone, I stammered out, "No, it's fine. I enjoyed our online chat. How are you?"

"Listen, I'm doing great since I spent my morning messaging you."

I smiled, excited as a kid in a candy store.

"So, tell me about yourself," Victor said.

After I explained my job and jewelry business, I shifted gears. "I guess I told you a lot through the e-mail, but I am pretty new, well, no, very new to the online dating thing. How long have you been on?"

"I've been on for about, let's see, three months or so. I usually don't have time to check my e-mails too much. I have my children every other weekend, so on my off weekends, I try to check my e-mail. It's been a pretty cool way to meet other people."

After the initial five minutes on the phone, Victor and I talked nonstop about so many things until I really felt like I knew him. Even though he did most of the talking, I didn't care. He had a boatload of funny stories about being a police officer; and his two girls, ten and twelve, sounded just as lively. He hadn't gotten around to explaining why he and his ex-wife divorced, but I was glad to know that she remarried. No baby mama drama, at least I hoped. "One thing I've learned from this online dating thing is that the sooner you go ahead and meet in person, the less time you waste if it doesn't work out," he said.

I certainly saw the logic in that and agreed to meet him at the Books-A-Million café on Sparkman. Before we got off the phone, we set a date to meet the following day.

Although I hadn't been as productive with my jewelry orders as I would've liked, I couldn't help calling Shay to share the good news about Victor. I felt like a girl with a teenage crush.

"Shay!" I said, hardly able to hold my excitement.

"Hey, Des, guess what?" she said.

"No, you wait. Me first. *Victor* is meeting me for coffee tomorrow after church!"

"Victor? Who the devil is Victor? Don't tell me you're meeting someone already? I told you, girl. See? Just have fun. I'm so excited for you."

"Okay, I just had to get that out. Maybe this Internet dating thing will be fun after all. Now, you go ahead with your news."

"Well, I am so happy with Paul. Can you believe that he brought me flowers this morning? I still had rollers in my hair when he stopped by. He couldn't stop telling me how beautiful he thinks I am."

I smiled, but somehow I always felt upstaged by Shay in one way or another. My excitement deflated as she went on and on about her knight in shining armor. I only hoped that Victor might be mine.

Since the bookstore had a local author there for a signing, more of a crowd had gathered near the café section, but I still could pick out Victor immediately. He looked somewhat recognizable from his pictures, but only somewhat. The police officer stood nowhere near the height he had claimed to be on the site. At no more than five feet nine inches, I would be his exact height with the two-inch high boots I had chosen. He stood up instantly as I approached. He extended his hand. "Why, Desiree, you look just like your picture."

"Oh, thanks," I said, not able to say the same back to him. I smiled cautiously, noticing that he had worn the same sweater in one of the pictures in the online album.

"Can I get you something to drink? I'm sorry I got started without you." He held his cup up.

I examined his drink. "What's that? Let me guess: a white chocolate mocha maybe?"

"You're good, but black coffee. May I get you a mocha?" he asked as he helped me with my coat and pulled my chair out. I could tell already that this date would be much better than any that I'd had in a long time.

As we made small talk, I noticed his long eyelashes curled enough to make any woman envious, but his prominent chin and dark, brooding eyes hardened his look, making him very masculine and attractive, even if he lacked in the stature department.

"You're a very beautiful woman, Desiree and you're wearing some very beautiful jewelry to match. Did you make that?"

"Ahhh, you remembered. Yes, thank you."

We closed the bookstore down, talking, laughing, and listening to one another. My heart fluttered, and I thought that just maybe Shay wouldn't be the only one falling in love.

CHAPTER 12

ISABELLA

*A word fitly spoken is like apples of
gold in pictures of silver.*
—Proverbs 25:11

To my surprise, my wait wasn't long.

"Why, Mrs. Morrison, how are we feeling today?" Dr.
Perkins asked.

I wanted to say "we" weren't feeling anything. I was
the one tired of all the discomfort and wanted to get my
test results. "Dr. Perkins, I'm doing okay. No better and
not really worse, I guess. Just wondering about the test
results."

"Yes, totally understandable. First, let me ask you,
how's the pain in your breast been?" Without waiting for
me to answer, she gently pulled my robe down. "Okay,
I'm just going to take a quick look." Dr. Perkins frowned.
"It looks like it's changed some and it's only been a few
days." She felt the tender area under my arms. "Hmmm.
Your lymph nodes still seem to be swollen."

The sound of my heart racing thumped in my ears.
Something didn't feel right. She didn't sound like things
were okay. She continued, "Mrs. Morrison, your mammogram didn't show any signs of a tumor."

I blew out a sigh of breath of relief. "I already told you
that I didn't have cancer, doctor."

Dr. Perkins raised her brow and continued, "However, it did show a thickening that is a concern. I am going to refer you to a surgeon who can do a biopsy on the tissue in that area of your breast. We need to know what it is we're dealing with here."

"A surgeon?" Now, I was surprised again.

Dr. Perkins struggled to be matter-of-fact but avoided eye contact. "Yes. The only way that we can rule out a malignancy is through a surgical procedure called a core biopsy."

"I thought that was the reason for the mammogram, to rule out cancer, I mean."

"Mrs. Morrison, the mammogram can show us quite a bit, but not everything."

"Oh, I see." I had never had surgery and rarely even got as much as a cold. Dr. Perkins read my mind.

"Nothing to worry about right now, Mrs. Morrison. We just want to know what course of action we need to take, so it's imperative that we find out exactly what this is and as soon as possible."

My muscles tightened. "Okay, well, I need to do what I have to do then."

Without hesitation, Dr. Perkins replied, "Yes, it is very important that this is scheduled and done without delay. I'm going to schedule your appointment myself. Just sit tight, and I'll have your appointment date before you leave. Oh, you can go ahead and get dressed. Relax. I'll be right back." I read the worry beneath her smile as she walked out.

Usually, I moved like lightning to get dressed after an appointment. This time was different. My body wouldn't move, yet I felt like a spinning top. I didn't feel that bad, and certainly didn't want a biopsy.

I trembled after I dressed and watched the feathery snowflakes blanketing the ground from the office window.

Snow in Alabama is rare, even in the dead of winter. The city can never prepare for it the way they do up North. Not enough salt trucks. And people don't know how to drive in the snow. Snow in Alabama. Cancer. Some things you can't prepare for, no matter how hard you try.

As she opened the door, Dr. Perkins, who apparently had been laughing with a colleague, caught the grave look on my face and abruptly sobered up. I hoped that wasn't for my sake. No matter what it looked like, as a woman of faith I believed God for good news.

CHAPTER 13

DESIREE

Howbeit when he, the Spirit of truth, is come, he will guide you into all truth: for he shall not speak of himself; but whatsoever he shall hear, that shall he speak: and he will shew you things to come.

—John 16:13

A watched phone never rings. Mama, as saved and holy as she was, hadn't seemed to let go of superstitions like these, and I'd always been mad that she passed the craziness on to me. After an hour of cradling the phone like a newborn baby, I set it back down on the base, telling myself that I was not watching, just waiting for a promised call from Victor. *I am not desperate,* I told myself over and over again. I stopped looking at the phone, and the phone rang. Mama was right, again. The only problem was that Shay said hello on the line and not Victor.

"Sooooo, things went well with Mr. Policeman?"

"Actually, very well. He's a little on the short side, but he's a really nice guy."

"Really? I know you like tall men, but keep an open mind."

"I am," I reassured her.

"Right, right, but you both are interested. That's the important thing. Listen, I wanted to invite you and Victor to come over for *Monday Night Football* tonight. I know it's a last minute thing, but it would be a great opportunity for you and Paul to meet."

"I do really want to meet Paul, but Victor hasn't even called today. I'm definitely not calling him. Oh, and I refuse to be the third wheel, so don't even ask about me coming without a date." My other line buzzed. "Oh, hold on, girl, it's the other line."

"No, you go ahead. That's probably him. See you for *Monday Night Football*, Des."

I chucked and clicked over to Victor. He immediately invited me to dinner, and accepted my invite to Shay's after dinner for *Monday Night Football*.

Things were finally looking up.

My dinner with Victor felt much like a polite game of tennis as we bounced the conversational ball back and forth. Everything moved with ease and comfort.

"I love teaching English at Alabama A&M. It's a dream job for me with the exception that I need to get my PhD. Without it, I'm restricted to teaching mostly composition, so I'd love to go back to school." Suddenly embarrassed by my chattiness, I picked up my glass and gulped down a swallow. "I'm sorry, Victor, I've been talking too much."

Victor's smile moved effortlessly across his face, and he reached across the table to touch my hand. As the small electric current flowed through my body by what should have been a small and insignificant touch, I smiled back, both wilted and energized all at the same time.

"Desiree, please don't feel like that. I like hearing about your life. It's a part of us getting to know one another."

"It's just that I'm not normally this talkative." I groped for words to fill the empty space that hung suspended midair. Victor oozed coolness that made up for what he lacked in stature. "So, tell me about your daughters." I took a much too large bite of my Creole chicken and watched Victor cut into his prime rib. He spoke while he chewed, but for some odd reason, it didn't annoy me. "Sorry to sound sappy, but my girls are really my heart. He held his knife and fork, motioning with them as he spoke. "Older one looks like me but acts like her mother." He let out a little sigh. "Can't have it all, right? Younger one? She looks like me and acts like me. She's a real charmer."

I faked a laugh, only half believable. "Oh, I see," I said, eyeing him playfully. Victor beamed while speaking of his daughters, and I tried to smile at all the appropriate places and even comment here and there.

"Now I'm the one who's talking nonstop." Victor noticed I was finished eating and glanced down at his watch. "We've been here almost two hours. Time flies when you're having fun."

"Sure does," I replied, not wanting the dinner to end.

"I guess we'd better head on over to your girlfriend's so we're not too late," he said, trying to discreetly pay the bill.

We walked, holding hands to the car, and continued conversing easily all the way to Shay's. As soon as we pulled into her driveway, Victor turned the headlights off but not the engine. I wondered if it was my imagination or if his eyelids had really lowered. With his eyes glazed over, he lowered his voice to a near whisper. "You are so beautiful."

"Thank you, Victor." I prayed that he wouldn't ruin things by coming on too strong, too fast.

"I'm usually not so forward, but I have to tell you, I am so attracted to you." He dragged out the word so a little too long for my taste, but still flattered, I smiled and made my dimples extra deep. Just like in one of those movies, he gently lifted my chin ever so slowly and said, "Hey now, look at me." He studied my face, gazing with such intensity that I didn't know if I could take it. Before I knew what was happening, his lips pressed against mine, and I didn't have time to decide if it was okay. Things were going faster than I'd expected, but I liked him. He eased his hand up the back of my shirt while he kissed me, and I knew it had to stop. I moved away and tugged my shirt down hard and fast. Victor settled back into his own seat, smiling like a cat who had just eaten a rat. "What's up, Desiree? I can tell you're into me. What's the problem?"

"The problem is that we don't know one another. We just met. We're in the driveway of my girlfriend's house. You're also going way too fast. Is that enough for you?" I crossed my arms. These men with their inflated egos and deflated character made me sick.

I straightened myself up, pulled the visor down, and groped through my handbag for lipstick.

"Okay, hey, my bad!" He put his hands up. "I respect you, Desiree. I remember you said you were in the church. I like that."

"Victor, I didn't just say that I went to church, I said that I'm saved."

He blew a long deep breath out. "Excuse me. I'm saved too, you know?"

"That's what you say," I said, unapologetically sarcastic.

"Come to church with me this Sunday, and you'll see."

I smiled. "You got yourself a deal. What church do you attend?"

"New Birth Revival Center on Smith and Glen." Before Victor got out, he said, "Just make sure you got your shoutin' shoes on, 'cause we have some church."

"Oh, I can't wait." I felt better as we made our way into Shay's house, like he had received the message. I wasn't that kind of woman.

Once we settled in at Shay's, I got a good look at her new man, Paul. Fair skinned, a slender build and dark eyes, just like she said. Even though Paul's hair receded, making him appear quite a bit older than Shay, it was in her "pretty hair" category. By the time the evening came to a close, I understood Shay's attraction to Paul. He doted on her every word, and if he called her "baby" one more time, I thought I'd have to leave. On the other hand, Shay's interest in sports fascinated Paul. He asked her things like, "Baby, you think they'll let Johnson go back in?"

She responded without even looking at him or blinking, "Sweetheart, you know ain't no way they letting that joker back in after that last crazy play. He did nothing the last two times they put him in." Paul rubbed her shoulders, back, and hands like crazy. They were a seasoned couple already.

Victor and I, on the other hand, had become like oil and water in just a few minutes' time. Clearly, something changed between Victor and me from the driveway to the front door of Shay's. Hopelessly and utterly silent through most of the game, the only thing I managed to comment on was a Coke commercial. I didn't know anything about football and really didn't care to.

"I can't believe Beyoncé is endorsing another thing. She's so overexposed," I said, sounding pathetic, especially when no one commented back. So, I took unnecessary trips to the bathroom to read through the old *Essence* and *Ebony* magazines in the rack and mainly to avoid falling asleep from boredom.

Victor rarely acknowledged my presence. He didn't flirt, put his arm around me, or throw out even one mildly endearing name my way. I felt the sting of his dismissal, but I refused to accept it. He was just into the game, I told myself.

During the ride home, Victor livened up a bit and
entertained me with stories of popular athletes and
seemed especially proud of knowing professional athletes
who I'd never heard of. As he talked, I found myself
fantasizing about what life might be married to a guy like
him. Right off the bat, I knew I'd have to tolerate sports,
but I was willing.

As he walked me to my door, he rested his hand lightly
on my lower back. When we got to the front door, I
stopped. "Thank you for a wonderful dinner and evening.
I had a good time, Victor."

"You gonna make me say good night out here in the
cold?" Victor blew into his hands.

The comment threw me for a loop. I didn't know what
to say for a second. As much as I wanted him to come
in, I knew that we had two different agendas. I wanted
conversation and company, and he had shown me that
he wanted much more than I was ready to give. "Listen,
Victor—"

He interrupted, "No sweat, no problem, Desiree. I
totally understand. No need to explain."

"But I want to explain."

He backed away slowly, still facing me. "I'll give you
a call about church this weekend. Had a great time,
Desiree. Your friends were nice." His face held a phony
smile while he made a clean getaway.

CHAPTER 14

ISABELLA

*Let us therefore fear, lest, a promise being left us of
entering into his rest, any of you should
seem to come short of it.*

—Hebrews 4:1

Forty-eight to seventy-two hours seemed like an eternity to wait to see if you had a disease that could kill you. I probably would've broken down and told Langley about the biopsy, but he hadn't come home. Again. I hadn't even told Desiree about the biopsy since it was outpatient and "minimally invasive" as Dr. Perkins explained. I just didn't want or need her worrying, especially if it turned out to be nothing.

When I got home, I was surprised by Langley's car in the driveway with the trunk wide open.

"Langley?" I called out. No answer. As I entered our bedroom, I found him rummaging through drawers, haphazardly throwing clothes in a large suitcase.

"Langley? Is everything okay?"

"Isabella, I tried to call you." He didn't look up at me.

"Oh dear," I said, groping to find my cell phone from my purse. "I had an appointment so I had turned it off and forgot to turn it back on. Where are you going? I didn't know you had to go out of town again so soon."

"It's not that." He threw clothes in his baggage as if he were going to miss a flight.

"Is everything all right with your mother?"

He stopped packing and bit his bottom lip. "She's fine, but . . . I am leaving . . . you."

"Okay. . . . Where might you be going? And what's the big rush?"

"I don't know how to say this, Isabella, so I'm just going say it." He exhaled deeply, wiping the sweat that had collected on his forehead. "We haven't been happy for a long time."

My purse slid out of my grip and onto the floor. I nearly joined it.

"The thing is, Isabella, we shouldn't spend the rest of our lives unhappy. Desiree is grown and doing well now, and it's blatantly obvious that our lives are going in two opposite directions."

I swallowed hard, but the lump remained lodged in my throat. My head spun so I sat down on the bed. "You're leaving me? Today? Just like that?"

He stopped moving and planted his feet. Then, he dug his hands deep in his pants pockets, suddenly a child. "Tell me you're happy, huh, Isabella? Tell me."

I challenged him. "Since when is marriage just about being happy? Love is more than a feeling. We both know that it's a choice, a decision we made, a vow we made before God, through thick and through thin, better or worse, to make it work, no matter what."

Langley chewed on his bottom lip, clearly angry that I resisted his plan and upset that I had the audacity to put the full weight of the blame on him. "Don't bring God into this, Isabella. That's something you always do when you can't communicate with me properly, effectively, appropriately."

I stood up, pacing the room. "That's your whole problem. You don't ever want to bring God into anything. I don't throw God in things to help me win a debate with you. If you had a real relationship with Him, you would understand what I'm talking about!"

He came back with fury. "Just because I don't live at that little hole-in-the-wall church you attend doesn't mean that I don't have a relationship with God. You don't know how much I've prayed for things to change around here. How dare you judge me! God is bigger than you think, Isabella."

"What kind of prayer you been partaking in that allows you to go meandering all across the city of Huntsville with who knows what kind of women? You don't have to have a theology degree to know that you don't have a faithful bone in your body."

His eyes widened and shoulders dropped. "You know?"

"Know what?" I demand.

He sat on the bed, holding his hands in his lap. "Know about my . . . my indiscretions?"

"You think I'm a fool, Langley? I've known for years." I searched his face for a hint of remorse. He only frowned, looking like I'd ruined his party, cheated and won at his game.

"I'm so sorry," he whimpered.

"Yes, you are," I hissed.

"I *am* sorry." He paused, finally looking at me. "I want this to be amicable. Of course, you can have the house and your car. You'll never want for anything."

"Langley, you don't believe in divorce; at least that's what you told me. We don't believe in it. And God hates it."

"Believe it or not, I've done some research on divorce in the Bible, and God did allow it. It's in the Bible you know," Langley stated with his uncanny ability to sound

arrogant even when he knew remarkably little about the
Bible.

"You talking about when Jesus said God allowed it
in the Old Testament because of the hardness of folks'
hearts?" I stepped closer to him, in disbelief.

He stood up. "That's not the point! I am simply saying
that there are times when divorce is the only option left.
God has already forgiven me, whether you think so or
not. I have exhausted all options, with the exception of
divorce."

"No, that's where you're mistaken. We've got lots of
options left. You just aren't up for exploring them, I
guess. Like how about us going to my pastor for marriage
counseling? Or, I know how you are about spreading
our business, so we could go away, just the two of us to
somewhere special, like to the Family Life Conference, or
we could even—"

"Stop it right now!" he interrupted. He lowered his
head and went back to throwing clothes into his bag.
"We're not doing any of that, Isabella. Don't be ridiculous.
It's too late."

"It's hardly ridiculous when you've been married over
thirty years."

"It is too late." He zipped his bag up, and we stood face
to face. He blurted out, "I've met someone."

"Someone" meant it wasn't a string of nobodies. With
a lump in my throat, I managed to say, "What do you
mean?"

"I've met someone who makes me happy."

He looked relieved, and I knew this was it. My husband
had finally decided to leave me. As usual, his timing
was impeccable. I didn't know if I had cancer, and he'd
dropped a bomb on me. I should've been the one to leave
him, but my fear of being alone kept me silent. I should've
confronted him decades ago, but my fear of this very

thing happening, kept me silent. I remembered that verse in Job that says, "What I feared has come upon me; what I dreaded has come upon me."

"You love her?" I asked, more because I didn't want a divorce than caring.

He pulled the suitcase from off of the bed and dropped it onto the floor, measuring his words. "I didn't mean for this to happen. I just can't help the way I feel."

"Do you love her?" I asked again, and waited for an answer that felt equally as agonizing as the forty-eight to seventy-two hours I needed to wait for my test results. He waited for the noise of a distant plane to fly by before he answered. I wanted to be on that plane instead of there, looking at the pathetic scene play out in front of me.

"Yes, I think so," he finally said.

My insides screamed, but he couldn't see me unravel. He wouldn't have that satisfaction. I headed to the bathroom because I didn't want him to forget his toothbrush. If he planned on leaving, I wanted him to take everything. I grabbed his toothbrush and threw it at him. He caught it, looking at me as if I were insane. I then snatched his cologne off of the dresser and threw that at him, too. When he caught it, I didn't say another word but began throwing any- and everything of his at him.

"Stop it, Isabella! What are you doing? Stop acting crazy!"

After tossing the case to his eyeglasses at him, I sucked in a deep breath and then exhaled. Langley's weird, jerky hand and eye movements toward the door were more than I could bear. He tried to stuff the items I'd thrown at him into the bag as quickly as he could to make his getaway without getting hurt. Before he could leave me though, I gathered up the broken pieces of me, grabbed my shoes and purse, and left before he could.

I thought I heard him calling my name. But if he called my name, it wasn't nearly loud enough.

CHAPTER 15

DESIREE

*Confidence in an unfaithful man in the time of trouble is
like a broken tooth, and a foot out of joint.*
—Proverbs 25:19

Mama cleans when she's upset.

I mess things up or eat when I'm troubled.

While Shay groped for the right words to tell me what I
already suspected, I peeled and picked at the loose piece
of my Formica countertop.

"This is hard, Des."

"Just say it," I said, holding my breath for a second.

"Okay, so here goes. Victor called me last night."

"Victor who?"

"Your Victor," she said with all the gentleness that she
could muster up.

"Why did he call you? How'd he get your number?"

Then, she unloaded. "You know how I have my Mary
Kay business cards out? He claimed his mother was
looking for a new rep while you were in the bathroom.
At first, I was cool because he really did ask about what
products to buy to surprise his mom. Then, he started
talking about other stuff. I'll spare you the details, but
let's just say he came on to me. I'm so sorry, Des."

I knew exactly what she meant, but still, I had to ask,
"What do you mean, he came on to you? What did he say?"

"What he said isn't really important, is it? He was just wrong."

"Tell me, Shay. Really, I'm cool."

"Are you sure you wanna hear?" I heard the hesitancy in her voice.

"Please just go ahead."

Shay let out a long deep breath. "You're mad."

"Of course, I'm mad! I'm embarrassed and everything in between, but it's not your fault. I need to know what he said. It's not like he's my man or anything."

"I know, but you've been telling me how much you like him, and I'm sorry that he's such a jerk. Are you sure that you want to know?"

"For the last time, tell me." My cheeks felt hot, and I wanted to cry. Still, I wanted to know.

"Girl, he is a total mess. He had the nerve to try to say that I was looking at him. That arrogant something said he could tell that I wanted him and that I kept trying to get his attention. I told him he was a liar, and the conversation was about to end. He went on saying how sexy I was and then some. I ended the conversation telling him he was crazy and where he could go for trying to talk to me behind your back. That brother's a piece of work."

I knew Shay was editing, trying to spare my feelings. I didn't want her to though. I wanted it all, every hairy detail. I couldn't let her hear the lump in my throat, the tightness in my chest, the pounding in my heart, or the splash of my tears hitting my newly destroyed countertop.

"Shay, you don't need to feel bad about this. I'm glad you're telling me because I was starting to feel some kind of way about him. You know what I'm saying? He was really trying to get physical fast, which is not happening. Now I actually feel better about not talking to him anymore. I know that wasn't all he said though. What else did he say?" I tried to make her feel comfortable, like I was okay.

Shay still proceeded cautiously. "He did badger me, saying that if I was worried about how you'd feel, not to worry because there never really was anything between you two anyway."

I tried to save face. "He is right about that. There wasn't anything between us. Besides, he was only after one thing and when he found out that he wasn't getting it from me, I guess he thought he'd try you."

"Just as slick and sly as all get-out. Don't worry or waste one minute on him, Des."

After I hung up, I inspected the damage I'd done to the countertop, throwing the scraps into the trash, downed two Twinkies, and rummaged through my clothing, pulling out my secret weapon, the black dress with the plunging neckline that everyone always complimented me on. "Oh, you've lost so much weight; what have you been doing to lose it?" they all said when I wore the black wrap dress, tight and loose in all the right places.

I reapplied my makeup that had dulled from the long day at work, and refreshed my curls that had shriveled under the duress of the phone call. The only evidence that anything at all was wrong with me were the deep creases in the brow that refused to relax, no matter how hard I tried.

As I drove over to Victor's, I prayed that I'd remember which apartment was his. I'd only been over once, and only briefly. I tried to think of a scripture to calm me but the only one I could think of was "the violent take it by force." I decided to leave out the "be angry and sin not" one.

Like a warrior seeking her enemy, I would confront the one who wronged me. Sure, I had often scoffed at other women with less class, dignity, and self-respect. They were those who ran wild, throwing accusations at their cheating boyfriends. I had never even thought about slashing tires, keying a car, or throwing bleach on a man's clothes. I was too much a lady for that behavior in the past, but where had it gotten me? Maybe now I did understand characters like Bernie in *Waiting to Exhale*. While Victor was just a date, not a husband or boyfriend, for me, he represented all the dogs, including my stepfather. I wanted justice; or at least confrontation.

Lexi, an old college friend, used to race over to her boyfriend Chester's, and at the slightest appearance of an infraction, she would let that brother have it. If he so much as looked at another woman, she was on him. No amount of rationalizing worked with her. I would plead with her to stop her from tearing his things up, telling him off, or embarrassing him in front of his friends. I thought of myself as her voice of reason. The tables had turned now, and I was tired of being the sick and tired woman, letting guys do their dirt with no consequence.

With no exact plan laid out except to go to Victor's house to confront him, I pulled in and surveyed the parking lot, looking for his car. Victor's Navigator was parked in two spaces in an already crowded parking lot. His arrogance extended to even parking. I couldn't believe it. I inhaled and exhaled, my breath labored in anger. I flicked my hair back from around my face and balled my fist tight, aiming toward door number 307. My nails dug into my palms. With my fist in midair, I stopped, deciding to not give him a heads-up that it wasn't a friendly visit. Instead, I gave a dainty knock. He might have been suspicious or anticipated the venom I planned on spewing out if I was loud. No answer. I knocked a little louder and then heard rustling. Victor opened the door, clearly stunned.

"Hey, Desiree, what's up, sweetheart? I'm surprised to see you here."

I bit my bottom lip. "Yes, I thought I'd come by and see what you were up to."

He didn't welcome me in but said, "You should've called. What made you drop by here?" He licked his lips, clearly rehearsing LL Cool J's tired sexy act.

"How could you try to hit on Shay?" I demanded.

"What did that girl tell you?" He chuckled and shook his head in disbelief. "I called that girl to talk to her about Mary Kay for my mom."

Before I continued, I remembered I was standing outside. Although I didn't want to come in, he still hadn't invited me in. His apartment was pitch black with the exception of the candle he held in his hand. I took a step back. "Do you have company, Victor?" It hadn't occurred to me to ask earlier.

He looked down and the smile dissolved from his face. "No."

I tried to look past him.

"They're supposed to turn it back on soon." Victor looked embarrassed.

"Turn what on?" I asked, clueless.

"My electricity got shut off. You know how it is. You get busy and forget to pay the bill." He shrugged his shoulders.

"Your electricity is off?"

The need to tell him off and give him a good piece of my mind took wings and flew away. Like cool butter on a hot plate, my anger melted with the strange turn of events. I smiled in disbelief at my stroke of good timing. God knew that I needed to see this for myself.

"I mean you're welcome to come in, Desiree." He looked embarrassed.

"Thank you for the invitation, but no thanks." I backed from the doorway. "Just so you know, Shay likes a man who can keep his electricity on."

"Cute," he said before he slunk back into his apartment while I reveled in the moment.

Before I pulled out of the parking lot, I called Shay and filled her in. We both laughed a little too hard for what the situation called for and promised to talk tomorrow, but the undercurrent tension was there. As much as I acted like I had it going on, I felt insecure. Men found her more desirable. Even with a boyfriend right in front of Victor's face, another man had chosen Shay over me.

Without warning, I crashed from the tiny high I had been on, and my giddiness evaporated before I had even made it home. I replayed every conversation that I'd had with Victor. I knew that I'd done nothing wrong, but I questioned myself. What had I done to turn him off? Where did I keep going wrong with these guys? When we met, Victor had seemed so sincere, so genuine, so interested. We'd had countless hours of phone calls. Although he never followed through on the promise to go to church together, things seemed fine.

Shay's sticky sweetness, unthreatening sassiness, hourglass figure, and love of sports made her the one men always wanted. Men looked in amazement at her expansive knowledge of players' names and stats. It drove me and men crazy in different ways.

I replayed the scene from a few weeks ago as I drove home. I'd dressed in jeans and a ruffled fuchsia blouse for the *Monday Night Football* date. With just a hint of fuchsia lipstick and a little mascara, I felt pretty. That is, until I saw Shay, a size ten, who had worn a black designer sweat suit, hugging her in all the right places. As usual, she wore minimal makeup, a long but fake ponytail, and smelled of fresh roses and lilacs. I remembered suddenly feeling frumpy.

During the game, Shay didn't or couldn't suppress her excitement. "Hinrich is just sick, man, just sick with them moves."

Sick? Where did that word come from? Because she grew up with four brothers, she got along great with guys and knew their language and genuinely liked sports. She was up off of her seat jumping around like I had never even seen her do at church when the spirit was high. I couldn't pretend to be into sports if I wasn't. To me, sincere or not, Shay came off like she was trying too hard; but, obviously, Paul, Victor, and a lot of other men felt differently.

When I got home, I raided the fridge, topping my binge off with a waffle ice cream sandwich. Against my better judgment, I got back on the dating site, remembering Mama's encouraging words: *"Sometimes you gotta kiss a lot of frogs before you find your prince."*

My spirits lifted when I noticed three new flirts and several e-mails from new men. I typed at lightning speed to so many men I should've been embarrassed. Before I knew it, the sun that peeked in through the curtains and a simultaneous hand cramp let me know that I had been online an unreal number of hours.

CHAPTER 16

ISABELLA

Yea, though I walk through the valley of the shadow of death, I will fear no evil: for thou art with me; thy rod and thy staff they comfort me.

—Psalm 23:4

My feet, heavy as two-ton weights, fought against me as I struggled to make my way to my car from the doctor's office. Dr. Perkins's words hit me with the force of a boxer's blow. With all the compassion she could muster up, she said, "Mrs. Morrison, unfortunately, the biopsy shows that you have breast cancer." She paused, trying to give me a second to absorb it before continuing. "More specifically, you have a rare type and very aggressive form called inflammatory breast cancer. The biopsy was tested by three different pathologists, and unfortunately, they have all come to the same conclusion."

After that I heard nothing, yet I knew she was still talking. My mind kept repeating the word "cancer" until she said, "First chemotherapy and then a mastectomy. We'll follow up with more chemotherapy and radiation after the surgery just to ensure that we've gotten it all. Let's say we start you right away on the first line of chemo, which is Adriamycin and Taxotere."

I nodded, but still couldn't catch up. Everything moved in slow motion. It was like a movie. I felt detached from my own body, watching everything happen above me. I didn't realize that I had asked a question until I heard my own voice.

"What's the survival rate?"

For the first time, she stumbled over her words. "I . . . I think it's better if you concentrate on beating this thing, Mrs. Morrison."

"Please, I need to know."

She frowned. "Only about two percent of patients survive five years, but let's not focus on the statistics. I think we need to focus on treating this as aggressively and quickly as we can."

I felt a pain unlike any I'd had before even though I understood that God numbers our days, not man. But this thing was much worse than I had imagined. Having trained myself to hold on to a Word from the Lord in trouble, I panicked when every single verse that came to mind seemed too trite and small for something like this. I'd instantly felt bad for all of the times that I'd recited scriptures to people who were going through heavy trials. I needed compassion and a listening ear. If I had been diagnosed with this a few weeks ago, before Langley left, it would've stung a little less, but now the diagnosis on top of his final rejection felt brutal. All at once, I understood Job a whole lot better.

I wanted to call Desiree, but couldn't bear her tears, worry, and pity. Still, I needed to talk to somebody who wouldn't fall apart by the news. My hands trembled as I drove while dialing Pastor Kingston's office. Fully expecting to get the church administrator or an assistant, I met Pastor Kingston's baritone voice on the line.

"Why, Sister Morrison, how are you?"

After hearing only those few words, I cried. Not a pretty, feminine cry, but a gut-wrenching sea of tears while telling him of my diagnosis. I even told him about the survival rate for people with my condition.

"Why don't I come to where you are, and we can have prayer? Or, you are more than welcome to come here, whatever would be best for you."

"Oh, Pastor, I can come to the church now if you're available. I'm so sorry to bother you, but I just can't seem to get myself together right now."

"Totally understandable, Sister Morrison. You're absolutely no bother to me; in fact, that's what I'm here for. Please be careful."

Pastor Kingston's office reflected modesty and humility with its amber-colored walls, obviously not painted by a professional but a well-intentioned member or deacon perhaps. They were decorated with his divinity school degrees and a picture of his wife and children. On the wall directly behind his desk a needlepoint-framed picture of the Lord's Prayer hung. He noticed me eyeing the prayer.

"My wife is pretty good at that, huh?"

"I'll say she is. I'm not too good at crocheting or doing needlepoint myself. Some people just have a knack for things like that." I twirled the Kleenex between my fingers, not knowing where to start. I lingered on the words in the Lord's Prayer, "Thy will be done on earth as it is in heaven." *Is this His will for me? A divorce and a terminal diagnosis, all at the same time?*

Instead of being seated behind his desk as I had assumed, Pastor Kingston directed me to take a seat on the small dingy loveseat in the corner of the room. He took a seat on the leather chair horizontal to me.

"Would you like my wife to join us? She's right in the sanctuary sprucing things up, so it wouldn't be a problem."

I knew that he was careful about meeting with women alone. He had to be. "Thank you for asking, but I am comfortable."

"Well then, I want to pray for you and let you know that I will continue to pray for you. God is in the healing business and there's nothing too hard for Him. I've seen how you operate and pray for others, Sister Morrison, so I know that you know this; it's just a reminder though. We all need to be reminded in times of adversity that there's not an infirmity that we can have that He hasn't been touched with. In the depth of our deepest despair, He is there. Just allow the Holy Spirit to lead and direct you. He'll give you peace that surpasses all understanding."

I wondered what that really meant now. Jesus never had inflammatory breast cancer as far as I knew, and He'd never gone through a divorce. Nevertheless, I shook my head in agreement, and he continued, "I have to admit that I am wondering what Brother Morrison's response to your current condition is."

I took a deep breath and explained to him that Langley had no earthly idea about my diagnosis, and I intended it to stay that way.

"Don't you feel like you should go ahead and tell him? He can be a help to you, can't he?"

"Actually, Pastor, no there's just no way he can help me. I haven't told him and don't plan to. As far as my husband, he can't do me any good."

Pastor Kingston leaned forward in his chair. "What is it, Sis Morrison? Is there something else you'd like to share with me?"

"I really have tried to be a good wife to Langley. I really have." I grabbed a tissue from the coffee table, dabbing my eyes.

"Of course you have." Compassion oozed from Pastor Kingston's voice, expression, and body language like no other, and I felt safe to pour my troubles out.

"I can't believe what I'm about to tell you because if anybody should be leaving, it should be me. But Pastor, my husband left me a few days ago for another woman."

Pastor Kingston's brow furrowed, deep in thought. He didn't say anything for a moment. Then, finally, he said, "Oh, Sister Morrison, I am so terribly sorry to hear this. I didn't realize that you two were having problems."

"We've always had problems, but I guess I'd learned to live with them, you know what I mean? Truth be told, the problems were pretty much there before we said 'I do.' All I've ever been to Langley is an arm piece and now that I'm getting older, his use for me is pretty much gone. He could hire a maid and get what I am to him."

"Why, I hardly can believe that, Sister Morrison."

I continued, "I've never been in the dark about that. He's no tyrant, believe me. I've gotten a thing or two from him."

"What do mean?" he said, resting back, arms folded.

Now, in confessional mode, I said what I'd never spoken aloud. "You see, Pastor, I wanted a better life for my daughter and me after Desiree's father died. I gave up on loving anybody else after that. Too much risk and pain involved. What I wanted at the time was for Desiree to have the very best that life had to offer, and I gotta be honest, I wanted a good life. You know, I didn't want to have to work so hard just to make ends meet. I can't lie. I wanted an easier life. Only thing is, Pastor, I just didn't count up the cost. I guess you can say that I'm paying the piper now. "

"We all make mistakes and fall short, every single one of us. I believe you did what you thought was best at that time. The important thing now is to repent if you haven't already and then move forward. Don't be too hard on yourself. Press toward the mark, in spite of Brother Morrison's choices. There's nothing too hard for God, no marriage troubles or sickness that can't be healed. God loves you and wants what's best for you and your husband. Remember, He's a very present help in the time of trouble."

"We were never supposed to get married in the first place though. The Word also says you reap what you sow. I married for mostly the wrong reasons and now I'm paying for that."

"Don't be so quick to settle on that now, Sister Morrison. Have you asked God to forgive you?"

"Too many times."

"Trust Him then. He's forgiven you. Satan loves to deceive us into thinking that we are slaves to the world's way of doing things, but it's not so. God's grace is sufficient, and His love covers all of our sins. I also know that God wants you both to seek Him and He will direct your paths. In spite of what wrong decisions we make, He can change things. He can make the crooked places straight."

"Yes, I know you're right." My head knew it, but my heart just wouldn't line up.

Pastor sensed that there was much more on my mind and asked, "What is it, Sister Morrison?"

"The Bible does say that if the unbeliever departs, we're supposed to let him because God has called us to peace, right?"

"Yes, it does say that, but I thought your husband had professed salvation."

"Professing and living saved are two totally different things."

Pastor Kingston nodded. "Just remember that we all make mistakes, and by no means am I suggesting that you should remain with him if he really wants out of the marriage. What I will say though is to stay prayerful and don't rush things. Let things cool down. You have an enormous amount of stress on you, so peace is what you need in the midst of this storm."

I tried to lighten the mood. "What I need is for this storm to disappear!"

"Yes, we shall certainly pray for God to remove it, but if He doesn't immediately, you have to know that this too shall pass and He will carry you through this time. In the meantime, your church family is here for you, day or night. My wife and I are here for you. You are not alone."

He walked to his desk and opened his drawer, handing me a small bottle of oil. "As you know, there's no magic potion here, but I want you to anoint your head with this oil every morning before you pray. The oil is a symbolic representation of our faith in Jesus Christ to heal, deliver, and set free." He put a dab of oil on his fingers and anointed my head before giving it to me.

"Thank you, Pastor." Even though I had plenty at home and used it faithfully before prayer time, I accepted the bottle, hoping this fresh and new anointed oil would come with some serious yoke-destroying power.

"Yes, of course, but why don't I give Brother Morrison a call and see if we can meet? I'd like to speak to him on your behalf if you'd let me. He should know about your condition. It might change his outlook."

My back stiffened, and I shook my head. "That's just it though. I don't want him to stay with me out of pity or charity."

"I totally understand your feelings, and I don't want to overstep my boundaries. However, he actually should stay in his marriage out of charity, which just means he should stay out of his decision to love you."

"I didn't mean that kind of charity."

Pastor Kingston nodded. "Totally understood. I'll be praying with you and for you. You have a lot to handle right now, so let me ask you this, have you spoken to Desiree about your diagnosis or the state of your marriage?"

I bowed my head. "No, I haven't told her yet. To tell you the truth, I never thought I had anything but maybe a bad spider bite or rash. Today I not only find out that I have cancer, but I have one of the most aggressive kinds. I don't know how I'm gonna tell her. She's all I really have besides my church family."

At fifty years old, Pastor Kingston, still young in my book, was wise beyond his years. He had a way of provoking folks to love and do good works minus judgment and condemnation. "I understand, but I think you will find that Sister Desiree is much stronger than you think she is. She'll want to be there for you in every way. Why don't you let her know what's going on?"

I couldn't control the steady flow of tears when I tried to speak, and I noticed tears clouding my pastor's eyes at the sight of me. I nodded in agreement. Pastor Kingston placed his hands on my shoulders and prayed so hard that I knew God had heard him if He hadn't heard me.

As he walked me to my car, Pastor reminded me, "God is sovereign. He knows and He cares. We may never know all the whys and hows, but God allows things to happen to His people for a reason. We're not here to understand all things, but we need to continue to fight the good fight of faith. Wouldn't be a fight without opposition, right, Sister Morrison?"

"I know you're right, Pastor. Thank you so much for your time. I do feel so much better."

He gave me a light embrace and said as I got into my car, "I'll be calling to check up on you, you hear now?"

I thanked him, and before I got on the Highway 565, I prayed again for strength before dialing Desiree.

After three calls over the course of the remainder of the day and no answer, I wondered if I should be worried. Desiree always returned messages relatively quickly, so I thought I'd give Shay a call to see if she knew her whereabouts. As I talked to Shay, the other line beeped. My heartbeat fluttered when I saw that it was her. I ended the call with Shay and then clicked over.

"Hi, baby," I said.

"Hey, Mama, I'm sorry I'm just now calling you back. It's been a crazy day."

"What's the matter?" I heard something in her voice.

"I've just got a slew of papers to grade, and the dean met with me today. Can you believe one of my students filed a complaint? He said the grade I gave him on his last paper was unfair. Sometimes I just wonder why the heck I do this. I barely get paid and instructors are so underappreciated."

"Don't be upset. It's just one of those things. Don't worry about it. Things will work out."

"You got that right, and guess what else, Mama?"

"What?"

"I don't know if Shay called you yet, but she told me that Paul asked her to marry him."

"Oh my! I thought you said that they'd just met. I just had her on the other line, trying to find out if she had talked to you. How long has she known this Paul fellow?"

"Not long, but apparently long enough. I know I'm her best friend and I'm supposed to be happy, but I'm so depressed. This will be her second marriage and I can't even get married once."

"Desiree, you don't need to be saying things like that. Better yet, don't even think like that. You'll hold up your blessing. It'll happen for you, honey."

"Mama, you don't sound like yourself. Something wrong?"

I didn't need to tell her now. The timing was off. I would tell her tomorrow when I could control my emotions. I needed to be strong for her. Tired and worn, I promised

her we'd get together for lunch the next day. I'd tell her
everything.

Before I went to bed, I prayed that the Lord would
help Desiree to be strong. If I ever needed her, I needed
her now.

CHAPTER 17

DESIREE

He shall not be afraid of evil tidings: his heart is fixed,
trusting in the LORD.

—Psalm 112:7

It was too late, but I couldn't resist meeting Kyron. He sounded so interesting and excited. I couldn't believe that I'd only met him. It felt like I'd known him for much longer than two days. After I pulled into the parking lot of the diner we'd decided to meet at, I decided that maybe it was a good idea to call Shay, just in case he turned out to be crazy. Somebody needed to know where I was and what I was doing.

"Hey, girl, what's up?" I asked.

"What are you doin' up, Des? It's ten-thirty; isn't it past your bedtime?" Shay chuckled.

"Ha-ha. Very funny. I do have an early class tomorrow and then I'm meeting Mama for lunch, but, girl, I had to call and tell you I'm meeting this guy at the City Café Diner."

"Come again?"

"I'll give you the details tomorrow, but his name is Kyron James. He's an attorney, girl."

"Oh, wow! That sounds like a good prospect, but isn't it odd to meet him so late?"

"You're one to talk. Don't get all weird on me now that you're engaged, Shay. It's not that late."

"I'm not. Just be careful, Des," Shay said, nearly making me nervous.

"I'll send a text when it's over, and we'll talk tomorrow." I hung up and freshened my makeup, anxious to head to the café.

The City Café Diner, with its checkerboard tiles, silver fixtures, and throwback red and white vinyl tablecloths was open all night and was a popular spot, especially for breakfast food. Since I didn't see anyone who looked remotely like Kyron's picture, I seated myself. As soon as the waitress got ready to take my drink order, I recognized him. I waved to signal him. Butterscotch skin and basketball player tall. He nodded, walking toward me, chomping hard and fast on his gum. His emotionless smile gave me the impression that either he was nervous or didn't like me. He slid in on the opposite side of the booth. "Kyron," he said, reaching for my hand. "Thanks for coming out so late to meet me, Desiree."

I held my hand out and smiled. "Oh, well, I know you said your schedule is pretty busy, so it's no problem. Nice to meet you as well."

After the waitress took our order, Kyron started the conversation. "So, tell me about yourself." He asked all the appropriate follow-up questions like a good attorney. I asked him the same. His answers, short, vague, and nondescript, made me notice that he hadn't complimented me at all, about anything. I comforted myself by remembering his education. Maybe he looked for depth like me and tried to get past the superficial.

Floating on a superficial cloud, much too light and airy to hold me for long, I came home from the date feeling good. Like I always did, I dreamed of my life married to Kyron, the attorney, who would insist that I couldn't work, and I'd insist that he'd drop that insane habit of chewing gum. Kyron would build me a house of my dreams and would love every inch of me just the way I was. I would be so inspired by his absolute and complete unconditional love for me that I would exercise and eat right with a diligence that I had never had before. We would then have two children who would behave beautifully and go to a private school. I would open a very posh and successful store downtown to sell my jewelry. Kyron, with a reputation for being one of Huntsville's best attorneys, would be highly sought after, but he would never forget his first obligation to his wife and children.

Things always came together perfectly in my dreams. Imagining a future with Kyron and any other guy I dated always invaded my thoughts and dismissed my good sense. Like a schoolgirl doodles the name of her crush on everything but the kitchen sink, I already etched Kyron, in a non-stalker kind of way, into nearly every facet of my life after one decent date. His polite hug and parting words, "I'll call you soon, okay?" replayed over and over again. I couldn't wait to hear from him again.

Over the years Mama had become the consummate hostess. With the shiny flatware one inch from the brocade patterned dishes, topped with a bird-of-paradise napkin fold, the table setting appeared eerily formal for what was supposed to be a routine lunch meeting. Two fancy chicken salads, garnished with glazed pecans and fresh avocado, iced tea, and one of my favorites, a home-made iced lemon pound cake, set my alarm bells off.

"Mama! My, my, my! Everything looks so good. Surely this isn't just for the two of us? You're up to something!"

"This isn't anything, but thanks, baby."

"Are you kidding? Just last week you didn't even heat the day-old Popeyes chicken when we had lunch."

Mama, sullen and quiet, didn't crack a smile. "Well, I know how much you like my chicken salad. I also know you don't have a whole lotta time, so let's go ahead and bless the food and eat."

After we blessed the food, I noticed Mama didn't touch her plate. "Mama, you okay?"

"Well, funny you should ask that, honey. Actually, I guess they say I'm really not too well right now."

"What's wrong? And who's they?"

"You know that spider bite I showed you a little while ago?"

"Yeah, what about it?" I drank a swig of iced tea to swallow my food down faster.

"It isn't any spider bite, honey."

I frowned. I felt my pulse begin to race.

Mama blew out a long breath. "I been to the doctor and she said . . . she said that . . . it's breast cancer, inflammatory breast cancer to be exact."

I couldn't move or speak, except to drop my fork. "What? When did they say this? Are they sure? How do they know for sure?"

"I didn't want to go upsetting you for nothing, but I had a biopsy. It's been confirmed a couple of times over. It's only been a few days since I found out."

"A few days? Really, Mama? Why didn't you tell me so I could go with you? I would've been there for you. I can't believe this." I stood up, pacing. "Where's Dad and what's he saying about all this?" I felt my heart dancing wildly in my throat. I wanted to hit the rewind button. It didn't feel real.

"This is a lot to unload on you, honey, but I want you to know that I'm okay. The good Lord is gonna carry me through this, so I don't want you to worry, but your daddy . . ." Mama stopped short.

I heard something strange in her voice. "What, Mama?"

"He's left, Desiree."

"What do you mean he left?"

"Ain't no kinda easy way to say this, but he's left me for someone else."

"What?" My heart pulsated from my throat to my head and an awful headache hit me as if I'd been hit by a baseball bat.

"Yes. I know you're shocked. I'm shocked. But I know the Lord has a good reason for all this." Mama began fiddling with the tablecloth.

I wanted to scream. After all I had done to protect Dad, I couldn't believe he could hurt Mama like this. "So, Mama, are you telling me that Dad doesn't know about the . . . the diagnosis?"

"He left before I got the diagnosis, but it really doesn't matter. I don't want him here if he doesn't want to be here."

"That's so not the issue, Mama. You need him here now. I'm going to tell him."

Mama shot up straight in the seat, elevating her voice. "Girl, you won't do such a thing! I may not be well right now, but I'm still your mama. This right here is between me and your dad, and I don't want him knowing nothing. Now that's it."

Shocked at the flash of anger, I tried to get a hold of myself. "Okay, relax, Mama. I won't tell him for now, but you have to tell him eventually. This could change things."

"I'll tell him in my time. I don't know how bad I want things to change anyway. Go ahead and eat, Desiree. Things are going to be fine."

I pushed my plate away. "I'm sorry. I'm just not hungry."

"Oh, I'm sorry. I should've waited to tell you until you finished."

"No! You waited too long to tell me. I want to be there for you." I wanted to be angry with her for shutting me out up to this point, but I knew that it wouldn't do anyone any good. Instead, I decided that I needed to act my age. "You're right. It's going to be all right, Mama." I had to hold my right leg down to stop it from jumping. I couldn't let her see how scared I was.

Mama began clearing the dishes, and I stood up to help.

"Thank you, honey. Are *you* okay, Desiree?"

I smiled. "Yes, Mama. Don't you think I should be asking you that question? I need to see everything: the medicine, paperwork, scheduling, anything that the doctor gave you."

Mama tried to sound upbeat, but I detected worry weighing down her words. "Dr. Perkins says the oncologist is the best one in the city. I believe she said his name is Dr. Sumner, and he's going to start seeing me real regularly. The chemotherapy will start in a few days. I know you probably got a lot of questions, but shoot, I got lots myself. I think I may feel better to tackle them tomorrow, but for right now, I need a little rest."

"Sure, Mama. We can talk about everything later. I'll come back after work. You just go on upstairs and get some rest. I got the rest of the dishes."

"I believe I will, baby. I know this is all a lot to dump on you at once, but I guess that's how life is sometimes." Mama pecked me on the cheek. "Thank you."

While Mama left to nap, I washed the dishes, trying to prepare myself to now be the one to clean up messes.

CHAPTER 18

ISABELLA

Rest in the Lord and wait patiently for Him.
—Psalm 37:7

Waiting. I'd never liked waiting for anything. I'd always been the one to tap the horn if the car in front of me moved a little too slowly when a red light turned green. I murmured to myself if the cashier was too slow or the line was too long, but this kind of waiting was different. I began to realize that cancer would make me learn patience. I had to wait a whole eight days for my first treatment. Now that it was here, Desiree and I pulled up to the building where I'd receive my first chemotherapy treatment. Desiree's leg always bounced when she got nervous, so I rested my hand on her leg, wanting to relax her. She returned a weak smile.

Cancer also makes a person rush almost as much as it makes you wait. If I wanted to beat this disease, the doctors told me that I had to treat it quickly and aggressively. I decided to do exactly as the doctors recommended, but placing my life in the hands of people I didn't know scared me. Just the day before, the oncology nurse had drawn blood because, according to her, "We need to make sure you're well enough to do the chemo."

I found out that I was just well enough to have toxic waste pumped through my body, and I just didn't know how to feel about it. But what else could I do? So much information had been thrown at me about treatments, medicine I would take, and side effects, my head spun. Just when I thought it couldn't get any worse, the nurse explained that she was ready to take me on a tour of the chemo room.

My knees nearly buckled as we entered the cool, sterile room displaying a tiny, pathetically decorated Christmas tree, dripping with tinsel and a few faded ornaments. Three patients receiving treatment held nonchalant expressions, but one looked as shell-shocked as I felt. Only one man chuckling at his reading material looked hopeful.

The nurse had tucked her mousy brown hair behind her ears as she explained that my first treatment would be in a private suite, as if it were a hotel or something. I wondered why my first treatment had to be done privately, but I didn't ask, halfway afraid of what the answer might be. Unable to shake the images of the bald heads we just passed, I swallowed hard and asked, "Nurse, how long will it take for me to lose my hair?"

Desiree closed her eyes and bit down on her bottom lip. The nurse, unfazed, as if she'd been asked the questions a million times, offered in a pseudo-compassionate tone, tilting her head to the side, "Mrs. Morrison, not all chemo patients lose their hair, but many do. Maybe you'll be one of the lucky ones. When we get back out front, I'll check your chart. There's a new medication that's effective for some patients concerned about hair loss. If it does happen though, it's usually gradual and takes a few treatments for it to, you know, come out. However, try not to worry about it. It'll grow back after your treatments are complete."

Desiree looked at me like she'd just seen a ghost, like she hadn't even thought about it. For me though, I had thought about it instantly, almost as soon as Dr. Perkins said I had cancer. Who would I be without my hair, my crown and glory? The nurse with no name continued, "We do recommend that patients cut their hair in a short hairstyle."

I didn't understand. "Might I ask why?"

"Mrs. Morrison, it can be a lot less dramatic if you do experience hair loss. I'm sure the doctor must've told you that even if you don't experience hair loss, the texture of your hair might very well change."

Rena Bailey. Just then I remembered going to see her after she had chemo. She had lost all of her long hair, and it started to come back in coarse and nearly white. She passed away before it fully grew back, and she didn't look at all like the woman I had known for years.

With a quick wipe, Desiree dabbed at her eyes and nose, trying to keep her sadness from me. I patted her on the back. "I'm sorry, Mama. I'm supposed to be comforting you."

"I'm fine, now. It's gonna be okay." I spoke the words. If only my heart would line up with my mouth.

Standing before the glass double doors, not ready to take my first chemo treatment but not ready to die either, I squeezed Desiree's hand, then my Bible, and entered what felt like the war zone.

After checking in at the front desk, we took our seats in the waiting area. Beside an older brown-skinned man, a tall, white mocha–colored woman about twenty or so rested her head on the older man's arm. Her face, still pretty, even with the red and blotchy spots from crying, held tiny specks of residue from tissue. The older man patted her gently, not saying a word.

The elevator music playing in the background didn't do much to ease any of us in the waiting room as far as I could see. Desiree grabbed a *Ladies' Home Journal,* offering it to me.

"No, baby, I brought this to read." I held up my Bible and started to read in First Timothy.

Eyes bore through me. I felt it and looked up. Did white chocolate mocha give me a dirty look? I told myself that she had no reason on God's green earth to be mad at someone she didn't know. I sure hoped she wasn't sick. I kept reading.

Fight the good fight of faith, lay hold of eternal life.

The hot glare bore into me again. With my finger holding my place, I closed the Bible. The angry eyes were piercing. I couldn't hold my peace any longer. I asked, "Do you look at everyone like that, or is that look reserved for me?"

Desiree gasped. "Mama!"

Tall white chocolate mocha sat up, cocking her head to the side, and the older man raised his eyebrows. "You actually believe that stuff in the Bible?" her puffy face demanded.

"Why, yes indeed, I do. What's not to believe?"

"Mostly all of it."

"Such as?" I questioned, intrigued by the nerve of the stranger.

Desiree whispered aloud, "Mama! Don't do this! Not here, not now!"

"Jonah got swallowed by a whale? Noah got two of every kind of animal in a boat the size of China and saved humanity? Not to mention that Jesus walking on water bit. It's just so unbelievable. And where are the miracles now? People aren't being raised from the dead or healed from terminal diseases like mine now, are they?" tall white mocha asked.

"I beg to differ, young lady," I said before the older man snapped.

"Simmer down, Kaylyn!" He made eye contact with me. "I'm sorry, miss, she's just upset."

The young lady looked into the older man's eyes. "What, Uncle Beau? I'm not saying anything wrong, just being honest."

Uncle Beau turned toward me. "Ma'am, I'm sorry for my niece's rude behavior, but she's under a lot of stress right now. I've been teaching her to live by God's Word, but she's goin' through somethin' right now with all the stress of what's happenin'."

Kaylyn chuckled sarcastically and said under her breath, "Stress? Is that what this is? More like a death sentence."

Desiree, now appearing to check out, kept peering at the three of us over the article she pretended to read. I knew she hadn't missed a beat.

"Honey, that's why you need to believe the Word and have faith cause the big C ain't bigger than God," I said.

"No disrespect, miss, but why are you here then? You believe all that in the Bible and you're still here, just like me." Kaylyn looked pleased with herself.

I raised my eyebrows but refused to let her rattle me. "I'm here, my dear, because God uses His people, places, and things to help, heal, and save us. Sometimes He just heals spontaneously and sometimes He heals through a process. We're going through the process, honey. We'll all understand it better by and by. 'Til then, our job is to trust Him, no matter what."

"Oh, brother! I'm so tired of all the clichés and scriptures people give. I need substance and evidence of your faith. You're strong in faith and you're sitting right here next to me who doesn't have it. I'm confused." She threw her hands up and slapped them down on her thighs.

Desiree closed the magazine. She shut her eyes. I felt that maybe she wanted the same answers Kaylyn wanted, but I couldn't be sure. I sat up even straighter in my seat and said, "The Word says that it rains on the just and the unjust. Trouble isn't just reserved for unbelievers. We all have to go through something."

"Yes, but why?" Kaylyn, now sitting on the edge of her seat, asked again, "Why? What's the benefit of going to church, reading the Bible, and praying if that's the case?"

My tongue tied and knotted. I wondered if I should tell her that we go through trials because they make us strong and build our faith. Maybe I should've told her that sometimes trials aren't really for us to get something out of them but for someone else to witness our faith during the test. Or just maybe the story of Job would encourage her heart and prick her faith. Truth was, though, I didn't have answers for her because I didn't have them for myself. It's so easy to put Band-Aids on other folks' trials. Just a few weeks ago, I would've had all the answers for Kaylyn, but my, how things looked different with an ugly monster staring me right in the face.

I finally just spoke from my heart and stopped trying to dig for the right answer. "It's not all about the Lord taking away all of our discomfort and pain. We all have it, but it's how we handle it that counts. We got to trust Him, no matter how dark the situation looks."

Kaylyn looked robbed, disappointed, and defeated all at the same time. She rested her head back on her uncle's arm as if I had extinguished the little remnant of hope she may have had. I was another Christian who had let her down. After all the church services, Bible Studies, praying and fasting, and volunteering, none of it prepared me for the prospect of suffering—my suffering or anyone else's, for that matter.

I couldn't let her go that easily though. "I didn't introduce myself correctly. My name's Isabella, and I heard your uncle say your name. Kaylyn, is that right?"

She nodded. Her uncle spoke. "Nice for us to meet you, Isabella. I'm Beau, Kaylyn's uncle."

"Nice to meet you both. This here is my daughter, Desiree."

Desiree smiled politely, and offered, "Nice to meet you."

"Kaylyn," I said with all of the gentleness I could muster up. "I am sorry I don't have all the answers you seem to be looking for, but I'm trying to make sense of all this myself. I'm gonna pray for you though. Prayer changes things."

Beau nudged Kaylyn. "Oh, thanks. At least you know how to admit you don't know everything just because you're a Jesus freak."

Beau shook his head in disbelief at his niece.

"Oh, she's fine," I said to Beau. I then said to Kaylyn, "Chile, that's a fool who thinks he or she knows everything. I don't know much, but I do know that He's gonna get us both through this," I said.

Kaylyn sat up again. The more Kaylyn discovered she couldn't upset me, the more she seemed to want to interact. "So, what kind of cancer do you have anyway?"

"I have inflammatory breast cancer, otherwise known as IBC. What about you, dear?"

"Wow. I'm sorry, I've actually read about that. I have breast cancer too, but it's not inflammatory. I'm here for my first treatment."

"Guess that means we got somethin' in common."

"Really?" Kaylyn perked up even more.

"This here is my first treatment too."

"Maybe you two can schedule some of your treatments together?" Desiree offered.

"As long as you promise not to preach to me," Kaylyn said to me.

"Well, I can't promise that I won't preach a little. See, He's been too good, but I'd like to do that if they'll let us." I dug through my purse and wrote my name and number on the back of an old receipt and handed it to her. "Now, why don't you call me as soon as you're feeling up to it?"

Kaylyn took the receipt and keyed in my cell number. My phone rang. Before I could pick up, she said, "Oh, it's just me, making sure that you had my number too."

"I guess I didn't think about doing that," I said, feeling a little silly to write my number down.

"Technology these days is something else, isn't it?" Beau said to me.

I shook my head in agreement.

Kaylyn seemed oblivious to the shift in the conversation. "I guess I've lived a sheltered life because I don't know anybody who's had cancer, let alone breast cancer. It would be nice to have a cancer buddy," Kaylyn said.

I still hadn't totally come to terms with the cancer diagnosis, but Kaylyn helped me to get there and quick.

"Kaylyn, your great-aunt Delores had cancer, but I guess you was too young to remember," Uncle Beau added.

"This is a new one for me too, so let's help one another through."

Desiree tapped me. "Mama, I think they just called you."

"Isabella Morrison, we're ready for you now," the nurse called again.

"I'm ready," I said, knowing deep down on the inside that God had a bigger plan that no cancer, chemo, divorce, or anything else could thwart. The Lord knew exactly what I needed to get me through, and by the looks of that girl's face, He knew that she needed a good dose of Isabella.

CHAPTER 19

DESIREE

For we wrestle not against flesh and blood, but against principalities, against powers, against the rulers of the darkness of this world, against spiritual wickedness in high places.

—Ephesians 6:12

Much like a frayed ribbon holding together a fragile, dilapidated box, I had decided to keep my father's secret in hopes that it would keep my parents' marriage from falling apart. I'd always known that Mama would never accept a husband who cheated. With her high morals and low tolerance for mess, Dad's infidelity would put the nail in the coffin of their rocky relationship. I just knew it.

At first, the secret I kept from my mother drove me to pull single strands of my hair out when no one paid attention. I would imagine my mother finding out that I had known all along and hadn't told her. The idea of her thinking I'd betrayed her was more than I could bear. I couldn't stand Dad from the beginning, but after I found out that he was cheating on my mother, I hated him. Yet, I loved my mother more. I knew how carefully she had carved out a better life for both of us, but mainly me. I had tiptoed on the tightrope, always teetering between telling and not telling.

Over the years, a strange thing happened. The weight of carrying the secret morphed into a strange sense of revelry in the power that it gave me over Dad. He was forever indebted to the stepdaughter who never told on him.

Mama had gone on a women's retreat with the church, something she did occasionally. Under normal circumstances Mama would have asked Aunt Josephine to come from Dothan to Huntsville, but she had gotten too sick to travel. With the house to ourselves, Dad and I interacted little, and when we were forced to, it was awkward and forced. He had told me that his colleague would be coming over to discuss business, explaining that he wasn't to be disturbed. I remember seeing a red BMW pull into the driveway and racing to the kitchen to grab a snack before retreating to my room. After watching television for a few hours, I realized that it was almost ten and decided to get ready for bed. Just as I lifted my blouse up over my head, my door creaked open. I gasped, realizing it was a stranger. I yanked my shirt over my chest to hide my bra.

"I'm sorry!" the strange white teenage boy said, shutting my door.

Shaking, I put my shirt back on, unsure of what to do. I then heard a light tapping.

"My dad is here! Go away! Now!" I yelled, aware that Dad would be in his office, much too far away to hear my cries.

Muffled by the door, the boy said, "I'm sorry. My mom is visiting your dad, and I was looking for the restroom."

I closed my eyes, relieved that it wasn't an intruder, but embarrassed. "It's the next door down!" I said, agitated. I had assumed that my father's colleague was a man. Even at my young age, I knew that something wasn't quite right about Dad having a female at the house at such a late hour. Still shaken, I sat down on my bed. After a few minutes, a light tap on the door returned. "Dad?" I called out.

"No, it's Hunter, your dad's friend's son. Can I talk to you for a minute . . . please? I'm bored out of my mind, and they're still having their stupid meeting."

I cracked the door. "Yes?"

Hunter dug his hands deep in his pockets, looking ashamed. "I'm terribly sorry about that. I was only looking for the bathroom. If it makes you feel any better, I didn't see anything."

"Well, you came a long way to find the bathroom. We have two on the main level." I knew that he was just snooping around the house.

"Oh, I guess that's probably what your dad meant."

"Dad would never tell a visitor to come up here, you know."

"Again, sorry about that. This house is just so big." He dug his hands deep in his pockets, looking at the floor. "By the way, what's your name?" he asked.

We stood in the doorway for at least fifteen or twenty minutes discussing school and music. At almost fourteen years old, I had really just begun liking boys, and my school was mostly white. I didn't discriminate. Hunter was cute, so I let my guard down. He noticed Monopoly on my bookshelf and asked if I wanted to play. I purposely left the door open, but invited him in to play.

After about an hour of playing, I yawned, wondering why Dad hadn't checked on me and why he had someone over so late into the evening. I explained to Hunter that I had to get up for school and needed to go to bed. I should've known something was off by his response.

"I know; how about I sleep here with you?" He chuckled.

"Yeah, right," I said. "Let's go downstairs and get our parents."

***

Hunter stood in front of the door, playfully blocking me from passing through. At first, I laughed with him, but when I realized that I really couldn't get past him, I got a little frightened.

"Move, Hunter! I'm not playing around now!"

With a smirk, he began to keep me back by holding me to him. Before I knew it, his hands and lips were all over me. I slapped, pushed, and resisted, but his strength proved too much for me. He kicked the door shut and groped under my blouse.

A wicked grin spread over his face. "You know you want this. Stop playing hard to get!"

The wild pounding of my heart flooded my eardrums and made me dizzy, but I didn't give up. I dug my fingernails into his skin, and the shock of it made him grimace. He shook me in anger. He flung profane insults at me, ones I'd never ever heard. When he said something about wanting to teach me a lesson, I knew that I was in trouble. I felt like it was all happening to someone else. I kept wondering where my dad was. He nearly picked me up and threw me onto my princess white sleigh bed. I kicked and cried until he dragged me off of it and onto the floor. Pinned, I struggled to move but couldn't.

"No! Dad." I cried for Dad's help but to no avail. I fought to turn my head away from his slippery lips that groped to quiet me with an open-mouth kiss. I had never imagined my first kiss would be like this. Over and over again, I prayed that Dad would come to my rescue. The only thing was, the more that I fought, the more it excited him.

"Shut up!" he hissed, tightening his hold, grinning.

I squeezed my eyes shut, fighting him and praying for the Lord to help me. Mama had taught me that. *"He preparest a table before me in the presence of mine enemies."* As soon as I opened my eyes, I spat in Hunter's face. He slapped me so hard that my face stung like fire. I grabbed his face with one hand and snatched the empty Coke bottle I had left on the floor just within arm's reach. I grabbed it, and in one swoop, I hit him on the head as hard as I could. He yelled out profanities, holding his head, while I wrestled out from beneath him, and ran, screaming for Dad.

"Dad! Dad! Help me, Dad!" I ran first to the office, then to the living room, sunroom, finished basement, kitchen, and then noticed the light coming from underneath one of the guest room doors. I stopped short for a moment, wiping tears, confused.

Afraid that Hunter could be on my heels, I grabbed the doorknob, turning and struggling, only to realize that it was locked. I beat on the door. "Dad! Dad!"

"What on earth is wrong, Desiree?" Dad asked, flinging the door open only enough to hang his head out.

Without thinking, I pushed the door open, pushing my way past him. As soon as I came to my senses, I realized that Dad had a sheet thrown around him. I saw Hunter's mother, groping to get her clothes on by the bed. Dad's face, flushed and guilt-ridden, contorted. "What's wrong? I'm sorry that you had to, uh, see this. It's not what you think. Wha . . . wha . . . what are you doing in here? Wha . . . wha . . . what's going on?"

Hunter's mom, a petite dirty blonde with smudged mascara, threw her blouse on and grabbed her purse and shoes, racing out without one word. Shirtless, Dad started toward me. I fell to my knees.

"Why?" I cried.

"I'm so sorry, Desiree. I'm so sorry. I can't explain it. I really can't."

"That boy . . . that boy . . . he . . ."

Dad frowned. "He what? That's her son. I'm sorry that I didn't tell you that he was here. I thought you'd be going to bed, and I didn't want to disturb you. What did he do?"

"He's bad, and you're bad too," I cried. Anger and disappointment replaced fear. What good would it do to tell one bad man about another bad one?

Dad covered his face with his hands. "He didn't do anything to you, did he? I'm sorry if he wasn't nice to you. I never meant for any of this to happen, Desiree. You must believe me when I say that. I love you and your mother so very much. When you're older, you'll understand things better. "

The more he talked, the less I listened. I didn't care that Dad begged me not to tell Mama about his cheating. He wasn't the reason I knew that I'd never tell her. Mama was the reason I wouldn't tell on him. Mama was also the reason why I knew I couldn't tell Dad about Hunter's assault. Dad would be compelled to tell Mama if I told him how Hunter had tried to force himself on me. I knew how much keeping the marriage together meant to Mama. I also knew that I'd have to forfeit having the appearance of a father if I let the cat out of the bag. It had become a special prize to be black and to come from a wealthy, two-parent household. Nobody knew that Dad wasn't really my father with the exception of people very close to the family.

Instead of disliking my stepfather, I hated him with the intensity of a catastrophic hurricane. My hatred was the worst kind. For years, I lay in wait for another misstep from my father, which never took long. Whenever he did or said something to hurt my mother and I knew about it, he paid a price. He always tried to make amends with his checkbook and not with his heart. I fully understood that I couldn't change his heart toward Mama or me, but I could cash his checks. Dad didn't know that he could never pay enough for what he had done to Mama or me.

What I wanted from a man wasn't a lot to some but more than what I'd seen from Dad and other men floating in and out of my life. *Is it really so difficult for a woman to have a saved, sanctified, Holy Ghost–filled man with a decent job and the staying power of a tube of Super Glue?* All of my experience with men had been ones with the stick-to-itiveness of a Post-it note.

I added Kyron to the long list of men who didn't bother to call back after the first date. Like all the others, I punished myself with the reasons why he didn't call. Too fat, too sad, too old, and a bunch of other too this and that and not enough whatever.

I also didn't talk to Shay about my man issues anymore. She was too happy about her engagement to Paul. She was too busy attracting my men to her.

I scrolled through the numbers on my phone. For one reason or another, I didn't want to call any of them, but I stopped when I came to Taye. Hadn't I erased his number? I called him. My heart skipped a beat hearing his husky hello.

"Hello Taye, it's Desiree."

"I know who you are, girl. What's up? I ain't heard from you in a good minute."

"Yeah, I know, things have been so busy with work and everything."

Taye didn't attempt small talk, and there was silence.

"Well, I was thinking about you and just called to see how you were."

"What'chu thinking about me now for? I called you like a stalker for months, Des."

"I know. I'm sorry about that. Guess I was traumatized by all that happened, that's all."

"I kept tryin' to tell you how sorry I was. I guess all that made me really wake up and get myself together. I'm back workin' now. My job called me back and, get this, I'm a supervisor now."

"Wow, Taye, that's really great."

"God has really been blessin' me, girl."

God has been blessing him? Maybe he really had changed. "I'm glad things are going so well for you."

"And you? What's up with you?"

"My mom is sick." I surprised myself by blurting this out, but I desperately needed a shoulder to lean on.

"Hey, I'm real sorry to hear that. You okay?"

Before I could answer, I heard a high-pitched female voice question him. "Hold on a minute," Taye said while he answered. I couldn't hear anything but muffled voices. Clearly, he had covered the mouthpiece to the phone, and I wished I hadn't called.

With his voice dramatically lower, Taye practically whispered, "I'm gonna have to go, but you know, Des, it was good to hear from you, girl. I'll say a prayer for your moms, okay?"

"Oh yeah, sure, you take care now."

I tossed the phone down and felt my cheeks warm in embarrassment. I, a female Charlie Brown, read the bubble captions over my own head. *Ugh! Stupid! Loser!* I had stooped to an all-time low by calling for comfort the same man who had abused me. As sorry as he was, even he had moved on, rejecting me.

Thinking about my man troubles took my mind off of Mama's illness and Dad's departure, but only temporarily. With Mama's first few chemo treatments done, I had been staying with her around the clock. Only recently had she begun to get pretty sick. I crept back into her room, careful not to let the door squeak as I checked in on her. Glad to see her eyes closed, I started to pull the doorknob shut but heard her whisper my name.

"Hey, Mama, go back to sleep. Just checking in."

She put the plastic vomit bowl on her nightstand and sat up. "Who can sleep? You sleep a third of your life away, you know, baby?"

I walked in, sensing that she wanted company. "I know, I know." Mama had been saying that to me since I was a teenager.

I helped her adjust the pillows behind her head and handed her a glass of water. "You still feeling really nauseous?"

"Yeah, but it's not as bad as I guess it could be. With the ache in my joints it makes it hard to sleep. I imagine I'll be feeling better soon. What'chu know good?"

My mother's optimism amazed me. My father had left her, and she had been diagnosed with cancer, going through chemo, all in a matter of weeks, and she was always concerned about me. I struggled for something good to tell her, and then I remembered that Shay had chosen her colors for the wedding.

Mama frowned. "What kind of wedding is turquoise, black, and white?"

I chuckled. "Actually, Mama, it's a new kind of fad. It's going to have a Tiffany's theme."

"Who the heck is Tiffany?" Mama said with great seriousness.

"The store Tiffany's."

Mama threw her hand up and shook her head, chuckling. "Aww, shoot, Desiree. Does she even own anything from Tiffany's? That girl's always trying to be more than what she is, at least to you, anyway."

Now that surprised me. Mama always loved everything Shay did or said, or at least I thought. "Well, she e-mailed me a picture of the cake she wants, and it's really quite pretty. It's a big Tiffany's package with a bow. She does have a Tiffany's necklace. Who cares if it's a knockoff?"

Mama shook her head. "Okay, what about you, dear? I know you been all worried about me for the past few weeks, but you met anyone nice?"

"There's nothing going on in that area of my life. Trust me, though, you'll be the first to know if there is." I glanced at my watch. "I think it's time for your medicine." While I went to gather her medications from the bathroom, her phone rang. I rushed out to get it, but Mama beat me to it.

"Langley, how nice of you to call," Mama said in a voice dripping with sarcasm.

Then, there was silence. I retreated to the bathroom but still listened.

"I've had better days. What do you want?"

The silence lasted for four or five minutes, and then Mama spoke again. "I reckon you can come back, Langley. It's your house, always has been and always will be, but you need to know things have changed for me."

It got quiet again for a few minutes. "Yes, we can talk about it tomorrow, but I can't make any promises about anything now. Okay, I'll be here."

I stood frozen in the bathroom. Dad's mind had come back from vacation. He had realized the error of his ways and wanted Mama back. One of my many prayers had been answered, but I just hoped Mama wouldn't mess things up. I knew that she wanted the marriage, and as much as I couldn't stand Dad, I did think that Mama needed him.

CHAPTER 20

ISABELLA

When thou passest through the waters, I will be with thee; and through the rivers, they shall not overflow thee: when thou walkest through the fire, thou shalt not be burned; neither shall the flame kindle upon thee.
—Isaiah 43:2

Langley wanted to come home.

After steadying myself from the bed, I sat up slowly, praying the nausea wouldn't rear its ugly head. I wanted to be ready for him and didn't want to look sick. I had mostly been in bed for days and wanted nothing more than to do some of my normal activities. A long bath, a cup of coffee with extra cream and sugar, and the newspaper. Only thing was, my dizziness made taking a bath and reading out of the question, and just the smell of coffee made me sick. My head felt strange and light so I sat back on the edge of the bed. I reached my hand around to rub the back of my neck. My stomach dropped when I reached my hand to my head. Way too large tufts of hair wrapped between my fingers.

I gasped for air, noticing an alarming amount of salt and pepper hair all over on my lavender pillowcase. Even though I knew this could, would probably happen, I wasn't prepared for the horror of it. I shot off the bed and almost tripped, running to the bathroom. I still had a good amount of hair there, but I knew it would fall out sooner than later. I reached up to stroke it and more hairs fell into the sink.

It's only hair, I told myself. *It will grow back. Don't be so shallow. You're more than your hair.* It didn't matter what kind of pep talk I tried to give myself. I choked, sobbed, and trembled at the loss of so much hair. My hair, my crown of glory, covered me even while Langley had not. People knew me by all of my long hair. Who was I without my hair?

After I took a shower and calmed down, I didn't dare comb it. I walked around the house tidying up things, careful not to move too much. I knew it was ridiculous, but I couldn't bear any more hair loss today. Besides, I wasn't near ready to break the news to Langley. His decision to come back home couldn't be grounded in sympathy for his sick wife. He'd have to come back because he wanted to; then I'd tell him.

All at once, fear, hurt, and anger choked me. Somehow, I'd thought I'd be different from all of the other bald patients getting chemo, fighting cancer. I felt like one of those silly women who thought that she could be the one to change the bad boy into a nice guy. I thought that I'd be the exception: one who'd not lose her hair to chemo.

For the first half of the day, I avoided the mirror after those initial examinations of myself. The second half of the day, I stared at my face, trying to imagine what my head would look like bald. I'd no longer be Isabella with the pretty hair. I knew as shallow as it was, it was the truth.

My oval, olive-colored face had really begun to show its age. Dark circles, worsened by just a few weeks of chemo, surrounded my large, dark eyes and the little crow's-feet appearing in the corners of them made me feel haggard. When I really looked at my face, I wondered why I had always been told I was so pretty. My features were rather ordinary. My lips, fairly thin anyway, with age appeared even thinner. My facial features weren't the thing that made others comment on my attractiveness. My hair was the main attraction, and I knew it.

At six o'clock on the nose, some wrestling with the door lock let me know he was back. I sat quiet and didn't turn to greet him. Instead, I stared at the pink shiny decorations on the tree while sitting purposely in his recliner.

I could hear the uncertainty of his footsteps as he drew nearer. "Isabella?"

"I'm here, Langley."

Langley stood towering above me physically but inwardly cowering. I waited for him to begin. An unexpected rage welled up in me that I hadn't known. I wanted to claw him, slap him, really hurt him. Yet, there was a big part of me that sighed with relief. With everything turned completely upside down, I silently welcomed the familiarity of my husband.

"My, my, my, doesn't the Christmas tree look lovely. I see that you've added quite a bit," he remarked, taking a seat on the sofa across from me.

"Yes, a lot has changed since you've been gone." I stared at him, noticing he smelled different, something like summer even though it was the dead of winter. Was it *her* smell?

He looked down into his lap. Langley frowned, studying me. "Isabella, are you feeling well?"

My stomach sank. Had he noticed my hair loss? "I'm feeling as well as can be expected. Why?"

"Oh, you just look small to me, that's all. Maybe a little tired."

My eyes bore into him. "What do you expect, Langley? It's not every day that a wife comes home to her husband packing up his things, telling her that he's in love with another woman!"

He appeared to swallow hard and put his hands to his temple as if he had a headache. "I am sorry for my behavior. There's really no excuse for what I've done to you, and what I've put you through over these past weeks. You have every right to be done with me and our marriage, but I have made a terrible mistake."

"Just how many mistakes have you made in our marriage, Langley?"

He smoothed out the wrinkles in his khakis and took a deep breath. "I am not going to lie to you. I have made many mistakes, and I am not proud. You must know that I have not meant to hurt you."

I chuckled sarcastically. "Really? Have you ever tried to love me?" Without waiting for an answer, I asked, "Exactly what has brought you to this epiphany?"

"Well, being away these last several weeks has allowed me to see what life would be like without you, and I don't like it. You see, Isabella, I have taken you for granted. I can say that I thought that I was in love, but it was nothing more than infatuation. You are the one I love."

I frowned, sensing a snow job. "So, why did she leave you?"

"What?" he demanded.

"I want to know why she doesn't want to be with you anymore. That's the only reason why you're here, isn't it?"

He didn't respond, but stared at me like I was a psychic. "I do love you, Isabella," he insisted as if he were trying to convince himself.

I eased back in his recliner, feeling tired and a bit more nauseous. "I think you feel comfortable with me, kind of like an old pair of house slippers."

He started to protest, but I stopped him. "But that's okay because I probably feel a lot of that same kind of way toward you. This whole thing is just as much my fault as it is yours."

He looked puzzled, but his eyes told me that he knew what I was saying.

Langley stuttered at first and then exhaled. "I want us to make our marriage work. We've put too much time in it to throw it all away. I am so terribly sorry for what I've done to you, what I've done to us."

"And her name is?" I questioned.

"Is that really necessary to know, Isabella?"

"Why yes, I think I should know her name in case I run into the woman you are in love with."

His voice, tight and strained, wavered. "I'm not in love with Amber. I love you."

"Oh, for goodness' sakes, Langley. Amber? How old is she with a name like that?"

"It doesn't matter now, Isabella."

The expression on his face revealed his shame, but I kept going. "Is she black? No, it doesn't matter, but I don't know many African American women named Amber. Come on, Langley, don't make me ask every single question that you must know I have."

"I met Amber at a golf tournament in Decatur. She's my age, and she's not black."

I swallowed hard, feeling clammy and faint. If I didn't care about his cheating, why was I feeling this way?

"What's the point, Isabella? I don't want to be with her. I want to be with you!"

"Why are you back, Langley? Tell me the real reason. If you want to have any hope of reconciling things with me, you've got to tell me. Be honest for once in your life."

"She didn't dump me. We mutually decided to end it."

It really didn't matter what he said. I knew I'd been right. She'd called it off. All it would've taken her was a few weeks to get a good taste of the real Langley. No woman in her right mind would put up with him.

"I'd like to take you to dinner. We can continue talking there."

"Actually, I don't feel much like eating. I think I'd like to lie down, rest my head a bit."

"Of course. If you don't mind, I'd like to stay here."

"Like I said, Langley, it's your house."

"It's our home. I'd like your permission to stay, Isabella."

"The guest room is ready for you. I'm just not ready for anything more right now."

Langley looked relieved and pecked me on the cheek. "Thank you. I'll make all of this up to you somehow, even if I have to spend the rest of my life trying."

CHAPTER 21

DESIREE

*Likewise the Spirit helps us in our weakness. For we do
not know what to pray for as we ought, but the Spirit
himself intercedes for us with groanings
too deep for words.*

—Romans 8:26

In the weeks since Mama's diagnosis, I juggled her
care, teaching, grading papers, and in spite of it all, I
hadn't slowed down my Internet dating. I looked forward
to Christmas break, one of the perks of teaching. I needed
time to recharge and fill jewelry orders. And do more
Internet dating. Every time I booted up my computer to
work, the temptation to chat with men whispered and
then screamed in my ear, and I always complied. One
date after another, on any available lunch or dinner, I'd
either chat or meet up with men.

There was Rodney, the pharmacist who appeared to be
on the drugs that he probably prescribed for his custom-
ers. His eyes darted around like an animal, and his hands
trembled while he sweated profusely. I knew not to take
Rodney any further than a lunch date.

Next, I went to the Air and Space Museum with Tim,
the former GM car salesman who had lost his job when
they shut down the dealership because of the company's
bankruptcy. All he did the whole night was lament over

his unemployment status and recent divorce. He'd even shed a tear when he spoke of his beloved ex-wife, who'd left him for his son's teacher. I'd ended up consoling him all night and was fearful that he might harm himself by the end of the evening.

I met William, a social worker, at the Russian Tea Room. Over our cups of white Ayurvedic Chai, he bragged about his six children by four different women. Never married any of them; he didn't believe in marriage. When I questioned why he would be on a Christian site, he explained his openness to other religions. "Oh, I don't judge like that," he said. "I'll date anyone, but I personally don't believe in marriage."

Ted, a mattress salesman, who posted a picture of himself from twenty years earlier and sixty pounds lighter, told me off when I let him know I didn't recognize him. We didn't make it to the table for lunch, of course.

I have to admit though, all of my dates weren't bad; at least at first anyway. Jesse, a gym teacher, had me excited for a while. With a muscular build, ebony skin, and hazel eyes, I became enamored with him from the jump. He asked for my number, but we only spoke once on the phone. He only sent texts. He sent songs every morning, videos sometimes in the afternoon, and gobs of corny and flirtatious text throughout the evening, but he wouldn't pick up the phone. When I finally caught on, finally figured out that he must be married, I sent him a good-bye text.

When Kiefer, a blue-eyed ash blond messaged me, I was skeptical and proceeded with caution. I hated to admit it, but it was true. So many African American men had issues. Gay, married, non-committal, or unemployed, I'd had enough. I had also heard plenty of horror stories about sisters having bad experiences with white men who only wanted to see what it was like to be with a black woman. However, loneliness had no color and love had many, so I gave in and met Kiefer out to stroll around in the artsy downtown Five Points area of Huntsville.

His athletic physique adorned with a model-like face, earth sandals, and mop of curly ash blond hair intrigued me. His first words, "Aren't you a doll?" not so much. All the same, Kiefer complimented me incessantly, even holding my hand as we window shopped. He treated me like a perfect gentleman would, and our conversation flowed well as we sipped tea at the tiny café in the health food shop.

I knew from his profile that he owned his own business, but I couldn't believe what it was. "You make cheesecake? Really?" I nearly choked on my tea.

Kiefer leaned in nodding, making way too many hand gestures. "Yeah, you know, I have a way of preparing everything with all organic ingredients. My secret is that I use tons of fruit toppings and very little actual cheese-cake, which automatically makes it much healthier."

I told him about my jewelry-making business, and although he was a bit Thoreau-like for my taste, we had enough in common. When he told me that he walked or rode the bus everywhere he went, I talked myself into giv-ing him a chance anyway. His apartment, he explained, was right down the street. He convinced me into stopping by his apartment for a cheesecake. He just happened to have one that a customer didn't pick up that he wanted to give to me. I felt light in my steps as we entered into his building and actually squeezed his hand. When we made our way into the aged and narrow apartment complex, I was taken aback by the litter strewn in the foyer and halls.

"Oh, it's not as bad as it looks," Kiefer said, noticing my upturned nose.

I wanted to turn back, but his easy, carefree nature reassured me to press forward. He smiled at me as he unlocked the door to his apartment.

A Beautiful Mind. That movie is the only thing I could think of as I stared at the writing on the wall, and I don't mean figuratively. Nearly the entire wall space was cluttered with taped-up notes and papers, lists, and even recipes. But most alarming on the walls was Kiefer's handwriting, which rang of a serial killer's graffiti. The sheer volume of it scared the daylights out of me. I stayed close to the door to make my quick exit.

"I know, I know," he said, noticing my frown and anticipating my questions as if he had done it a million times before. His studio apartment leaped out of an episode of *Hoarders,* except that there appeared to be an organization to the chaos. Piles were separated according to subject, he explained: clothes, shoes, books, papers, empty food boxes, Styrofoam egg cartons, brown paper bags, CDs, LPs, and more. "I'm a stickler about my things," he added.

Kiefer maneuvered his way around the heaps to reach the untidy kitchenette area. He talked nonstop as he boxed up the tiniest tiny cheesecake that I'd ever seen. No wonder it was so low in calories. He walked it over to me. "The walls need to be painted anyway, and there's no sense in wasting paper when I can just use all the blank space of a wall."

"I see," I said, eyeing an unusual mosaic of pictures, including Angela Davis, Nikki Giovanni, Jimi Hendrix, and even the Black Panthers.

"I love black people. I think that you're all so beautiful. So expressive, moving, and poetic," he said, staring into my eyes. He thought he'd given me the biggest compliment.

I thanked him for the cheesecake, knowing I'd never taste it. There was just no way I'd eat anything coming from a crazy living in such a chaotic space. Needing to make a clean break, I explained that I needed to get back home.

"Oh, I'm so bummed. Do I get a little chocolate kiss?" he asked.

I coughed, backing out slowly but steadily, explaining that I never kissed on the first date. When I saw a flash of anger overtake his face, I made a quick exit. And needless to say, that was my last encounter with crazy but cool Kiefer.

At least a handful of my dates were really good dates, guys I would've loved to see again, if only they had asked for a second date. It didn't matter too much though because if I wanted, I could have a date almost every night of the week. The string of bad dates hadn't brought me any closer to a potential husband, but they had left me with plenty of unfinished jewelry orders.

The lure of potential suitors had my adrenaline on high speed, much like a drug. I couldn't wait for another opportunity to meet someone new and get one step closer to the rest of my life. Aside from Mama's health, my thoughts rested almost solely on meeting and dating men. Logically, I knew that all of the men in the world couldn't change having to face Mama's illness, but emotionally, dating gave me the mental break with reality that I needed to keep me going. I actually had something to look forward to.

Every spare moment I had I spent scrolling through profiles of men in my area. I had gotten savvy with the whole thing, sending winks, smiles, flirts, and a host of other ridiculous little icons to complete strangers, all the time praying that I'd never come across any of my former or current students. I became addicted to how my self-esteem soared with my iPhone buzzing with new messages from men.

As I got ready for a new date, I reveled in the anticipation of our possibilities. Much like the others, I didn't know much about Phillip, except that he was an engineer at Redstone Arsenal, had no kids or previous marriages, and that he seemed to be attractive from the pictures posted on the site. Tall, lean, and academic looking, Phillip had a responsible husband look to him.

Phillip and I had reluctantly agreed to meet at Beale Street, a new shopping center in the city. In spite of the fact that we knew it would be hectic with last-minute shoppers, we both had at least one thing in common: we loved Chinese food, and Beale Street had the best. Afterward, we'd agreed on catching a movie.

Before entering the restaurant, I took a deep breath, trying to fight the nervous excitement. Immediately I spotted a tall brown man in a tweed sports coat and loafers coming toward me. He looked exactly like his pictures except that I hadn't remembered him wearing glasses.

I smiled and walked toward him. He extended his hand toward me and held on to it lightly. "Desiree, I instantly knew it was you."

"I hope that's a good thing, Phillip."

"That's a great thing." He lightly held my arm. "Come on, this way to the table." He helped me with my coat and pulled my chair out.

While we waited for our meal, Phillip answered, "A little about myself? Hmmm, I'm not terribly exciting, Desiree. Let's see. I'm an aerospace engineer, a contractor for Lockheed. I transferred here from the DC area. I'm an only child but wasn't spoiled any more than your average only child."

I smiled.

He took a sip of his drink. "I'm proud to say that my parents have been married for well over forty years."

"That's a blessing and an accomplishment for any marriage these days. So, what about you? Why haven't you married?"

He disregarded my question, but it didn't matter because our conversation flowed beautifully. By the time our meals arrived, Phillip surprised me again with his manners and asked, "I'll bless the food, okay?"

I bowed my head, and while he blessed God for the food, I blessed Him for what seemed to be the best date I'd had yet.

As Phillip poured more soy sauce on his orange chicken, he explained, "Oh, yes, I'd forgotten. Earlier you asked why I haven't married. My parents really have been excellent role models for me in the marriage department. They always taught me to wait until I know it's right. Shoot, at my age, which, by the way, is thirty-eight, I can say that I probably have met a few women who would've made wonderful wives for me."

I raised my eyebrows. "Really? So, what's the problem then?"

He chewed his food, took a swig of Coke, and dabbed his mouth with his napkin before answering. "You see, the problem hasn't been with the women. It's point blank been with yours truly. I think the timing just hasn't been right for me. I was really focused on school, getting my master's, and then advancing my career. And the main thing was, I just wasn't mature enough to make the commitment to marry."

"And now?" I asked, feeling fairly confident that he wouldn't think of me as desperate for asking.

He smiled at me. "And now, Ms. Desiree, I think I'm ready for that next step. Just need to meet the right one, that's all. Women my age tend to have a lot of baggage, if you know what I mean? On the other hand, younger women have a little too much growing up to do for me to deal with."

"What do you expect, Phillip? At our age, people do have a past," I said, only slightly agitated.

"Sooo? Tell me about your past, Desiree."

I replaced my chopsticks with a fork. "My past is probably also pretty boring compared to some my age, which, by the way, is thirty-four. I've had a couple of serious relationships, but mostly not. It's harder for women, especially ones who have high standards."

"Don't be so hasty now. Women think it's so easy for us, but not so."

I rolled my eyes and smiled.

"So, no kids?" he asked.

"No kids, Phillip. Did you think I'd lie on my profile?"

"Don't even go there! Do you know how many women I've dated who lie on those? Oh, and I don't even want to talk about the anger and bitterness when you date those baby mamas."

Again irritated, I nodded. "I'm not saying that they're right, but come on, they probably have plenty of legitimate reasons to be angry at men. As for me, I'm not a bitter black woman, but it's frustrating. It really is true that all the good men seem to be taken."

"Hmmm. I don't think I'm so bad." He grinned.

"That, Phillip, remains to be seen," I flirted.

Phillip and I talked so effortlessly that we skipped the movie and got hot cocoa at Starbucks after strolling the shops. I didn't want the date to be over and was surprised when he said, "Well, I guess I do need to let you go since it's getting late, but I don't want the night to end."

"I've really had a good time, Phillip."

He placed his hand on my back again as we crossed the parking lot to get to my car. "I have to tell you that I'm glad I didn't have any professors who looked like you in school, because I never would've finished."

"Oh, yeah, right!"

He playfully put his arm around me. "I am so serious. You are so pretty, smart, and yeah, I like the confidence and sassy in you."

I smiled.

He smiled too. "I feel lucky to have had the opportunity to go out with you. Guess that site may have been a good idea after all, huh? Kudos to your girlfriend for talking you into it."

"All right already, Phillip. You really know how to lay it on thick."

He blew into his hands, clearly cold from the December chill in the air.

"Where are your gloves, mister?"

"I don't need gloves when I have you to keep me warm, right," he said, grabbing my gloved hands in his as he leaned lightly into me in front of my car.

We were inches away from each other and I inhaled the hot chocolate smell on his breath. Just when I opened my mouth to say something, his lips met mine, softly and gently. Then, in a flash, he backed up and opened my car door. "You better go. I'll call you tomorrow. Be safe going home and thank you." He kissed his two fingers and turned them toward me before jogging off to his car.

Of course, common sense told me that he would be like all the others who I had been interested in: he wouldn't call again. But, the hopeless romantic in me won out as it always did, and I melted just reflecting on the easy conversation, the hand lightly caressing my back and the kiss, not to mention the good physique, job, and manners.

I heard Mama's voice: *If it sounds too good to be true, it probably is.* I hushed her voice and floated home, praying that Phillip rested on the same cloud I had landed on. Maybe we'd dream of each other tonight. Maybe Phillip could crowd out the dismal reality of Mama's cancer, my parents' fragmented marriage, and my own loneliness.

While unlocking the door, the phone rang and I took a nose dive across the couch in my attempt to answer.

"Hello?" I tried to sound soft and feminine and not like I had nearly killed myself, hoping it was Phillip.

"Hey, baby, what'chu all outta breath for?"

"Hi, Mama, just walked in," I huffed.

"Good gracious, girl, it's almost eleven o'clock. Where on earth you been?"

"Went to Beale Street." I hoped she wouldn't ask me anything else. I didn't dare tell Mama about Phillip. Mama might get her hopes up, and more importantly, she'd want to know how I met him. She would flip her lid if she knew I was meeting men on the Internet.

"This late?"

"Mama, remember, it's the holidays. You know the stores stay open late."

"Oh, of course. Now don't you go spending your hard-earned money on me and your daddy. We got everything we need."

"I know, Mama. How are you feeling?"

"I'm better today than yesterday, but I surely hate thinking about the chemo treatment that's coming the day after Christmas. Just when I'm starting to feel some better I've got to let them put that poison in me again. Don't make a lick of sense."

"I know, but it'll be over soon," I said, hoping she'd believe what I didn't.

"I hope so because I can't stand losing my hair."

Little pins pricked me all over and the hairs on my arms stood up. "Your hair? Mama, you didn't tell me you were losing your hair!"

"Yeah, I thought maybe, just maybe, it wouldn't happen to me, but it's gonna be okay. I'm fine."

"I'm so sorry, Mama." I felt like an ice skater on a lake of thin ice, but I kept on. "We'll have to get you a real nice wig if it keeps coming out. Shoot, Beverly Johnson has such wonderful and sophisticated ones. Geneva wears them all the time."

"Oh, I appreciate that, honey, but Kaylyn and I are going to go out after our next chemo treatment and hunt for some good ones together. We talk at least once a day, you know."

"I knew that you all were spending time together, but I don't have to be jealous of this girl, do I?" I only half joked.

"Honey, she's becoming like another daughter to me." Mama chuckled. "We talk on the phone every day now. She's such a sweet girl. You should come with us, Desiree. She's really a lot of fun. She could be the little sister you never had."

Fun? I hadn't heard Mama say that anyone or anything was fun in years. My muscles tightened, and I realized that I cringed inside every time Mama mentioned Kaylyn's name. "Mama, I'm glad that you're having fun with her, but to be honest, I really don't see how you can talk and spend so much time with her. She seems so negative, and God knows, you don't need that right now. She's not even saved, for goodness' sake."

"Oh, Desiree, that's why I make every effort to talk to and spend time with her. And she's really not negative when you get to know her. We are all a product of our experiences. She's just had some bad ones. Both of her parents have passed away, and she's only got her uncle to care for her. Imagine that? No mom, aunt, or sister to help her through breast cancer. God knows, though. I feel like I have a purpose with her, you know what I'm saying?"

I mumbled, "Yeah, sure."

I decided to leave Mama alone about her friendship with Kaylyn. I knew it would fizzle out eventually, and it did seem to take her mind off of her situation. I changed the subject. "So, Mama, I figured I would have Christmas dinner catered. Don't even think about cooking."

"Now you know I'd have to have one foot in the grave not to cook Christmas dinner."

"But, Mama—"

"But, Mama, nothing. I've already done quite a bit today to prepare for it. You just swing by tomorrow if you can, and lend me a hand."

"Of course, I'll help, but you don't need to overdo it this year. It's just me, you, and Aunt Gert, right?" I hesitated. "I mean, is Dad home now and will he be around for dinner?"

"He's back. If your daddy is around, then he's welcome to join, but as always, Aunt Gertie is coming."

Aunt Gertie, Mama's mother's sister, somewhere near ninety, was the spriest woman I knew, young or old. She lived in a residential home, busying herself taking care of other ailing elderly people, most much younger than herself. Before she got sick, Mama visited Aunt Gertie several times a week. Lately, I had been forced to visit but only went when I felt like I could handle her Bible quizzes. For as long as I could remember, I had to recite the books of the Bible before we could start any visit. When I was about twenty and feeling like I knew a lot, I had come home from college to visit. I walked in her room to find her spraying a bottle of bleach spray, wiping the bathroom down.

"Aunt Gert?"

She glanced up, frowning, "Hi, baby." She then whispered, "It smells like pee in here all the time, you know?"

I giggled until she said roughly, "Okay, baby, go ahead."

"Auntie Gertie, please, I know the books of the Bible and I'm too old to be doing this now." I then asked her how she had been feeling.

"Say them." She grinned through pursed lips.

"I'm too old to be—"

"Say them, Desiree!" she interrupted, slamming her spray bottle down.

I opened my mouth to give her a piece of my mind but stopped short, realizing that I would never win this battle. I regretted coming but couldn't back out like I wanted. Instead, in very controlled tone, I spat out the books of the Bible. Instantly, the heavens opened up, and Aunt Gertie tossed her cleaning rag to the side to embrace and kiss me on the cheek. "Auntie Gertie has missed her baby, Desi!"

Aunt Gertie's Bible drills annoyed me, but I had to admit that her love of the Word of God fascinated me. Her ability to apply the Word to any and every life situation amazed me. The only thing was, I didn't feel like Aunt Gertie this Christmas. With Mama's illness, I couldn't handle her drama. However, just like I knew that there was no getting Mama out of cooking dinner, there was no way of avoiding good old Aunt Gertie. I knew that I'd have to pick her up for dinner and dreaded it. "Anyway, Mama, how are things with you and Dad?"

"Well, I think they're as good as can be expected."

"What does that mean?"

"He's here, but it'll take a mighty long time for things to get back to the way they were."

"You have told him about the . . . I mean, that you're sick, haven't you?"

"That's something that I'm not ready to discuss with him yet, Desiree."

"Please tell him, Mama. I'm sure he knows the very best doctors. He can help you. Besides, maybe there's a better oncologist than the one you have."

"Let's just try to have a decent Christmas, and I'll tell him after my next treatment."

"That's not fair, Mama! It's been too long. Please tell him."

"I'll not have him sticking around because I'm sick. I'm going to do it in my time. And fair? We don't need to talk about what's fair."

Mama yawned, and I let her go, wanting her to rest.

Only I didn't go to sleep. I reached for my computer and logged on to the dating site. If things with Phillip didn't work out, I needed a backup.

CHAPTER 22

ISABELLA

If we suffer, we shall also reign with him.
—2 Timothy 2:11a

The smell of burnt toast and the smoke detector going off woke me up. I knew this to be a part of Langley's lame attempt at reconciliation. If it were only as easy as him fixing me breakfast. Over the years, I always jumped to Langley's every beck and call. Guessed I'd always felt like I needed to earn my keep, especially after I stopped working as his office manager.

The thing was, any job I could've gotten years ago would've been menial work to him and just embarrassed him. Years ago my friend Angela had started her own business cleaning homes, and I was mighty excited for her. When she asked if I'd like to help, I jumped at the chance. Once Langley found out, he flipped out. "No wife of mine will be cleaning other people's homes. Do you have any idea how that would make me look?"

I heard a light tapping at the door, but I didn't move. I felt tired of jumping, trying to earn my keep, hold his attention, and make a real godly marriage all by myself. The door creaked, and in he walked with a tray of food and even fresh flowers. I pretended to be asleep, hoping he'd just leave the tray and go.

"Isabella?" he whispered. "Isabella, wake up. I've brought you something to eat."

I opened my eyes but without my glasses, he looked foggy and actually a whole lot better that way. "Oh, you didn't need to bother with that. Thank you."

Langley sat uneasily on the bed. "I was getting a little concerned. Never known you to sleep past eight. It's ten."

My medications either seemed to give me insomnia or make me sleep like a brick. "Yes, guess you got that right. I can't believe that I've slept so late. I'm tired."

I was sure he heard the word "tired" in more than one way. He looked concerned. "Well, now, you just go right ahead and enjoy your breakfast, Isabella."

I started to sit up, but I remembered. Alarmed that my hair might have shed more, I stayed glued to the bed. Even with it pinned up, I didn't know what to expect. Langley watched, waiting for me to eat.

"I do appreciate the breakfast, but can you put the tray over on the dresser? I need to freshen up a bit first."

Clearly disappointed, he set the tray on the dresser. I saw that he wore his golf attire, a crisp Polo shirt and heavily starched khakis.

"Going golfing today?"

"Ummm, well, I thought I'd go to practice at an indoor range if you wanted to rest. Or I could stay?"

Lord, if I ever wanted him to go, it was then. All the Saturdays I had practically begged him to take me to an antique mall or a little weekend getaway, and now I wanted him to leave. The sight of him nearly made me sick, yet what would I do without him?

Instead, he sat back down on the bed. "I was hoping to continue our conversation."

"About?"

"About our marriage, of course." A thick cloud of dense tension hung in the atmosphere, suspended until he broke the silence. "Like I told you before, I do want our marriage to work, and I am sorry if I've made you feel that I didn't want it."

Was he kidding? What kind of backhanded apology was he offering up? Still, I couldn't get into this with him. I was still lying flat on my back, fearful about my hair loss. As usual, me and my husband were on two separate pages. I was trying to save my life and he was halfheartedly trying to salvage scraps of our broken marriage. "I can't really talk now, Langley. I need to use the restroom, but after I shower and dress, we can talk."

He looked surprised that I waited until he left to get up. I thanked him again for the breakfast but couldn't avoid the churning in my stomach. Nausea had become an unwelcome visitor at the worst times. When he closed the door, I said a quick prayer and sat up slowly. I took a deep breath and looked back at my pillowcase. More hair, but not as much since I had pinned it tightly to my head, a futile attempt to hold on to every strand for as long as possible.

After I showered, I looked at my hair and knew that I'd have to comb it and pin it up carefully as I had been doing. The thing was, when I began to carefully pull the bobby pins out, clumps of hair fell into the bathroom sink. By the time I had taken all of the pins out, I no longer recognized my reflection. A dying woman stared back at me. This was all too fast, too unbelievable for me to grasp hold of. Hot tears slid down my face. Before I could collect myself, I felt a presence. I gasped.

Langley stood speechless.

I covered my mouth with my hands and sobbed. There were just no words between us. Stunned, he held his mouth open. Then, he held both of my arms, facing me. "Isabella, what is going on? What's wrong with you?"

I shook my head violently, totally unprepared for this confrontation. This would change things. I knew it would.

"Is it stress from our problems causing you to lose your hair? What is it? Please tell me so I can help!"

I didn't say anything, and he stared at the clumps of hair on the sink and held me tight. I cried, melting in his strong hold. I felt him shaking so hard that it scared me more. It really was that bad. Langley seemed to sense that it was more serious than stress. After all, the man knew things I didn't know.

When I calmed down, I explained my inflammatory breast cancer diagnosis and treatment plan. Langley looked as torn up as I felt. He tried to recoup from the shock, but his hands still trembled.

After about an hour or so, he threw down his husband hat and put on Dr. Morrison's, one that I knew he felt much more comfortable wearing. He said he would take me to the University of Texas MD Anderson Cancer Center, known to be the best hospital for cancer care in the country. His good friend specialized in the field. "In these types of matters, it's wise to seek the best, and Dr. Christopher Weiss is *the* best."

I listened and nodded, knowing that this time I wanted to listen to the Lord and my own heart about my health care. For too long, I had allowed Langley to control every nook and cranny of my life. This was my decision and I needed some things to stay the same. I liked and trusted my oncologist. Besides, Langley's guilty conscience wore like a banner across his face every time he looked at me, something I had wanted to avoid and the main reason I didn't want him to know about my diagnosis right now. I didn't want or need his sympathy.

"I don't know a great deal about inflammatory breast cancer, but I do know that it's one of the most aggressive forms of breast cancer. It's very rare," he said.

I nodded. "Only one to three percent of all breast cancers are IBC."

Langley bit his bottom lip and shook his head, clearly deep in thought. "I just can't believe this. I'm sorry, Isabella. I would've been there for you. Why didn't you tell me?"

"Why? You can't be serious. I don't want you to be here for me because you pity me. I reckon things will be fine. The Lord hasn't forsaken me. Even through this, He's sovereign. He's a healer and deliverer."

"Do you understand how serious this is? I mean, it's very serious." Langley appeared to draw back, looking smaller than he ever had.

I massaged my temples, wondering if he understood that in spite of the fact that I didn't tout degrees, I didn't come in on a load of turnip trucks. "Langley, there is almost no part of my body that is untouched by cancer or the medications to combat the cancer. As I am speaking to you, my mouth has sores as a result of the treatment, so yes, I do realize the seriousness of the diagnosis."

He hadn't heard anything I said and continued, "You see, what happens is that the cancer cells block the lymphatic vessels in the breast. The blockage in the lymphatic flow leads to the inflammation—"

I cut him off. "I'm perfectly aware of what I got. While you were off gallivanting around with your girlfriend, I've had to deal with doctor visits, getting poked and prodded every which way, taking chemo and throwing up buckets of vomit."

He had finally heard me.

With his shoulders hunched, Langley crumpled in the chair. "I'm sorry, I only meant—"

I interrupted again but this time I spoke softly. "I've been diagnosed with Stage IIIB, which isn't good but it could've been worse. The oncologist says it's in the dermal lymphatic system, and thank the good Lord, the cancer hasn't spread to other organs. Anyway, I'll get chemo for the next three to six months, depending on how it goes. After that, I'm going to have a double mastectomy and then more chemo and radiation. After that, maybe Tamoxifen, a hormonal therapy."

"Well, how are your side effects?" I raised my eyebrows, and he said, "Well, of course there's the hair loss, but what else are you experiencing besides the mouth sores?"

"Doctor says I'm handling it well so far, but it sure doesn't feel like it. I'm nauseous a lot but the medicine helps with that some. Lately, I've been having some stinging and weird feelings in my hands and feet."

"Hmmm. Sounds like neuropathy."

"I'm tired a lot, so I'm gonna lie back down. I've just got to rest."

"Of course, Isabella, but one more question for now."

"Yes?" I asked, returning toward the bed.

"Does Desiree know?"

"Yes, of course. I couldn't have made it without her. She's been my help through all of it. She's been real strong, but you never know with her. She hides so much, and I haven't a clue why."

Langley's face turned ashen, and he shot up, turning the bed down, insisting that I rest before cooking. He sat down next to me and gently touched the side of my face. "I want you to know that you're not alone. I'm going to be right here with you."

I stared into his eyes, looking for the truth, desperately wanting, needing to believe him, and just when I teetered on the edge of trusting my husband, he turned his eyes away from me. Langley didn't love me the way a husband was supposed to love his wife, but what could I do at this point? As a sick woman with a husband who agreed to stay, I should have felt blessed.

He tucked me in, but before I drifted off to sleep, I heard his car start and back out of the driveway.

CHAPTER 23

DESIREE

*For nothing is secret, that shall not be made manifest;
neither any thing hid, that shall not be known
and come abroad.*

—Luke 8:17

"Merry Christmas, Mama!" I knew that Mama looked forward to my tradition of calling first thing on Christmas morning.

"Merry Christmas back to you, baby! Your dad is right here. Would you like to speak to him?"

I heard an excitement in Mama's voice that had been rare since her diagnosis, and I didn't want to dampen her spirits. I hesitated, but still couldn't do it. "No, I'll tell him when I get there. So, I guess that means that he's staying for dinner?"

"Why yes, he is, honey."

Talking to and seeing Dad ranked last on my to-do list. After all the years that I had held his secret like a ball and chain, he unloaded on Mama at the worst possible time of her life. I had no words for him. "Mama, I wanted to see if you were up to having a guest. It's no problem if not. I know you're not feeling the greatest, it's just that he—"

"He?" Mama's voice hit a high note.

"Yes, Mama." I smiled. I knew that if I had a guest it would take some of the pressure off of all of us for dinner.

"*He* can come on. The more the merrier!" I could hear Mama's smile over the phone. "Details, baby."

"He's just a friend, so don't press him, please, Mama!"

"What's his name and what does he do? Where'd you meet him? Do I know his people?"

"Oh, Mama, you're making me nervous. He's just a friend now. His name is Phillip Madison. You don't know his people because he transferred here not too long ago from DC."

"DC?" Mama's voice dropped. "A city slicker, huh? Be careful, baby."

I ignored the disappointment in Mama's voice. Always a strong advocate for Southern men, she turned her nose up at anyone from elsewhere. I didn't see a difference when it came right down to it. Men were men.

"Phillip is an aerospace engineer and works at Redstone Arsenal. He sounds like he comes from a good family."

"Well, I guess we'll see. Main thing is that he's saved." She was quiet for a second. "He is saved, isn't he, Desiree?"

I didn't want to tell her that we hadn't quite gotten to that conversation yet. I'd have to withstand an hour lecture on how I should find that out before his first name. Instead, I lied: "Of course, Mama. I wouldn't date anyone who wasn't."

Mama seemed pleased, and I got the green light to have Phillip over for Christmas dinner. "Don't worry. I'll pick Aunt Gertie up for dinner. How's the dinner coming?"

"Well, we did just about everything last night. Thank you so much for staying so late. This was the easiest Christmas dinner I've ever had. The turkey and macaroni and cheese are done, just heating up the ham. I'll wait to stick in the homemade bread. You just don't forget to bring those sweet potato pies out of your fridge."

"Yes, ma'am, but you know me better than that; no way I'd forget those."

"Desiree, you be sure to wear your hair down. Men like long hair. I can't stand when you put it in that ponytail thing. You better enjoy that hair."

"I'll wear it down, just for you, Mama." Usually her advice on how to wear my hair annoyed me, but now I wanted to appease her. Seeing Mama's hair loss broke my heart, especially because it was our most similar trait. "Have you found a wig you like?"

"I did, but it's so uncomfortable that I'm just gonna wear a head wrap. I don't want Aunt Gertie getting all worked up. I have no intention of telling her anything, so do us all a favor and continue on the path of not telling her a thing."

"Oh, Mama, I know how you feel about that. You don't want to tell anybody anything. It's okay to need and want help sometimes. Aunt Gertie is a praying woman, and she should know."

"Just let me do things in my own time, Desiree."

"If you don't stop saying that . . . So, does that mean Dad still doesn't know about you being sick?"

Mama paused for a second. "Honey, he knows. I didn't want him to know just yet, but he does."

Both shocked and relieved, I asked, "Your hair, right?" Without waiting for her to answer, I asked, "What did he say?"

"You know your dad, always trying to fix stuff. He's upset. I can tell, but you know he's strong. He's all right. I don't wanna talk nothing more about cancer today. Today is Christmas. I'm so happy that God sent his only Son for us. Jesus and joy is all I got time for today. Now you just get yourself, Aunt Gertie, and Phillip on over here by two, you hear?"

"I want to know how you're feeling today though, Mama."

"Baby, I'm fine. You just make yourself pretty for Phillip."

I called Phillip to invite him, and I was surprised by his eagerness to attend. Since he'd decided to stay in Huntsville for Christmas, he didn't have family in town. He agreed to pick me up and seemed happy to pick up Aunt Gertie, too.

The doorbell rang promptly at one o'clock. When I opened the door, the light scent of Phillip's woodsy cologne along with his kind smile caused an unfamiliar giddiness in me. He wanted to meet my family, called me regularly, had a good job, and no baby mama drama.

"Whew! Girrrl, you have the potential to drop a brotha to his knees! That red is killing me softly, and I didn't know you had all that hair." He stepped in and caressed a curl between his fingers. "Oh, that is your hair, isn't it?"

"I didn't buy it, if that's what you mean."

"I'm glad it's real, but it doesn't matter. You look stunning. What a Christmas treat you are."

"You need to stop." I smiled coyly on the outside, but on the inside, my stomach did somersaults and back flips. "Let me grab my coat, and Lord knows if I forget to bring the sweet potato pies, Mama will have my hide."

"Sweet potato pies?" Phillip asked.

"Yep, Mama didn't have room in her refrigerator."

"So she made them, huh?"

"I helped a little."

"Women these days don't know how to cook. It's a shame," he said playfully.

"What's a shame is that you East Coast brothers are supposed to be so enlightened and you're saying the same things the Southern guys say. I'll have you know that I do cook, as if you couldn't tell from looking at me."

Phillip eyed me up and down. "Mmmmmm. Yes, ma'am, you got it all in the right places."

I raised my eyebrows and put my hands on my hips.

"Don't start things you don't want to finish." His eyes landed on my curves. He snapped himself out of it and asked, "So, should I be nervous to meet your parents?" When I didn't respond immediately, he closed his eyes. "Oh, no, what am I in for?"

Phillip helped me put on my coat. "No, really, they're good people. They'll like you."

"Somehow, I'm not convinced."

"Like I mentioned on the phone, we have to go on South Parkway to pick up my Aunt Gertie. She's the one you need to worry about."

"I see. You mean she's not a sweet little old lady?"

"You have no idea, Phillip."

"No problem. I think I can handle Aunt Gert," he said as he helped me with the pies and headed out the door.

The conversation flowed so effortlessly that I felt like I had known Phillip all of my life; that is, until we picked Aunt Gertie up from the residential home. As soon as we pulled up in front of the home, I spotted Aunt Gertie leaned against the glass door in the lobby. I couldn't believe that her gray hair stood at attention as if she'd put her finger in a light circuit. Her Don King–like afro had grown since I'd seen her last and it needed serious shaping up.

Phillip started to get out of the car to help, and I instructed him that under no conditions could he get out of the car. Aunt Gertie would be offended. Phillip laughed me off, exiting to assist her. I told him to wait at the car. I got out to hug her and figured I'd help her on the sly; after all, she was past ninety, couldn't see well, and had to use a cane. She shooed me and flung her skinny arms frantically, motioning for me to get back in the car.

As we walked to the car, I said, "We're going to have to go to the beauty school next week and get your hair shaped."

She shot me a deadly gaze. "You don't know the latest, do you? This here is natural. Everybody's doing it these days. Look it up. It's in all the pictures."

I had called her to tell her that I had a male friend coming along so she wouldn't be surprised. Still, she peered over her cobalt blue glasses, eyeing Phillip suspiciously.

Phillip, who hadn't listened to my warnings, attempted to open her door, but Aunt Gertie beat him to it. She rushed in the car and slammed her door with the strength of a twenty-year-old. Before I could introduce her properly, she started in. "Young man, do I look like a feeble old woman incapable of takin' care of herself? You need to mind your business." Aunt Gertie didn't take kindly to people treating her like an old lady.

Phillip chuckled with a hint of a condescending tone. "Why of course not! I just wanted to treat a beautiful woman like you with your due respect. Chivalry is not dead with me, ma'am."

Aunt Gertie pursed her lips. "Hmmph! Desiree, did he say I look dead?"

"No, ma'am. Aunt Gertie, this is my friend Phillip."

"Okay, so now is your name from Philip in the Bible?"

I cringed, knowing that Phillip was in for it. I had only been out with him once, and I was beginning to think that maybe this meet the family day wasn't such a good idea after all. I mean, I really liked the guy.

Phillip said, "Nice to meet you. Actually, Phillip is a family name. I'm Phillip the third."

"So, it ain't got nothin' to do with the Bible? What you know about Philip in the Bible?"

"To be honest, not much."

Aunt Gertie's haughtiness came through unmistakably. "Philip was one of Jesus' disciples. Seem like you ought to know at least that. He was one of the first traveling evangelists to spread the gospel. He helped with the food distribution. You mean you never heard none of that? You saved?"

"Auntie Gertie!" I pleaded, looking back at her.

Oblivious to my frantic look for her to ease off, she kept on about Phillip. Her blue plastic frames looked cracked on the side and she had clearly used duct tape to hold them together, so I used that to try to slow her down.

"Looks like you need some work done on your frames. You should've called me so I could take you to Sears Optical. It's about time for your appointment anyway."

"I didn't forget," she said, ignoring my suggestion.

"Forget what? Your appointment?" I asked.

"You need to go ahead and recite the books of the Bible," she said, ignoring my comment.

Fortunately, I had remembered to tell him about my aunt's ritual, so he seemed delighted by my singsong list of the books of the Bible.

"Quite impressive!" Phillip chimed.

"Did you remember Habakkuk?" my aunt asked.

"Yes, ma'am."

"I don't think you said Habakkuk."

"Yes, Auntie, I said Habakkuk." I tried hard not to let the irritation overtake me; we hadn't even made it to my parents'. Phillip, on the other hand, was amused.

"I never heard of that book of the Bible," he said lightheartedly.

Oh, Lord Jesus, rapture me up from this car, was all I could think.

She shot Phillip a dirty look. "Habakkuk is a very important book of the Bible and you don't know it even exists? Your parents didn't bother to take you to Sunday

School, huh? Shame how parents are too lazy to teach children simple lessons in the Bible. You see, Habakkuk didn't understand why God seemed to let the wicked go unpunished, and I sho' do understand his dilemma." She shook her head so much that her afro swayed with her words. "We just got to know that God will answer all of our questions. The Lord told Habakkuk to 'Write the vision and make it plain upon tables, that he may run and readeth it. For the vision is yet for an appointed time, but at the end it shall speak, and not lie.'" Auntie took what I call a hallelujah break. After a litany of hallelujahs and thank you Jesuses, she went on. "Though it tarry, wait for it," she said emphasizing "wait." "Because it will surely come, it will not tarry."

Auntie had made herself happy right in the car and began speaking in tongues. The amusement slowly left Phillip's face, and he looked a little scared. I reached over and touched his arm. "It's okay. She's just got a touch from the Holy Spirit."

He whispered and smiled. "Remind me not to let that Holy Ghost touch me," he joked.

"What did he say, Desiree? That's the devil or one of his imps. That's not one of Jesus' disciples talkin' 'bout he don't want the Holy Ghost. Oooh weee, this is bad! Watch out, Desiree. You don't see like I do."

I didn't stoke the fire and say anything but, "Faster," to get Phillip to step on the gas. By the time we pulled up into the driveway, I felt both exhausted and relieved. Mama would calm Aunt Gertie down for sure. As we walked to the door, Aunt Gertie asked, "Did you remember Philemon, Desiree? I don't think you said Philemon."

"Oh, look Auntie! There's Mama!" I said as Mama opened the front door waving.

"What's that thing your mama got on her head?" Aunt Gertie asked. This time, I deciding ignoring her would be best. Mama knew how to deal with her.

As we walked up to the front door, Phillip said, "Desiree, your parents have a beautiful home."

Aunt Gertie picked the strangest times to hear perfectly. She was several feet in front of us and I couldn't even believe she had heard him. "That's what the favor of God will do in your life. You could have some nice stuff too, but you can't join in, you gotta be born in. If you get saved and Holy Ghost filled you can be blessed too. That's the truth."

Thankfully, Mama and Dad greeted us. Dad conveniently avoided eye contact with me, but he did muster up a peck on my cheek. His warmth toward Phillip eased my nerves because Dad usually made sure to be extra stern with any male I got up the nerve to bring around them. As for Mama, she smiled from ear to ear, especially when Phillip handed her the poinsettia with a big red bow. It didn't hurt that Phillip said as soon as we walked in, "Mrs. Morrison, the food smells delightful and I hate to say it, but it smells better than my mother's and Mom's a great cook. I can tell this is going to be wonderful." Mama liked him instantly, especially since I'd told her that he was an engineer. It didn't hurt that he looked and spoke just the way Mama liked.

Dad led Phillip to the family room for hors d'oeuvres, and I overheard them chuckling about the car ride with Aunt Gertie.

Mama helped Aunt Gertie put her overnight bag in the guest room and strongly encouraged her to take a little nap before dinner. There was no way anyone but Mama could get her to do that. I heard Aunt Gertie in the distance, "Take that silly thing off of your head, Bella. You got company over."

While I busied myself by slicing tomatoes and cucumbers, Mama sauntered back into the kitchen, wearing an apron over her stunning emerald green dress with her hands planted firmly on her hips. "Now, I don't know what foolishness happened in that car on the way over here, but it has got Aunt Gert all riled up. She thinks your friend is a pure . . ." She paused and then whispered, "Heathen."

I opened my mouth to explain, but Mama put her hand up in a halt motion. "Don't even explain. Baby, I'm beginning to think she needs to be put on some kinda medication. She's getting a tad worse every time I see her. I wanna say she got some kinda dementia or something, but that'd be the strangest form I'd ever seen. Woman acts like she don't have a lick of sense about anything but scriptures. She even tried to fight me about takin' a nap, but I imagine she'll be all right after she gets a little rest."

"Mama, she embarrassed me so bad!"

"You can't let that ruffle your feathers. Aunt Gertie used to prophesy like nobody's business. God's given her a gift now. When everyone was telling me to marry Langley, she was the one telling me not to do it. She's a good, saved woman, but just a little off because of her age. Shoot, I pray the Lord lets me get there. She's blessed." Mama's thoughts seemed to wander off for a second. "Don't be fooled now, daughter. Ain't no need in be embarrassed. Everybody got at least one somebody in the family that got some serious issues, including your Phillip." Mama pulled the candied yams out of the oven, admiring her masterpiece.

"They smell divine. When did you make candied yams?" I asked, wondering how Mama could be so sick and do so much.

"Don't you worry about that. Who heard of Christmas dinner without candied yams?"

"Mama, you shouldn't have, but I'm glad you did. Look at those marshmallows, pecans, pineapple, and raisins; there ought to be a law against it."

Mama loved people loving her food, and I'd always been front and center for almost anything she cooked. She always concerned herself with making the food look as good as it tasted. "Presentation is important," was one of her mottos.

"I just hope your friend likes everything."

"He will, Mama."

"Soooo?"

"Soooo what?" I asked.

"You really like this fella?"

"Ma, I don't know, we really just started dating."

"You just make sure to always look your best and make him chase you, Desiree. You do look so pretty, but I was hoping you'd wear that fuchsia. It's so feminine."

I couldn't stand how Mama could make me feel like a teenager at my age. She meant well, but I never felt good enough. There was always something not quite right about me. If I got an A- in school, she wanted to know why it couldn't have been an A. If I lost ten pounds, she wanted to know why it couldn't have been fifteen. Instead of responding like I normally did, I decided to ignore it.

"You didn't say anything about this old thing I got on my head."

I had noticed it but didn't know how to bring it up. "Oh, you look very pretty. I like it. When did you get that head wrap? It matches your dress perfectly."

"Honey, Kaylyn dropped off a whole hatbox full of the headscarves last night. She says she has way too many."

It seemed like Kaylyn and her Uncle Beau had invaded Mama's life like the plague. She spoke of them every day.

Mama and I brought the final dishes to complete the table setting. "Just beautiful, Mama, but aren't there too many place settings?"

Before she could answer, the doorbell rang. "Oh good, that must be our dinner guests, Kaylyn and Beau."

I stood there dumbfounded, wondering why Mama hadn't mentioned them coming before now.

"Girl, please get that silly look off your face. Kaylyn called me last night, and she's been having such a time with that chemo. Since they didn't have plans, I told them to come on over here. She's such a sweet thing. Guess we both got company for this Christmas." Mama looked more excited than I'd seen her in a long time as she rushed to the door.

My idea of a cozy Christmas morphed into a looming nightmare. I didn't want to spend Christmas with Kaylyn or her uncle. Something didn't feel right about either one of them. Before I went out to meet our guests, I sank my teeth into one of Mama's hot, buttery homemade rolls, took a deep breath, and put my game face on.

CHAPTER 24

ISABELLA

It is the glory of God to conceal a thing: but the honour of kings is to search out a matter.
—Proverbs 25:2

"Langley, do you mind blessing the food for us?" I asked as we all held hands around the Christmas dinner table.

If looks could kill, I'd have been dead as a doorknob with that look Langley shot my way. I knew that he didn't like to pray out loud, especially in front of guests, but I didn't care. He needed to make changes to repair the damage he'd done and working on his relationship with the Lord had to be the first thing. Langley cleared his throat and stammered as if I'd asked him to preach a sermon.

"Gracious, Heavenly Father, who art in heaven who hath gathered us here today . . ."

I opened my eyes, squinting to see if he was really serious. Beau's eyes were open too, looking at Langley in amazement. I couldn't believe he was trying to impress everyone.

"You hath bestowed so many miraculous blessings upon us and the food we have before us is one of them. Thou art kind, merciful, and we give you thanks for this day in fellowship that we have come together to celebrate. Amen."

"Sweet Jesus, forgive him. He doesn't know what he's doing. Amen," Aunt Gertie said, unapologetically.

I didn't know if it was my imagination, but I thought I heard a collective sigh of relief that we had made it through the blessing. Langley's prayers never really sounded or felt like sincere ones. He used any opportunity where he might have to pray to display how lofty his speech could be. His God seemed to be a little farther away and distant for my taste.

After everyone fixed their plates, I couldn't help noticing that Desiree and Phillip seemed to be in their own world chatting between themselves.

"Why, Ms. Isabella, this is the juiciest ham and best dressin' I done had in years," Beau said while chewing.

I blushed, but Langley winced. He hated when people talked with food in their mouths. It didn't take a rocket scientist to know that Beau rubbed Langley the wrong way. Beau, on the other hand, seemed totally oblivious to it, and kept trying to engage him in conversation.

"I don't believe I've ever had dinner with a doctor. Guess if you don't count that time I was in the hospital with kidney stones, and the doctor walked in."

I smiled. Langley's smug glare followed Beau's light and relaxed laugh.

"Kaylyn, you're eatin' like a little bird. You feelin' okay, honey?" I asked.

"I'm fine, just don't wanna overdo it. Everything is fantastic," Kaylyn said, looking thin and frail.

When Aunt Gertie got bored with giving Phillip the evil eye, she turned her attention to Kaylyn.

"You can't overdo eating, honey. Get you some potatoes and gravy," Aunt Gertie instructed Kaylyn.

Kaylyn ignored her command, and I tried to divert Aunt Gert's attention. "Aunt Gert, you ready for some more mashed potatoes?" I asked.

"Nope, no more. You usin' milk in those. I'm lactose intolerant, you know that. Give me gas."

Beau chuckled, and Langley looked disgusted.

Aunt Gertie got Kaylyn's attention again. "Hey, there. Is that the style with them scarves you and Isabella got on your heads? Maybe I need to get me one. I just don't want to look like one of them foreigners."

Kaylyn's face reddened but she spoke. "Ma'am, I thought you said you were a Christian."

Aunt Gertrude stiffened. "What's that got to do with anything?

I got up quickly, deciding it was time for her to get back to the guest room to settle herself. When I touched her arm, she shrugged me off. "I ain't gettin' ready to take no more naps. What'chu think I am, some old lady or somethin'? The chile asked me somethin' and I intend on answerin'. Yesss, indeed I'm a Christian, but I don't wanna look like no foreigner. Too much to deal with bein' colored and havin' folks thinkin' you might blow somethin' up, too. So you see, missy, there ain't nothin' ungodly about that."

Kaylyn jumped at the opportunity to respond. "Seems like you're being judgmental and prejudiced. That's wrong, isn't it? Just because someone is foreign doesn't mean that they're going to blow something up, now does it, Ms. Gertie?"

"Ohhhweee! You young folk think you're so smart, but you don't know a lick of nothin'! The Bible says not to let your good be evil spoken of—"

I interrupted. I knew this could go on forever with Aunt Gert, so I eyed Kaylyn. She read my eyes and offered, "I'm sorry. I certainly didn't mean you any disrespect."

Aunt Gertrude looked mildly satisfied by Kaylyn's pseudo-apology but had to have the last word. "You a Christian?" she asked Kaylyn.

"Here we go," Desiree quipped from the other side of the table while Phillip's eyes widened.

Kaylyn tossed her greens around in her plate for a second and said, "I don't know."

Uncle Beau gulped down his whole glass of lemon water without saying a word.

Kaylyn continued, "I don't see any difference between people who claim to be Christians and those who don't. Really and truly, Christians are some of the most narrow-minded people I know."

Beau interjected, "Now, Kaylyn, this is not the time."

"Now, you and I agree on something," Langley said.

Kaylyn searched Aunt Gert's weathered face the same way she had done mine that day we had first met in the lobby. Aunt Gert put her wrinkled hand in the air, her mouth open wide enough to nearly engulf the table.

"Let me tell you somethin'. I didn't mean nothing about that headscarf thing. This is a real serious thing though you talkin' about. They ain't no real Christian if they blend in with the world. There oughta be a difference between clean and unclean. He's gonna come like a thief in the night and He's gonna separate the sheep from the goats, that's for sure."

"Aunt Gert, let's get you some dessert," I said, taking her nearly empty plate away.

"I don't want no dessert right now, Isabella." Aunt Gertie shook her head and muttered, "Askin' me about dessert at a time like this?"

"Okay, so He's separating us according to what?" Kaylyn asked, sincerely wanting to know.

"Oh, sweetheart," I said. "It's all about your faith in Him. The believers and unbelievers will be separated. Aunt Gert is right. It's a serious thing."

Aunt Gert rose up from her chair. "You know Jesus said, 'Every plant, which my Heavenly Father hath not planted, shall be rooted up.'" She looked directly into

Kaylyn's eyes. "You don't let the devil deceive you into thinkin' God ain't real. Daughter, Jesus is tellin' you straight from His Word, 'Come unto me, all ye that labour and are heavy laden, and I will give you rest. Take my yoke upon you, and learn of me; for I am meek and lowly in heart: and ye shall find rest unto your souls. For my yoke is easy, and my burden is light.'"

"Rest? That sounds nice. I'm pretty tired," Kaylyn whispered as her eyes filled with tears.

As crazy as Aunt Gert could act, the Word had pricked Kaylyn's heart.

"Yes, the rest that you need comes from Him. He's got the answers that you're looking for, so stop looking for people to do what only God can do." With that, Aunt Gertie shuffled out of the room mumbling, "Lord Jesus, you know what she needs. Help her, Lord. Time is short. Hear her prayer, Lord." She made her way out of the dining area and into the family room and she hollered out, "Somebody tell me what channel *Sanford and Son* is on."

Just then, we heard the doorbell ring. "I got it," Aunt Gertie called out. She shuffled back into the room. "Police here for you, Langley."

Stunned, we all fell silent, except Langley, who wiped his mouth and excused himself. I got up to follow him to the front door, and he stopped me. "It's fine. You stay here."

"I'm sure it's nothing," I said, trying to reassure everyone and myself. As Desiree, Kaylyn, and I cleared the table, Langley came back, trying to appear cheerful. "It was nothing to worry about. They're looking for someone, that's all."

"What you done now, Langley?" Aunt Gert shook her head.

Langley rolled his eyes. "Isabella, please take her to her room."

"Nobody need to take me to nowhere but to King Jesus. You the one that need to go somewhere and get saved."

"Come on, Aunt Gert, let's get you settled. I'll find *Sanford and Son* for you."

As I led her out, Aunt Gertie fussed in a loud whisper, "I told you that he ain't no good for you, Isabella, but don't nobody want to listen to me. Now, look. You got the police comin' to your house on Jesus' birthday."

By the time I came back out to join everyone in the living room, Langley had disappeared. I took Desiree aside. "Where's your father?"

"No idea, Mama. What were the police here for? Did he tell you?"

"He didn't." I sighed. "I'm gonna go see what's going on. You keep everyone entertained."

I found Langley in his office. "What are you doing?" I asked.

Startled, he stopped rummaging through the papers on his desk and massaged his temples. "Isabella, what are you doing in here? Please go back. Everything is fine."

"Not until you tell me what the police visit was all about."

"Oh, it wasn't the police. Aunt Gert just saw a uniform. It was a situation at the office. I'm going to have to see a patient."

I knew he was lying. "So, can you explain why you're acting so strangely? I know that it was the police." He began stuffing papers into his briefcase.

"For the last time, it wasn't the police! I don't know what you're making such a big deal about. I have a lot of things on my mind. Work has been stressful, and your illness . . . and everything else, but I'm fine." He shot a quick smile my way, trying to calm down. His erratic behavior made me afraid for him. He pecked me on the cheek, and told me he had to leave to take care of some business.

"On Christmas Day?" I asked, only he didn't hear me, or he acted like he didn't, and left out through the back door.

CHAPTER 25

DESIREE

Beloved, believe not every spirit, but try the spirits whether they are of God: because many false prophets are gone out into the world.

—I John 4:1

After we left, Phillip couldn't wait to start in on her. "Your Aunt Gert isn't playing around about her faith, is she? I've never experienced anybody like that. Your family cracks me up. That woman is a straight out of a Tyler Perry movie."

I smiled for a second and stopped. "Aunt Gertie is a devout Christian, and to tell you the truth, I've always respected that about her. She lives the life she preaches about, and I'll admit, she does go overboard sometimes, but her intentions are good." It was one thing for us to laugh at Aunt Gertie as a family, but it was a whole different ballgame when someone from the outside was laughing at her expense.

Phillip then added, "That dude Farmer Beau clearly has his sights set on your mom. I'm serious, man. You could write up a script on today and send it in, police visit and all."

"I'm glad you find us entertaining, but we're hardly a Tyler Perry movie. This was a very out of the ordinary Christmas, Phillip." I tried hard not to sound as offended as I was.

"What was up with your dad? The police didn't arrest him, did they?" he asked, still looking quite amused.

"Listen, everything is fine."

"Awww, don't be upset." He chuckled, shooting glances at me while driving.

I stared out the window, trying to control my temper.

"Lighten up, baby," he said as he put his hand on my thigh. "I'm just happy to have spent Christmas with you."

"Well, don't make fun of my family if you want to get anywhere with me."

"I'm just joking. Trust me, we all have our issues. It'd be worse if you spent time with my family. You'd be bored to tears."

When we pulled into my driveway, he pulled a box out of his coat pocket. "I know we haven't known each other long, but I really like you, Desiree. I saw this and thought of you."

"Awww, Phillip, that's so sweet of you. I feel bad. I didn't get you anything."

"Remember, I told you. I already have my gift, even if it is wrapped a little too tight."

"Very funny. I could get used to this," I said, opening the box. "Pink leather gloves? These are gorgeous! My favorite color! How sweet!"

"Wow! I wasn't expecting this type of reaction. I remembered you saying you liked pink and I want those hands of yours to stay just as warm as your heart."

"You are so full of it, Phillip, but thank you." I tried on my gloves and then asked, "Would you like to come in? We can watch a movie or something."

"Sure, I thought you'd never ask."

"Well, it's just an invitation for a movie and conversation, so don't get too excited." I didn't want to send him any mixed signals.

***

After the movie, I yawned, wanting him to know I needed some sleep. I had to be at Mama's first thing in the morning to take her to chemo.

Phillip massaged the back of my neck. "You tired, baby?"

"I am. Mmmmm, it feels good, but I think that's enough." I pulled away.

He pulled me back to him. "I just wish the evening didn't have to end so soon." He kissed me softly, and I smiled.

"Well, it's late, and I have a busy morning," I said, pulling away to stand up.

"I don't have to go, you know," he said, standing up, facing me.

"Oh, but you do," I said, smiling politely but with unmistakable firmness.

"You're a hard sista, Desiree." He pulled me to him. I hugged him back, but his tight embrace felt a little uncomfortable. I couldn't seem to wiggle out.

"Phillip." I tried to pull away again.

He nuzzled my ear. "I love how you say my name. Let's go to your room."

"No, we're not. I said no." I was annoyed that he could think about me like that. I wondered what kind of women he had grown accustomed to dating. I also wondered if he really thought a few dates, conversations, and a pair of pink leather gloves warranted me sleeping with him. He kept his arms around me with a pressure that scared me.

"Come on, Phillip. Let's not end the night on a bad note. Let me go."

He loosened his grip. "Well, you can't blame a brother for trying now, can you?"

Irritated, I got his coat and walked him to the door. He held him arms out for another hug.

I folded my arms across my chest. "Thanks again for the gloves."

"I don't get another kiss?"

I wondered if I had gotten a little too defensive too fast. My past molestation and Taye's assault had a way of rearing its ugly head a little too often. I thought about it and leaned forward to peck him on the cheek. He looked disappointed. "You might need to adjust your expectations, Phillip. I'm not going to be intimate with anyone before marriage. Been there, done that. I'm doing things the right way so if you—"

"Whoa, slow down." He put his hand up, smiling. "Good things come to those who wait, right?"

"That's not at all what I said."

"I heard you. You're a nice girl, Desiree. I understand." He pulled me to him again and returned the peck on my cheek. "I know the best is yet to come. I'll call you tomorrow," he said before leaving.

I didn't act like it, but a tingle swept through me. He was a gentleman, maybe in the rough, but still a gentleman after all.

When Mama and I arrived at the doctor's office for her chemotherapy treatment, I tried to fix my attitude to be cordial to Kaylyn and her uncle. Mama lit up when she saw them. Before we got to them, I whispered, "Mama, did you know they were gonna be here?"

"Oh yeah, baby. Remember, I told you we were scheduling as many appointments together as possible. It really makes things so much easier when you don't go through it alone."

"You're not alone, Mama," I said insulted.

"Oh, you know what I mean," she offered, shrugging off my hurt feelings.

"Don't you look pretty, dear," she said to Kaylyn, dressed in a fuzzy yellow sweater and tight jeans.

Beau sat up. "Hope you don't mind me sayin' so, Isabella, but you're lookin' real good yourself today." Mama glowed with her lavender turtleneck and matching headscarf, but I didn't like the way Beau complimented her.

"Oh, now, you hush," Mama said blushing, clearly amused.

Suddenly I didn't like Mama's reaction either. I didn't like that Dad wasn't there. There was a whole lot for me not to like lately.

Mama gushed over Kaylyn, feeling her warm forehead. I found it silly, considering Mama's own frail condition. "You look a little peaked, dear. Make sure you drink a lot of fluids and rest; nothin' like good rest."

"I'm fine, Ms. Isabella," Kaylyn said, gushing over Mama's concern.

After Kaylyn and I greeted one another, she tried to make conversation. "Ms. Isabella tells me you make real pretty jewelry. Maybe you could show me some?"

"Oh sure, I'd like that. Only thing is, I have to warn you, I've been called gaudy. I like chunky jewelry so that's my signature."

Kaylyn chuckled, eyeing my necklace. "Well, if you gotta be called something, gaudy isn't all that bad. I love your style. Those purple stones are beautiful."

I had forgotten which piece I'd worn and looked down. "Thanks. They call these healing crystals. Of course, I don't believe in that stuff. I'll bring some pieces the next time for you to look at."

Mama interjected, "You sure don't. God is the only healer. Anyway, Kaylyn, you know how we had talked on the phone about going wig shopping again? After that, let's meet at my house and, Desiree, maybe you can come over and we can have a little jewelry party. I'll get some of them petits fours and make some tea."

Mama's relationship with Kaylyn irritated me, but I couldn't pinpoint exactly why. I felt like a jealous child. Kaylyn's name had suddenly become a part of every conversation with Mama, and while at times I did appreciate the shift in her attention away from me, it was beginning to get old. Apparently, Mama hadn't remembered that I had asked her to go wig shopping.

"That's cool. Just let me know what time," I said.

Beau quipped, "I do hope I'm invited."

Beau's presence made my skin crawl. He reminded me of a leech or a tick, just lying in wait for Mama. He didn't fool me with his kind act.

"Uncle Beau, you aren't invited. Bad enough, I got to have you coming with me to all these appointments. Plus, it's a girl thing; you wouldn't understand." Kaylyn waved him off.

"Girl, your ol' uncle's just playing around with ya."

A nurse came out and called both of their names.

"Oh, well, good. Desiree, you don't wait around here, honey. I know you got stuff to do. I'll call your cell when I'm done."

Beau cut in, "Now I don't mind droppin' you off at all, Isabella. Ain't no use in Desiree hanging around when I'm gonna be here."

I stared at Beau in disbelief and gave him a phony smile. "No, thank you. I'll be back here, Mama. I want to take you home."

Beau and I sat, mostly in silence, until I left for the vending machine. After two and a half long hours, Mama finished her treatment first. After Mama assured Beau that Kaylyn would be done shortly, I left to take Mama home. I rode home, trying not to sulk about her newfound enthusiasm over Kaylyn and Beau. She talked about

Kaylyn like she was the daughter she'd always wanted. And Beau, he knew a woman starved for affection when he saw one. I tried to warn Mama.

"Mama, you do know that Beau is interested in you."

She waved me off. "Oh, he's interested in me all right. He's interested in me helping to get his niece saved. He's happy to have a mother figure for her since her mom passed away and all. Beau is harmless, honey."

"Harmless as a serpent," I quipped.

Mama laughed as we pulled into her driveway. "Really he's as wise as a serpent and harmless as a dove, now that's what the Word says. He's saved, you know. He knows I'm a married woman, and he respects that. Don't you worry about me. I see your dad is home, so he'll get me settled."

After refusing to allow me to walk her in, I got back in the car, headed for home.

I didn't know how Mama's situation could be much worse. A fractured marriage and terminal diagnosis at the same time is enough to make anyone fall apart. I marveled at her strength but wondered how long it would be before she would start to unravel. Even though I hated to think of meeting with Dad alone, I had to do it. He had moved back home, but still remained distracted and aloof.

Phillip kept me sane. His consistent calls and date nights filled most of my empty spaces. Still, I couldn't totally stop corresponding with men on the sites. Mama had advised me long ago not to ever put all my eggs in one basket.

To my surprise, when I pulled up at my house, I recognized Phillip's car parked in my driveway. I pulled up beside him and rolled the window down. "What in the world are you doing here?" I asked, smiling on the outside but frowning on the inside.

"Uhhh, decided I'd take a chance and stop by. Just got here and realized that you weren't here. I'm sure you need to get settled in. I'll stop by another time."

"I guess it's okay. I do wish that you would've called though. You can come in, but just for a little while. I have tons of things to catch up on."

He grinned from ear to ear. "Hoping you'd say that."

When we got in, I prepared him an iced tea. "So, I don't remember you saying that you had vacation time off for Christmas break," I said.

"I have today off, but it's back to the daily grind tomorrow."

I handed him his glass. "I see. Phillip, I'm glad to see you, but—"

"Oh, here we go," he said as though he'd been through this before.

"Excuse me?" I didn't like that he'd said that one bit.

He sat on the sofa, stretched out, a little too comfortable for my taste. "I know, I know, I won't stop by again without calling. Sometimes I just like the spontaneity of dropping by."

"I'm glad that you enjoy being spontaneous and all, but I don't care for unexpected visitors."

"Live a little, Desiree. Besides, I thought we were moving in a positive direction."

"Let me put it to you this way, if you come by again without calling, you won't get in my door."

He sighed. "I get the picture. Didn't mean to upset you."

An unnatural quietness fell over the room. I tried to shake the uneasiness by reminding myself that Phillip was a great catch. It wasn't every day I had an attractive engineer wanting to spend time with me. He seemed different though. Every now and then, he said things that were off and out of sync. I'd tried to ignore it, but coming over unannounced let me know that I really didn't know him.

Phillip patted the empty seat next to him, signaling for me to come closer to him. I didn't want to. He had thrown me off by coming over, but if he was really a good guy, I didn't want him to think I didn't like him. I inched closer, shooing the little voice inside my head away.

He put his arm around me and whispered in my ear. "You are beautiful, and your hair . . ." He sniffed. "It smells like sunshine."

I laughed. "You're trying really hard, Phillip. And, tell me, exactly what does sunshine smell like?"

"Fresh, warm, and wonderful." He laughed at himself and pulled me closer.

"I'm no poet, but you don't smell so bad yourself."

He kissed me, and I fell into it, a little too freely. Being desired felt good. After all, how many women named Desiree don't want to be desired?

While we kissed, I felt his hand run inside the back of my blouse, and I grabbed his hand. I tried to wiggle away, but he pulled me close to him without removing his hand. I fell into the kiss again until I felt him trying to undo my bra. I turned my head away from the kiss, jolted back to reality. "Come on, Phillip. Wait," I said softly but firmly. I had gone down this road before with a few of my ex-boyfriends and always regretted giving myself to a man before marriage. I had a lot of spiritual growing to do, but I resolved after the breakup with Taye that fornication wouldn't be something I'd have to repent for again.

Phillip, unfazed by my protests, kept groping, and I struggled to stop him. Just like the time at the door, he came on much too strong.

"I can't, Desiree. I want you so bad," he said in a raspy, low growl.

I grabbed his arms, only I couldn't move them. "Phillip, this can't go any further. I don't wanna lead you on."

"I can tell that you want me, Desiree. Stop teasing. Stop playing hard to get. That's what you've been doing, you know."

This time, I raised my voice. "I have not! Stop it!" I was sure that I didn't want anything with him ever. I'd fought Hunter and Taye. I wasn't afraid to fight Phillip.

He panted, his wild eyes blank. I didn't know this stranger in my house.

"You know you like to play hard to get, girl," he said again, now pressing his massive hands on my back.

My anger exchanged itself for fear. "You're hurting me, Phillip," I cried, slapping his meaty hands from their forceful grip.

"I am not," he hissed. "You know you want me." He pushed his body on top of mine, and we toppled off of the sofa onto the floor. All of my attempts to get free of him were useless. I could barely breathe or even move.

He smashed his lips on top of my mouth, muffling my cries, while he tugged forcefully, pulling my pants off.

I squeezed my eyes shut, and I was a teenager again, fighting off Hunter. I screamed and fought, but Dad didn't come to save me. Mama didn't come. No one heard. *This is it,* I thought. The thing I feared the most was the thing that would happen to me.

I prayed and opened my eyes, hoping to see something to use as a weapon as I had done before. Nothing was within reach. Confused and dazed, I had the out-of-body experience that people talk about who are near death. I never believed it. Until then.

I saw myself, a limp body under the weight of a monster. I didn't want to die, but knew that I couldn't live knowing I hadn't fought.

Yea, though I walk through the valley of the shadow of death, I will fear no evil. For thou art with me.

The Spirit of the Lord strengthened me, and when he tried to put his mouth on mine again, I bit his lip until blood ran down his chin.

He hollered profanities I'd never heard him use, and he drew back, slapping me with such force, I couldn't believe that I didn't black out. I knew he had won and stopped fighting.

When he finished, he kissed me on the cheek. "Why don't you go and take a shower?"

He posed it as a question but I knew it was an order. I trembled, stumbling my way to the bathroom.

When I got into the shower, I knew that I wasn't supposed to rinse the residue of him off of my body, but I felt used, dirty, and violated. I wanted all traces of him gone so I scrubbed until my body felt raw.

I stepped out of the shower and wrapped a towel around me. I shook so much that I could barely turn the doorknob to see if he was still there.

"Are you here?" I called out.

No answer, so I said his name again. I flung open my drawers and threw on clothes. I needed to find my cell phone, but my mind went blank. I couldn't remember where I put it. Long ago, I had let go of my landline.

I crept out to the living room. An eerie silence filled the house, sending a shiver up my spine. For the second time, I had been victimized in my own home. Was he still there? I knew he would probably kill me if he heard me call the police, but I had to either get my phone or get out of here.

Tears gathered at the corners of my eyes, clouding my vision, as I made my way into the living room. I searched the rest of the house for him. With him nowhere in sight, I ran to lock the door and checked the other door and windows. I peeked through the curtain. He and his car had vanished.

I spotted my purse on the kitchen stool and dumped out the contents until I found my phone. I sank onto the floor, sobbing, and started to dial 411. I hung up, hearing information.

I stopped. Was it 511? I tried to calm down and think. Then, I remembered. *911*. Before dialing, I thought about the fact that there were no visible signs of a struggle in the living room. Aside from the coffee table being pushed to the side, nothing was out of place. I did notice something that hadn't been there before. On a sheet of paper lying on the coffee table, he had left a note that read:

> *Desiree, I had such a nice time on our date. Let's do it again soon.*

I threw the note down, shaking, and nearly vomited. A gut-wrenching cry escaped from my lips. I knew the voice was mine, but it sounded primal, unlike me.

Gasping for air, I knew I had to call. I just had to catch my breath and think of what to say. Confident that the physical evidence was washed down the drain, I knew it would be my word against his. I thought about explaining how I'd met him on an Internet dating site. About how I had let him know where I lived. How I really didn't know a lot about him. About how I had invited him in. How I had kissed him and flirted with him. About how charges against him could affect Dad and his precious reputation. Dad would be humiliated to know that his daughter had been dating men on the Internet. And then there was Mama. How the stress of it could impact her health. She would be ashamed of my behavior too. I had never told her the truth about how Phillip and I had met. About how it would affect me personally and my career at the school. And about how it was all my fault.

I put my phone down. I saw the red marks across my face, arms, and legs. I knew that I had evidence that something terrible had happened, but I didn't know if telling would be worth everything else that I'd have to go through. I could just let it go. Or could I?

Just then, my doorbell rang. My breathing suspended for a moment. Had he come back? I shrank down and didn't move a muscle, hoping he would go away. I picked my cell back up, ready to dial for help.

Then I heard a female voice: "Desiree, I know you're in there. Open up or I'll be forced to use my key!"

I jumped up and opened the door, expecting to see Shay but saw both her and Geneva open-mouthed and wide-eyed by the large bruise on one side of my face and other smaller but equally swollen and reddened bruises across my arms and legs. They came in at once, and I fell into their shocked embraces.

CHAPTER 26

ISABELLA

*For God so loved the world, that he gave his only
begotten Son, that whosoever believeth in him should
not perish, but have everlasting life.*

—John 3:16

I couldn't make heads or tails of Langley's sudden burst
of attentiveness to my every beck and call. Instead of
spending a whole heap of time trying to figure things out
though, I used it to my advantage by asking him to attend
church with me. I hoped that our marriage would change
from the inside out since we had perfected the reverse.

He promised he would come but with a pained
expression he said, "Not this Sunday, Isabella. I have a
conference in Tampa, but I will promise to come the next
Sunday."

My heart sank, but just a little. Instead, I chose to
delight myself in knowing that Kaylyn and I planned a
shopping trip for church clothes. She planned to go to
church with me, and I wanted to buy her an outfit or two,
for inspiration.

When I answered the door, she appeared bright-eyed
and ready to shop. Beau grinned, waving from the car,
and I actually caught myself giggling. He had a way of
giving me attention, and I felt it on the inside, much like
I had with Ray.

"Ms. Isabella, my uncle actually tried to come along on our shopping trip!" She shook her head. "I mean, really, Uncle Beau is a trip."

I smiled and welcomed her in.

"He tried to get out of the car, telling me he wanted to walk me in. I made him stay in the car. I keep reminding him that you're a married woman."

I sighed. "Yes, I am, aren't I?"

Kaylyn eyed me, and we both smiled. "I'm just glad that today we don't need your Uncle Beau or Desiree to cart us around. I'm having a good day and feel the most like myself that I have in a good while now."

"Uncle Beau won't let me drive, whether I'm having a good day or not, so I'm glad for the break."

We left out for our shopping trip, but got tired a lot sooner than we expected. Kaylynn told me about her favorite Italian restaurant, a quaint place, with a cozy atmosphere, so we ate there. As we talked about our treatments, church, and life in general, the topic of men came up.

"I've never been one to fall in love easily," Kaylyn said.

I drank a sip of tea. "Oh, is that right? In all of your twenty-two years?"

"Actually, I am twenty-three, and I'll have you know that tons of women my age have been in love multiple times by now."

"I guess you may be right, but it's perfectly okay if you haven't."

Kaylyn bit a piece of pizza. "I don't think much of men. Generally speaking, they're mostly dull and shallow."

I chuckled.

"Really, and besides my Uncle Beau, I don't know one good one. They all cheat."

I frowned. "You don't really believe that, do you, Kaylyn?"

"Oh, I do. I would say that 99.9 percent of them can't be faithful to one woman in or out of marriage. That's why, even before the cancer, I wasn't with anyone. I really don't see much of a need for them. And by the way, I'm not a lesbian."

"I hadn't even thought of that," I said. "It does trouble me that you feel that way about men. I think there are more faithful men out there than you think. Unfortunately, I can't say that I don't understand why." My thoughts drifted to my unfaithful husband, father, and grandfather while Kaylyn talked.

"I think it's a shame that men are so unworthy of trust. You can't even trust preachers."

I raised my eyebrows. "I suppose some are unfaithful, but I'd like to think that that's rare."

"Oh, I know you don't believe that, Ms. Isabella. Think of all the televangelists and how many fall from grace. It's basically an epidemic."

"An epidemic? Oh, I don't think so, honey. Now we just have so much technology we find out about it. Maybe it's a little more common than I'd like to think, but, baby, try not to focus on the bad. When you do, you can always find it. At the end of the day, preachers are men too, in need of Jesus, just like me, you, and everyone else."

Kaylyn's lips tightened and she crossed her arms over her chest. "What's the point of preaching to others when you don't have yourself together enough to be faithful? Aren't they supposed to be held to a higher standard of accountability? It's crazy. That's one reason why I don't need to join a church. If Jesus is so powerful, He ought to be able to keep a preacher from fornication and adultery."

I said, "Well, He can and He does when one wants to be kept."

Kaylyn rolled her eyes and sucked her teeth.

I continued, "When a person sins, regardless of what the temptation is, they have the power through Christ to avoid it. The Word says that 'God is faithful, who will not suffer you to be tempted above that ye are able; but with the temptation He'll make a way of escape that you might—'"

"'He'll make a way of escape that you might be able to bear it,'" Kaylyn finished.

"Impressive," I said.

"Not so much. Uncle Beau loves reciting verses to me. I'm sure he doesn't think I listen, but I do. I also research and study things for myself. If this verse is true, why are so many men unfaithful?"

"I do wish I had all the answers, but I do know that when we allow our flesh to overtake us, sin takes dominion. We have to stay in the Word and be obedient to it. There are some good men out there. Don't give up."

Kaylyn's expression looked pained, but she didn't say anything.

Instead, I asked, "Did someone hurt you in the church?"

She looked down. "I don't want to talk about it."

"Okay, that's fine, but if someone did do that, let me tell you that I'm so terribly sorry about that. He was wrong."

Tears splashed onto her blouse. I wanted to go hug her, but she hung her head and began to speak. "I was thirteen and I had gone to a revival with my best friend Linda who had just gotten saved. She kept nagging me to go, and I only agreed because she was my friend. I didn't grow up in church, not really. The preacher's words touched me. I knew I needed to have the free gift he spoke of. I needed to be saved. I needed Jesus to save me. As soon as he made the altar call, I went up. I didn't even need Linda to come with me."

She took a sip of her drink and continued, "After I joined, the church van came every Sunday, picking me up and even came for Bible Study and choir rehearsal. Everything seemed perfect until I started having trouble at home. Mama and I were getting into it about everything. I didn't know what to do. Linda recommended that I meet with the pastor. I did, and at first, he was great, praying with me and really helping me. He gave me money to help pay my lunch and a few times he gave me enough money to buy a new dress for church. I felt really special but things began to change. He started touching me, but it seemed more like how a dad would touch his daughter. Before I knew it, I was being molested by the pastor."

"Oh, dear, I'm so very sorry that happened to you. Did you tell anyone?"

She wiped her nose. "I told Linda, and she got mad. She didn't believe me. My closest friend didn't believe me. I was so messed up about the whole thing, I told Mama. Do you know what my own mother said to me, Ms. Isabella?"

"What?"

"She called me a liar, and said she was tired of me always trying to get attention. And I needed to keep my little narrow behind home from now on."

I got up from the table and went to put my arms around her. No wonder the girl had so many issues with her faith. "It's going to be okay, honey. It really is. There's no God in what he did to you, and just know that he is accountable to God for what he's done to you. We are all accountable to God for the things that we do and say. That's why it's so important to forgive. Just like he's accountable to God for what he's done, you're accountable to him for how you handle it. You've got to let go of the anger."

She shook her head. "Ms. Isabella, I'll never forgive him for what he did to me, never."

I placed both hands on her tear-streaked face. "You have to forgive so you can be forgiven. Put all of your trust in Him, not people. We all fall short. That's why we need Jesus, but God, He never fails."

I sat back down while she dabbed at her eyes. "I'm probably just as hurt by Mama's reaction as what the pastor did to me. Do you know how it feels to be angry with your mother and she's dead?"

"Well, I wish that I didn't know, but, baby, I do know. I was mad at my own mama for her shortcomings for a long time, but it tore me up inside. I had to let it go, not just for her but for me and my own child. Believe me, I understand you feeling that way, but just don't let the hurt cause you to be bitter, especially toward God. He didn't orchestrate that mess. The devil did."

"Well, that's a lot easier said than done now, isn't it?" She folded her arms and looked away.

"Nobody said it was easy, but it is necessary for you to get all that the Lord has in store for you. You got a lot to deal with right now, and Lord knows that you don't need to have this issue holding you down. Have you ever thought about seeing a counselor or maybe even joining a support group?"

Kaylyn looked at me, uncrossing her arms. "I thought about it, but no. I guess I've just wanted to leave the past in the past. Since my diagnosis, I've done a lot of reading on rape though. I guess I've just wanted to try to deal with it. I have found a little bit of comfort knowing that I'm not alone. Did you know that a woman is raped every two minutes in the US? And by the age of eighteen, one in four girls and one in six boys will be victimized? I had no idea that most victims are assaulted by someone they know: a friend, an acquaintance, a relative, or even the neighbor next door."

"Those are terrible and shocking statistics, but I think you need to consider going to a professional to work through things. Even attending a support group could be a good start. You shouldn't have to work through it on your own any longer. Meeting others who have experienced the same things might be really eye opening. When we can lean and depend on one another, it can make things better. You know what I mean? Look at us. As terrible as breast cancer is, it brought us together."

A tiny smile broke through Kaylyn's otherwise distraught face. "Okay, so I guess you've made your point."

"In the meantime, just remember that each of us is accountable to God for the things we think, do, and say on this earth. Nobody can escape that. God will deal with each us in His own way. You just have to forgive though, baby. Things we can't do for ourselves, well, let's just say that God is the master at helping us do them. He's able to help you. He doesn't want you bound by the bad things others do to you. It's a trap. No matter how bad it is, we have to surrender all to Jesus. I'll be praying for you and with you. You just pray for the Lord to help you to forgive those who've hurt you. You haven't been able to do it on your own, but that's when God works best."

I could tell that Kaylyn considered all that I had said. I just had to make sure that I did the same.

When I walked into the church, Beau waved me down, grinning, in stark contrast to Kaylyn's stony countenance.

"I'm so sorry y'all had to wait on me. I hope you hadn't been here long."

Beau chuckled. "Aw, don't worry 'bout it at all, Ms. Isabella, we ain't been here long."

Kaylyn rolled her eyes. "I beg to differ, Uncle Beau. We've been here nearly thirty minutes!"

"Oh, my! Please accept my apology," I said regretfully, checking my watch.

Kaylyn explained, "No, wait. It wasn't because of you, Ms. Isabella. Why does Uncle Beau have to be everywhere so doggone early? Drives me totally crazy. I can't wait until he'll let me start driving myself around again. Be glad that you can do that for yourself, Ms. Isabella." Kaylyn's medications often made her nauseous, dizzy, and lightheaded, so her doctor recommended that she not drive. Truth be told, they'd given me the same instructions, only I knew when I could drive and when I couldn't. Besides, I didn't have someone like Beau to look after me.

Beau stood, cheerful and unfazed by Kaylyn's little rant. I couldn't help returning his smile. Kaylyn could be tough on folks, especially her uncle, but I knew he was her rock. Since her mother's passing, Beau had become like a parent.

"Have you two seen Desiree yet?" I asked.

They both shook their heads no. After we scanned the sanctuary and I didn't see her, we took our seats. As the service progressed, I tried not to let the cares of life weigh me down, but my family was in utter chaos. Now, Desiree appeared to be slacking off from Sunday service.

Beau tapped me. "Ms. Isabella, you all right now? You don't look so good."

I assured him that I felt just fine and noticed how much he seemed to be enjoying Pastor Kingston's sense of humor. He grinned and even chuckled aloud. He was always so happy. After Pastor Kingston told a lighthearted and amusing story, he began his message entitled, "It's Time to Clean Your House." As he related the cleanliness of the homes we lived in to our spiritual houses, Kaylyn sat at attention too, soaking in the message like a sponge.

Pastor Kingston said with his voice rising to a crescendo, "If I came to visit some of y'all, your house would probably look fine on the surface, but what if somebody were to open a closet door, peek under a bed, or, heaven forbid, in your basement? Amen, lights."

"Well now, Pastor," someone blurted out.

"Go ahead," another member coached from the rear of the sanctuary.

"I got news for somebody. I'm not the one droppin' in on ya. No, it's not me, but there is One who's always there whether you recognize His presence or not. Let me tell you, He sees what's in that spiritual closet of yours. He already knows what's under the bed and in the basement. He even knows the secret places like under your mattresses. Nothing is hidden from Him. Luke 12:1–3 says, 'Beware ye of the leaven of the Pharisees, which is hypocrisy. For there is nothing covered, that shall not be revealed; neither hid, that shall not be known. Therefore whatsoever ye have spoken in darkness shall be heard in the light; and that which ye have spoken in the ear in closets shall be proclaimed upon the housetops.'"

Pastor preached on, encouraging those proclaiming the name of Christ to live righteous and holy lives. He explained how offensive it was to the name of Christ and all He stood for to profess salvation and live like the unsaved. "We are to be the light and salt of the earth. Oh, if we would only realize the impact we have on one another's lives when we don't live clean and upright lives. Somebody is watchin' you." Pastor Kingston pointed out toward the congregation. "Somebody you may not even know is looking at you."

As he drew his sermon to a close, Pastor lowered his voice almost to a whisper. "I know some of you must be sitting there thinking, 'My house isn't so clean, Pastor. How do I clean it up?' Well, cleaning up your spiritual house isn't as difficult as you might think. David lets us know in Psalm 51:17, that 'The sacrifices of God are a broken spirit: a broken and contrite heart, O God, thou wilt not despise.'"

He slowly closed the Bible and picked up his handheld microphone from the stand. "Ask the Savior to help you this morning. Come on. Repent and ask Him to cleanse you from any and all unrighteousness. He is the only One who can present you faultless before His presence in glory. Won't you come? He's waiting on you. Won't you come? Come on," he implored with an outstretched hand as he walked out into the aisles of the congregation.

Tears rolled down Kaylyn's face, so I prayed that she would give her life totally. Through our many conversations, I had learned that Kaylyn's problem with Christianity stemmed from her dysfunctional childhood and from seeing the hypocrisy from those who claimed to be Christians. The sermon, tailor-made to suit that girl, had convinced her. Beau reached to squeeze my hand when Spirit of the Lord moved her out of her seat and down the altar. The music played softly while Pastor Kingston prayed for those at the altar, and I noticed he spent a good amount of time talking and praying with Kaylyn. He motioned for the music to quiet down, and spoke into the microphone.

"God is a good God, Saints of Zion."

The congregation chimed, "Yes, He is."

Others responded, "All the time."

Pastor Kingston smiled. "The Lord has drawn two of His into the fold. Ah, yes, He's good. Go ahead and praise Him."

Applause broke out across the sanctuary.

"We oughta be glad about it. What the devil meant for evil, God turned it around for His good and His glory. Angels are rejoicing over our two candidates for baptism. I want to give the two who have repented of their sins and confessed their belief in the Lord Jesus Christ as their personal Savior, a chance to say something if they choose."

Kaylyn took the microphone first. With tears streaming, she took a deep breath and began. "I want to thank God for saving me today." Before she could continue, people, including Beau and I, stood up and clapped.

"I've been pretty angry with God and wondered if He even exists, to be honest. Like the pastor was saying, I've seen a lot of people who act like they're Christians, but they do pretty un-Christian things. I just have never wanted anything to do with that."

"Well," someone from the congregation called out.

"I've gone through a lot even though I'm not that old, and I had, well, I still have a lot of questions, but I believe that God has forgiven me for my sins. I just want to start living my life for Him, and I'm excited to see what He has in store for me."

"Hallelujah!" Pastor Kingston rested his hand gently on Kaylyn's shoulder. "I'm going to be here to help you with questions you may have, and where do we get our answers from church?" he said, turning toward the congregation.

Various voices from the congregation rang out. "The Word!"

"Okay now, that's the answer I was looking for." He turned back to Kaylyn, staring directly into her innocent eyes. "Jesus is our rock and anchor. The Word of God is our sword, so we're gonna work so you can equip yourself by wearing that whole armor of God. When you got that armor on, you can quench those fiery darts that come to rob you of the faith God has given you. Amen?"

Kaylyn answered enthusiastically, "Amen!"

Pastor Kingston embraced her, and Kaylyn's new life began at that moment.

Mine, on the other hand, slowly kept unraveling.

CHAPTER 27

DESIREE

Let him ask in faith, nothing wavering. For he that wavereth is like a wave of the sea driven with the wind and tossed.

—James 1:6b

Having to endure a trip to one of the places I'd least like to be, except for my own wedding, was a bridal store. I tried to remind myself that being Shay's maid of honor was an honor, not punishment. Since the attack though, the thought of a man, any man, made me ill. I didn't even know if I wanted to be married anymore. Why Shay couldn't be sensitive to what I'd been going through amazed me. It had only been two weeks since she and Geneva appeared at my door after Phillip assaulted me.

They'd both tried to text and call me but couldn't reach me. Shay had sent me a text to tell me that she would use her key because she wanted to borrow one of my necklaces for a date with Paul. Geneva had been in the neighborhood, dropping off tomatoes and cucumbers from her garden to me and another friend. They'd come almost at the exact same time, and Shay even noticed an SUV bolt from my driveway.

After they'd calmed me down, Geneva and Shay demanded to know what had happened.

I shook and found myself unable to speak for at least a minute or two.

"She's in shock," Geneva said, "I'm calling the police."

Shay wailed, "What happened, Des? Please?"

I screamed, "Put the phone away! Put the phone down now!"

Geneva didn't listen and began to speak. I jumped on her, pushing the phone away from her ear to the ground. Startled, she grabbed my shoulders and then held her hands up. "Okay, okay, just tell us what happened."

I told them everything, except that I was raped. I told them that I'd fought him off. Shay and Geneva eyed one another suspiciously. Geneva got up to get me a glass of water and made me take a swallow before saying, "Honey, I'd like to believe that you won this fight, but it doesn't look like you did. It needs to be reported either way though."

I refused to look at them and explained, "I did fight him off. I did. He didn't do anything but rough me up a bit. That's all. I'm not stupid, you know. I'd report him if he raped me."

Shay cried, "No, Desiree! You won't even look at us! He did! Why don't you let us call the police?"

I sobbed, slumping my shoulders. They knew me too well. "I don't want to. I can't. It's my decision, and if you do call, I won't tell the truth. I have too much to lose to go down that path. Mama's sick, and it'll make things worse for her. You've got to understand. I'm okay now."

They'd talked to me for over an hour, trying to convince me to report Phillip. I had thought it through though. It was as much my fault as it was his, and I didn't want to do it.

Oblivious to my despair, Shay interrupted my thoughts. "For heaven's sake, Desiree, you must like one more than the other." Shay spun around for the ninth time on the platform in front of the beveled mirrors, holding her play bouquet for effect. I yawned, slouched down on the sofa meant for the happy viewing audience.

"How rude, Des! This is a very important day for me. It's not every day that a woman picks out her wedding dress."

I sat up, mildly aggravated, especially since this wasn't her first wedding. For the second time, I'd have to endure Shay, the Bridezilla. "Are you sure you want to wear white?" I asked.

When Shay swung around toward me in a Scarlett O'Hara kind of way, the expression on her face let me know that I had said the wrong thing. "Do you really think He makes all things new?" she asked in disgust.

"Oh, don't be offended, Shay. I'm just saying, you know how some folks are. I just don't want you to fall apart if someone says something about the white."

She shrugged and sashayed back toward the dressing room, but not before turning around to say, "I couldn't care less what they think. Oh, and is it really they or you?"

"I'm sorry, guess I'm a little tired. I told you that I like the A-line ones the best on you. They look so regal."

She put her hands on her hips and stopped. "The problem is, four of the wedding dresses are A-line."

"Well, it does cut out five," I quipped.

"You don't like this fishtail?" Shay said, swinging to show her backend.

For forty-five minutes, I oohed and aahed at most of the dresses Shay tried on, struggling to play happy, hoping that she didn't feel any more of my misery. When we finally finished and got into her car, Shay unloaded. "Desiree, you've been pulling away for the last couple of months, even before what happened to you. Everyone has been telling me to leave you alone and to stop pushing you to cooperate. I can't because you're my best friend, my maid of honor."

She paused and then continued, "I'm sorry about all that's happening in your life, especially the assault and your mother's health. I just feel that you need to report the rape. That's too much for anyone to have to deal with, just too much. I'm also terribly sorry that you haven't found the love of your life, Des, I really am." She wiped the tear that had fallen from the corner of her eye. "However, I've been through a lot, and I've finally found happiness with Paul." Her voice cracked. "You're supposed to be happy for me. I'd be happy for you. I have to know, are you angry with me for introducing you to the Internet dating thing? I'm so sorry—"

I touched her arm. "Please stop apologizing for that. I did it because I wanted to do it. I let my guard down and let Phillip into my home. I didn't know him well enough for that. For the millionth time, it wasn't your fault."

"It just seems like you're angry with me," Shay insisted.

"I'm not angry with you," came out of my mouth, but my heart did feel a twinge of anger at Shay; only it wasn't for the reason she thought. I didn't see why Shay could get married twice, and I couldn't get married once. It didn't seem fair that she found happiness while I got the bottom of the barrel. What had I done so terrible to deserve being molested as a teen and now assaulted and raped? Why couldn't I be the one to wear a white dress this time? Why couldn't she be the one helping me to get ready for my big day? Why did I always have to be Shay's and everyone else's flunky? Furthermore, I didn't understand how she could expect me to be happy at a time like this.

Shay's phone buzzed, but she didn't pick it up. "I'm going to say this because I love you and I don't want bad feelings to come between us." She inhaled and exhaled. "You've done almost the same thing before every important event in my life, Desiree. Think about it. In my first marriage, you looked sad in all the pictures; so sad that anyone who looked at them asked, 'What's wrong with her?'"

"Oh, Shay, you knew that I had a virus that day!"

She continued, "When my son was born, you made sure that all of the attention was on you, not me or him!"

I raised my voice, seething in anger. "Are you talking about when I fell as I raced into the hospital to see you and sprained my ankle? Really, Shay?"

She matched the rise in volume of my voice. "Every single time I tried to talk to you about how painful the divorce was to me, you made sure to tell me how much worse your situation was being alone. You actually said, 'At least you found someone to marry you.' Why can't you ever just be compassionate toward me without telling me how lonely and sad your life is?"

Her words hit me with the force of a tsunami, and when I opened my mouth to respond, a cry instead of words escaped. The angry look on Shay's face left as quickly as it had appeared and sympathy replaced it. Shay groped in the back seat for the box of tissue and cried with me. "I'm sorry, Desiree. I just want you to be happy too. You so deserve it, and I don't know why things have happened for you like this. I didn't mean any of it. I'm just so stressed out by what's happened to you, your mom, and all of this wedding stuff. I'm so sorry, please don't cry."

I shook my head, trying to tell Shay that it wasn't her, but still the cries that I had muffled all these months unleashed like a broken dam, and they wouldn't stop. Almost on cue, rain began to beat down on the windshield, as if to give me permission to let go. Shay rubbed my back and tried to console me the best she could. After a while, she seemed to recognize that she wasn't the reason for my breakdown. Shay's eyes, reddened and sad, showed her deep and genuine concern. "Is Ms. Isabella okay?"

My head pounded as I blew my nose and tried to gain my composure. "I'm sorry, Shay. I've never meant to hurt you."

"I know, Des. I'm sorry too. I can be so self-centered," she said, rubbing my back again.

"Yes, we both can," I said, and we both laughed through our tears. "You know, Mama's in the hospital. Her doctor is saying that her prognosis isn't good."

"I know she's had an incredibly hard time lately," she said, sensing more.

"I am just tired, Shay. I'm trying to be there for Mama, but she makes it hard. She's gotten so close to Kaylyn, and it's just crazy."

"You know Ms. Isabella likes to be in control of things. She's not in control of a lot now, but Kaylyn needs her. I think aside from their commonality in the struggle, they also get different things they need from one another. I know that you want to be there for your mom, but I think, even in her illness, she wants to be there for you. Tell her what's happened, Des. Let her in."

"No way. Mama will make sure that the jerk is in prison, which, by the way, is where he needs to be. But she would also blame me and, even worse, herself. I just can't take that. I'm already blaming myself enough. And it's not just that. As small as this city is, and as large as Dad's practice is, my parents would be all over the news too, and God knows there's already enough going on with Mama and Dad. It's just all too much."

Shay's shoulders sank. "I understand what you're saying, but your parents love you. They'd want to support you and help you through things. Shoot, it may help to bring them together."

"Are you kidding, Shay? They're living in two different worlds and they have for a long time. Besides, I'm not a child. I've got to deal with this in my own way."

"I'm glad you got the security system installed. So, has the creep tried to contact you?"

"No, thank God. I've taken myself off of the site, indefinitely." I held up my key chain, dangling the pepper spray.

"That's good, but I just want you to know that it's not your fault, Des. That jerk needs to pay."

"I don't know about that. You and Geneva have been great, really. I appreciate everything, but I have to work through things a little bit at a time."

"I just wish you would listen to Geneva and me, even now, Desiree. It's not too late for him to be punished for what he did. People get put away for a very long time for things like this."

"I know, I know, you've said it a million times, and Geneva is just driving me insane with her phone calls and threats to report it. I just don't want that, not now, not ever. I can't believe you and Geneva showed up at my house at that moment and at the same time."

"You can't tell me that God isn't real. He meant for us to be there for a reason. Think about that."

"I'm thankful for you showing up, but I just don't want to be pressured."

Shay sat, pondering. "Well, I don't think you've made any decisions that I haven't made myself. I feel terrible."

Suddenly, Shay snapped her fingers and brightened up. "Desiree!"

"What?"

"I have an idea, but first, let's go see your mom."

I didn't try to pry it out of Shay because I knew how she got when her wheels started churning. I just snapped my seat belt in place and tried to enjoy the ride.

When Shay and I got to Mama's hospital room, I heard her laughing and let out a sigh of relief; that was, until I discovered that Kaylyn was the source of her happiness.

"Hi, baby, and Shay, honey, how are you? How are the wedding plans comin' along, girl?"

We both kissed her on the cheek. Kaylyn got up and said hello. After we greeted her, Kaylyn said to Mama, "Well, I guess I better be going."

Mama practically lifted her weak body up from the bed in protest. "Oh, I won't hear about that, Kaylyn. You sit yourself right back down, and visit with us. You're all my girls."

Kaylyn smiled. I winced. I never had Mama alone these days. Mama pointed to the bouquet on the table. "Desiree, baby, look at the pretty flowers Kaylyn brought to me."

I put on my plastic smile. "Oh, they're so pretty. How'd you know Mama's favorite flowers were pink roses?"

Kaylyn flung her arms up in the air. "That's the funny thing; I didn't know. I told Ms. Isabella that I was in the flower shop looking to see what kind of flowers reminded me most of her, and I just happened to pick her favorite. Isn't that something?"

"Yeah, isn't it?" I muttered. Shay nudged me with her elbow, still smiling.

"I think what kind of flower you like says something about your personality. For instance, I know I can stick you like a thorn if you aren't careful." Mama's eyes narrowed playfully. I knew she wanted to divert the conversation from sickness.

"You got a favorite flower, Kaylyn?" Mama asked.

"I just love daisies. They're like freedom to me." Kaylyn smiled dreamily.

Mama closed her eyes. "Hmmm. . . . They're simply beautiful but often underestimated."

"And they wilt easily without enough attention." Kaylyn laughed.

Mama let out a weak laugh. "Guess that's true about all flowers."

"Except maybe the dandelion," I chimed in. "Guess that's mine."

Mama and Shay frowned. Kaylyn grinned. "Girl, please, I think dandelions can be beautiful in the right places, and furthermore, they can be quite beneficial. They have a lot more attributes than most people think. Uncle Beau is an expert when it comes to gardening."

I couldn't help but notice Mama's raised eyebrows at the comment.

"Well, I think dandelions are unruly and just a serious nuisance to everyone. The best thing for them is pesticide," Shay joked.

We all laughed until Mama turned toward Shay and asked, "What about you, dear?"

"Oh, Ms. Isabella, you already know that I love those calla lilies. I'm gonna have a ton of them for my wedding so you gotta get well quick so you can be there."

"I wouldn't miss it for the world, Shay," Mama offered wistfully.

I raced to Google calla lilies from my iPhone and pounced on the opportunity to get Shay back. "Let's see now, it appears that calla lilies can mean a pig's ear in Afrikaans."

Everyone chuckled except Shay, who jabbed me in the arm.

Mama closed her eyes for a moment, and moaned a bit. I rushed to her side. "Are you okay?"

She nodded, but her eyes told another story.

"So, Mama, what did the doctor say today?" I felt her clammy head.

"He said my blood count was way too low, so they are going to transfuse me today."

"A transfusion?" I asked.

"Oh, don't worry about it too much, Desiree. You know that I've had so many transfusions that I can't count. Nine times outta ten, as soon as they're done, I feel like a new person. She'll be fine," Kaylyn said, trying to console me.

"Yeah, baby, Kaylyn here has been through the wringer much more than I have. She oughta know."

I nodded, but my stomach turned in agitation. Kaylyn's situation didn't exactly compare to Mama's. Kaylyn didn't have inflammatory breast cancer, the most aggressive and deadly type. She also had her youth on her side. Mama's episodes of hospital stays and treatments had gotten longer and more serious faster than I could've imagined.

Kaylyn's tone, bubbly and hopeful, informed me of Mama's status. "I just happened to be here when the doctor came in, and he said that if all goes well, she should be home in a day or two."

"Great news then," Shay said, always the willing party to fill silent spaces.

Mama avoided any further discussion about her health and asked Shay again about her wedding. Shay, Mama, and Kaylyn chatted almost nonstop, and Shay even pulled out a few pictures of wedding dresses she had tried on.

Mama then turned her attention to me. "Baby, you look almost as tired as me. You okay now, sweetie?"

"Uh, I'm doing well, Mama."

"Don't you worry about me. I'm fine. I need to know that you're happy, which brings me to you, Shay. Surely, you know somebody at your job or church you can introduce to my daughter."

I rolled my eyes.

Shay looked uncomfortable. She blurted out, "Oh, Ms. Isabella, it's hard these days. Like they say, a good man is hard to find."

I didn't want to have this conversation now or ever, especially around Kaylyn.

Kaylyn added, "I'm so thankful for your mother, Desiree. I've been learning so much at the church. Pastor

Kingston has been doing a whole series in Bible Study called Saved and Single. He's been doing some fantastic teaching on how a man should be the one to find a wife and how we, as women, just need to wait and trust God. There's so much I hadn't even thought about."

This girl really got under my skin. Did she really think she was dropping knowledge to me about my church and my pastor? She just joined the church, and she had become more involved while my attendance had only waned.

Mama tried to sit up a little. "Desiree, I left you a message a few weeks ago because I thought you might be interested. Kaylyn has jumped right on it and I thought you two could really get a lot out of it with you being young and all."

"Maybe we could go sometime. I get tired of having Uncle Beau driving me around sometimes. Ms. Isabella says we live pretty close to one another."

"What'chu sayin' 'bout me, girl?" Kaylyn's Uncle Beau came in Mama's room without even knocking. I hated how familiar they had become with her. He then greeted everyone with a hearty hug and laugh.

"Hey, Unc! Guess you're here to pick me up."

"Yes, but more importantly, I had to come up to check up on sweet Isabella."

Mama's cheeks turned red. "You oughta stop that, Beau. You're just too much."

He lightly tapped Mama's headboard. "You just take care of yourself and get plenty rest. We'll surely be back tomorrow."

"Don't y'all go outta your way. I'm fine now, ya hear?" Mama said, actually trying to smooth her tufts of hair down. Mama's voice sounded different around Kaylyn and Beau. I couldn't put my finger on it, but I thought maybe it sounded more like how she sounded when she visited home in Dothan with her extended family and old friends.

Kaylyn got her purse. "Ms. Isabella, I gotta come here tomorrow for my routine blood tests, so it's no trouble. Just call if you need us to bring you anything, unless of course you get out of here before I get here."

"Okay, now then. I'll just say, thank you kindly," Mama said with the politeness of a true Southern belle.

As soon as they left, Shay sensed that I needed a moment alone with Mama and left for the cafeteria.

"Now, baby, I want to hear all about what's been goin' on with you," Mama said.

I started to talk again about my classes, but in a few short minutes, Mama fell into a deep sleep. I pulled the blankets up around her, kissed her softly on the cheek, and quietly left.

CHAPTER 28

ISABELLA

But he was wounded for our transgressions, he was bruised for our iniquities: the chastisement of our peace was upon him; and with his stripes we are healed.

—Isaiah 53:5

With all of the chemo treatments done, the doctors had finally decided that the time was right to have a mastectomy of the infected breast. I felt ready for them to get as much of the cancer out of my body as they could, but losing a breast made me scared. Another part of me would be gone.

My eyelids refused to open, but I came to enough to hear a man's baritone voice. I strained to hear whose voice it could be and comforted myself, knowing it was Langley.

"Bless this woman, God. She's a faithful servant, and we know and trust you to be a healer. Let your divine will be done in this situation. We need you, Lord."

No, it couldn't be my husband. He didn't like to pray out loud. It had to be Pastor Kingston. I started to thank him, but a moan was the only thing that came out. I felt a gentle stroke on my shoulder. "Now, you don't worry about nothing, Ms. Isabella. You gonna be just fine. Desiree and Kaylyn went to the cafeteria but they'll be right back. Your husband was here but had to leave for a few minutes. He'll be back too."

Beau. He never ceased to amaze me. I wanted to thank him, but the drugs had my mouth dry and locked shut. My eyelids felt like lead, and they refused to open and cooperate. Only a tear or two squeezed through and fell down my face. I felt him wipe the tears from my cheeks with a soft tissue.

"One day at a time now. You'll be talkin' soon enough. You just rest and know that everything is gonna be okay."

I nodded and drifted off to sleep again, too drowsy and drugged to see if my breast really was gone.

I'd been in the hospital for almost three weeks, sick with infection and fever. They hadn't even been able to remove the drainage tubes from the space where my breast had been. Delirious and broken, I knew that I probably wouldn't recover. The only thing that beat back thoughts of death was Beau. Like clockwork, he came every day. Nothing seemed to scare him off. Vomiting, irritability, and a host of other unpleasant issues couldn't keep him away. While Langley rushed in and out, being more of a doctor and less of a husband, Beau filled in the gap.

Desiree was there but not present. She seemed lost, afraid, and shell-shocked about the whole thing.

Once again, God had kept death from me, and I had gotten well enough to go home. As I collected my things, Beau knocked.

"Hello, sunshine!"

I waved him off, like I always did. "Aren't you funny?"

He took off his cap and pushed back his wavy salt-and-pepper hair with his hand.

"I told you they were releasing me today. There was no need to come up here. Langley and Desiree will be here shortly."

He sat down in the nearest chair to the bed, and I took in his scent of Irish Spring soap. "Aww, I know that. My day wouldn't be the same if I didn't check in on you. I can't do this when you get home. I might not be too welcome, if you know what I mean."

I smiled, wishing that he would but knowing that Langley could hardly stand Beau's presence. He treated Beau like he was a gnat or a fly swarming around him.

"I appreciate you for being such a special friend, Beau."

His face reddened, and he looked down. "Why, I appreciate you, Isabella."

"I don't know why. I haven't been any good to anyone."

"Oh, now, don't you say that. You're doing good to a whole heap of folks, me included."

For some reason, his presence made me feel womanly and girl-like all at the same time. I could be vulnerable with him, and it felt refreshing. "I haven't told anyone this, but I get scared, you know?"

He nodded.

"My outlook is very grim; guess you know that by now. The statistics are all against me. I'm so tired of all the sympathetic, apathetic, and hopeless looks from doctors. I know that you have your hands full with Kaylyn, and Desiree does have her stepfather, but will you please check in on her every now and then, when . . . when I'm not here?"

Beau leaned in toward the edge of his chair. "You don't talk like that, you hear me? If somethin' happened to you, of course I'd see about Desiree, but you need to keep fightin'. I tell Kaylyn about every day that she's gonna be okay. Those doctors don't have the final say, but you know as well as I do that the Lord does. When those thoughts of death come in tryin' to rob you of your hope and joy, you fight back with the Living Word. You ain't alone either. I'm prayin' and a whole lot of folks are believing God for a miracle. He's still in the miracle-working business. God doesn't change."

After he said a short but powerful prayer for me, I forced a weak smile and offered my hand out. He took my hand in both of his rough hands and caressed them. He looked into my eyes and I saw then that he loved me. Not for the outside, but in spite of the outside. I melted in his eyes, not saying a word until a voice dropped us both into reality.

"What's going on here, Isabella?"

I pulled away from Beau. "Hello, Langley. Nothing at all. Beau was just leaving."

Beau stood up and a grim expression overtook his typical jovial nature. He gave Langley what looked to be an extra-firm handshake and said at the door, "Dr. Morrison, take extra special care of her, you hear?"

Langley bit his lip and balled his fists at his sides before turning to look at me.

"Thank you for everything," I said.

"I'll be checking on you real soon, Isabella," Beau answered, not wanting to leave and not bothering to say good-bye to me or Langley.

"My love to Kaylyn," I called out as he left, not wanting him to leave either.

Langley paced the floor of the small hospital room. "What is going on with you and that Fred Sanford character, Isabella?"

My throat tensed. "He's not a character."

"You know what I mean. I'm insulted. He's got a lot of nerve telling me to take care of you!"

"Somebody needed to tell you that, Langley."

"Don't start a scene, Isabella! I've made sure that you've seen the very best doctors in the city, and I've come to see about you every day."

I whispered, "I'm more than what's on a flipchart."

"Of course you are. You think I don't know that?" He sat down in the seat Beau vacated, and his leg shook. "I'm doing everything in my power to help you to live. This is a very serious disease, and not many people can survive it. It's the most aggressive—"

I raised my voice. "Stop! You don't need to tell me what I'm suffering through anymore! I know that sixty to seventy percent of patients don't live past five years with this disease. I'm the one who's been taking chemo, radiation, and endured multiple hospital visits. I'm the one who has chest burns from the radiation. I'm the one who lost her hair, her breast, her marriage!" I began to cry, and Langley looked as if he'd seen a ghost. Right then, Desiree walked in.

"Mama, what's wrong?" Desiree asked, rushing to my side.

I sucked in all my tears, gasping at my daughter's appearance. "Your hair! Where's your hair?" I managed to get out.

"I cut it. Just wanted something new. Now, are you okay?" Desiree stated a little too nonchalantly.

"You cut your beautiful hair?" I said, stunned, not really asking.

"What has gotten into both of you?" Langley asked, staring in disbelief at the both of us.

"Both of you, please calm down. It's only hair. It'll grow back, right, Mama?"

I nodded, still frowning.

"What's wrong with me wanting to look more like you? Besides, I donated it to a charity for women suffering with cancer. They make wigs out of it."

I thought of my nearly bald head. She wanted me to feel better. She didn't want me to lose my hair alone. I tried to sound calm and said, "That's mighty generous of you, honey, but that's a big sacrifice. I mean, it's a lovely cut, but you just look so different." I studied her asymmetrical bob with honey highlights. The cut did make Desiree look more mature and chic.

Desiree kissed me on the cheek. "I understand. You'll get used to it. Mama, my hair felt like a weight, and I'd considered cutting it as soon as you began losing yours. I want people to see me, not just my hair. I've never seen you as clearly as I have since you've lost your hair."

I didn't understand everything that she said. She didn't get that losing my hair wasn't what changed me, but the cancer had. I decided to let it go though. I didn't want to upset her.

Desiree changed the subject and asked, "You're still coming home today, right? I mean there's no other news, is there?"

"No, not at all. I'm just a little emotional about everything. Everything is right on schedule. Let me get my shoes on."

Langley got up. "I'm going to make sure that they have your discharge papers ready."

Desiree gathered my plants and flowers together. "Mama, are you sure that you should be coming home now? Is something hurting you?"

"No, honey. I'm excited to be coming home. It's just all these medications and weeks here. I just want things to go back to normal."

Desiree looked skeptical, but she didn't question. I noticed the gray circles around her eyes, and she looked like she'd lost weight but not in a healthy kind of way. The stress was getting to her. I felt worse, knowing that she'd done something impulsive like cutting her hair for my sake.

"Desiree, how are things with you? I've been so down for the past several weeks that I haven't seen about you."

She loaded the plants on the cart and started to take my things out of the closet. "I'm doing fine, Mama. I'm concerned about you. It's not a fun thing to see your mom sick or sad."

"Oh, I'm sorry about that. It's all the drugs. I'm sure of that."

"It's not fun, but it's totally understandable. I just want to get you home."

"It just seems like something else is bothering you," I said.

She avoided eye contact. "I'm just concerned about you and busy with school and jewelry orders."

I didn't know what was going on with her, but I knew when she was hiding something from me. She would never tell me unless I got well enough for her to feel like I could handle whatever it was. At that moment, I decided that I would fight hard for my life. I would do as Beau reminded and fight with the Word, no matter what it looked like. My daughter needed me. My extended family and friends needed me. Kaylyn and Beau needed me, and I needed them. Something about the look on my daughter's face ignited my spirit, and let me know that my work wasn't finished.

Whether I felt good or bad, I began reciting healing scriptures out loud. I understood that since Satan is the prince of the air, I had to fight the sickness upon me with His Word. I woke up in the morning and said from Psalms 103:2–3, "'Bless the Lord, O my soul, and forget not his benefits: Who forgiveth all thine iniquities; who healeth all thy diseases.'"

When I felt tired and in pain, I meditated on the story of Hezekiah and how he was told to set his house in order because the sickness he had would kill him. I remembered how Hezekiah prayed and cried out to the Lord, reminding him of how he had served him and walked upright before him. Then, the prophet told Hezekiah what the Lord told him in 2 Kings 20:5.

I have heard thy prayer, I have seen thy tears; behold, I will heal thee.

When I thought about that prognosis of less than five years, I remembered how the Lord added fifteen years to Hezekiah's life and I just got happy.

At night, when I got fearful that I might not wake up in the morning and see another day, I would say, "'But unto you that fear my name shall the Sun of righteousness arise with healing in his wings,'" from Malachi 4:2. Not even Langley and his strange looks at my recitations could stop me. I remembered Job who was healed and delivered. I read over again how Jesus healed the sick. I even thought about how Paul perceived that the crippled man in Acts had the "faith to be healed."

I'd prayed too long and studied my Bible too much to give up because of my bad situation. I hadn't gone to all the church services and worshipped and praised God for years to leave my faith behind and not have the hope that the Holy Spirit had given me just because man said I was going to die. My determination was sealed. I would be an overcomer and trust God. Shadrach, Meshach, and Abednego had told King Nebuchadnezzar that God was able to deliver them out of the fiery furnace and that even if He did not, they still would not cave under the pressure. They trusted God, no matter what, and that's exactly where I was.

I couldn't tell a soul, but the one thing I had lost faith in was my marriage. While Langley doted on me in a phony, unnatural way, he didn't seem to notice that he repulsed me. My illness had blown the cover off of our façade of a marriage. I just had to find the right way and time to let him know.

I had been home for about two weeks when Pastor Kingston paid an unexpected visit to our home. Langley welcomed him in and led him to the back patio where I sat reading.

"Why, Sister Morrison, don't you look better!" Pastor Kingston said.

"Oh my, Pastor, I'm such a mess right now." I placed my book on the table and greeted him.

"Now, don't you get up. I've wanted to come for quite some time since your release, but my schedule has been so busy lately. I was delighted that your husband invited me over to talk to you both."

I shot Langley a look. Since when did he contact Pastor Kingston? And why hadn't he told me?

Langley offered Pastor Kingston a patio chair beside me. "May I offer you a sweet tea or lemonade, Pastor?" Langley asked uncomfortably. He was hardly used to entertaining men of the clergy.

Pastor Kingston, easy and warm, said, "Lemonade would be nice, Brother Morrison. Why thank you. So tell me, Mother Morrison, how are you doing?" He didn't ask like most people who just wanted a "fine and thank you." Pastor Kingston really wanted to know, and his sincerity cut straight through any thoughts of a mere polite answer.

"I feel some better than I did, but I am still mighty tired."

"That's to be expected. You're going through a lot right now."

Pastor Kingston turned to Langley, who had given him his drink but hadn't taken a seat and was lingering in the patio door entrance. "And how are you, Dr. Morrison?

"Oh, thank you for asking. I'm doing well, and you?"

"I'm doing fine, but I do have to admit that I'd love to see you over at the church. Actually, I was thinking about having a wellness conference at the church. Diabetes, especially juvenile diabetes, has been such a problem in the church. Would you consider doing a seminar for us?"

Langley stammered a bit. "Why sure, Pastor Kingston. Just tell me when. I am also very concerned with the number of children diagnosed with diabetes. I'd love to be a part."

"Come on and sit down, Langley," I coaxed. Surely he had asked him over for a reason.

Langley sat down but at the edge of the seat.

"You have both been on my mind," Pastor Kingston said, attempting to make conversation. Pastor Kingston appeared totally unfazed by Langley's apparent discomfort with his presence. "Brother Morrison, I have had the pleasure of meeting with your wife quite a few times over the past several months."

"Yes, she's shared that with me," Langley said, using his doctor voice.

"She's expressed a great deal of concern about her illness and the state of your marriage, and I want both of you to know that I have been praying."

"Thank you, Pastor," I chimed.

"Yes, thank you," Langley offered.

"No thanks necessary. From our sessions and my friendship with your wife over the years, Brother Morrison, I know that she understands that Satan wants to attack our faith by allowing us to cave to temptation and doubt God's goodness and love for us."

"Certainly," Langley said with his brow furrowed, still in physician mode.

"Brother Morrison, I take my profession seriously, just as you do, I'm sure."

"Why yes, of course, Pastor Kingston." Langley shifted in his seat.

"I'm going to get right the point," Pastor Kingston said. "Are you saved?"

Langley removed the doctor's mask and almost became childlike in an instant. "I believe in God," he said defensively. "Always have, always will. I grew up going to Sunday School and going to church every Sunday."

"Good, then you know that being saved is quite different than being religious."

"What do you mean?" he asked with sincerity.

The pastor folded his hands together, leaning in toward Langley. "What I am asking you is if you really believe with your heart that Jesus Christ is the Son of God? Do you believe that He is the Savior of the world? Do you believe that God sent His only Son on earth to be born of the Virgin Mary and that He died on the cross to save us from all of our sins? Do you believe that He rose from the dead so that we all might have eternal life?"

"That's quite a mouthful, Pastor, but yes, I believe in all of that." Langley cowered a bit in his chair.

I sat, praying that Pastor wouldn't let Langley off so easily.

"Hmmm ... that's wonderful news. I do want to remind you that Romans 10:9 says that if you confess with your mouth and believe in your heart, you are saved."

"Well, I do believe in Jesus, Pastor. I guess I just haven't connected all the dots."

"What do you mean?" Pastor Kingston asked, taking a sip of his lemonade.

"I don't want to offend you, Pastor, but I don't think it takes all that my wife does, for instance, to be saved. I don't have the time or patience to spend every free moment in church. All I have to do is confess and believe, and I've got that covered."

"That's right in a sense, but when you truly believe in your heart, other things follow, like bearing fruit for Him.

The Bible says in Romans that 'faith comes by hearing, and hearing by the Word of God.'"

"So then, you're saying that I need to go to church. I understand."

"Yes, I'm saying that, but it shouldn't be simply out of obligation or religious duty. You should desire to fellowship with a local body of believers to hear the Word of God, which will help to increase your faith and help you to be accountable."

Langley shifted again in his chair and folded his legs, putting his hand up on his head as if he were in a business meeting. Pastor Kingston, undeterred by Langley's countenance, continued, "So many people have a skewed view of what the church is here for. The cares and temptations of life will destroy you if you are not anchored in the Lord and His Word. In no way do I want to overstep my boundaries with you, but as the head of your household, Brother Morrison, I want to encourage you to lead your family in prayer. Seek His will for your lives together. Pray for your wife's healing together. Attend church together regularly. Get in Bible Study. Do some things to actively hear from God so that He can give you both direction."

Langley, deep in thought, finally put his guard down. "You've given me a lot to think about, Pastor."

"Clearly, you have been a superior head of the household in one sense." Pastor Kingston put his hands up and looked up at our massive home. "However, I believe that being the spiritual head is a much higher calling that God has given husbands. You see, it's so much more than providing material things."

"Of course, I do know that much, Pastor Kingston. It's just that this," he said, looking up at our home, "has required so much from me. It doesn't seem appreciated. In fact, it seems minimized."

"I've always told you how much I appreciate how you've taken care of us, Langley," I said.

"It's more than just words, Isabella," Langley quipped.

"Yes, indeed it is," I said.

Pastor Kingston closed his eyes for a second. "I hear what both of you are saying, but what I think needs to be done right now is a whole lot of listening. I think that we can accomplish a lot if you, Brother Morrison, would make your petitions known to God and then just listen to what He's saying."

Langley frowned. "I don't believe that I've ever heard God's audible voice."

"Most of us haven't, but we can hear what the Holy Spirit is saying to us if we open our hearts and minds to Him. He leads and guides us into all truths."

While Pastor Kingston continued to talk to us and prayed for Langley and me, I noticed Langley's eyes filling up with tears, in a state of remorse and repentance. I, on the other hand, had run out of tears for our relationship. I hadn't told a soul, but I wanted out of the marriage, and there was nobody who could change my mind, not even Pastor Kingston.

CHAPTER 29

DESIREE

He that dwelleth in the secret place of the most high
shall abide under the shadow of the almighty.
—Psalm 91:1

"Is it me, or are you changing, Mama?" I asked.

"People do change, baby. Really, God is the only One who doesn't. This cancer has really made me appreciate each day that the Lord has given me, and these stark white walls are something you've been wanting me to change for years. For the first time, I don't care if your dad likes it or not!" Mama looked around at the vaulted ceilings. "I just think Beau is a little too up in age to attempt these high ceilings."

"I am glad that you're finally doing it, but are you sure that it's a good idea to have Beau do it? You know they say it's not wise to do business with friends." I couldn't believe Mama. She pushed Beau and Kaylyn on Dad and me mercilessly.

"Who said that? I ain't never said that now! Shoot, if friends are really friends, they can be the best to do business with 'cause you can trust them."

I couldn't stand the effect Beau had on Mama. Suddenly, the word "ain't" had crept into her vocabulary. She sounded more and more like Beau and less like the mother I'd known all my life.

"Besides," she added, "Beau's a professional painter and handyman. He will do a good job. The way I see it, he can bless me, and I can bless him."

I guessed Mama forgot that she told me Beau offered to do it free of charge. I just hoped Mama would pay him money so he didn't expect payment in other ways. There was just no way I could make a big fuss out of it though. Mama's fragile and worsening health scared me, and I wanted her to be happy, even if it meant I had to put up with Kaylyn, her long-lost and perfect daughter, and Beau, her wannabe husband.

The doorbell chimed, and I opened to find Beau, clad in his usual attire of overalls, and Kaylyn, dressed in a neon orange T-shirt knotted at the waist and ripped jeans. They hugged me respectfully and embraced Mama warmly.

"Oooh weee, Isabella, you smell like lavender and vanilla!" Beau said, nearly drooling over Mama.

"Beau, get out of here!" Mama flirted back, adjusting the tail of her headscarf draped around one shoulder.

Beau clapped his hands. "Let's get this party started!" He shook the paint can up and flipped open the can.

"Desiree, do you think it's too bright?" Mama asked, looking at the paint color.

Before I could answer, Beau jumped in. "Woman, this is not too bright, for the last time. It's café au lait, just warm and bronze like you."

Mama chuckled, "What am I gonna do with you, Beau?"

"I can think of lots of things." He grinned.

"Oh, Beau," Mama said, like a schoolgirl.

Kaylyn held her cheeks. "How embarrassing! Uncle Beau, can you just paint? I'll start cutting the edges," Kaylyn said, grabbing a brush, avoiding eye contact with me.

"Oh no, you don't, young lady," Beau said, snatching Kaylyn's brush out of her hand.

Before Kaylyn could respond, I asked, "What's that supposed to mean?"

"Oh, I don't want Kaylyn or your mother anywhere near all of these paint fumes. They need to stay upstairs and visit with one another. In fact, all three of you need to let the men work," Beau said.

"That's not what I'm talking about. I'm talking about flirting with my mother."

Beau's smile faded. "Why, I'm mighty sorry, Desiree. I didn't mean nothing at all—"

I interrupted Beau. "Mama *is* married."

"Desiree, calm down." Mama touched my arm, and then she turned to Beau. "She's just overly protective right now."

I fumed but bit my tongue. Mama ignored me and took Kaylyn's hand. "Excuse me, young lady, but your uncle is right. No painting for you!"

"I love to paint, and I'm feeling good today. I really want to help! I *am* an adult," Kaylyn pleaded.

"She's sayin' the same thing that I said on the way over here. Ain't no way you're painting! I won't allow it any more than I'll let Isabella!" Beau started stirring the paint with a wooden paint stick.

Kaylyn looked to me. "I don't get why they don't understand that when I feel good I want to do things that I want to do. I want to help."

"If she wants to paint—" I started.

Now, Mama interrupted me. "The paint fumes aren't good for you or me."

"Oh yes, right," I whispered, remembering.

Beau chimed in again. "Besides LeRoy and Deonte are gonna be here any minute. They'll do the high, and I'll take the low."

"Isn't that the truth," I said under my breath. Kaylyn heard me and grinned. I had already put a good dent in the guest bathroom by painting it a soothing lavender. Mama hadn't wanted me to do it, but the artistic side of me loved doing things like that. However, I had second thoughts about proceeding with Beau and his sidekicks.

"Besides," Mama added, "I'm not feeling the best today. Desiree, can you pick up my prescription from the drugstore? I've got plenty of other things besides painting that you and Ms. Kaylyn can help me with."

"Mama, of course, why didn't you tell me that you needed something?"

"I just did. Besides, it will give you and Kaylyn some time away from us old folks."

I didn't want or need time alone with Kaylyn and didn't want Mama and Beau to be alone either.

Kaylyn, energetic and ready, said, "Okay, that'll be fun. Do you mind a Starbucks run?"

"Why not?" I said flatly, seething at the prospect of leaving Mama alone with Beau and having to put up with Kaylyn.

From the moment we got in the car, Kaylyn ran her mouth. Her nervous laughter and complaints about her uncle controlling her life, her stalled college career, and lackluster love life all took place within the fifteen-minute drive to the drugstore. I nodded, smiled, and mmhmmed at the appropriate places, but inside I wondered what Mama saw in her that was so intriguing.

During the ride home, she finally got quiet. The abrupt shift in her demeanor made me ask, "You okay?"

She stared out the window. "Yeah, I was just thinking about how lucky, I mean, how blessed you are to have both of your parents. I mean, your mom, I would've loved to have her for a mom."

I knew she wanted me to ask about her mom, but I didn't want to get sucked in on her problems. I had quite enough of my own. Since the assault, feeling sorry for myself and Mama filled all my empty spaces, crowding out room for anything and anybody else. After a few seconds of silence, she continued. "My parents never married. My dad left before I met him, and my mom passed away several years ago. She basically drank herself to death. Cirrhosis of the liver. She drank like she wanted to die, and me, well, I've never touched the stuff. I love life, and still, I'm stuck with cancer."

"I'm sorry to hear about your mom, Kaylyn," I said, genuinely sympathetic. "Things will work out for you. Just keep the faith."

"Yeah, my faith is growing, and your mom has been a big part of that. Ms. Isabella sure has changed my life and for the better."

"Thank you. Yeah, I guess Mama does seem to have that effect on people." Mama had been so busy making an impact on Kaylyn and helping her through her tough time, she hadn't even recognized the pain I was in.

I had to admit that even though Mama's relationship with Kaylyn and her uncle irked me, and I wanted Mama to myself, I couldn't deny that I was starting to like her a little.

As we pulled into the driveway, Kaylyn asked, "Where's Uncle Beau's truck?"

"Maybe he needed something," I said as we made our way up the house. Since the door was locked, I rang the doorbell. Nobody answered so I found my house key and entered.

A paint-covered brush seemed to have been dropped carelessly on the drop cloth. "That's weird. Uncle Beau would never leave the brushes full of paint like this. He's real meticulous about things like that," Kaylyn thought out loud.

"Mama!" I called out.

She didn't answer, so I walked upstairs to check on her, figuring that she must've been napping. I didn't find her in her room, bathroom, or anywhere. Had she and Beau gone off somewhere alone? I called out louder and searched the whole house. I dialed Mama's cell, and heard it buzzing. My stomach dropped. Mama didn't go anywhere without her phone.

Kaylyn's phone rang. "What? Okay, hold on," Kaylyn said to me, handing me her cell. "Uncle Beau wants to talk to you."

Out of breath, Beau huffed, "I'm sorry to tell you this, but your mama was just sitting on the step, and we was talkin'. She just passed out. Came out of nowhere."

"What? Is she okay? Where is she?"

"I believe that she's okay. I just scooped her up and raced her to Huntsville Hospital. I figured I could get her here way faster than any ambulance could. They're checking everything now."

"I knew I shouldn't have left. I'm on my way."

"Is she okay?" Kaylyn asked, running on my heels back out of the front door.

"I gotta call my dad," I said, dialing his number on the way to the car.

After I made sure that Dad was on his way, I cried. "Jesus, please let her be okay," I prayed the whole way to the hospital. Kaylyn reached her hand over to touch my arm, knowing not to say anything.

Once we got to the waiting room, the hospital admissions receptionist told me that I needed to wait. While waiting, Beau filled me in. Mama had come to on the way to the hospital, insisting that he take her back home. Beau had the sense not to listen to her.

Beau, Kaylyn, and I sat in the cold waiting room mostly quiet until Dad raced in looking frazzled. "Desiree, how's your mother?" Dad asked.

I stood up. "They're running tests, and they've already said she's going to be admitted. The emergency room doctor said he's put a call into her oncologist, so I guess we'll have to wait. They won't let me go back."

"We'll see about that," Dad said, ignoring Beau and Kaylyn.

Beau stood up to shake Dad's hand. In paint-covered overalls with speckles of paint all over his face, hands, and arms, Dad shook his hands swiftly and uneasily, wiping his hands conspicuously on his pant leg afterward.

"I hope you don't mind me waiting, Langley," Beau said.

Dad's sour facial expression didn't get past Beau, but Beau stood straight and undeterred.

"Beau, right?" Dad said.

Beau nodded and smirked.

"Desiree told me that you brought my wife to the hospital. Thank you. It's not necessary for you to stay though. I'm going to go see about her now." Dad left to speak to one of the receptionists who let us back to check on Mama without delay.

After about fifteen minutes, we both returned to see if Beau and Kaylyn were still there.

"How is she?" Beau asked, scooting to the edge of his seat.

"She's okay," Dad said.

I glared at him, knowing that he purposefully didn't offer details. Even though I didn't care for either Beau or Kaylyn, I knew that they loved Mama and deserved to know her status.

Kaylyn closed her eyes, holding her chest and whispered, "Thank God."

"Well, I know you all must have other things to do, but thank you again for your help. There's really no need for you two to stay here. Desiree and I can take it from here, and we'll call to let you know her status as soon as we know something."

Kaylyn and Beau didn't budge from their seats. "No disrespect, Dr. Morrison, but Ms. Isabella has stuck by me every single time I've been admitted into the hospital, and I'm gonna stay until I get to see her," Kaylyn said.

Beau added, "If it's just the same to ya, I reckon we'd both like to see her."

Dad eyed Beau. "Well, that won't be for at least a few hours. Once they stabilize her, she'll be transferred to a regular room."

Kaylyn gasped. "Stabilize her?"

I spoke up. "Listen, they're not exactly sure what's going on, but they know it's serious. We have to wait for all the test results to come back."

"We'll be here, so please keep us posted," Beau said, wringing his cap in his hands.

Dad spun around and walked toward Mama's room. I stood, not knowing what to say to Beau or Kaylyn.

Dad called after me, "Come on, Desiree."

"We're praying," Beau said.

I thanked him and followed Dad.

By the time Dad and I got back to the room, Mama was gone. They had moved her to intensive care. The oncologist had come and told us that they had discovered a blood clot in her lung. I couldn't believe it.

"Is she going to be okay, Dad?"

He looked past me, and stuttered out, "We need . . . we need to pray, Desiree."

I couldn't remember Dad telling me that we need to pray about anything. I noticed the tremor in my hands as I pushed through the waiting room doors to update Beau and Kaylyn about Mama's condition.

Kaylyn and Beau appeared equally shocked, but I convinced them to go home. Dad didn't want it, and I didn't want to rock the boat. After I promised to call with any changes, they assured me that they'd be there first thing in the morning.

Before Dad and I entered Mama's room in the ICU, a female doctor with bleached blond hair and a crooked smile tried to stop us. "Dr. Morrison, how nice to see you," she said.

Dad smiled faintly but didn't break his stride. "Hello, Dr. Winston. Likewise."

"Is that it? Really, Langley?" she called back.

When Dad didn't stop moving, I asked, "What was that about? And how did you go from Dr. Morrison to Langley in two seconds?"

"No worries, Desiree. I don't have time for her chitchat right now. She's a colleague. Known her for ages, and she's not one you want to be entangled with."

I let it go. I had Mama to think about.

We passed through the sliding glass door of Mama's room. I had to catch my breath at Mama's condition. Her face, wearing an oxygen mask and hint of a smile, looked gray and almost lifeless. IVs ran from her arm and only the high-pitched beep shattered the silence.

"Don't try to talk, Isabella. Just relax. We're here and everything is going to be fine," Dad said.

I rubbed her leg softly. "I love you, Mama. You're going to be fine. You just need some rest." Mama closed her eyes and fell off to sleep.

Dad fussed with her oxygen, and then thoroughly examined her IVs. He read through her charts at the bottom of her bed.

"What is it, Dad?" I whispered.

"I guess I didn't know that she was still doing the Tamoxifen with the hormone therapy. That would explain the pulmonary embolism, but it could also be from the drugs they gave her to treat the anemia some time ago. This is so frustrating, Desiree. The medications that they are giving to treat the cancer are nearly killing her. There's got to be a better way." Dad angrily slid the chart back onto the clip at the bottom of the bed. "I'm going to speak with her doctor. I'll be back."

I knew Dad wouldn't be able to sit still. He dealt with fear by leaving.

In the quiet of the hospital room, I sat and let my mind actually think about my life without Mama. My life, like a blank canvas before me without Mama, just had no laughter, no colors, and no joy. As much as I hated thinking about it, I couldn't keep pretending like she didn't have a terminal disease. I had to face that she had the most aggressive form of breast cancer.

The hair that Mama took so much pride in had been replaced by only sparse strands here and there. Her slender curves had disappeared into a frail body, struggling to fight off cancer while withstanding the countless treatments and medications that she needed. Dad had lamented that she may have done better fighting the disease without so many of the harsh medications battering her tired frame. She couldn't take much more of this. I knew it, and Dad knew it.

I prayed for Mama, but doubt crept in as it always did whenever I prayed for healing. I didn't know if God would hear me without faith. I knew that without faith, it would be impossible to please Him. Yet, I couldn't get my faith to kick into gear. No matter how many scriptures I read and how much I prayed, I fought with the facts, statistics, and grim prognosis. Sure, I believed Jesus healed the sick and raised the dead. It was also easy for me to believe that the disciples healed and delivered people after Jesus' resurrection. I just didn't know how many people were being healed now.

I had wholeheartedly accepted and believed that God would heal a couple of close family members, but they had still died. Still, I had faith to believe that God would heal a fellow friend and colleague who had been diagnosed with lung cancer. Chip, a devout Christian, left a young wife and three little children behind. If God didn't see fit to extend Chip's life, who would He heal?

I prayed for the Lord to help my unbelief, but thoughts of the rape and how I had prayed for the Lord to not allow it to happen tormented me. He hadn't heard my cries then, so why would He now with Mama's situation? Yet, I begged God silently to intervene on her behalf. If my faith waned, I knew Mama's hadn't. She trusted God with no reservations.

Dad couldn't reach the doctor and came back frustrated. "Come on, Desiree. Let's go down to the cafeteria."

After we got our food, he blessed the food in a way he had never done before. "Lord, thank you for sparing my wife's life today." He paused and continued, "We're so grateful for the mercy and grace you've shown us today. Now as we prepare to eat, we ask you to take out any infirmities and bless it, in your name we pray. Amen."

Shocked, I couldn't remember a time when my dad prayed without a thee or thou. His prayer touched me.

"Are you okay?" he asked, scooping up a bit of cottage cheese.

"Good as can be. You want some of this cheeseburger?"

"Aww, no, thank you, sweetie. You enjoy. I have been meaning to talk to you, and although these aren't the most ideal circumstances, I have a few things I'd like to share with you."

I took a swig of Coke, bracing myself for what was coming. I didn't want him to drop anything heavy on me. I just couldn't take anymore.

Dad pushed his tray away from him. "Desiree," he began.

Dr. Winston, the same woman we had seen outside of Mama's room, walked up to our table holding her tray. "Why, Dr. Morrison, who might this be?" she interrupted.

Dad cleared his throat. "This is my daughter, Desiree."

I smiled and extended my hand to meet her. "Nice to meet you."

When she shook my hand, her hands felt cold and so thin that I could feel her bones. Dr. Winston's crooked smile returned, and she asked, "Do you mind if I join you?"

Dad's eyes widened. He remained speechless, so I scooted over and welcomed her in the booth.

"I'm just crazy about your father. He's such a help to so many children." She flipped her stiff blond hair, exposing at least an inch of black at the root.

Dad didn't attempt small talk. Although I didn't feel like making small talk with Dr. Winston, I felt compelled since Dad appeared to have lockjaw. "Will you be at the health and wellness fair for children that Dad's been organizing?" I asked her.

She picked at her salad. "No, I don't believe that I know about that. Please fill me in, Dr. Morrison. I'd love to be involved."

Dad coughed, cleared his throat again, and nodded slowly. "I'll have to be in touch with you; maybe later on this week when we both have more time."

"Well, you just make sure you call me about that. I'll be looking forward to it," Dr. Winston said. Her face warmed but held deep lines and the dark black eye shadow aged her even more. She made small talk about the weather, golf, and the bad hospital cafeteria food.

Dad, engaging only a little, looked at my food as if he wanted me to eat faster. I couldn't figure out if he wanted to hurry to get back to Mama or just didn't want to converse with Dr. Winston.

The more she spoke, the more familiar Dr. Winston's face looked, but I couldn't place her. Finally I asked, "Have you been to one of my parents' parties? You look a little familiar."

Before Dr. Winston could respond, Dad answered looking stunned and suspicious. "I don't think so, Desiree. Jill, I mean, Dr. Winston has never been to our home."

Dr. Winston held up her Styrofoam cup almost as if it were an alcoholic drink, unsuccessfully hiding her crooked grin. "No, wait one minute, Dr. Morrison. I believe I did come once years ago when we were working on the golf charity event committee. Let's see . . . maybe ten, fifteen years ago even."

"I don't think so. Surely I would've remembered that," Dad muttered.

I tried not to make snap judgments about people, but I didn't like her. I finally began to connect the dots. Maybe Dr. Winston was one of Dad's affairs. It explained Dad's discomfort and her snarky attitude. I didn't care about any of Dad's drama. I had Mama to see about. I tossed my napkin on my tray. "Dr. Winston," I said, "it was terribly nice of you to join us, but my father and I need to discuss important family business right now. If you'll please excuse us."

"Yes," Dad chimed in. "Um, thank you for joining us."

Dr. Winston's nice nasty grin let me know that she wasn't quite finished torturing Dad. Although I couldn't blame her, I couldn't believe that she refused to leave. Dad, seated on the other side of the booth, stood up, tray in hand, ready to bolt out. I, on the other hand, sat on the inside of the booth and couldn't leave until she got up. "So, Desiree, are you married?" Dr. Winston asked, looking at my bare ring finger. "I have an absolutely delicious son. He's a handsome doctor in Raleigh, and let me tell you, he loves women with a bit of a tan, if you know what I mean."

"Thank you, but Dr. Winston, I prefer my men to have a bit more than a tan."

Dr. Winston belted out a phony, forced laugh while she rummaged through her purse to find her wallet. Dad closed his eyes for a second and demanded, "Come on, Desiree. Let's go. Please excuse her, Dr. Winston."

Dr. Winston waved Dad off and opened her wallet. She flipped through her pictures and shoved a picture under my nose. "You really ought to consider Hunter. He's quite a catch."

When I saw his picture and heard his name, alarm bells shot off like fireworks. It was him. The hairs on the back of my neck stood up. The room tilted and spun. I almost pushed her out of the booth and raced out. I heard Dad calling my name, but I needed air. I needed out.

CHAPTER 30

DESIREE

Be not deceived; God is not mocked: for whatsoever a man soweth, that shall he also reap.
—Galatians 6:7

Like a whistling tea kettle, I had reached my boiling point. Anger replaced my hurt. I craved justice. My anger toward Mama for marrying a man she didn't love festered. That, I decided, got to the root of the problem. Dad's cheating was just a byproduct of them choosing to be together for all the wrong reasons. I hated Dad when I thought about the fact that he might have known something happened to me. Yet, I just didn't know. I couldn't be so sure. He had been so scared for his own misdeed that maybe he hadn't considered me. Any way it went, he didn't put me or Mama before his own selfish desires. Like a dutiful daughter, I had held it all in for so long, but knowing that Dad still had some kind of relationship with the same woman from years ago ripped all the hope I had for mending fences with him.

The rape pushed me over the edge. Things had to be exposed, once and for all. In desperation, I had tried to block out what Phillip had done, pretend it hadn't happened; only fear wouldn't let me. It swallowed me up and spit me out at every turn. Plagued with headaches, sleepless nights, and daily worry, I knew I couldn't go on much longer.

Danger lurked around every nook and cranny of my life. Every time a male student came to my office or stayed after class to talk, my palms got sweaty and I trembled, unable to focus. Even walks from the parking lot to the school buildings and back were sheer agony, so much so that I rarely left campus unless I had decided to leave for the day. Male colleagues that I had once been so friendly with, I now steered clear of. In the middle of almost every night, I woke up in a cold sweat, mentally running or fighting for my life. Before I pumped gas, I'd sit, scope my surroundings, and make sure that I had one finger on the trigger of my pepper spray ready to strike. I didn't even think of going to the gym or a movie if it meant I'd be alone. Trips to the grocery store, which I'd always found so pleasurable, had lost their thrill. I'd toss things into the basket as fast as I could, praying that I wouldn't run into Phillip. I didn't feel too much better at church, but since women outnumbered the males by quite a bit, I still attended. I sized every man up, no matter where I was, wondering if he could be a potential rapist. All of this propelled me to make the decision to attend the rape counseling center.

Phillip wasn't a scary, threatening-looking guy. In fact, he was a guy who I had thought wouldn't hurt a flea. Clean cut, well dressed, and attractive. He had done and said mostly all of the right things. I mean, I knew that rapists weren't always those men waiting in bushes to attack, but Phillip seemed as though he wouldn't steal a stick of gum, let alone rape someone. He could probably get just about any woman he wanted without raping her. I didn't get it.

My hands shook as I typed in the Google search bar, statute of limitations on rape in the State of Alabama. I clicked on the link that listed crimes and the statutes of limitations on them. Then I saw what I was looking for. "No limit for filing charges of rape in the State of Alabama." I couldn't believe it, but as good as it sounded, I knew evidence would be necessary. I didn't have a shred. It would be his word against mine. I hadn't taken pictures of my ripped clothing or the bruises on my body. I refused to allow Shay or Geneva to take any because I didn't want them to have control over the situation. I needed to be in control. The sight of the torn clothes had sickened me, and with no thought of pressing charges, I threw them away that night. It was my word against his, and I had enough sense to know that it didn't mean anything in a court of law without evidence.

For hours, I read statistics and court cases of date rape and sexual assault. I had considered myself so informed, yet I discovered that I knew so little. In the State of Alabama, an average of almost 90 percent of rape victims know their assailants. I couldn't believe that the majority of rapes take place in or near a victim's home. I found out that I had become a textbook case for date rape.

With Geneva and Shay knowing about the rape, they had made things more difficult and easier at the same time. They never stopped reminding me of how God worked it out so that they both came the very same day at the same time. I only wished that God could've had them come sooner, before Phillip had the chance to attack.

After a staff meeting at the university, I had to deal with Geneva on my heels, asking, "How about lunch?"

"I have so many research papers to grade. Thanks, but I'll take a rain check." As I walked toward the parking lot, I saw a woman in the distance waving in what looked to be our direction. I looked behind me to see if she could be waving to someone else. As I drew nearer, I stopped short.

"Geneva, please tell me that it's not Shay! What are you two up to?" I asked, now annoyed.

Geneva struggled to keep up with me. "Oh, girl, chill out! We only want to take you to lunch. You're getting skinny on us pretty fast. Let's go to Landry's since that's your favorite."

I stopped short, holding my hands on my hips. "I don't want to go to lunch. I'm not hungry, and like I said, I have papers to grade."

Geneva looped her arm around mine and pulled me toward the parking lot. "Come on now! Shay and I have come up with a plan, girl!"

I knew that between the two of them I had no chance of refusing, so I gave in, resolved to eat in silence. I didn't want to talk about what had happened anymore, and I certainly didn't want to try to press charges.

While we ate, Shay updated us on her wedding plans. I could tell she gave a restrained version, not wanting to appear too happy considering my circumstances. Geneva, more reserved and serious, finally got to the point of the meeting.

Geneva wiped her mouth with her napkin and said, "This is the deal, sweetie. We have tried to find this Phillip character online, and we thought he'd disappeared totally."

Before she could continue, I spat out, "Stop, please! I want you both to leave it alone! I don't want anyone to do anything!" Tears sprang up and I dabbed at them with my napkin.

Shay, seated next to me, tried to console me, rubbing my back. "He can't get away with this, Des, he just can't!"

Geneva, calm and cool as a cucumber, appeared unmoved by my emotions as she opened up a pack of sweetener and poured it into her coffee. With attitude and determination, she pursed her lips, took a swig of coffee, and said, "Oh, something is going to be done to that man, whether you agree to it or not. You can either cooperate or not."

I frowned, totally enraged.

"Listen, Desiree," Geneva said, "I'm gonna need for you to get your sista girl back. Now, we can go the police or we can go to the 'POPO.'"

"Who the devil is the 'POPO'?" I asked, only half wanting to know.

Geneva shook her head. "You buppies kill me. The 'POPO' are the po-leece, in other words, they're the down-low police."

Without warning, my tears and Shay's sadness turned to faint smiles. Geneva, on the other hand, didn't crack a smile and said, "Go ahead and explain, Shay."

Shay took a deep breath. "So, as you know, Paul is an undercover investigator."

I rolled my eyes and fought to remain silent.

Shay continued, "When I told Paul what happened—"

"You told him? Oh, Shay, how could you?" I said, wanting to strangle her.

Geneva frowned at me. "Calm down, Desiree, and just listen."

I wanted to leave, but I knew it would only make things worse between the two of them.

Shay continued, "Anyway, when I told Paul, he did agree that it would be very hard to prosecute him, considering the whole thing. He didn't say it was impossible, but it would be very hard for you to go through. It would also boil down to your word against his."

"Yes, exactly," I said, crossing my arms.

"Geneva and I tried to find him online but couldn't. Fortunately, you had sent me that picture of him from your phone after you first met. So, Paul gave it the IT guy at the station, and he found him on two other dating sites, but he had a different name."

My eyes widened. "What? You mean to tell me that Phillip isn't his name?" I couldn't believe it.

"His new name is Warren." Shay wrestled through her purse and pulled out a paper, pointing to his name. "Warren Hampton."

Geneva shook her head and mumbled, "What a jerk."

"Okay, so here's what we're going to do. Paul has a lot of friends in the department, if you know what I mean. He's got people who owe him favors," Shay said, lowering her voice.

Geneva butted in, "Listen, honey, we're going to cut to the chase. He's agreed to set up a sting operation."

"Huh, you two are crazy! What do you think this is, a Lifetime movie? No. Absolutely not!"

"We weren't even going to tell you because we knew that you would protest. But, Des, he can't get away with that. He'll do it again to someone else. He needs to be taught a lesson!" Shay pleaded.

"It's just not right! The Lord says that vengeance is mine; I will repay. It's not up to me to retaliate. And besides, Paul would risk his job doing something that crazy."

Geneva spoke up, straightening her wig. "It's not you doing the repaying; it's us. The Lord works through people. Besides, the Bible does say that you reap what you sow."

"And," Shay added, "don't worry about Paul's job. Like I said, he's practically running things. He knows what he's doing."

Their argument was compelling. I did hate him for what he did to me. I did want him to pay. I did want to be around to see him pay. And, most importantly, I wanted him to know that he could never do this to anyone else.

I took a deep breath, and for the first time in a long time, I felt alive. "Okay, what's your plan?" I asked.

***

I shook like a leaf as the three of us sat in the back of Paul's unmarked police car. Paul, originally from Detroit, had a laidback, raw, and rough quality. Nothing warm and fuzzy about him. Paul didn't appear to take any mess. As a lead investigator, Shay reassured me that he knew the law inside and out. While we waited outside of the house being used as an undercover female police officer's home, Paul got on his digital radio, signaling to the other officers at the scene that a car of his make and model was approaching. My stomach ached. My entire body trembled as I sat sandwiched between Geneva and Shay.

"Okay, the suspect is pulling in the driveway and preparing to enter the residence," Paul said into his headset.

Geneva, Shay, and I held hands as Phillip got out of the car.

"It's okay," Shay whispered.

I didn't want to look, but I couldn't turn away as Phillip rang the doorbell of his supposed date. Tears slid down my face as I caught a glimpse of her and knew that he would make his move. Phillip and the undercover officer had gone out on three dates, and this was supposed to be their first date at her house, which wasn't her house at all. The undercover officer, a petite African American woman wearing tight-fitting clothes and glossy ruby red lips, opened the front door. Phillip held flowers behind his back for his date, just as he had done for me. She hugged him, and the door closed.

After a little over two hours of waiting, night fell and Paul went to the unmarked van where he could view the tape from the secret video cameras installed throughout the house. The three of us sat, at first nervous, but hopeful. As the minutes passed, I felt the hope dissipate, and I sulked, feeling defeated and embarrassed by all the hoopla. He wouldn't be stupid enough to do it to another so soon.

"It's okay, honey. They're going to catch him eventually. It may not be today, but he's not going to get away with it," Geneva offered.

"Let me tell you something about my man," Shay said. "He would not be spending this type of time, having all these folks involved unless he's on to something. He does not play when it comes to men mistreating and abusing women. He had never shared this with me before last night, but his mom was a victim of domestic violence. I hardly did any convincing about all of this, Des. He wanted to help. Plus, he found out that so-called Phillip had domestic violence charges filed against him about a year ago, but the woman dropped them."

"Look!" Geneva's eyes widened.

The three of us watched as Paul and another undercover officer from the van ran up to the door with their hands on their weapons.

"Sweet Jesus, please protect them," Shay whispered while we all watched in horror and disbelief.

Paul keyed in the front door, and they both bolted in. Within minutes, Paul and the other officer directed Phillip out of the house in handcuffs. While they made their way across the lawn toward the van, I nudged Shay and Geneva. "Let me out! Quick! I want to get out!"

They both tried to stop me, but I screamed, "Let me out now!"

Shay nearly fell out and I jumped out. Geneva followed.

"Phillip!" I yelled at the top of my lungs.

Paul and the other officer made Phillip stop. Phillip squinted, trying to make out who I was. I crept up toward him.

"Phillip! Warren! Or whatever your real name is"—I choked back tears—"I can't stand you for what you did to me!"

When Phillip realized it was me, he looked as if he'd seen a ghost. He looked down, avoiding eye contact.

"How many women have you done this to? How many? How many?" I screamed, sobbing.

The female decoy came to me first. "It's okay, honey," she said.

A neighbor stood on her front porch in her robe, trying to make sense of all the fuss, but I didn't care. "I hope you rot in jail!" I screamed. Geneva and Shay rushed to my side as they led him away. I fell to my knees, not caring about more neighbors who had also come out to observe the spectacle.

The female officer knelt to me and cupped my face in her hands. "It's okay. He's not going to be able to hurt anybody for a while, and hopefully ever again because of your courage."

I tried to whisper a thank you out to her, but I only made wailing sounds. I hugged her, and she rocked me.

By the time I had the strength to stand, I noticed Geneva and Shay had tear-streaked faces but were smiling. Not needing words, we held each other.

The other officer had taken Phillip to the station, and Paul stood leaning on the unmarked car with his hands folded, deep in thought.

I wiped my face and went to him. "Paul, thank you." I couldn't say anything that I wanted to say except that. Tears welled up again, and I managed to say again, "Thank you so much."

Paul, stoic and strong, unfolded his arms and stretched them out to me. I stepped to him and hugged him like I'd never hugged another man since my biological father. He then took me by the shoulders. "I know you don't want to press charges, but pray about that. Now that they have some hard evidence that he attempted to assault a female, you're more likely to be heard. Just think about it."

I nodded. "I will."

"Oh, by the way, you'll never guess what the dude's real name is."

"What?"

"Amnon."

"You're kidding."

"What's so special about that name? I've never even heard of it," Shay asked.

"Isn't he a bad character in the Bible?" Geneva said.

"Sure is," I answered. "Amnon raped Absalom's sister, Tamar," I answered.

Shay quipped, "Folks need to watch what they name their children."

I agreed in silence, but on the way home, I couldn't help but to think about the meaning of my own name.

CHAPTER 31

ISABELLA

The flowers appear on the earth; the time of the singing of birds is come.

—Song of Solomon 2:12

"I'm so thankful to God that you're home, Ms. Isabella," Kaylyn said, fluffing pillows around me. "It's a perfect day. I've never heard so many birds chirping."

"I hear 'em. They woke me up early this morning. Honey, I'm thankful. The devil counted me out, but God said, 'Not so!' I didn't think I'd get to see home again."

"You're a fighter, just like me. I knew that you'd be back home. I just knew it," Kaylyn said, sitting on the chair next to the bed.

"I just love the idea of seeing you while Desiree's at work, but I'm tired of all the fuss. You're young, and you have lots to do besides seeing about an old lady," I said.

"Oh, Ms. Isabella, there's nothing I'd rather be doing, believe that. We're a team. Besides, when I'm hanging out with you here, you can make sure that I keep up with my studying. I am so excited to be back at Alabama A&M. My counselor says if I go to school full time for the next two years, I can graduate!"

"That's wonderful! God is good! Now that you're on track for school, the only thing that seems to be missing is a male friend, if you know what I mean."

Kaylyn stood up, grinning from ear to ear. "Well, I guess I can tell you now that you're so much better."

"Tell me what? You been holding back on me? Child, you better put some kinda excitement in my life. All folks want to talk about with me anymore is cancer, medicine, and my treatments. I need to hear about what's really going on. People don't want to talk to me about nothing but sickness. I'm tired of that."

"Amen," she piped in. "Oh, I thought I was gonna scream at Uncle Beau last night. I'm so sick of being sick. I want to be normal for a while. *He* doesn't treat me like I'm sick."

"Okay, missy, spill the beans. Who's this *he?*"

Kaylyn beamed. "His name is Marvin, and he's a mechanic at his dad's shop. He takes night classes at Calhoun Community College. I met him when Uncle Beau took the truck in for service. He kept coming in and asking all kinds of silly questions. Uncle Beau wasn't having it at all, until Marvin sneaked and didn't charge him any labor for the brake job! Uncle Beau thinks he's pretty much okay now."

We both laughed. "So Marvin is kind of a smooth fella, huh? What does he look like?" I asked.

Kaylyn held the bedpost, gazing into the distance. "He looks like a young Denzel to me."

"Really?"

"Really! He's about six feet tall and the color of chocolate milk, heavy on the chocolate. Ms. Isabella, the man has perfect skin and dark ebony eyes."

"He certainly sounds like he's attractive, but you know I gotta ask the most important question."

"Before you ask, let me tell you. He's not only saved, but get this, he's a minister from Huntsville Heights Baptist. He's the first guy to tell me that my hair is cute as short as it is. He thinks the pixie cut shows off how pretty my face is." She giggled. "He calls me his Halle Berry. Isn't that a trip?"

"Well, that's quite a pair, Denzel and Halle!"

She ran her fingers through her short hair. "It's taken a lot of getting used to, but it's so much better than being bald and having to wear a scratchy wig or scarf."

"I know that's right. I'll be glad when mine grows back a little more. I don't want to be a downer, but you did tell him about your illness, didn't you?"

"Oh no, Ms. Isabella. I'm not trying to scare him off. I just want to be normal with him for a bit. He can't tell I'm sick so I've sworn Uncle Beau to secrecy. I want you to meet him, but please swear you won't say anything. I'll tell him soon."

"I don't swear, but I won't let the cat out the bag. I'm so happy for you. You deserve every little ounce of happiness life has for you and even more. I can't wait to meet Marvin. Maybe we can plan a little dinner. I'll give you and Desiree instructions about how to cook my pork ribs, baked beans, potato salad, and do you like coconut?"

"I love coconut, so don't say coconut cake!" She clapped her hands together.

"Good. I'll teach you how to bake my grandmama's coconut icebox cake—four layers of moist decadence. You'll have Marvin hooked when he finds out you cooked it."

"Mmmmmm! I can't wait to invite him, Ms. Isabella. You just gotta get lots of rest and take those blood thinners exactly how they say. Both of us could stand to gain a few pounds, so dinner is just what the doctor ordered!"

"I can't wait to meet Minister Marvin, the mechanic."

She got up and plopped across the foot of the bed. "Ms. Isabella, it's none of my business, but I'm just wondering if you think that you and Dr. Morrison are going to work out."

"Wow, you really cut to the chase. I don't remember saying that we were having any problems."

"I hate to tell you this, but it's painfully obvious that things aren't the best. I guess that's another positive thing cancer has done for me. I realize that I don't have time to play. I gotta get straight to it, you know what I'm saying? We have this one life to live here on earth, and I don't want you to spend it being unhappy."

"Indeed, I do." I struggled to sit up in the bed. "My plan has always been to stay married until death do us part, but I don't know now. People change, and some things just can't be fixed no matter how much you'd like. You're right about being sick though. It does make you see things quite differently. "

"So, Uncle Beau has a shot?" Kaylyn asked.

My eyes widened. "I'm not sure how to answer that question. I am a married woman. If things were different, well, maybe. He's a very nice man and a golden friend. I'm so thankful that our paths have crossed. Beyond that, I just can't say what the future holds; only God knows."

"I understand, Ms. Isabella, but in my perfect world, you and Uncle Beau would be together. You know that, right?"

I couldn't respond to that. Things weren't going as I'd planned, and I had held my marriage together by not considering other options. "I'm just glad to have you in my life, young lady. Is there something else on your mind, Kaylyn?"

"Actually, there is something. You can't breathe a word of it to Uncle Beau or anyone. You know how I told you about the abuse?"

I nodded.

"Well, about a month ago, I took your advice and joined a rape and incest survivor group."

"Oh good, Kaylyn. That's good news."

"Yes. I see a counselor there as well as attending group therapy. They're having an open meeting next week for survivors and their significant other, meaning husband, mother, sister, friend, et cetera. I know that it's probably too early to tell, but only if you feel well, I'd love for you to consider joining me."

"I wouldn't miss it for the world. So, does your Uncle Beau know about the abuse?"

"No! Are you kidding me? He'd flip his lid. It's been years, and I don't want a big production of it. I just want to heal. Between God's Word, the church, you, and now Marvin, I just want to get better, from the inside and out!"

"Don't we both," I said.

At Langley's insistence, the doctors changed two of my medications, which made a remarkable improvement in my energy level. I was finally able to be up and about for two to three hours at a time. Assured that the session wasn't for me, Langley agreed to drop Kaylyn and me off at the counseling office. Much like an AA meeting setup, the crisis center's counseling room had posters and art filling up nearly every space on the walls. One read: I listen when a girl says no. Do you? Another huge banner read: No Means No!

Women and their families straggled in as Kaylyn and I took our seats toward the middle of the room facing the easel. There seemed to be no one age or race represented. Women, both young old, black, brown, or white, came in filling the empty seats. What I thought would be a small group actually turned out to be quite large. By the time the leader began the meeting, at least thirty to forty people were in attendance.

Kaylyn bit her fingernails and shot a nervous grin now and then while the leader introduced herself and thanked the family members and friends for coming.

"That's Christy," she whispered. "She was abused terribly by an ex-husband. Now she's a leader here at the center. She's been really great to talk to."

I nodded while Christy rattled off alarming statistics. "Approximately sixty-six percent of rape victims know their assailant, and about forty-eight percent of victims are raped by a friend or acquaintance. So you see, an assailant is rarely the person who jumps out of the bushes. He is the acquaintance, neighbor, date, boyfriend, and yes, he can even be your husband."

While Christy dimmed the lights and started the slide presentation about sexual assault, I looked to my right as a few ladies rustled about to take their seats. I squinted, not believing my eyes. Desiree, Shay, and Geneva got seated on the other side of the room! I tried to attract their attention, but they concentrated on settling in and watching the presentation. I wondered why they were here, and who had been abused, Geneva or Shay. I felt so sad to think that either one of them had been raped or abused but proud that my daughter could be so support-ive of her friends. I tried to wave again, but with Desiree sandwiched between them, it was futile.

After the slideshow, Christy turned the lights on, and Kaylyn yanked my shirt, pointing to Desiree on the other side of the room. Immediately, Shay spotted me, nudging Desiree. As if she'd seen a ghost, Desiree's mouth opened and I could see her chest moving up and down. She closed her eyes, not bothering to wave. Geneva looked over and smiled, acknowledging my presence. Just then, I noticed Geneva's arm around Desiree, as if to console her.

I trembled and panicked all at once, trying to process Desiree's presence. Surely she wouldn't react like that if she were merely supporting a friend. I wanted to bolt across the room, snatch her out, and ask her what happened. I knew that I shouldn't though. I needed to stay calm. Getting her attention to signal her to leave the meeting and talk to me was useless. She wouldn't look my way. I felt dizzy and sick. Horrible thoughts and scenarios swirled around in my head. I couldn't move and didn't trust my body to cooperate at that moment.

After about fifteen minutes of the presentations, Christy continued, "So you see, family and friends, you are such an important part of the recovery journey for your loved one. They are not to blame for what's happened to them. It's not their fault. They don't need your condemnation, but they do need you to believe them, accept them, and walk with them through the difficult process of healing. Sexual assault is one of the most underreported crimes in the United States. Some studies suggest that less than twenty percent of all sexual assaults are reported to the police. One of the reasons why it is not reported is because it is very unlikely to lead to an arrest and conviction. As you all know, whether it's reported or not, the effects of a sexual assault can haunt survivors for a lifetime, especially if they don't seek treatment. That's why I'd like to thank you for taking the courageous step to seek help."

Applause echoed around the room from seemingly everyone but Desiree and me. For a while after Christy said these words, everything moved in slow motion. I didn't want to believe that my only daughter had been raped or abused. However, when survivors began to tell those stories, I tried to gain my composure and listen, for Kaylyn's sake and maybe for my daughter's.

Kaylyn surprised me when she pulled her iPad out and went to the podium. She hadn't told me that she would be speaking. She fidgeted with her iPad for a few second and began, "Like many of you, I feel like my life is the story of a survivor. When I was a teenager, a man, one who I, along with many others in the community highly respected, raped me."

Kaylyn zeroed in on me, took a deep breath and continued. "I didn't want it to happen, but he had become like the father I never had. He counseled me about the issues I was having with my mother. He bought me things and took me to get ice cream and things like that. I felt fortunate because he only selected certain girls in the neighborhood to treat this way. I was special. For once, I had the attention of a man. Little did I know, I had fallen into the hands of a child molester. By the time I discovered that I really needed help, he had moved on to another girl."

Tears streaked her face, and I wanted to grab her and my daughter and hide them to keep them safe, but I sat still, clutching my purse to my chest.

"I did try to tell my friend, and I told my mother. Neither believed me. I've kept all of these feelings on the inside for so long. Some people say that you can actually get diseases from bad feelings being locked inside. I'm not sure, but maybe that's what has happened to me. I don't want that to happen to any of you." She looked directly into my eyes and I nodded to her, prompting her to continue.

Kaylyn put her iPad down on the podium. "I've been ashamed, angry, distrustful, sad, and even guilty. Maybe if I'd told someone who'd listen I could have saved other girls from being abused. I'm thankful that God is a healer. He has given me an uncle who's as good as gold, and he's been teaching me to trust. I'm so thankful. He's given me a mother like I've never had. Thank you, Ms. Isabella. And a sister I've never had. Thank you, Desiree. Thank all of you for listening and for your support during my journey toward total restoration."

Once again applause filled the room as Kaylyn made her way back next to me. I smiled and patted her on the back. While I sat through the remainder of the meeting, I couldn't focus though, wondering what had happened to Desiree and why I hadn't noticed the signs.

CHAPTER 32

ISABELLA

*And call upon me in the day of trouble: I will deliver
thee, and thou shalt glorify me.*

—Psalm 50:15

After the group meeting at the crisis center, I exchanged
hugs with Desiree, Shay, Geneva and Kaylyn and then
politely but firmly pulled Desiree aside to let her know
that we needed to talk. Desiree agreed, and after we
dropped Kaylyn off at her house, we finally had some
alone time.

Desiree turned the music off from her car radio. "Okay,
Mama. Just don't ask me any questions that you don't
want the answers to."

"What's that supposed to mean?" I asked, trying not
to get an attitude. "Of course I want to know what's
happened to you. Why were you at the meeting? Someone
has violated you?" I tried to keep my voice from elevating
but couldn't.

Desiree drove, not flinching. "Yes. The answer is yes."

I swallowed hard. "Oh no! Who did it and when? What
happened?"

"It was a date, Mama. And it was a couple of months
ago."

I touched her shoulder. "And you didn't tell me?"

"I didn't tell anybody. Well, I mean, I didn't want to tell anybody."

"You told Shay and Geneva before you could tell me? I don't understand." I tried not to cry but couldn't help it.

"Please don't do that, Mama. I'm sorry. I haven't wanted to worry you. You're sick. You've got so much going on. The last thing you need to worry about is me."

I pulled myself together. "I'm not too sick to want to know something like this. I want to help you. I just wanted to be there for you."

"Mama, you almost died. I know you wanted to be there for me, but you are now. That's what important, right?"

"What happened? Who was it?" I asked nearly holding my breath.

"Mama, I'd rather not discuss the details. It's hard right now. What I will tell you is that it was a date situation. He's been arrested on other charges for attempting to assault someone else."

"So, you haven't filed charges?"

"No, I'm not ready for that."

"What do you mean you're not ready for that? You better go ahead and get ready."

Desiree pulled into the driveway and took the keys out of the ignition. "I don't want that right now. It's my choice, and I have a lot of things to consider. Besides, I can't prove a thing."

"Well, if he's tried it with someone else then—"

Desiree snapped, "Mama, I don't have proof. I'm not filing charges now and that's all I can tell you right now!" She yanked the keys out of the ignition.

In all of her life, Desiree had never spoken to me out of turn. I didn't allow it to offend me though. "Who did it?" I asked again.

"I'd rather not talk about that," she said, biting her bottom lip.

"Who did it?" I pleaded.

"Phillip, Mama," she whispered.

"Phillip? The engineer?" I couldn't believe it. I hadn't picked anything up from him, but I remembered that Aunt Gertrude had.

She looked at me. "Yes, Mama, the engineer."

"Where did it happen?"

"Why do you want to know?" she hissed.

"I don't know. Maybe there's evidence or something," I said, confused.

"This isn't a crime show, Mama."

"Just tell me where and I'll let things alone for now," I said.

"In my home."

"You let him come to your home alone? I told you to never do that, ever!"

"I'm not a child, Mama. You've told me not to do a lot of things."

"For your own good, Desiree."

She rolled her eyes. "Yes, I know. I should've listened. And yes, it's my fault. I am dealing with that."

"For heaven's sake, no! I'm not saying it's your fault. I'm just saying that it's not safe. None of this is coming out right. I know I said that it was the last question, but I do have another one."

She crossed her arms across her chest. "Okay."

"Were you a . . ."

"A what?"

I fidgeted with my blouse, unable to say the word.

"A virgin? Is that what you're asking me?"

"Well, yes."

"No, I wasn't."

I sank down into the seat and practiced the deep breathing techniques I had learned during labor. Although I'd pretty much figured out that Desiree had given herself to someone in that way, I'd still clung to the hope that she hadn't.

"I know that I'm a huge disappointment to you, Mama. However, I have never slept around. Just so you know, I'm also a huge disappointment to me."

"Desiree, why would you say that? You're far from a disappointment to me. I'd hoped that you'd wait before giving yourself to someone in marriage, but it's done. Nobody is perfect. We all make mistakes, but I'm proud of you. The rape wasn't your fault, not at all. He needs to be punished for what he did though." Without warning, my head began to spin, and I felt faint. "I'm not feeling well at all."

"Come on, Mama. This is all too much for you. This is what I didn't want to happen. I'm just fine, and I want you to be well."

Desiree helped me in the house and gave me my medications. We didn't talk about the rape anymore. Before I knew it, I fell into a deep sleep.

As I lay in the bed, the sun that crept through the curtains shined a bit too bright. I couldn't imagine that I'd slept the rest of the afternoon and night away into the next morning.

Suddenly, the days started blending right into another. I couldn't tell how many days I'd been in the bed, mostly sleeping. People started visiting, and I noticed that they all talked too loud. The television stayed off because the sound had become too much for me. I despised the jiggling of pills spilling out of the bottle into my hand, and I nearly cried every few hours when I forced myself to swallow them down. As my health deteriorated, I had come to the realization that death loomed before me. My faith was strong but my body was not. All I could do was sleep, and I wanted to be left alone.

Desiree or Langley must've called my doctor who probably rarely did house calls. I knew Langley had pulled some strings. The doctor instructed Langley to call hospice. I knew that much.

I couldn't stand the light tap on the door that would come every few hours, no matter who it was from. Still, I tried to cling to my Southern hospitality and religion when I heard the light tapping. "Come in," I whispered.

Kaylyn, who hadn't missed a day of coming to see about me, said, "She insists on seeing you."

I didn't bother to ask who she was.

"Mother Morrison, I had to come to see you. It's Georgia," she said as if I couldn't see her.

My head felt heavy and I couldn't sit up. "Hello, Georgia. You can have a seat here beside me. Pull the chair up."

Georgia examined what little she could see of me. "You don't look so bad," she said.

I didn't know why that struck me as funny, but I laughed. And I laughed until she laughed too. We both laughed until we cried. Georgia grabbed a few tissues from my nightstand, handing me a few and keeping one. She looked into my eyes and pulled me close to her and hugged me. Her large frame swallowed me up, and I closed my eyes. I went limp in her arms, and she rubbed her large hands circling my back, melting my hurt away. I smelled lemons and mint from my grandmother's housedress. I felt my sister Jo's raspy voice comforting me. For those minutes, I felt like God Himself was telling me to rest.

When Georgia let go, she gently caressed her hand over my now all-gray hair and leaned me back onto the pillow without a word. Her smile at me wasn't full of pity or sorrow, but compassion. I soaked it in, basking in its glow. She pulled the blankets up under my neck and sat back in the rocking chair. As she rocked back and forth, the creak in the chair sounded sweet, lulling me into a deep, peaceful sleep.

When I awoke, Georgia was gone. In fact, I didn't know for sure if she was really there until Kaylyn came in and reassured me that she had been and left. It was almost as if Georgia's visit had been that of an angel because I felt more refreshed and rested than I'd felt in a while. I started to protest when Kaylyn opened the curtains, but it felt nice to get a little natural light in the room.

"The doctor says you need to eat more, Ms. Isabella. Iron-rich foods will do you good, so Uncle Beau made a pot of his famous pinto beans. I made some sautéed spinach."

"That's so kind of you, but, honey, I can't eat a thing. You two didn't need to go to all that trouble for me. You got to be takin' care of yourself. How you been feeling?"

Kaylyn helped me to sit up and directed me to the rocking chair while she changed the sheets. "Don't you even try to get me to stop changing these sheets either. You'd do the same thing for me, right?" Kaylyn said, stripping the sheets.

I smiled. "Thank you, dear. So, I refused to change the subject. How are you feeling?" I asked.

"Well, I'm not feeling bad at all. Besides Uncle Beau, I guess you'll be the first to know that they found some more cancer."

"Oh, honey, no. I'm sorry," I said.

"Yeah, but the doctors have reassured me that it doesn't appear to be much to worry about. I just gotta do another round of chemo," she said much too casually.

"It's gonna be okay. I hate being so sick that I can't help you. I feel so helpless. I am praying though. God is going to see you through."

"I know. I really believe it. For once, I'm not worried about it. He's going to do it for you too."

"Yes, I believe that He can."

"He will!" Kaylyn corrected.

"So, I know that you told me that you and Marvin are getting really close. Don't you think you'd better tell him about your illness now?"

"It looks like I'm not gonna have a choice. We see each other every day." She smoothed the wrinkles out of the comforter in wide strokes.

"That's so good. I'm mighty happy for you, Kaylyn. You just be honest with him."

"I'm scared to tell Marvin, but he says he's in love with me."

"That's wonderful, and if he really loves you, he'll stick it out with you. Don't you worry about that. Just tell him, so your relationship is open and honest from the jump."

"Who's in love with somebody?" Desiree asked softly, appearing in the entrance of the bedroom.

We hadn't really addressed our issues. I had felt too overwhelmed and sick to bring it up, but I felt ready. I didn't know how long I had left, and I couldn't have her misreading my feelings about her.

Kaylyn grinned. "Hey, Desiree, what's up?"

"Boy, I haven't seen any sun in this room for days. It looks nice, and thanks for changing Mama's bed, Kaylyn. How are you two?"

"I'm doin' some better, but Kaylyn here was just givin' me the update on her and Marvin."

"I see," Desiree said, shaking her head. "It's like that now?"

Kaylyn smiled again. "Yep, it's just like that. He's wonderful. I just hope he stays wonderful when he finds out about my diagnosis."

Desiree looked skeptical. "Oh, he doesn't know?"

"No, not yet, so say a prayer for me," Kaylyn said.

"It will be fine. He loves you, so it'll be fine. I'll be praying though."

Kaylyn took a seat on the floor and Desiree entered, sitting down on the edge of the bed. She eyed my medications. "Mama, you did take your afternoon meds, right?"

"Of course I did, baby. Kaylyn made sure of that. So, how are you?"

"I'll be glad when spring break comes. I'm a little tired, but I can't complain. Other than that, I've been helping Shay get ready for her wedding."

"A wedding? I love weddings. I can't wait to get married," Kaylyn said, smiling.

"Looks like one may be closer than you think," Desiree offered.

Kaylyn's face clouded. "I don't know why I can't just have a normal life. I'd always dreamed of getting married, having kids, and the white picket fence. My childhood was so totally messed up. I just wanted to have a real family, like you all have."

"You'll have that, baby. You just take things one day at a time," I said.

"I've only recently begun to dream about it again. Marvin has opened up my eyes to so many new possibilities. I have met so many breast cancer survivors with my kind of cancer, so I know with the Lord's help, I can beat it."

I nodded. "You will."

"Definitely, and you will too, Mama," Desiree said.

"I don't know what I'd do without my uncle. My Aunt Caroline and Uncle Beau took me in after my grandmother passed, and they've been great parents. Uncle Beau's had a hard go of it since Aunt Caroline passed away from a sudden heart attack, so we've been pretty much connected at the hip since."

"He's told me about his wife. She sounds like she was a wonderful woman. I know that it's been hard on both of you."

"Yeah, she was so sweet, just like you, Ms. Isabella. You remind us both of her."

"I know that's a compliment, and I thank you for it."

Kaylyn looked deep in thought. "I do have a question for you two though. You know, Uncle Beau and Aunt Caroline made me go to church, but it was boring, really no young people. I'm wondering about some things."

"Okay, such as?" I said.

"I want to know why bad things happen to good people. I want to know why God allows babies to die. I want to know why even people who are strong in the Lord have to suffer and die. Why would a God who loves us allow us to experience pain, disease, and heartache?"

I generally kept the upper hand with Kaylyn. Over the past months, I'd been able to share and explain scriptures with her, only I didn't have answers to her questions this time, not completely anyway. I had some of those same questions myself.

Desiree jumped right in when she realized that I was silent on the subject. "I can't believe you're asking this question at this time, Kaylyn. I've been struggling with this very issue. I mean, there's so much going on that is so bad."

"Exactly," Kaylyn chimed.

"Well, the Lord is showing me that His perfect plan was for us to walk in fellowship and harmony with Him. If we understood everything about God, He wouldn't be God. So, we're not going to have all of the answers in this life, but He reveals things to us in His Word, His people, and through our experiences. I do believe that in the beginning we weren't made to experience pain, heartache, and suffering. Think back to Adam and Eve in the garden. Everything was perfect until the Fall of Man."

"What do you mean by the Fall of Man?" Kaylyn asked.
I added, "The Fall of Man just refers to the book of Genesis in the Bible. Initially, Adam and Eve were obedient and innocent. After they were tempted by the serpent to eat from the Tree of Knowledge of Good and Evil, one that was forbidden by God, they disobeyed God and ate of the tree."

Desiree continued, "As a result of their disobedience, Adam and Eve became ashamed of their nakedness and were expelled from the paradise. At this point, original sin was committed and with that, the fall of man. Because of this original sin, all of mankind is born into sin. The world is in a fallen state and is not the world God intended for us to live in. For example, we have diseases, accidents, natural disasters, and sin all around us because of the original sin."

"I'm not trying to be funny or anything, but what's the point of Jesus then? Isn't He supposed to be greater than all of the evil?"

Desiree amazed me by her knowledge of the subject. I nearly held my breath waiting for her to answer.

"Kaylyn, the Lord has been revealing to me through His Word and prayer that Jesus is our one and only way back to God the Father. Jesus *is* greater than evil. Through Him, we have access to eternal life—a life with no sickness, no disease, no natural disasters, no heartaches, no pain, and no death. It's actually really exciting."

Kaylyn looked unsure. "Okay, I know I've sinned, so maybe I got what's coming to me with this cancer, but what about newborn babies, people who are truly innocent?"

"That's just the thing," Desiree answered. "None of us are innocent. We are all born into sin. I was just reading in Romans 3:23 where it says that we have all sinned and come short of the glory of God. Romans 7:24 says something like we are all dead in trespasses and sins. When bad things happen, it doesn't have to be because of a sin you've committed, although sometimes it is. Mama, do you remember where that scripture is when the disciples ask Jesus about why the man is blind?"

I got my Bible off my nightstand and looked in the concordance. "Okay, here it is in John 9:1–12." I read how the disciples had asked Jesus if a man who had been blind since birth was afflicted because of a sin committed by him or his parents. Jesus told the disciples that he wasn't blind because of a sin committed by him or his parents. I read on about how Jesus healed the man.

Desiree said, "This is just one of the many examples of the Bible that let us know that tragedy and suffering don't necessarily have to come from one specific sin. God allows things to happen, but as believers, we are to trust that He will and should get the glory out of it. Through it all, we have to believe and trust in Him, no matter what the cost."

Kaylyn added, "Maybe God allowed the man to be born blind so that others could see Jesus heal him."

"You're getting the picture, Kaylyn. Hey, Mama, may I see your Bible?"

I smiled and handed it to her. She flipped the pages until she settled on Romans. "There's a scripture that comes to mind in Romans 5:12. It says, 'Wherefore, as by one man sin entered into the world, and death by sin and so death passed upon all men, for that all have sinned.'" She skipped to verse 15. "'But not as the offence, so also is the free gift. For if through the offence of one many be dead, much more the grace of God, and the gift of grace, which my one man, Jesus Christ, hath abounded unto many.'"

Kaylyn asked, "Okay, so Adam, one man, caused sin to enter into the world and the sin would really sentence us all to death, but Jesus' death makes it so that we have access to eternal life?"

I answered, "Exactly, Kaylyn. Until Jesus returns, we all have to face death one day. We don't know all the whys, but one thing is certain: we will experience a permanent separation from Him when we die if we don't accept Him as our personal Savior. He was the perfect sacrifice for our sins."

Kaylyn said, "I'm not gonna pretend that I understand all of it, but this has helped. I'm so glad that God used you both to help me. I guess I've never really thought about it like that."

"Desiree, baby, I can tell you've really been studying and searching the Word. I hadn't thought about it quite like that either, even bein' saved all these years. Some things we can't really ever understand no how, but we gotta be ready. All things work together for the good," I said, echoing her sentiments.

Kaylyn stood up proudly and recited, "'All things work together for the good of those that love the Lord and are called according to His purpose.' I do know that I probably wouldn't be saved without the illness. Don't get me wrong, I don't like it and pray that the Lord heals me daily. But the thing is, even in something this terrible, He has turned it around for His good. I am so thankful for you both."

When I searched Desiree's face, I saw that she had felt compassion for Kaylyn. My daughter got up and embraced Kaylyn.

CHAPTER 33

DESIREE

*For I reckon that the sufferings of this present time
[are] not worthy [to be compared] with the glory which
shall be revealed in us.*

—Romans 8:18

Mama had been readmitted to the hospital for almost
three weeks with little to no improvement. In spite of my
new insight as to why God allows bad things to happen to
good people, I nearly crumbled under the pressure. The
doctors insisted that they were making her comfortable
and even reassured us that once we got her home, we
could call on hospice. Dad and I couldn't bear the thought
of calling hospice for Mama. We still believed that the
doctors could do something.

Falling apart at the seams, Dad moped around,
unshaven and unkempt. He refused to see patients or
do anything much except sit by Mama's bedside. The
intelligent, arrogant, and proud man my stepfather had
always been vanished as Mama's health deteriorated.
Most people probably thought that Mama needed Dad,
but her sickness allowed me to see how much he'd really
depended on Mama.

There were so many things wrong with Mama that
almost daily her most serious medical issues grew worse

or mutated into something different. She had developed lymphedema, cellulitis, a possible blood clot, as well as terrible side effects from the latest drug, lapatinib. Even her surgically implanted chemo port got infected.

I tried to be strong for her, but I had to admit that my heart felt faint. I didn't know how much more her body could take.

Mama would have small bursts of energy when she would talk and laugh, but they were few and far between. There was mostly just the hum of the machines hooked up to her and the occasional swing of the hospital door as people came in and out, filling the dead silence. She had even stopped requesting to hear sermons and gospel music.

I graded papers while Mama slept, astonished to read yet another narrative about a family trip to Disney World. After three C papers in a row, I was ready to take a break until I read the title of the next one, "Hope with Leukemia," by Jessica Stuart. Cancer popped up everywhere I turned, rearing its ugly head, slowing progress. Just as I set the stack of papers onto the nearest table, Dad came in. We had had little to no conversation for months unless it was about Mama. After several minutes of small talk about Mama, Dad cleared his throat and jammed his hands in his pockets.

"Desiree, why don't you get something to eat?"

I wanted to jump at the chance to get away from him, but I didn't want to leave Mama. "No, thanks, but I'm not hungry."

He fiddled with Mama's machines like he always did. Just then, the door swung open. An African American male nurse entered and greeted me. "Hello, there. I've met you, Dr. Morrison," the nurse said, shaking Dad's hand. "But I didn't meet you. I'm guessing you must be Mrs. Morrison's daughter, Desiree. You look just like your mother. She's told me a lot about you."

"Yes, that's me, in the flesh. I hope it was all good. Is everything okay?"

"Everything is fine. I'm Roman and I'm going to be her nurse for the next shift." Roman walked up to the bed and checked her machines and tubes.

"I just checked everything, and it looks good," Dad said.

Roman smiled, looking at me. "I appreciate that, Dr. Morrison, but I still need to check for myself or I'll risk my job security."

I smiled back.

"Mrs. Morrison, I need to ask you some questions about how you're feeling, all right now?" Roman asked as he gently tapped Mama. She didn't move a muscle.

I came to the opposite side of the bed. "Mama, the nurse wants you to wake up for a minute, okay?"

Her eyelids only partially opened. "Okay, I'm sorry. Seem like I'm always so tired."

Roman slowly lifted Mama's hospital bed and began to ask her a few questions. I felt a little weird with Roman. I hadn't had much contact with a male nurse; yet, I liked his confident manner, kind expression, and woodsy cologne. After Roman asked Mama a few questions, he took a few quick notes on his clipboard and said, "Okay, well, I apologize for interrupting your nap, Mrs. Morrison. However, I think I smell your dinner tray coming."

"Well, I best be goin' back to sleep then," Mama whispered.

Roman chuckled. "I know what you mean, but it's important for you to try to eat. Let's make a deal. If you don't see anything you like on the tray, buzz me, and we'll see about getting you something else, okay?" He cleared her tabletop and pushed her bed tray in front of her.

"Thank you," Mama said.

"It's no problem." Roman turned to me and smiled, flashing his straight teeth, which exposed a tiny gap and deep dimples. "Really, let me know if either one of you wants or needs anything."

"Thanks so much," I said.

He walked briskly to the doorway and stopped short. "Oh, it's nice to meet you, Desiree. Pretty name," Roman said, leaving the room.

Mama perked up some. "What'chu think about him, honey?"

"Oh, Mama! I don't believe you."

"Did you see the way he looked at you? I think he's sweet on you, and I didn't see no ring either."

Dad, awkward and silent for the most part, finally said, "Why don't I let you two ladies chat a bit? I'll be back so you can grab a bite to eat in about, let's say, twenty minutes, Desiree?"

I nodded, glad for him to leave. Mama and I could continue our conversation without the uncomfortable presence of Dad.

"Mama," I said, "he was only in here for a second, and you know a lot of married men don't wear rings for one reason or another." I had no interest in meeting anyone. I knew that I'd never do Internet dating again and felt resolved to live my life without male companionship; at least, for a very long time.

An orderly entered the room and put Mama's tray in front of her. The orderly lifted the plate cover and Mama gasped. "My word, what happened to that chicken?" In spite of it all, Mama tried to keep her sense of humor. The orderly laughed as he made a quick getaway.

"You want me to get the nurse to get you something else?" I asked.

Mama raised her eyebrows. "Why not?"

"Oh, Mama, do you really want something else?"

"No," she admitted. "I just thought it'd be fun for you."

"I don't think that you're as sick as they say, fooling around like that." I cut up her chicken, seasoned her carrots and mashed potatoes, and added sugar to her tea while she picked at her food.

"Desiree, since we're here alone and I've got a little energy, I want to talk with you a minute," Mama said, putting the cover back on her uneaten meal.

I sat back in the chair, hoping that she wouldn't bring up the Phillip ordeal.

"Being sick like this has a few advantages because you think of so many things you don't have time to think about when you're well," Mama explained.

"Like what, Mama?"

"I love you more than my life, Desiree."

"I know that." I nodded, not wanting to have this conversation.

"Just let me say this now. I was hard on you in a lot of ways, but it's always been because I love you, honey." Mama took a tiny sip of her tea. "I know I've said things about your weight over the years, and those things, I see now, have hurt you. I just thought it'd be better comin' from me than the world. I didn't want you to be disadvantaged in any way, but it was wrong. As long as you're healthy, weight doesn't matter."

"I know this, Mama. Please, you don't need to explain anything," I said, feeling uncomfortable and like Mama was giving me a deathbed confession.

She continued, "I should've reversed it and been that safe place for you to land. I just wanted you to be tough and the best that you could be. I couldn't see that you were better than the best all along."

My eyes filled with tears.

Mama took a tissue, dabbed at her eyes, and reflected, "I brought a lot of baggage from my past to you, and I'm sorry. As much as my grandmother loved me, she got some stuff wrong, and I passed that on to you. I want you to be happy, and happiness isn't just about being with a man. There's more to it. You got to have the Lord at the center of your life. I mean you got to let Him love you and you gotta love Him with your whole heart, not just a part of it. Then, He fills you with His love and it spills out so you love yourself and other people unconditionally. That's what God's love can do for you."

Mama dabbed at her eyes again and her voice cracked when she said, "I made a mess of things marrying your dad for mostly the wrong reasons. I've repented, and I'd be mighty sad to know that you'd go and make the same mistakes. Only reason you need to marry a man is because it's the good Lord's will. Don't do it for money, 'cause you're afraid of being alone, or for any other reason." Mama took a deep breath and stared into my eyes. "Oooh, sweetie, if your daddy Ray could see how pretty and smart his daughter is, boy, he'd be so proud and happy. You wait until God sends you a man like your daddy. Please don't ever settle for less than what God has for you."

"Thank you, Mama," I said, wishing that she'd stop. It felt too final, too much like the end.

Mama leaned back onto her pillow. "You don't need to thank me. It's the truth. You've been through a lot over this past year, but the good Lord has kept you. You don't let what happened to you make you fearful. You can be careful without being fearful. Whether you decide to press charges or not, I support you. I'm sorry for pressuring you to do something you're not ready to do."

"Please, Mama. I know that you only want what's best for me. I understand," I said.

"You'll understand so much better when you have a child. And that will happen, baby. Trust me. I feel it in my spirit. If you have an aching in your spirit to be married, God will fill that desire in you. Just trust Him."

Mama continued. "I have surrendered everything to Him, Desiree. But I don't feel that my time is long, and I want you to start talking to me. You've had a lifetime of listening to me, and I'm so sorry I didn't listen more. I'm listening now, and I don't want there to be any unfinished business left between us, whether that time I have is long or short."

The last thing on earth I wanted to do was to upset Mama, but I did have a few things that I wanted to say. I wasn't prepared to unload about Dad, but I did ask her about my biological dad. "Mama, when I was really young, I remember overhearing you and Aunt Jo talking about Daddy."

"You did?" Mama asked.

"Well, I remember Aunt Jo saying that you killed Daddy by making him move from Dothan to Huntsville."

Mama smiled. "Ahhhh, yes, I do remember her saying that. You heard that? Oh no! That's terrible that you heard that. What you must have thought all this time!" Mama took a deep breath. "Jo, along with both of our extended families, had a fit when Ray and I decided to move to Huntsville. Me and Ray both made that decision, and truth be told, Ray talked me into it. Jo was mad as fire when we moved, and she thought I was behind the move. I loved my sweet sister but that girl could make you pay when she was mad. Baby, your father had a heart condition from childhood. I don't know why, but it was just Ray's time to be with the Lord," Mama explained.

I felt relieved, but before I could respond, Dad walked in with an armful of flowers.

Mama looked weary but smiled anyway. "Those are lovely, Langley, but you shouldn't have done that."

"The least I could do for you, Isabella." He came in and put the flowers on the windowsill.

I knew that this was my cue to leave them alone, so I headed to the cafeteria to get something to eat. On my way to the elevator, I ran into Beau.

"Hey there, Desiree!" he greeted me.

"Hello, Beau," I said, attempting to shake the cool tone from my words.

"How's your mama doin'?" he asked, twisting his cap in his hands.

"She's about the same, not too good. Actually, I'm sorry that you came up here right now; Dad is talking to her now."

I could see Beau putting two and two together. "Oh, I see," he said. Beau's brightness faded quickly. "So, you headed home?"

"No, I'm going to grab some dinner from the cafeteria."

"Oh, do you mind if I join you? I don't want to interrupt. I think I'll stick around for a while so I can just at least say hello to her," Beau said.

"I don't mind," I said, knowing that I really did mind him joining me. The thought of Beau made me cringe, but I couldn't say no. I had gotten to accept Mama's relationship with Kaylyn, but Beau still grated my nerves. He and Mama were like two peas in a pod, while Mama and Dad were polar opposites. Beau wanted to be with my mother and I knew it. Her sickness and marriage were really the only things keeping them apart. Sometimes, I didn't even think Mama's marriage to Dad was what kept them apart since it seemed to be hanging on by a string.

Once we made it to the cafeteria, we went through the line. I realized that Beau didn't meet a stranger; he was a real happy camper. He smiled and spoke to everyone as if he'd known him or her all of his life. When we checked out, he even insisted on paying for my dinner, despite my protests.

I had opted for the Alfredo and a gelatin cup. Beau had a plate of fried chicken, potato salad, beans, rolls, and corn on the cob. He could barely fit the huge slice of sweet potato pie and drink on his tray. I began to eat, but Beau reminded me to say grace, which he said aloud. "Lord, you been good to us today and every day. Heal Ms. Isabella and Kaylyn. Bless this food and sanctify it, in Jesus' name. Amen." As soon as Beau said "Amen," I swallowed the bite of food I had taken and tried not to look embarrassed that I could forget to bless my food. Beau grabbed the hot sauce and began shaking it all over his chicken with an intensity that even I couldn't appreciate.

"That's a lot of hot sauce," I said, looking around to see if anyone was looking at him.

"Yeah, love the stuff," he said, biting into his chicken.

"So, how's Kaylyn? I haven't seen her in a few days," I said.

Beau finished chewing but left bits of crust around his mouth. "I ain't gonna tell Isabella. Don't want her worryin', but Kaylyn is in this very hospital. She's gonna be fine though. They're just running some tests. That chemo takes so much outta her, you know?"

"Gee, I'm sorry to hear that. I had no idea. I thought she was in remission. I'll be sure to visit before I leave."

"Well, don't you worry about her. She's young and the doctor says that this is pretty common. Just say a prayer for her. Kaylyn's worried about your mom and wants to see her, but I told her to stay put for now. I'm just gonna be real about this. As you know, your mama's cancer is very aggressive. There's so much more they can do to help in Kaylyn's situation. We need the Lord to work a miracle for your mom."

I knew that he was right. I just didn't want to face Mama's situation. It was all too much too fast. "Yeah, we do," I said. "I'll have to drop by to see Kaylyn before I leave. Thank you for telling me."

Beau talked with his mouth full. "I'm glad that we're having this time to talk, Desiree."

"Me too," I said, not meaning it.

Beau swallowed his food and finally wiped his mouth with his napkin. "Isabella and I have gotten really close over these months, you know?"

I looked away, but said, "Yes, I know."

"I am going to cut to the chase. I know that she's married. The thing is, she's told me that she's thinking of divorcing your dad when she gets better. I'm sure that she's told you."

I stabbed my spoon into the gelatin cup. "As a matter of fact, she hasn't shared that information with me," I said, shocked that Mama would tell Beau and not me.

Beau's eyes widened. "Oh, I'm sorry then. I didn't know. I just figured that she'd told you since you two are so close!"

"Apparently we're not as close as you or I think," I said.

Beau frowned. "I can see that this has taken you off guard, Desiree, and I'm sorry for that. You know that your father and mother have had a boatload of problems—"

I interrupted. "Which wouldn't be your business."

Beau nodded. "Yes, you do have a point, but I care deeply for your mother. I just wanted you to know that. I never thought I'd feel this way again after my wife Caroline passed, but God has blessed me—I mean, us."

"I'm sorry. I don't know what you mean by 'us.' Does Mama know how you feel?"

Beau cleared his throat. "I have told her some. Let's put it like this, we both care deeply about each other."

"Beau, no disrespect but my mother is fighting for her life. She has no time to think about divorce, separation, or your feelings for her. Besides, has my mother told you that my father desperately wants to reconcile with her?"

Beau pushed his tray away and said, "Isabella did mention that he wanted to work things out, but she's told me that the marriage is pretty much over."

Upset that he refused to let the conversation go, I raised my voice. "She may have said this to you, but it's not over legally. I don't want to overstep my bounds with you or my mom, but like I said, my mother is in no state to even entertain a relationship with you or anyone else. Her life is in the balance right now. As you reminded me, she has the deadliest form of cancer. If you care about her, leave her alone."

Beau hung his head, looking hurt, and said, "I realize the seriousness of her condition, and that's one reason why I need to be honest with you and her. I intend on helping her fight this so that we can possibly have a future together. Please forgive me if I seem a little self-centered by bringing all of this up with her in the hospital. I've come to realize how precious and short life is, and I don't intend on wasting a minute of it."

I lowered my voice, now almost pleading. "Please, Beau, I'm asking you not to complicate things for my mother or our family. You really don't want to put yourself in the middle of this thing with my parents. Let them work this out without outside influences."

Beau leaned in toward me. "Desiree, your father hasn't been there in all these years for your mom. She's told me so. I can help her fight this. If she really understands how much I love her, she might have more incentive to fight."

"Don't think so much of yourself, Beau. You're a nice man, and my mother recognizes that. I recognize that, but things are complicated. Furthermore, my mother is not alone. I've always been right here for her, and my dad is trying his best to find his way back into her heart so please, for the sake of our family, leave us alone." I got up from the table, leaving my tray and Beau behind, thinking how much I hated this hospital cafeteria.

CHAPTER 34

ISABELLA

Fear thou not; for I [am] with thee: be not dismayed;
for I [am] thy God: I will strengthen thee; yea, I will
help thee; yea, I will uphold thee with the right hand of
my righteousness.

—Isaiah 41:10

"Ms. Isabella, Ms. Isabella, please wake up!"

I opened my eyes and a blurry face appeared. I rubbed my eyes slowly, trying to wake up. After almost three weeks in the hospital, days ran together.

"Oh, please wake up, Ms. Isabella."

"Kaylyn, dear," I said groggily. "It's so nice to see you."

"Can I lift your bed up a bit?" she asked with excitement that clearly couldn't be contained.

"Sure, honey, sit me up." The medications kept me in a fog, but I tried to regroup for her sake. I had begun to feel better over the past few days, but I knew not to be fooled by that. My health stayed up and down, depending on the day.

Kaylyn waved her left hand in front of me. "Guess what?" she sang.

"Hmmm, let me guess," I kidded.

"Oh, can you believe that Marvin asked me to marry him, Ms. Isabella? Can you believe it?"

"Yes, as a matter of fact, I can. Now keep that hand still so I can see it." She held her hand up close, and I examined the small round solitaire, brilliant and clear as crystal.

"Oh my! Kaylyn, that's a beauty. He done good with that now."

"I am so happy," she cried. "Okay, Marvin is right outside in the hall. If it's okay, he wants to come in to say hello."

"Girl, I'm a mess. Hand me that brush over there," I said, pointing to the wall shelf. I brushed the little bit of hair that I had and put a dab of Chapstick on my parched lips.

Kaylyn said cheerfully, "You look fine, Ms. Isabella!"

"Don't have your fiancé in the hall, for Pete's sake. Let him in," I told her.

Marvin appeared to blush as he walked in, grinning from ear to ear. "Hi there, Ms. Isabella."

"Hi, yourself, Marvin. I hear that congratulations are in order."

"Yes, ma'am," he said, nodding.

"I am so happy for both of you. Kaylyn has told me so much about you. You got a good girl here," I said.

"Absolutely, ma'am," he said, smiling.

Kaylyn grabbed his hand and they gazed into each other's eyes, reminding me of how Ray and I had been so many years ago. "So, I know it's early, but have you all talked about dates yet?" I asked.

They both began to speak at the same time. Marvin offered, "You go ahead, Kay." He even had a little pet name for her.

She smiled. "I've always wanted a big summer wedding, but Marvin here wants to do it now."

"Well, you've got time," I said, so sad to think that I probably didn't. I hoped that I could be there to witness her dream coming true, but I just didn't know.

***

Most of the time I stayed in a fog, too tired to think clearly about things. But, in the moments by myself in the hospital room, I reflected on my life, prayed, and recalled scriptures from memory. I was so thankful for all the years I had read and studied the Word because I could see the words on the pages in my mind. Scriptures flew across my mind one after the other. Psalms 103:3–4 would rush in like a hurricane, blocking all negative thoughts.

He who healeth all thy diseases; who redeemeth thy life from destruction; who crowneth thee with loving kindness and tender mercies.

Then, I'd remember all the times when Jesus healed the sick and even how Paul healed the cripple that "had the faith to be healed." I remembered so many of the sermons I'd heard over the years, ones I'd never even realized that I'd committed to memory. I remembered that Pastor had preached a dynamic sermon about Jesus giving power to the disciples "to heal all manner of sickness and all manner of disease" from Matthew 10:1. I meditated on His Word day and night, whenever I was lucid, even though I couldn't read it. The Word was hidden in my heart.

I knew that the doctors had given up, but I believed God more. I believed that God was able to do exceedingly and abundantly more than I could ask or think. Sure, I couldn't deny the sickness that ravaged my physical body, but I knew it was just my shell. Sickness couldn't touch my spiritual wholeness. For the very first time, I truly understood what Paul meant when he said, "To live is Christ to die is gain." Either way, I had the victory, but I believed God could heal me. I just didn't know if He would.

***

Beau's visits were few, but when he did come, I would get a renewed spark of energy. His presence made me feel relaxed and protected. Beau didn't put on any airs or have anything to prove. He just was who he was, and I felt good being me.

I had been up sitting in the chair by the window, drinking a cup of black coffee, when I heard a tap on the hospital door.

"Hello, Isabella," he said in an unusually serious voice.

"Beau, come on and have a seat. I actually had the stomach for some coffee. Never thought I'd see a morning without it, but since this cancer, I'd lost my taste for it."

"Well, I'm glad you can enjoy that then," Beau said, pulling a chair next to me.

"You seem serious. Is Kaylyn okay?" I asked.

Beau crunched his hat in his hand. "She's okay. She's getting testing done to make sure that the cancer hasn't spread, but all is well."

I smiled. "Well, good for her then."

Beau frowned. "It's just that I've been doin' a lot of thinkin' lately, Isabella."

Relieved, I asked, "So, what is it, Beau?"

He stared down into his lap, then into my eyes. "I know this isn't appropriate, and I'm all about doing the right thing at the right time. But, the thing is, I'm gonna bust if I don't let it out."

"Okay," I said as I set my coffee cup down on the table.

"I've just got to let you know how I feel about you," Beau blurted out.

My stomach dropped. I didn't want to know and wanted to know at the same time.

"Isabella, I know this timing isn't the best, and I know you're still married. I just want you to know that I have strong feelings for you."

"You've told me that. Remember, I've told you that I care a lot about you too, Beau." I fidgeted with the hospital gown.

He placed a hand over mine to get me to make eye contact. "No, it's more than that." He leaned in toward me, and suddenly, I could hear myself breathing.

"I'm in love with you, Isabella," Beau confessed.

My mind told me to snatch my hand away, but my heart wouldn't let me. I'd never seen Beau so serious, and the truth was that he had ignited so many feelings in me that I had thought were gone. He made me laugh. I felt comfortable spending time with him. He was my friend. Still, I was married, and more than that, I didn't know how much longer I'd even be around. The odds were stacked against me. All the statistics and doctors told me so. I'd read far too many stories from IBC patients online, only to find a note attached at the end from a loved one, regretfully notifying others of their passing. I didn't know if it was realistic to hope about life after cancer. I squeezed his hand before gently sliding it from his grip.

"Beau, I do hope this is not one of those deathbed confessions." I smiled, trying to lighten the moment.

He frowned. "Heavens, no, Isabella. You're gonna make it now, ya hear me? You keep fighting now. It doesn't matter what the doctors say. It's about what the Lord says. He says to live, Isabella. Live." His gray eyes sparkled.

I nodded. "Thank you for sharing your feelings with me. Thank you for being such a good friend and confidant. I do have feelings for you, but quite frankly, I've got so many things to deal with before I can even think about exploring those feelings. For one, I've got to make it out of this hospital."

"Yes, of course, Isabella. I just want you to know that I'm here for you, and I'll be here, waiting, no matter how long it takes."

My breath left me for a second. When Langley had left, years of loneliness had unfolded ahead of me, but now, even with Langley back and the prospect of being healed still meant years of loneliness in my book. Beau scrambled everything up. He gave me so much to hope for; only thing was, I didn't think I'd be around for it.

I swallowed the lump that had formed in my throat before I spoke. "Beau, why couldn't I have met you earlier? If I only had known then what I know now. What I have learned is that I can't base my actions on my emotions. Shoot, if I did, I'd . . . Well, never mind. The point is, my feelings have run me off into a ditch more than once or twice. I've got to make sure that my words and actions line up with the Word, regardless of what Langley's mistakes have been. I'm accountable to God for my actions. And, quite frankly, I have to face the fact that I may be closer to meeting my Maker than not, and I don't have time to mess up. Do you understand what I'm saying?"

Beau looked away, deep in thought. "I understand perfectly, and your explanation is just one of the reasons why I feel the way I do about you. I did go against your daughter's wishes by coming here to tell you how I feel, but I just couldn't help it. I'm going to give you and your family space, but I'm here if you need me."

He took my hand again and brought it to his lips, softly kissing it. I closed my eyes, wanting to savor the moment because I felt the end of things coming fast.

I dreamt that my hair hung down my back, long, dark, and wavy, just like it was when I was in my twenties and thirties. Carefree and light, I walked down the street just like one of those models on a shampoo commercial. It wasn't that farfetched either. My great-grandmother had done a magazine ad for Madame CJ Walker's hair care products. In our family, hair meant status. My dreams took a nasty turn to a nightmare when the wind blew and my hair fell out in clumps. I felt naked and afraid.

"Isabella? Isabella?"

"Beau?" I asked, trying to wake up.

"No, Isabella. It's me—your husband," Langley said, clearly disgusted.

"I'm so sorry," I said, trying to wake from the fog.

Langley put a cool cloth on my forehead and stroked my face gently. "It's okay. You just had a bad dream."

My eyes tried to focus on him, but I couldn't. I thought I heard Desiree. I tried to speak but my tongue felt as heavy as lead. My eyelids refused to stay open. There was so much I wanted to say. I tried to hold my arms out to speak for me, but they too betrayed me. I decided to stop fighting.

CHAPTER 35

DESIREE

Precious in the sight of the LORD is the death of his saints.

—Psalm 116:15

Calla lilies decorated the entire pulpit, windowsills, and every nook and cranny of the overcrowded sanctuary. People came from all over, and the pastor had said that he'd never had so many people in the sanctuary that the deacons had to turn people away for fear of a fire hazard. Even though it wasn't proper protocol for an occasion like this, mostly everyone wore white to represent purity and heaven's rejoicing at the homegoing of a saint. I stared at the lifeless body and couldn't believe how many lives had been touched by such a humble and gentle person. I couldn't believe how fast everything had been. There hadn't even been time to call hospice. I nearly collapsed at the news. She was gone too soon.

Dad surprised me by sitting between Beau and me. Dad and Beau did have one thing in common on this day. They both sat stoic but wore red, tear-streaked faces and puffy eyes. With her wedding only weeks away, the mourning over Kaylyn's sudden passing was widespread and shocking.

In a miraculous turn of events, Mama rallied and was well enough to go home after almost a month in the hospital. Kaylyn, who had only been in the hospital a few days, had been home well before Mama's return home. With Mama home less than a week, Beau called to say that Kaylyn had been hospitalized due to pneumonia, Mama had sprung out of the bed into action. Armed with her anointed oil and a burst of energy, we rushed to the hospital to be by her side.

Weak but smiling, Kaylyn still managed to be upbeat, even in intensive care. Only two of us were allowed to visit at a time, so Marvin and Beau had allowed Mama and I to go back to see her together.

Mama had said as soon as she entered her room, "Oh, sweetie! You don't fret about anything. I'm gonna anoint you with oil, and pray for you. This is going to pass."

"Yes, ma'am, I believe it will," Kaylyn said with a faint voice and cough.

After Mama anointed her and we prayed, Mama went to the foot of the bed and slipped Kaylyn's socks off and massaged her feet. Kaylyn closed her eyes, and I thought she had fallen asleep.

"Desiree," Kaylyn whispered.

I jumped up from my chair, going to Kaylyn. "Yes?" Kaylyn coughed again, and I said, "Don't try to talk, Kaylyn. Save your energy."

Her voice, raspy and hoarse, scared me as she whispered, "I want you to be my maid of honor."

I held my hands to my chest. "Me?"

"Yes, who better?" Kaylyn asked back.

"Of course, I'd be honored," I said, realizing that I hadn't even been kind to the girl until very recently. I couldn't believe that with all of the friends she had her age, that she would ask me.

"I've always wanted a sister, a real sister," she explained.

"Yeah, me too," I said, realizing that I also had always wanted a sister. I had let my jealousy over her relationship with Mama keep me from really getting to know her.

Mama chuckled. "Well, this is gonna be a great wedding! You stop talking now, dear, so you can save your energy!"

"Okay," Kaylyn whispered. "But, Ms. Isabella, do you mind seeing if I can get some ice chips?"

"I'll do it, Mama," I said.

Mama instantly declined, rushing out. "I'll be right back. It's nice to be able to do a little something for someone else for a change."

When Mama left, Kaylyn's smile faded into a pained look.

"You okay? You need a nurse?" I asked.

With Kaylyn's breathing labored, she answered, "No. I just wanted to talk to you for a second. I'm not so sure that I can kick this infection. This feels different than the other times."

"Oh, don't say that," I said.

"I'm just being real, Desiree. I hope that God will heal me. I want to live. I have so much to live for, but just in case, I have to tell you this. I've spent so much time being angry and unforgiving. I don't want that for you. We're really so much alike, you know. Your mom tells me so often. Let the negativity go and live your life. Every day is precious, with or without a relationship with a man. Love God, and love yourself. I know that I haven't been saved long, but the Lord has done a lot for me in a short time. He has shown me that the closer I draw to Him, the more I love Him, others, and, yes, myself. When you get that special man God has selected especially for you, it's just icing on the cake, not the be all and end all."

Just then, Mama rushed in with the ice chips. "At your service, baby."

Looking back, I should've known that she knew it was the end, but it just didn't seem possible. Young, happy, and hopeful didn't mean long life. She finally had peace and a God-ordained relationship with a man who loved her for her.

All that time, I had been preparing for Mama's passing, not Kaylyn's. As I admired the beautiful wedding dress that Beau had decided Kaylyn would wear for her homegoing service, a tear fell. As the lid of the casket closed, I clutched Mama's hand as she let out a whimper of mourning.

Pastor Kingston broke the solemn mood with his kind smile and calming presence as he took the podium. He used his handkerchief to wipe the small beads of sweat that had collected on his forehead. Silent for a few seconds as he scanned the droves of people who spilled out into the vestibule, he took a deep breath and began. "In the Apostle Paul's letter to the Philippians, he writes, 'Christ shall be magnified in my body, whether it be by life, or by death. For me to live is Christ, and to die is gain.'"

There were a few faint amens across the sanctuary as he continued, "I might mention that Paul is imprisoned while he is writing this letter to them. He is in an uncomfortable state, yet he writes this joyful letter, encouraging the Philippians. He says, 'I count all things but loss for the excellency of the knowledge of Christ Jesus my Lord: for whom I have suffered the loss of all things.' Oh, yes, Paul has the understanding that in all of his accomplishments, and they were many, nothing compared to the joy of knowing Jesus as his personal Savior."

Pastor Kingston reached under the podium and took a sip of water. "I had the pleasure of pastoring this lovely young woman, Sister Kaylyn Simms. I think I would be remiss if I didn't add right here that she would've been in just a few short weeks Sister Kaylyn Smith." All eyes rested on Marvin who had his head hung in grief, tears streaming down his face.

"My brother Marvin," Pastor said to him. Marvin wearily looked up into Pastor Kingston's eyes. "Few of us are or ever will be acquainted with the pain that has met you at such a young age, but rest assured that God knows and He cares. He hasn't left you alone. As much as your heart hurts, I am confident that your life is better for having known and loved Kaylyn."

Marvin nodded.

Pastor Kingston looked to Beau and said, "Brother Beau, God knows how faithful you've been to Him, and you will surely be rewarded for your unconditional love, compassion, and care for your niece. Kaylyn shared her love and appreciation with me for you on so many different occasions. She treasured having an uncle who stepped up and willingly became a father, caretaker, and friend to her."

Beau wept openly, nodding his head in affirmation.

Pastor Kingston then addressed Mama. "Mother Morrison, you truly lived up to your title of Mother in your relationship with Kaylyn. She loved you as a mother."

Pastor Kingston then continued, "In the short time I knew Sister Kaylyn, she grew by leaps and bounds becoming a spiritually mature person. She found so much delight in teaching the children Sunday School and helping out in the nursery. I have to tell you, Church, as excited as she was about getting married and her future, I don't have a doubt that, just like the Apostle Paul, nothing was more important to her than her relationship with Christ." Again, amens echoed throughout the sanctuary. Mama patted my knee in agreement.

"I had the pleasure of counseling her, and her growth far superseded her years," Pastor Kingston said. "We studied the Book of Job together, and I can tell you without reservation that over the last couple of months she came to understand her suffering in another way.

She didn't see her suffering as God's judgment for some sin she committed. While this can be the case for some of us, she grew to understand that was not the nature of her condition. She not only understood that her illness was God's way to teach, discipline, and prune, but also grew to appreciate that her sickness caused her to truly trust God for who He is, not just for what He does. Oh yes, family, His power is perfected."

Pastor Kingston stepped away from the podium and explained, "When I last visited her in the hospital and she was able to speak with me, she quoted Job from the forty-first chapter: 'I know that thou canst do every thing, and that no thought can be withholden from thee. Who is he that hideth counsel without knowledge? Therefore have I uttered that I understood not; things too wonderful for me, which I knew not.' Now, I'm going to tell you that in spite of my seminary training and years of pastoring, this young lady imparted some godly wisdom into her pastor through her suffering." There were a few lighthearted chuckles from the congregation and Marvin, Beau, and even Mama cracked a smile.

"When things like this happen, we are faced with our own mortality and the brevity of life. We are faced with tough situations that should cause us to examine ourselves and our faith. Some things we will never understand, especially when we are bound by our own human limitations and our own sense of fairness and justice. However, we must humble ourselves to God's omniscience, omnipotence, and omnipresence," Pastor Kingston said as he walked back to the podium.

Pastor Kingston preached on until I felt the heavy burden lighten on all of us as he continued. "Congregation, Paul says in Romans, 'For I reckon that the sufferings of this present time are not worthy to be compared with the glory which shall be revealed in us.' As much as we all love Sister Kaylyn, she is in glory and I don't hesitate to tell you that as much as she loves all of us, if the good Lord gave her the opportunity to come back, she wouldn't. She's happier than she's ever been here on earth." Again, a few light chuckles fell across the room.

"As I close, I must address the beautiful calla lilies throughout the sanctuary. I've never seen so many in all my life and I've been told by her fiancé that calla lilies were one of her favorite flowers. In fact, it is my understanding that she had planned to have them for her wedding. Well, I happen to know a little bit about flowers, and like you, I know that calla lilies are often the flowers people have at homegoing services, but I also know that calla lilies are popular wedding flowers. The calla lily symbolizes elegance, majesty, and beauty, but most importantly, in my opinion, the calla lily symbolizes rebirth and resurrection."

Pastor Kingston put the microphone back onto the stand and said, "Let's reflect on Sister Kaylyn's life and the commitment she made to repent of her sins and live a holy, saved, and sanctified life as a born-again Christian. Let's reflect on Jesus and His life, death, and resurrection. Sister Kaylyn would want that. I'm going to leave you with these final words from I Thessalonians 4:13–18. 'But I would not have you to be ignorant, brethren, concerning them which are asleep, that ye sorrow not, even as others which have no hope. For if we believe that Jesus died and rose again, even so them also which sleep in Jesus will God bring with him. For this we say unto you by the Word of the Lord, that we which are asleep and remain unto the coming of the Lord shall not prevent them which are asleep. For the Lord himself shall descend from heaven with a shout, with the voice of the archangel, and the trump of God: and the dead in Christ shall rise first: Then we which are alive and remain shall be caught up together with them in the clouds, to meet the Lord in the air: and so shall we ever be with the Lord. Wherefore comfort one another with these words.'" Pastor Kingston gently closed his Bible, and the choir sang as the processional began.

After I reassured Dad that I'd take Mama home after the repast, he left for home. Once Dad left, I watched Mama, though weak physically, transform into a strong tower for Beau.

"Beau, you need to eat a little something. It'll help that headache," Mama said, handing him a fork.

"Did you get yourself somethin' to eat, Desiree?" Beau asked.

Before I could answer, I heard a deep voice. "Hello, Desiree."

I looked around, only to see Margaret, who chatted incessantly. Then, when a man standing beside me moved, I saw him and my heart skipped a beat.

"Roman!" I hated that I sounded so excited, but I couldn't take it back.

"Good memory you have, Desiree," Roman said as he greeted Mama and gave his condolences to Beau. Roman then asked me, "Would you like some punch?"

"Sure," I said, as he signaled for me to follow him through the dense crowd.

Roman handed me a cup of punch and after I thanked him, I said, "I'm surprised to see you here."

"Well, although Kaylyn was never my patient, she was in to see your mom so often that I really got to know her. The hospital staff all loved her. She was special."

"Yes, she really was," I said, hoping I wouldn't tear up again.

Roman dug his hands in the pockets of his crisp black slacks. "It's tough because I try to be professional and not get too attached to patients, but people like your mom and Kaylyn make it impossible, you know what I'm saying?"

"Yeah, I'd imagine it would be difficult. I could never do your job. I'd be a wreck. On the other hand, I know your job is rewarding. I'm sure that your patients appreciate you so much. I know that Mama sings your praises."

Roman smiled. "So, I don't know much about you, other than what you mom has shared."

"Well, that means you know everything," I joked.

"She didn't share too much. On another note, your mom seems to be doing remarkably well for what she's been going through. It's really miraculous. You just don't see people rebound from IBC. In spite of what a lot of people think, there is a God and He is real."

"Yes, it's a miracle in my book. As you know, we were prepped to call in hospice only weeks ago. Now, she's up and walking," I said, observing Mama from a distance.

"Believe me," Roman said, "the word of your Mom rallying like this has amazed everyone in the hospital. The news has spread like wildfire."

"I don't call what has happened to Mama a rally, so I'll have to correct you. I call it Mama's healing in motion," I explained.

"Okay, amen to that! Well, I celebrate with you as the Lord continues to restore her to good health!" Roman added.

"So, obviously you're a Christian?" I asked.

"Born, raised, and born again," he stated as he pulled his cross out from around his neck for me to see.

I eyed him. "No offense, Roman, but anyone can wear a cross."

He pushed his cross back under his shirt. "Point well taken, but I live the life. No, I'm not perfect, but I'm saved by God's grace through faith."

I knew not to get too impressed with his words, and asked, "This might be personal, but if you don't mind me asking, how do you reconcile all the bad stuff you see on a daily basis with your faith?"

"It's not too personal. Really, you've struck a nerve, Desiree. I know what God can do, and not just because of what I've seen or haven't seen at the hospital," he said, leaning against the wall.

"What do you mean?" I asked.

"About six years ago, I was in a terrible car accident. By the time they got me to the hospital, I was barely hanging on. Apparently they called my parents, and I had praying parents, and a praying grandmother! I'm told that I flat-lined, and Mama and Daddy rebuked death and told it to keep his ugly hands off of me!" Roman shook his head and chuckled. "Well, look at me now! I know firsthand that the prayers of the righteous availeth much! I can't get my bullhorn out at work about it because it could cost me my job, but when I feel the Lord prompting me to share my testimony of bringing me back from death, I share it."

"That's awesome, Roman. God is so good, yet I wonder why He couldn't have spared Kaylyn. She was so young and had so much to live for, you know what I mean?" I asked.

"Yeah, some things we just can't understand, but God is just. When we pray, He hears our prayers, but He is God. He has the final say. When I see tragedy and triumph, I try to handle them both the same."

I frowned. "What's that supposed to mean?"

Roman explained, "I just mean that God is in control of it all. When there is tragedy, I understand that for whatever reason, God has allowed it. He can get the glory out of it if we let Him. It was Kaylyn's time, as difficult and painful as it is to understand. You mom, on the other hand, God is saying that it's just not her time yet."

"Well, it's a bit of an oversimplification of things, but if it works for you, then go with that," I said, hoping that he wouldn't take offense.

"Yes, I know it seems that way, but God gives us peace, even in the midst of things we may not ever understand in this life. He can do it. I've been praying for Ms. Isabella, and I trust God. Just continue to trust Him, and it will be okay, anyway it turns out."

I smiled. "You're not so bad for a male nurse."

"Hey! What's that supposed to mean?" he said, chuckling.

"I'm just joking. I'm just not accustomed to seeing male nurses much," I explained.

"Yes, I hear that a lot. What about you? What do you do?" Roman asked.

"I teach English composition at A&M."

He took a step back in disbelief. "Oh, I'm scared of you! English is not my subject."

"I can understand that. You know, years ago in graduate school I worked as an advisor in the School of Nursing and I'll tell you one thing, you all have to have so much math and science. I talked with so many students who labored over anatomy and physiology."

He nodded. "A&P can be a nightmare for a lot of students, but I loved it."

"I can't stand science," I said rolling my eyes.

"You're making me work hard, Desiree. I'm trying to find some things to have in common with you," he confessed.

Butterflies danced in my stomach. *Did Roman just flirt with me?* I wondered but decided to try to ignore it, not wanting to take a chance on another man. We stood like two teenagers groping for something to say for a few seconds, but Roman broke the silence.

"So, Desiree, I know this isn't the best place to ask, but I don't want to risk not seeing you again. Could I get your number? Maybe you'd consider going out with me—even though I'm a male nurse?" His dimples enlarged while he bit his bottom lip.

Without thinking, I blurted out, "Sure. Let me see if I have a card on me." I went to pull my wallet out of my purse and spilled my cosmetic bag and its contents onto the floor. Before I could bend down, he had scooped it all up and handed them to me. My face burned with embarrassment, but I thanked him. "You are just a real helper to me, my family, and friends," I joked.

"My pleasure and I hope to be able to do more of that, especially for you," he flirted.

I pulled a business card out from my wallet and handed it to him.

"Thank you," he said while reading the business card. "Hmmm, Desi's Designs, huh? So you make jewelry, too? I'm impressed. I actually have a side business as well."

"Really? What do you do?" I asked.

"Woodwork," he said, taking his wallet out to hand me a business card.

"I'm equally impressed. Boy, you take care of the sick and do carpentry work. You and Jesus have some things in common."

"Very funny. I like your wit."

I smiled. "Well, everybody can't handle it, that's for sure."

"Desiree, I'm so sorry we had to meet up at this type of occasion, but I am thankful to have run into you. If you'll be free tonight, I'd love to call you. I'm not back to work for two days, so maybe we can get together sooner rather than later?" he said as he put my card into his wallet.

"I'd actually like that," I said, amazed that I felt comfortable enough to allow him to call me. I felt a peace that I hadn't felt with other guys.

"Good," Roman said. "You have made my day, Desiree."

Mama, never one to miss anything, made her way slowly over to where we stood.

"Okay, you two, folks are clearing out of here. Beau is heading home, and I need to do the same. You all need to continue your chat over a date. I'm sorry to interrupt, but I need to lie down a spell," Mama said, looking tired. Roman explained that he understood and excused himself, promising to be in touch. When he got out of earshot, Mama said, "Now that fella is so sweet on you. Mark my words."

"Mama!" I said, not wanting her to put any pressure on either one of us.

"Mama nothin'. I know a man who's interested when I see one. I know his people from up in Decatur. They're real good Christians. I'm tellin' you, he's been raised right. Just give him a chance, daughter."

"Mama, I intend on doing just that," I said surprising both myself and Mama.

CHAPTER 36

ISABELLA

Confess your faults one to another, and pray one for another, that ye may be healed. The effectual fervent prayer of a righteous man availeth much.
—James 5:16

Kaylyn's death had been a cruel twist of events. I couldn't help wondering why the Lord would spare my life and allow hers to end so soon. She had so much life in front of her. Older and sicker by all accounts, I didn't understand why the Lord had chosen to take her and not me first. Still, I knew that God was in control. Since He had me here, He had things for me to do, and I intended on doing them. The doctors wouldn't say that the cancer was in remission, only that it seemed to be at a standstill. I knew it was all God's miraculous healing power.

"Mrs. Morrison," the oncologist had said, "this is just unheard of with IBC patients."

I knew that I was a walking, talking miracle. I had a testimony. I still dealt with a host of medical issues, but I believed God, taking my health and marriage one day at a time.

Just as I requested, Desiree took me to the health food store on the other side of town. When I realized how close we were to Langley's office, we decided to drop by and see if he wanted to join us for lunch. Things weren't back to normal between us, but I made a promise to myself. I would not make any rash decions.

"Mama, do you think we should call Dad first?" Desiree asked.

"No, let's surprise him. He's been so good at surprising me with such nice things lately," I said.

Desiree tried to convince me to wait in the car and save my energy, but I wanted to see his face happy for a change. Langley would never expect me to drop by for lunch. I had stopped doing that years ago. When we walked in, the new receptionist, LeAnn, greeted us warmly. "Hi there! You'll be glad to know that he's in and not busy," she said.

"Oh, good," Desiree said with a hint of sarcasm.

Desiree tapped twice on the door, and I turned the knob without waiting for him to tell us to come in. Instead of looking happily surprised by our appearance, Langley's facial expression turned into a look of horror. Seated in the chair facing his desk was a man who appeared to be about the same age as Desiree. LeAnn hadn't mentioned that Langley had a visitor.

"I'm sorry, Dad. I didn't know you were busy," Desiree apologized, ready to close the door.

I chimed in, "Yes, we'll sit in the waiting room until you're done."

"Oh, no," the man said. "I was just leaving."

When he got up and started to walk toward the door, Desiree gasped and pointed. "It's you!"

Langley came around from behind his desk, trying to make sense of what was happening. The stranger stopped, squeezing his eyes shut as if he were in pain. Langley stuttered, "Wha . . . wha . . . what are you talking about, Desiree?"

The man then tried to rush toward the door, but my daughter slammed it shut. "What's your name? What's your name?" she demanded.

Langley answered, "This is Hunter."

Desiree charged toward Hunter, crying out, "It's you! You attacked me! I could never forget your face."

My heart pounded, and I didn't know what to do. Was this the man who had raped my daughter? I was confused because I thought she'd said that it was Phillip. I dug in my purse to get my phone to call the police. "I'm calling the police! You mean to tell me that's the man who assaulted you?" I asked.

Desiree, who stood nose to nose with Hunter, barked out, "Yes, I mean, no, Mama. It's not what you're thinking. Do not call the police!"

"Hunter assaulted you?" Langley put his hand over his forehead. "What is going on here? Sit down, Hunter! Desiree, please calm down. Let's figure out what's going on."

Hunter didn't move and also didn't deny Desiree's accusations. Langley repeated, almost yelling, "Sit down, Hunter!"

Hunter plopped down on the chair and hung his head. I turned to my daughter. "Please tell me what's going on!"

Desiree stepped toward Langley and Hunter. "Mama, Hunter is the son of an acquaintance of Dad's." Desiree spat her words out in disgust.

"Okay?" I said, not understanding. "He attacked you?"

Desiree stared into space and spoke with clarity. "I was a teenager, Mama. Fourteen to be exact. You had gone to a women's retreat. Dad banished me to my bedroom for the evening, explaining that he had a colleague from work coming over."

I walked over and took a seat on the sofa to steady myself. "Okay," I said, looking at Desiree and then Langley.

Desiree's voice shook as she spoke. She explained, "I was changing my clothes for bed and my door opened.

It was him!" Desiree pointed to him and continued, "He apologized profusely and so much so that I figured he was okay. I mean, Dad had let him into our house. I discovered that he was Dad's friend's son, so I felt comfortable. He explained that he had been looking for the restroom. Against my better judgment, I invited him into my room. He wanted to play a board game while he waiting for his mother to finish the so-called meeting."

Hunter rolled his eyes and crossed his arms.

Desiree continued, "With no warning, this animal began trying to kiss me. He fought to get . . . to get on top of me." Tears began to roll down her face. "He would've raped me, I just know it, if I hadn't hit him over the head with a bottle!"

I traded turns glaring at Langley and then Hunter. "How could that happen?" I asked.

Desiree paced the floor and said, "There's more, Mama. After I hit him over the head, I ran to find Dad, only to discover him in bed with Hunter's mother!"

"What? Sweet Jesus, help me!" I said, not wanting to believe that I'd left my teenage daughter in harm's way, not wanting to believe that she'd been exposed to such vile activity at such a young age. I couldn't believe that Desiree had kept all those secrets from me.

Dad looked sick. He came face to face with Hunter. "Is this true?"

Hunter refused to say a word, so Langley addressed Desiree and me, saying, "Listen, both of you, listen. I didn't know about that! I simply didn't know about Hunter doing that to you!"

Desiree yelled, "You didn't try to find out either! You didn't want to know, Dad! It would've messed up everything for you!"

"Desiree, you mean to tell me that you didn't tell me? I could've helped you," I said, steadying myself by holding on to the desktop.

"I know that now, Mama, but then, all I was thinking about was that I couldn't let the marriage break apart. I couldn't break your heart like that."

"Oh, Desiree!" I said. "You've been through so much!" I walked over to Hunter and demanded, "How could you attack my daughter? What's wrong with you? You need to go to jail for what you've done!"

"What do you have to say for yourself, Hunter?" Dad asked, raising his voice.

I jumped in and said to Langley, "The nerve of you to ask him! What do you have to say for yourself? You've allowed my daughter to be molested. She's carried around this awful weight for years! Then, you allowed some miscellaneous woman into our home, had sex with her, and my daughter knew about it? All this time, I have tried to protect her, and you'd already contaminated her with your lies, betrayal, and abuse. You have hurt her, us, for the last time, Langley!"

Langley rushed over to me. "Isabella, that was almost twenty years ago! I've changed! Please forgive me! I had no idea that Hunter had done that to her."

"You've changed, Langley?" I asked. "Then, why the devil is this man who molested my daughter here with you now? What's the connection? Are you saying that you are not seeing this man's mother? Please don't try to keep playing me for a fool!"

Hunter, who had remained mostly silent, cleared his throat. "Desiree, I did do that to you, and I'm so sorry. I was an immature kid, and I misread your signals. I've thought about that whole thing so much over the years. I hope you'll find it in your heart to forgive me. I'm not a monster. In fact, I'm a responsible, law-abiding citizen. I'm a respectable physician."

Desiree sobbed, fighting hard to choke back tears, and said, "What do you want? You want an award for that?

You attacked me! My whole life was affected by what you did to me," she yelled. Then, she turned to Langley. "And most of all, what you did to me, what you allowed to happen to me! What you did to Mama!"

Langley held his face in his hands.

Hunter fought back tears and said, "I can't imagine what you all must think of me, but just so that you know, I would never hurt a woman. I mean, I have never hurt a woman since then. That hit on the head grew me up fast. I was a stupid kid with raging hormones. I am sorry."

Desiree wiped her face and raised her voice again. She turned to her dad. "So, it doesn't explain why he's here now!"

"He . . . he . . . he's here now because—" Langley started.

"Because he's my father," Hunter finished for him.

"What?" Desiree and I asked in unison.

"I . . . I . . . it's true," Langley managed to say.

Desiree shook her head violently. "There's no way. He's white!"

"Things aren't always what they look like. I guess I look more like my mother," Hunter quipped.

I stared at him, and sure enough, I saw it. In spite of his white skin and ice blue eyes, he was a dead ringer for Langley. His long face, sad mouth, gangly frame, not to mention his thick glasses told the story. I couldn't believe it.

"Oh, God, have mercy on me. My own brother molested me?" Desiree fell back onto the sofa. I went to her and sat down, holding her in my arms.

"All these years you've had a son?" I whispered, trying to take it all in.

"I know, and I'm so sorry that you found out this way. I really was going to tell you," Langley offered in his pathetic way. "I didn't know myself. All these years and I didn't know that I had a son. She kept it from me. I only found out because Hunter got into a skiing accident and needed a blood transfusion. We both have O-negative blood type, and his mother had to tell me to save his life."

I looked at Hunter, hoping for the truth. Hunter nodded and explained, "It's true. I thought that the man I knew as my father was my biological dad. Sure, we don't look anything alike, but I never suspected that I wasn't his. My mother confessed it all to me after I'd had the accident on Christmas Day. The only gratitude I can give her is for helping to save my life. Otherwise, I want nothing to do with her. She's robbed all of us in one way or another."

"Don't look for me to pity you, Hunter," Desiree hissed.

Langley walked up in front of Desiree and me and knelt down, explaining, "Remember when that policeman came to the door on Christmas Day? He wanted to tell me that my son had been in an accident. Well, that policeman was Jill's brother, who's a police officer. Since I'd blocked Jill's number, she'd sent him over to tell me about Hunter's accident. Isabella, the only reason that I didn't tell you right away is because I'd just found out about your diagnosis. I didn't want to do that to you. I couldn't lay that on you when you've been so sick."

"There have been so many lies. Why should I believe that?" I asked.

Hunter interjected, "Because it's the truth. I know that Langley, my dad, has been struggling with the right time to tell you about me. As for me, I've been trying to absorb the fact that my dad isn't my dad. And, I'm black, half black. I've always felt different, but Mom has always told me that I looked like her side of the family. I guess she was thankful that I came out looking white because it helped keep her marriage to my dad intact for as long as it did."

"And we should believe you because . . . ?" Desiree asked.

"Lord, have mercy on us all," I murmured.

Langley stood up and continued, "So, the truth is, Jill and I had been involved for years. We had to keep our relationship secret because she was married. For years, I begged Jill to leave her husband. She refused. I finally realized that I needed to move on when I found out she was pregnant. I had no idea that I was Hunter's father. That was when I met you, Isabella. That day, nearly twenty years ago, we did get together briefly. When you came in on us that day, Desiree, the affair ended until about a year ago. Jill and I ran into each other at a conference in the hospital. She explained that she'd transferred back to work at Huntsville Hospital and that she was newly divorced. That's when Jill convinced me that it was time for me to leave my marriage too. I knew that neither one of us has been happy. That's when I'd decided to leave you, Isabella."

Langley hung his head but continued. "I was selfish. I know that. Everything seemed like it was going to be perfect. We were finally going to be together. The only thing was, when Jill and I got together, she revealed that Hunter was my son. I didn't believe her until she began to show me pictures of him throughout the years. Then, I saw the resemblance. I just knew that he was my son. Then, the anger came. I couldn't stand her. What kind of mother would keep a man from his only son? I couldn't stay with her, so I came back home."

"So, let me get this straight," I said, "you came back to me because Jill had betrayed you?" I couldn't believe that Langley could be so calculating and selfish. Something clicked. I finally realized that I'd never known the man I'd been married to for all those years.

Langley continued to explain, "I couldn't do it. I didn't want to be with Jill. She disgusted me. As crazy as it sounds, I felt betrayed. I missed out on having a relationship with my son because of her lies."

"It seems like there's some reaping what you've sown. I'm just horrified that my daughter, our daughter, had to suffer the consequences of your philandering. You want to talk about disgusting? It's disgusting that your cheating and lying has caused so much pain to Desiree."

Desiree blurted out, "You and *her* seem like two peas in a pod to me."

Desiree then turned to Hunter, "So, Hunter, how does it feel to know that you molested your sister?"

Hunter now hung his head in shame, and Langley pressed his fingers into his temples.

Desiree kept at Hunter, saying, "So, just out of curiosity, Hunter, let me get this straight, you had no idea that you were part black?"

"No, I really didn't. I mean, look at me." Hunter threw his hands up. "I've always had my suspicions that my dad wasn't really my dad. My mother's infidelities have never been a secret. Something has just never felt right."

"I've had about all I can take for right now. Come on, Desiree. We've had enough for a lifetime today," I said, trying to collect myself.

Langley tried to stop me, but it was too little, too late.

Beyond superficial things, for nearly two months, Langley and I hadn't spoken much since the revelation of his affair and newly discovered son. When you've almost died like I have, you can somehow put even the most vulgar things in perspective. I no longer had the energy to put into things that I couldn't change.

When I walked down the steps, he said, "Isabella, you look nice this evening."

I crinkled up my face in disbelief. A housedress, short gray hair, and a bare face had never been appealing to him before. He didn't fool me. Langley didn't want me. He just didn't want change. Staying married felt easier and more comfortable to him, that I was sure of.

"I can get you some tea or coffee if you like," I offered.

He sat down in his recliner. "No, thank you. Why don't you let me get you something?"

I sat down on the sofa across from him. "I don't need a thing. I just want us to talk. My health is better than I'd ever expected, and I can think more clearly than I've been able to do in months. Maybe it's the warmth of the late spring, or maybe it's just that it's time for a change."

"I know, and I think it's wonderful. We can get our lives back to normal now. I've got some things to share with you as well."

"Back to normal? Langley, our normal is a life I'll never go back to."

He scooted to the edge of his seat, clasping his hands together. "No, you misunderstood. Not that normal. I only meant—"

I interrupted, "I think I understand. I just want us to be clear. I have to admit that I didn't think that I was going to make it out of the hospital. I had so much time to think about things, and I've repented for so many mistakes I've made. I've told you before, but I'm truly sorry for marrying you for so many of the wrong reasons. Not all of the reasons were wrong, but the main thing is that God never told me to do it. Something deep inside kept telling me not to, but I ignored that voice and married."

"I think I know where this is heading, and I want you to know that I fully understand the gravity of the mistakes I've made too."

"Langley, I appreciate all of the apologies and I know you're sorry. I can't forget all the hurt and pain. I forgive you though, and I hope you forgive me."

"I forgive you, Isabella, if that makes you feel better, but there's nothing to forgive," Langley said.

"I've done a lot that I need forgiveness for. I am sorry for marrying you to take care of me and Desiree and not because I loved you the way a woman should love her husband." I took another deep breath and he leaned back into the chair.

I continued, "Right before Kaylyn passed away, I was intent on saving the marriage because that's what I thought would be the right thing to do. I'd thought that I would be wrong to sever a relationship that you wanted. After all, I was the one to remind you that we made a vow before God."

"That's right." He nodded.

I said, "I was the one who reminded you about the fact that Jesus said, in the Bible, that people were granted divorces only because of the hardness of their hearts. I thought that I would and could stay on those grounds. I thought that I had made my bed and had to lie in it, so to speak. I was willing to sacrifice my desires for the good of the marriage and commitment to God. I was willing to sacrifice it because you seemed willing to work on us."

"Absolutely! I am willing to do whatever it takes to make us work, Isabella," Langley announced.

I ignored his comment and explained, "Like I said, after Kaylyn passed away, I began thinking about how no man knows the day or the hour. We don't know when He's coming back, and we can't know how long we have. We have to make each moment count. We're not promised tomorrow."

Langley blew out a long sigh. "Isabella, please get to your point. I'm really suffering here."

I smiled and said, "I called your doctor friend, Jill, yesterday, the woman you've been having an affair with, Langley."

He looked white as a ghost. "Okay, and why on earth would you do that? Why did you do that? How did you get her number?"

"She's called here before, and I simply wrote the number down. She knows that you don't love her the way she loves you, but you continue to sleep with her and lead her on. Apparently, the fact that she's betrayed you hasn't caused you to lose your attraction to her."

Langley shot up in disbelief. "She's a liar! How dare you believe her! I've been with you for months, showing, no, begging you to work things out with me. I love you and want our marriage. Surely you don't believe her. She wants me to leave you and marry her. Because I refuse, she is on a mission to get me. She's like a female stalker!"

I calmly continued, "Jill apologized for all she had put me through, but she wanted me to know that you have no intention of being faithful to her or me. She understands you very well."

Langley beat his fist on the arm of the chair. "I have committed my life to the Lord, and I may not be perfect, but I am trying. I feel like David at times. I don't always make the right decision, but I do have a heart for God. Doesn't that count for anything, Isabella?"

I sighed. "It counts for a lot, but it doesn't mean that I should stay married. My decision is based on what the Lord has revealed to me about you and me."

Langley stood up and paced the floor. "Oh, what a cop-out! I know that idiot Beau is behind this. What kind of life do you think you'll have with him, Isabella? He can't give you what I can give you, not even close."

"You're right," I said, "he would never give me what you've given me. Besides, this has nothing to do with Beau, and you and I both know it. I have never been unfaithful to you; I've made other mistakes, but I've never been unfaithful. We can both better serve and honor the

Lord apart. I have asked for the Lord's forgiveness, and I believe that He has forgiven me." I opened the side table drawer and took a pen and divorce papers out. I got up and placed my hand on his shoulder.

"I'll always have love for you, Langley, but it's time for us both to let it go once and for all." I handed him the papers and pen.

He shook his head and refused to take the papers and pen. He let tears roll from his face without wiping them and pushed my hand away. Langley then stood up and hugged me. The hug was unfamiliar because it came from such a sincere place. He held on to me and wept like a baby. When he let it out, I could see relief wash over his face. I had lifted the burden of me from his life.

When he finished holding me, Langley signed the papers without bothering to read anything and quietly left the house. I cried but felt ready to begin the rest of my life.

CHAPTER 37

DESIREE

*Be completely humble and gentle; be patient, bearing
with one another in love.*
—Ephesians 4:2

Shay's wedding, the soiree of the summer, was magical.
The Tiffany blue theme fit her electric personality, only
calmed by Paul's quiet strength. For the first time, I felt
nothing but sheer joy for Shay's dream come true. Shay
deserved love.

Roman had accepted my invitation to the wedding
without hesitation. We talked, laughed, and danced the
whole reception away. I ended up having to drag Roman
off of the dance floor because the three-inch heels Shay
insisted on for the bridesmaids had my feet throbbing.

"You need a spot on *Dancing with the Stars*," I said to
Roman.

"You're not too shabby on the floor, so you can appear
with me," Roman joked.

As we left Shay and Paul's wedding reception, I gazed
up into the evening sky. "Wow," I said, pointing up.
"Every star seems to be out tonight. I've never seen them
shine so brightly."

Roman grabbed my hand and looked up too. "They are
shining especially bright. I think it's just for us," he said,
squeezing my hand. "Des, it's much too nice out here to

leave now. How about we take a walk around the lake?"
he asked, motioning toward the horseshoe-shaped pond,
curved around the back of the hotel.

"Sure, as long as you don't mind me taking off these
shoes. My feet are killing me," I said, slipping both heels
off. Roman then pried my shoes from my fingers and
insisted on carrying them for me.

As we walked, we could hear the thumping of the party
music from the inside the reception. "I don't think that
reception is going to be over anytime soon," I said with a
chuckle.

"Well, I think it's good to enjoy something that's really
worth celebrating. So many bad things happen in life.
It's great when God brings two people who love Him and
each other together in marriage," Roman said, taking his
blazer off. He wrapped it around my bare arms.

"Thank you." I relished the feeling of being cared about.

"So, Desiree, summer will officially be over in two
weeks."

"Don't remind me. Back to the daily grind of classes,
grading, and meetings."

Roman put his arm around me, pulling me close as
we walked. "For me, that means less time with you. I've
gotten spoiled with your ability to see me around my
schedule, but I plan on doing all that I can to see you just
as often."

"Well, I guess reality had to set in sometime." I didn't
like the thought of seeing Roman less.

"Come on. Let's sit on the bench." Roman pointed to
the ducks on the pond and laughed. "I guess the reception
has them up late too."

"Oh, right." I tapped him playfully on his arm. We
sat quietly for a few minutes, just watching the ducks.
It surprised me that the silence didn't feel awkward,
just peaceful.

"I've been thinking about some things, Des. I was calculating how long we've been seeing one another. I counted three months and three days exactly."

"Wow, you're good." I couldn't believe he knew how long we'd been together to the day.

"I'm glad you think so too," he joked.

"What*ever!*" I said, bumping him lightly.

Roman loosened his fancy bowtie, and his expression changed. He took a deep breath. "Everything has happened fast for us. It's never been like this before for me. I mean, I told you that I was in love with you a month ago. I've never felt quite like this about anyone. I'm amazed that it's all happened so fast."

"I told you the same."

"I'm just saying that I had decided when I rededicated my life to the Lord there would be no more dating just to be dating. It just leads to too much other stuff," he explained.

"Yes, you've told me, and I know firsthand."

"I've done a lot of things in my past that I'm not terribly proud of when it comes to relationships, but God's mercy really covered me."

"What do you mean?" I asked, wondering if I'd be let down by a man again.

"I have slept with women, and some of those weren't necessarily women I'd even had real relationships with, you know what I'm saying?"

"You were a player?" I asked.

"I'm serious, Des. I'm ashamed of that. I'm never going to go down that path again. Listen, I've prayed and prayed about my relationship with you. God has given me so much peace and reassurance about you. You are what has been missing from my life, Desiree."

I stared into his eyes, praying that this all wasn't some sort of crazy dream. "Are you trying to make me cry, Roman?"

He lifted my chin up to face him. "I never want to make you cry. I just want to make you happy. I want to spend the rest of my life trying to make you happy, Des. I don't want to scare you, but I have a question I need to ask you."

My heart raced wildly as Roman knelt down on one knee and reached in his back pocket, pulling out a small black box. "Desiree, would you do me the honor of agreeing to be my wife?"

I covered my mouth with my hands. My eyes filled with tears of joy and I nearly fell onto him. "It's so soon!"

"I know. That's why I want us to pray right here, right now, before you answer. Listen to what the Holy Spirit is leading you to do, and whatever the answer is, it will be the right one."

"Pray here?" I looked around.

Roman took his jacket from around my arms and laid it on the grass. "Kneel down," he instructed.

I felt a little silly at first, but we were alone, and I needed to hear from the Lord. He knelt down beside me and intertwined his fingers with mine.

"Lord, we come to you tonight seeking your wisdom. You've given me what to do, and now, I ask you to let Desiree know your will."

As Roman continued to pray, tears streamed down my face, but only because I'd never felt so much peace about anything. I knew that it wouldn't make sense to others. An engagement would be much too soon for them, but I knew at that moment that God had blessed me with my future husband. When Roman finished praying, I embraced him.

"Yes, Roman, God says yes, so I say yes."

He laughed and wiped my tears while he sat down next to me to slide the ring on my finger.

"Oh, it's so beautiful! People are going to think that we're crazy!"

He kissed me and held my hands in front of him. "People don't matter. What matters is that the Lord has given us His blessing. These past few months have been the best I've ever had. I love you, Desiree."

"I love you too, Roman. I can't wait to spend my life with you."

"I want us to pray one more time today, to seal the deal."

It all felt like a dream. His love had taken me by surprise and taught me to trust Him totally. Only in right relationship with the Lord could I be in right relationship with a man. I knew that through Him, all things really were possible.

Roman held my left hand and rubbed his fingers over mine. He closed his eyes and I did the same. "Lord, I know that you have given me confirmation over and over again about this woman who is to be my wife. We are asking you to continue to give us your peace and your direction as we get ready to spend the rest of our lives together. Thank you for giving us your love. Thank you for bringing us together. We promise to be loving, honest, and patient with one another. Be at the center of all we say and do, now and always. Give us the strength to endure what people might think about our decision and just give us direction and peace. I thank you for Desiree and the love that you have given me through her. In Jesus' name, amen."

Roman opened his eyes. "Oh, Des, you're gonna have to stop crying. This is happy," he said, smiling while again wiping my tears.

"I do need to be honest with you about something, Roman. It may change everything. It really just occurred to me that you may not want to do this if you know."

His face, still relaxed and unmoved, let me know that it probably wouldn't matter, but I still needed to tell him. He sat back on the bench. "Okay, tell me."

Even though Roman and I had both confessed how we had committed fornication in the past, we both resolved that we would never let this sin work its way into our relationship. Yet, I hadn't told him about the assault.

"It's . . . it's just that something very bad happened to me." I looked away from his confused expression. "Well, for a while I got on an Internet dating site. I was dating guys. I thought I was being careful. There was this one guy who seemed to be nice, but he turned out to be a monster." I took another deep breath. "He took advantage of me."

Roman covered his hand over his mouth for a second, clearly stunned. "You mean you were raped, Desiree?"

I folded my arms over my chest, wanting to disappear. "Yes, I was."

From there, Roman asked me questions, and his emotions ran the whole gamut. He paced in front of me, wanting details, and then sat back down, consoling me in his arms. "I'm so sorry that it happened to you, Desiree. I still don't understand why you didn't file charges. He needs to be punished for what he's done." Roman stood up again, balling his fist. "If I could only get my hands on him."

"Please don't." My stomach tightened. I'd never seen Roman like this.

He seemed to read my thoughts and sat down again. "I'm sorry, Desiree. It's just not fair. I wish that I could've protected you. It's not your fault. The creep needs to be put in jail."

"Well, thanks to Paul, he's had to suffer some of the consequences of his behavior." I then explained what happened and how Phillip had been arrested. I even explained the whole mess with Hunter and Dad.

After Roman calmed down, he whispered, "Listen, this doesn't change the way I feel about you. You have to know that. I'm glad you told me though. I want to help you heal from these things, so we can have a healthy relationship. Everyone has things that they have to deal with. It's just dealing with them in the right way. I'm so glad that you're going to group counseling. I'd like to come with you sometime."

Full of shame and regret, I hadn't known how Roman would react. He seemed to sense my pain, and just let me vent. I hadn't really realized that I needed to grieve over all I had lost with men. I explained, "Even though my daddy passed away, he left me. That's what it felt like, Roman, like he left me. And my stepfather, Hunter, and Phillip, they betrayed me in the worst kind of way." I blew my nose, both angry and sad that the happiest day of my life had been infiltrated by ugliness.

"You've had some difficult situations with men, Des. I think that's why you have what comes off as a hard exterior, but I'm glad that you're being honest with yourself and me, and, most importantly, with God. All men don't leave. All men don't deceive and betray. I'm not going anywhere, and I'm not going to hurt you."

"I believe you, Roman. Counseling has helped me to understand that although my daddy passed away, he was a good man. He wouldn't want me to wallow in self-pity or be in an abusive relationship. I'm even getting to where I understand my stepfather better. He's not perfect, but I can say that he does love me. Even in his mistakes, I know he does. I just have to understand that without a right relationship with God, he can't really know how to love himself or anyone else."

Roman listened, and I felt the weight of trying to carry things alone ease from my shoulders. I knew that Roman could handle it because he knew how to cast things on the One who could bear anything.

CHAPTER 38

ISABELLA

These things I have spoken unto you, that in me ye might have peace. In the world ye shall have tribulation: but be of good cheer; I have overcome the world.
—John 16:33

With the For Sale sign firmly planted in the ground, I watched the movers load the final boxes into the moving van.

Desiree called from outside, "Mama! Mama!"

"I'm here in the garage. What'chu want, girl?"

Desiree huffed, "Somebody's here to see you."

"I parked on the side of the house. Didn't want to get in the way of the movers," Beau said, gripping and twisting that same old cap.

With my hands on my hips, I playfully scolded, "You need to quit standin' there like that and grab a broom. I don't plan on paying nobody else to clean this house. Hope you got on your work boots, Beau."

Beau's shoulders fell at ease. He chuckled and pulled his cap down on his head. He grabbed the push broom from the corner of the garage. "Isabella, you sho' know how to keep a man on his toes."

"I'm mighty happy to see you, but yeah, you done right by puttin' that hat back on. Looks like you need a haircut."

"Oh, Mama, you and your hair issues," Desiree chided.

I'd found a small two-bedroom ranch right outside of the county line. It took me a little longer to get to church, but I loved the peace and quiet. Beau helped me get my garden together, and he didn't seem to mind the thirty-minute drive it took to go walking with me daily.

We didn't talk much about our feelings that summer. We just helped one another to make it, one day at a time. I didn't know exactly what the future held for me or Beau, but I didn't try to figure things out. For once, I just lived life to the fullest. Our grief over losing Kaylyn was only paralleled by our blossoming love for each other, and I was so grateful the Lord had given me another chance.

CHAPTER 39

DESIREE

Weeping may endureth for a night, but joy cometh in the morning.

—Psalm 30:5b

Roman and I began premarital counseling with Pastor Kingston who had been overjoyed with our wedding, planned for December. Mama told every person she knew and any strangers she encountered that I was getting married. Let her tell it, Roman walked on water.

With a renewed dedication to the Lord, I saw things differently. I wanted to fulfill my purpose. Mama's illness, Kaylyn's life and passing, and everything in between let me know that God had given me a life to be used to glorify Him.

As much as I enjoyed my jewelry business, I slowed down long enough to hear what God wanted me to do. He gave me the idea to start a nonprofit business designing headscarves and head wraps for women who suffered from hair loss. I used jewels, studs, and stones in headscarves, making them unique, bold, and ornate. Roman and I even came up with a two-toned pink head wrap, named a Kay-wrap, adorned with the breast cancer ribbon in pink rhinestones. The wrap had become so popular that the National Breast Cancer Society endorsed Kay and Bella's headscarves, buying thousands to give to runners in the upcoming marathon.

So much had happened in a year. For the first time, I had help setting up my vendor table at the Harlem Renaissance Festival. Roman hung the Kay and Bella's Jeweled Headscarves sign, calling out to me, "Des, look who's coming!"

I looked out to see Lionel Banks, now the Huntsville City mayor, leading a news reporter to my booth. I stood up quickly, straightening my blouse as they headed toward me, camera in tow.

Mayor Banks explained into the reporter's microphone, "Desiree Morrison is a remarkable woman with a business that means something special in the city of Huntsville. The ramifications of her unique idea have spread across our community and our county. The thing that I love so much about her business is that she's teaching women to feel beautiful about themselves from the inside out, while in the midst of suffering through debilitating diseases like cancer. The city applauds and supports her efforts."

"I see," the reporter asked, her interest now piqued. "What made you start Kay and Bella's Jeweled Head-scarves?"

I wiped the sweat from my upper lip before the camera turned toward me. "My mother, Isabella, is challenged by a very aggressive breast cancer diagnosis, IBC, and a dear family friend, Kaylyn, also had breast cancer. While Kaylyn is no longer here with us, I watched her and my mom struggle to wear wigs that were uncomfortable. The chemotherapy makes the scalp very sensitive for many, so headscarves can be a great alternative. We began to discover how difficult it can be to find headscarves that matched both their outfit and personalities. Because I already had a talent with making jewelry, I decided to use the jewelry to embellish the headscarves."

The reporter nodded. "What a fabulous idea! You know, I have an aunt who has alopecia. I'll be sure to get a few for her. I may even get one for myself," the reporter said, admiring one and holding it up in front of the camera.

"Yes," I continued, "you don't have to be suffering from any condition to wear the scarves, but Kay and Bella's Jeweled Headscarves was born out of a desire to use a gift that God has given me to help women who suffer with cancer or any other illness that affects their hair. The softness, yet fiercely bold nature of the headscarves has been something to resonate with women struggling with hair loss. On this journey, I've had the wonderful opportunity to meet so many beautiful women with incredible courage. They have taught me that, as trite and cliché as it might sound, beauty radiates from the inside out. These two women, Kay and Bella, taught me the importance of real love, beauty, and truth."

The reporter nodded and then tuned to face the camera. "I'd like to encourage everyone to get over here to the Harlem Renaissance Festival to see this inspirational and very talented businesswoman. Oh, and you certainly don't want to miss the opportunity to see Mayor Banks."

Mayor Banks smiled with his cool swagger and put his arm around me. "Great job," he whispered in my ear.

The camera stopped rolling, and I noticed Mama and Beau waving as they walked toward me. It hadn't occurred to me until that moment: I realized that I'd never seen Mama smile so much. Beau also looked different to me. Instead of being a threat to the destruction of Mama's marriage, I saw him as an avenue to her happiness. In an instant, all of the bad feeling that I had about Beau dissipated. I nearly cried. I knew that it was all God. He changed how I saw everything and everyone.

I pulled out one of my scarves that I'd designed with Mama in mind labeled The Joy Jeweled Scarf, and wrapped it around my head. The scarf, the color of a bright yellow sun, had bright orange rhinestones and tur-

quoise beading as blue as the sky. I had labeled all of the
scarves different names, according to how the inspiration
for the design came. I remembered what Mama had told
me on one of her very bad days. "Desiree," she said, "just
remember, in the worst of times, joy can be the fullest.
You just have to look for it."

When Mama came to the booth, I didn't focus on
her grim prognosis, the looming divorce, or even her
questionable relationship with Beau. I saw her smile, and
I saw joy.

DISCUSSION QUESTIONS

1. Why do you think Desiree decides to continue her relationship with Taye in spite of the fact that they have so little in common? Why does she settle? Why do so many women settle in their relationships? Desiree laments that all the good African American men are married, gay, or unemployed. Is this true? Do all men cheat? Should a woman lower her standards to fit the men who are available? Why or why not?

2. Why does Kaylyn struggle with her faith? Have you ever witnessed abuse or been abused by someone in the church? How has this affected your faith? How can we help others who have been victimized by people in the church?

3. Desiree doesn't feel comfortable making the first move with men, but she decides to try Internet dating. Is a woman initiating a relationship with a man when she uses the Internet to date? Is Internet dating appropriate for Christians? Why or why not? Why do you think there's such a stigma attached to people who choose to participate in Internet dating? Do you think it's fair? Is it riskier to date on the Internet? Why or why not?

4. Desiree loves her best friend, Shay, but also struggles with feelings of jealousy toward her. Have you ever struggled with being jealous of a friend? Is it possible to love someone, yet feel jealous of him or

her? How can we get eliminate feelings of jealousy? Do you think Desiree worked through her issues of being jealous of Shay? If so, how did she do it?

5. Desiree constantly ignores that small voice inside of her head, cautioning her about potential suitors. Have you ever been like Desiree and ignored that small voice? Why does Desiree ignore the voice? Why have you ignored it? What has the outcome been? How can you identify whether the voice is that of the Holy Spirit, fear, or something else?

6. Is Isabella's relationship with Beau appropriate? Why or why not? Is their relationship considered adultery? Why or why not? What is adultery? Can a person cheat on a spouse without any physical contact?

7. Isabella has an epiphany when she receives her cancer diagnosis. She realizes that the way she's always responded to others going through adversity hasn't always been helpful. Isabella had prided herself in giving others scriptures to comfort them and discovered that that might not have been the best way to respond to others going through hard times. How has going through a trial changed your perspective when dealing with others going through a valley experience? As Christians, what are some appropriate ways to respond when someone is going through a devastating situation?

8. Isabella and Kaylyn are both diagnosed with breast cancer and have their own questions about healing. Kaylyn doesn't understand how a loving God could allow bad things to happen, and she also wonders why, if God is real, He doesn't perform miracles anymore. Is she right? Does God still perform miracles? Isabella wonders why she is left and Kaylyn is taken. Do you think it is God's will for every sick

person to be healed? Can you find scriptures to support your answer whether you agree or not? Why does God heal some and not others? When God allows a loved one to pass away, how can we help one another to stay grounded in faith?

9. Do you understand Desiree's decision not to report the molestation, physical assault, or date rape? Why or why not? Do you think her decision to not report the rape is realistic? Why do so many women refuse to report abuse? Does Desiree bear any blame in her molestation, rape, or abuse? Why or why not?

10. Isabella finally decides to divorce Langley, but says that she's asked God to forgive her. Did Isabella need to ask for forgiveness for divorcing Langley? Why or why not? Was Isabella justified in divorcing him? Why or why not? Is divorce ever acceptable for Christians? If so, in what situations? If not, is there scripture to support it?

11. After Desiree's intense turmoil, she gets greater clarity about her purpose in life. For example, Desiree decides to use her jewelry making talent to help others feel better with her jeweled headscarves. Why do trials often have a way of crystallizing our God-given purpose? Are you fulfilling your God-given purpose? If not, why not? If so, did trials clarify your purpose?

What We Believe:

—We believe that Jesus is the Christ, Son of the Living God.

—We believe the Bible is the true, living Word of God.

—We believe all Urban Christian authors should use their God-given writing abilities to honor God and share the message of the written word God has given to each of them uniquely.

—We believe in supporting Urban Christian authors in their literary endeavors by reading, purchasing, and sharing their titles with our online community.

—We believe that in everything we do in our literary arena should be done in a manner that will lead to God being glorified and honored.

We look forward to the online fellowship with you.

Please visit us often at:

www.uchisglorybookclub.net.

Many Blessings to You!

Shelia E. Lipsey,
President, UC His Glory Book Club

UC HIS GLORY BOOK CLUB!

www.uchisglorybookclub.net

UC His Glory Book Club is the spirit-inspired brain-child of Joylynn Ross, Author and Acquisitions Editor of Urban Christian, and Kendra Norman-Bellamy, Author for Urban Christian. This is an online book club that hosts authors of Urban Christian. We welcome as members all men and women who have a passion for reading Christian-based fiction.

UC His Glory Book Club pledges our commitment to provide support, positive feedback, encouragement, and a forum whereby members can openly discuss and review the literary works of Urban Christian authors.

There is no membership fee associated with UC His Glory Book Club; however, we do ask that you support the authors through purchasing, encouraging, providing book reviews, and of course, your prayers. We also ask that you respect our beliefs and follow the guidelines of the book club. We hope to receive your valuable input, opinions, and reviews that build up, rather than tear down our authors.

Biography

MaRita Teague is the author of the novel *The Taste of Good Fruit,* and has been a contributing author in various publications. She has a bachelor's from The Ohio State University and a master's in English from The University of Alabama in Huntsville. She enjoys ministering to women, teaching college composition and freelance writing and editing. MaRita lives in the Washington Metropolitan Area with her husband and three sons. To learn more about MaRita, visit her blog, *Abiding in the Vine, Writing to Bear Fruit,* at: MaRitaTeague.wordpress.com and follow her on Twitter @MaRitaTeague.